To Monica
+ Chuck

Best
Mark Sublette

GUARDIAN OF THE CORNFIELDS

A CHARLES BLOOM MURDER MYSTERY

MARK SUBLETTE

 JUST ME PUBLISHING

Published by Just Me Publishing, LLC.

Library of Congress Control Number: 2019912595
Guardian of the Cornfields / Mark Sublette
ISBN 978-0-9998176-2-9
1. Fiction I. Title

Quantity Purchases
Companies, professional groups, clubs, and other organizations may
qualify for special terms when ordering quantities of this title. For
more information, contact us through www.marksublette.com.

Cover design: Patrick Travers
Layout and production: Jaime Gould
Author photo: Dan Budnik

Printed in the USA by Bookmasters
Ashland, OH • www.bookmasters.com

AUTHOR'S NOTE

The books in the *Charles Bloom Murder Mystery* series are all works of fiction. Any resemblance to any individuals or names are strictly coincidental unless otherwise described in the author's notes.

All characters in *Guardian of the Cornfields*—including artists, trading post characters, the art, fossils or fossil dealers, galleries, or museums exist only in my mind. The Native American characters and references to any of their religious practices or beliefs are fictional; any relationship to real life—by name, clan, or description—is purely coincidental.

The story of Everett Ruess and his travels are, for the most part, accurately portrayed in this novel. The rustlers and the manner and place of his death are fictitious. For further reading about Ruess, I recommend David Roberts' excellent biography *Finding Everett Ruess: The Life and Unsolved Disappearance of a Legendary Wilderness Explorer* (Broadway Books, 2011).

Maynard Dixon, Dorothea Lange, and other well-known artists mentioned in this book had real relationships with Ruess, however, no Dixon painting was given to Everett Ruess, at least to this author's knowledge. Dixon's trip to Kayenta to visit John Wetherill, and his final poem, "At Last," are built around known facts for the most part, though there is no evidence Dixon ever got lost in the desert or discovered a Nasazi stronghold; those details originated from my imagination.

Paige Williams, author of *The Dinosaur Artist: Obsession, Betrayal, and the Hunt for Earth's Ultimate Trophy* (Hatchette, 2018), was immensely helpful, as was her September 2018 lecture at the Tattered Cover Book Store in Denver. While the characters associated with the fossil hunters or dealers are completely fictitious, the dinosaur species, geographic locations, and price structure for sales of their bones are based on factual information.

The Maynard Dixon Museum does exist in Tucson, Arizona, inside Medicine Man Gallery. While all characters associated with this portion of the book are fictitious, the pricing of Dixon's work and information about his inventory log information are based in fact.

For more information about Dixon's life, excursions, and body of work, see my richly illustrated book *Maynard Dixon's American West: Along the Distant Mesa* (Just Me Publishing, 2018).

The Historic Toadlena Trading Post, a central component of all the Bloom books, is a working trading post that exists as described on the Navajo Nation. This historic shop specializes in Toadlena/Two Grey Hills weavings, and is well worth making the effort to visit. I would like to thank its proprietor, author Mark Winter, and his wife Linda, for their invaluable insights as well as for Mark's editing prowess. The Brown family of Toadlena's careful reading of the manuscript has helped insure the cultural nuances of the Diné are more accurately portrayed.

I have added a glossary of geographical, Navajo, medical, and art terms that will hopefully make any unusual words more accessible to readers.

All the photographs of Santa Fe and the Navajo reservation were taken by me to serve as points of reference for each chapter. Other images are courtesy of Mark Sublette Medicine Man Gallery. I hope the images will help the reader experience the same sense of place and moment in time I experienced when I took them.

No book is complete without a great cover, and I'm most appreciative to Patrick Travers for his graphic design skills and to Jaime Gould for her remarkable book layout and attention to detail. I'm also grateful for Patricia West-Barker's careful manuscript editing and thoughtful suggestions.

CHAPTER 1

BEYOND THE WETHERILL TRADING POST

Everett's face radiated warmth, a welcome reminder he was once again at home in his beloved Arizona desert. San Francisco, with its cacophony of sharp noises, odd odors, and colorful art was no doubt stimulating, but not as viscerally rewarding as the great outdoors.

The human landscape of the City by the Bay couldn't compete with the solitude, or the late fall colors, on the high desert mesas lining the Navajo reservation. The remote terrain pulled at Everett's heartstrings, and was more soothing than a human touch or gentle kiss. The young man acknowledged he was a recluse, someone who had trouble connecting with others—unless, of course, he wanted to—but Mother Nature never asked anything of him but respect.

Nearly two years had passed since the young man's last Arizona walkabout; a year spent reflecting on nature's intrinsic order would bring back his inner balance, and—as his Navajo brethren would say—allow him to once again walk in beauty. In the desert, he would hear no more about the Great Depression or impending doom in Europe. Being outdoors and sleeping among the stars or in the occasional abandoned hogan were the order of the day.

A bead of sweat trickled down Everett's ruddy check and bounced off the colorful painting he was examining for the umpteenth time since he had received the gift.

The painting, tucked away in his burro's leather saddle pack, was tightly wrapped in a pair of semi-clean long johns, their warmth not needed on this particular November day. Chocolate's ears twitched incessantly as the last crop of mosquitoes assaulted him. The hotter than usual weather would break soon, Everett thought: The thin cirrus clouds grazing Navajo Mountain foretold a change about two days out.

Covering the painting with his underwear would not be of much help in a wet environment, but somehow the painting's security blanket made Everett feel less concerned. Traveling the backcountry could be dangerous business. Twice in 1932, all of his belongings, including one of his burros, had tumbled into the Colorado River—a near-death experience that cost him a substantial amount of gear, ruined his most recent watercolors, and damaged his camera beyond repair.

Four years of continuous exploration of the remote Navajolands of Arizona had given Everett wisdom beyond his twenty years. Extra precautions were in order when it came to protecting his most prized possession—a 16- by 20-inch oil painting executed in 1922 by the famed western painter Maynard Dixon. The young artist had traded Dixon a favorite poem and three woodblock prints, including *Square Towerhouse*, his best work to date, completed on a trip to Monument Valley.

The trade was clearly weighted in Everett's favor, and he understood Dixon was being magnanimous in making the swap; the Dixon painting was worth at least $50 even in the depths of the Depression. Dixon and his wife Dorothea Lange, the famed photographer, were fond of the young man from the time they first met him and Everett reciprocated their feelings. He was enthralled with the subject matter of Dixon's painting, and asked him endless questions about how he had come to create such an intriguing study.

The plein air painting—composed of blood-colored, juniper-topped jagged cliffs with ancient Anasazi ruins discreetly incorporated into the iron-stained rock face—was a road map of sorts for the young explorer to follow, the key to his journey to find Dixon's lost Anasazi ruins and their untouched multistory buildings.

Dixon said he had captured the scene in vivid detail with the oil study while traveling near Combs Ridge, inside the Navajo reservation on the Arizona/Utah border. Dixon also told Everett he was the first white man to visit the hidden ruins, which were perfectly preserved—boasting that even old man Wetherill, the long-time trader in Kayenta, did not know of this place.

The Wetherills had opened Oljato, their trading post, in 1906, when the nearest white neighbors were seventy miles away. Three years later John Wetherill, a great explorer in his own right, led the Cummings-Douglass expedition to Rainbow Bridge and was among the first whites to see the natural wonder. His wife, who spoke Navajo, had heard about Rainbow Bridge from the Natives, who had been aware of it for centuries.

Dixon, a lowly artist, loved the fact that he could tease the good-natured trader about his own important find, and refused to let Wetherill in on the painting's secret location. The idea that Everett, an itinerant artist barely out of his teens, might best the old man also had great appeal for Dixon: "The artist should be recognized as an explorer and discoverer of remote wonders," Dixon told Everett. "You need look no further than Catlin or Bodmer for proof of that. These hidden ruins are a rare find in a world soon to be overrun by tourists," Dixon said, handing his prized oil study to Everett as if he were knighting him and sending him on a quest for the Holy Grail.

With two mules and an ample supply of food and equipment, Everett Ruess was prepared for the adventure of a lifetime. He had stocked up at a fair price at John Wetherill's trading post near Kayenta a few days earlier and celebrated his coming adventure by splurging on one non-essential item: an old ingot Navajo bracelet studded with three round, green Cerrillos turquoise stones. "A tie to the land and its inhabitants," he declared to Wetherill as he slipped it on his wrist.

Everett's November purchases were welcome income, and John and Louisa Wetherill were happy to oblige the young explorer, even if the trip seemed foolhardy. Winter was coming and Dixon's ruins were hidden away in some of Utah's most remote wilderness. Many traditional Navajos and Utes did not like the white man trespassing on their ancestral lands, and Wetherill warned Everett to be wary of strangers; even packing heat, he said, was no guarantee of safety. The backcountry recognized no sheriff or law, and traveling alone was a risky proposition for a twenty-year-old white boy in 1934—even a white boy with plenty of desert experience.

The old trader had been kind to Everett and spent a couple of days telling him stories of the Navajo and what things were like before Arizona became a state. He also described in detail the four months that Dixon and Lange had spent with him in 1922, emphasizing Dixon's travels around the northern part of the Navajo reservation and how the painter had found an obscure slit in a sheer wall that led to a small island of odd, red-bluff formations along an ancient seabed.

Plastered into the semicircular slot canyon were a series of untouched Anasazi ruins. The tops of the mesas were overgrown and guarded by what Dixon described as "old growth vegetation nursed by slow seeps of water"—an apparent lifeline for the ancient Puebloans who had called this remote outpost home. To see the place from a distance was impossible unless you were high above it in an airplane, so finding the passage to the slot canyon would require determination and luck from anyone not born in the area. The Navajo avoid these ruins, Wetherill said, as they fear the Nasazi *chindi*, or ghosts, that occupy the abandoned homes.

Wetherill was proud Dixon had managed to uncover such a fantastic find, even if the only proof was his sketches and his word. The old trader had searched numerous times since he first heard Dixon's tale, and had yet to uncover the location—much to Dixon's delight. Now sixty-eight, Wetherill's exploration days were all but over. But he reported Dixon's story to Ruess as if it had taken place just yesterday, rather than a dozen years earlier.

"Dixon borrowed a favorite buckskin mare of mine who was good on her feet," Wetherill said, "and he took her deep into the heart of the Navajo Nation. He was gone for nearly four days while Dorothea stayed put, taking photos around Monument Valley. She never worried a lick. 'That man might be gone for a month for all I know, but the desert is his temple and sometimes he needs a lot of redemption,' she joked.

"Myself, I was worried for Dixon. Lots of bad stuff can happen if you don't have your wits about you—and even if you do, the snakes, bugs, Indians, or Mother Nature herself might knock you off your high horse.

"I pretty much figured out where he went," Wetherill continued. "There is a set of canyons resembling the red backbone of some giant beast a day's ride from here, and Dixon's canyon must be somewhere off this formation, about another half-day's ride north. East of there is a series of cliffs, maybe ten miles out. Dixon told me he had stopped to rest his horse when he noticed small dust bunnies floating in the air, all lit up in the late morning light. He worked his way through a set of thick trees—juniper, I think he said—then popped out into a small cul-de-sac of magnificent orange cliffs stained with ribbons of iron that he was sure had never been seen by any white man.

"Well, you can imagine my surprise when Dixon shared his large, detailed drawing and your oil study with me, claiming he was going to blow the studies up big, maybe into a 40- by 50-inch painting. And he already had a title picked out for the work: *The Guardian, Beyond Wetherill's Reach*.

"Well, we both had a good laugh and shared a forbidden whiskey the night he got back. That son-of-a-bitch never did let me in on whether he was pulling my leg or not, but the details of those studies makes me believe those ruins exist. Hell, he probably painted a larger version of it like he threatened, if only to get my goat."

Wetherill's story matched up with one Dixon had told Everett six months earlier. Everett believed the ruins existed and was sure he was going to rediscover them and best John Wetherill, the most accomplished explorer of the Southwest to date. If a twenty-year-old could find the hidden ruin, then the Wetherill gag got even better in Dixon's mind.

Dixon made Everett promise if he found his ruins he would do a small oil or watercolor and drop it off at the Wetherill Post as a gift from the two of them. The long-running joke would continue, with the working title now: *The Guardian, Beyond Wetherill's #2.*

Filled with clues, the intricate Dixon painting was a map of sorts, telling the story of unique formations in an isolated setting. The sheer red walls ringed by old growth juniper, and the multistory Chacoan, and later Kayenta, ruins attested to generations of human occupation and possible conquest.

There was one important detail Dixon shared with Ruess but not Wetherill: the ruin contained what appeared to be dinosaur teeth the size of peaches scattered among the sherds of prehistoric pottery, including a group protruding from a half-collapsed kiva, which he surmised had some ritualistic meaning.

Dixon commandeered one of the finer intact teeth and pointed it toward the opening to the canyon slit, placing it on a small tower of Anasazi rocks he had appropriated from the site. If they could unravel the clue, the tooth was a gift and a marker for the next people brave enough to find the desolate ruin.

The imagery Dixon painted had completely captivated Ruess, and he was determined to see the place for himself, swearing he would not return until the ancient buildings and the remains of the beast that bore those teeth had been found.

"What purpose did they serve for the Anasazi?" he wondered. "Those teeth would be a great Mesozoic find unto themselves."

Everett Ruess saw his path as more than that of a poet, writer, and artist; he considered himself an explorer in the true sense of the word. He would be gone for months if necessary. He might only be twenty years old, but after two years traveling alone in remote areas of Arizona, the desert had become his school—thirst and hunger his homework. Staying alive long enough to graduate meant packing enough water and food for three months, even while planning for two.

The first leg of his journey would focus on finding Dixon's ruins. A few days of hard travel and he would be in Bluff, Utah, then continue on to Davis Gulch, traverse the treacherous Hole-in-the-Rock gap, and set up a semi-permanent camp for the winter. Once the burros were fed and a brushwork corral constructed, he would return to the Combs Canyon area of Southern Utah and Northern Arizona on foot, carrying only food, water, cigarettes, a paint box, and his Dixon map for the journey of a lifetime. Ruess would test his mettle. Dixon had made the journey on horseback; he would do it on foot!

What the young vagabond couldn't imagine was he wasn't the only one who knew of Dixon's ruins—and the others wouldn't take kindly to visitors of any kind.

CHAPTER 2

I AM EVERETT RUESS

Remembering his experiences in San Francisco a year earlier helped Everett manage the physical difficulty of climbing the taxing grade from Kayenta to Bluff, a multiday, almost seventy-mile journey. The summer and fall months in the big city had left him with many moments for reflection. Edward Weston, Ansel Adams, Rockwell Kent, Dorothea Lange, and Maynard Dixon were his mentors in art, photography, writing, and nature, spurring him on a trip for which he had been waiting patiently—and now the adventure of a lifetime was finally underway.

The fact that Maynard Dixon, an acclaimed artist, had traded a cherished painting with him was unbelievable—more than Everett could have imagined when he knocked unannounced on the Western icon's studio door, interrupting him at work.

Dixon cut an impressive figure standing in the narrow door jamb—a black Texas Stetson hat riding low on his head, a hand-rolled cigarette in one delicate hand, a brush dripping blue paint on the oak floor in the other, an ever-present sword cane nestled by his side should some unexpected trouble be waiting for him around the bend.

The studio was everything Everett had imagined: Navajo blankets draped over every surface, ancient Pueblo pots stacked in each corner, a magnificent eagle-feather headdress hanging from an oversized easel dominating the interior.

A large canvas of men fighting in monochromic blue and gray hues graced the splattered easel—unusual subject matter for Dixon, but the Depression was affecting the subconscious of the nation, even that of the great Maynard Dixon, who had recently switched from painting expansive landscapes to more somber urban scenes of poverty and riots.

Everett admired both Dixon's and Lange's artwork. They were high on his list of people he must meet, so, when the artist opened the studio door, the young man just said, "Hi, I'm Everett Ruess. I travel the desert, paint the barren land, and write poetry inspired by nature. You, Mr. Dixon, have been my muse in all these desert travels."

The bravado of the unannounced visit didn't seem odd to the young man, who never lacked in self-confidence when it came to art or to meeting important artists. Finding age-appropriate peers to bond with was an entirely different matter; Everett was a freak in his own mind, comfortable interacting only with the far end of the creative spectrum.

Dixon, a lanky California native, was an impressive figure. No city slicker, he was indeed a man who knew himself well. The established artist saw a kindred spirit with piercing blue eyes, face partially obscured by a floppy hat wrapped in a snakeskin, rattle and all, staring back at him. An untucked, faded orange shirt and worn boots that spoke of long roads traveled was something Dixon understood; more words were not needed. Both men were explorers of the desert who sought truth in nature through their art and writings.

Ruess's impromptu meeting with Dixon quickly progressed from polite conversation to in-depth discussion, a meeting of two like minds. One day turned into two weeks; they had bonded over the call of isolated places few whites understood in 1933.

Both Dixon and Lange fell under Everett's spell. Undoubtedly, the ambitious kid reminded Dixon of himself, with his love of adventure and all things Indian. Lange recognized a younger, more virile version of Maynard, who now was pushing sixty, with constant smoking taking a toll on his asthmatic lungs. Dorothea saw Ruess as a lost son. A thin body that needed fixing and his inquisitive nature triggered Lange's maternal instincts, a rare occurrence for a seasoned observer of the human condition. She heaped food and concern on Everett as she documented the young explorer's existence with photos, somehow recognizing his genius could be fleeting.

Ruess soaked up Dixon's teachings about the simplicity of composition, color, and the importance of perseverance, giving the younger man a crash course in becoming a true artist. Everett's parents' insistence that he attend college was no competition to the gravitas of Dixon's intense mentorship. This was something Dixon understood, having only lasted three months at the California School of Design when he was about Ruess's age.

"Teachers can scare the crap out of you," Dixon told Everett during one of their hours-long talks. "Arthur Mathews did that to me, and it can keep you from finding your true inner voice if you're not careful. Your gut instinct to go to the desert is right. Don't worry about the authoritative naysayers; just listen to your own artistic self."

Everett Ruess returned to the present moment, content in the late afternoon light of the Canyonlands. Dixon's voice telling him to go to the desert echoed in his mind as he slowed his pace. The burros, following Ruess's lead, halted instinctively. He fished deeply into one of the saddle packs and retrieved a slightly bent portrait Lange had taken of him, one that seemed to capture something special. Everett smiled back at his reflection, the grin vanishing as he felt the shadow of an inner flaw.

"How odd it is to look at one's self in admiration," he thought, "a sin considering the beauty around me." But soon his smile reappeared; as he tilted his head backward and extended his arms, the photo pointed to the sky.

Everett turned slow circles in the crimson dirt, admiring the abundant mesas, the distant vistas, the land waiting to be conquered. As he turned, Everett sang to the heavens:

> "I know the real person, not a caricature of me.
>
> "I'm Everett Ruess, wanderer extraordinaire.
>
> "How sad others don't see, know what I know.
>
> "Trapped in their banal existence
>
> "With no beauty to guide them, unlike me!"

The young man plopped down on a mushroom of fine dirt and began writing furiously in his ever-present diary. A cascade of unconnected thoughts pulsed through his mind until a faint whiff of gray smoke broke the vagabond's trance—the smell of men in the distant red mesas.

"Bluff, Utah by late afternoon tomorrow," he thought. "But for now, a camp is in order. I have writing to finish." He knew that deep rest would be unlikely; his dreams of adventure were too powerful for the boy who rarely slept even when tired.

✳ ✳ ✳ ✳

Bluff was not much for the eyes, a humble Mormon-founded town that had somehow managed to keep a local theater alive. The bold red lettering on the marquee read *Death Takes a Holiday*, starring

Fredric March and Guy Standing. Everett had loved March's performance in *Dr. Jekyll and Mr. Hyde*, for which the actor had received an Academy Award.

The title of the film also struck a chord with Everett. Death was a real possibility traveling alone in the remote Southwestern terrain. Everett did not fear dying—in fact, he embraced the possibility—but a precious quarter would be well worth the price of admission. Spending two bits for entertainment was a luxury in 1934, when that same money would cover the cost of two packs of Lucky Strikes.

Everett decided he could forgo cigarettes for the next week and smoke only after meals. Smoking was a new habit he picked up in San Francisco, and Dixon incessantly puffing on his own hand-rolled Indian tobacco hadn't helped the cause. It could be six months before he had the opportunity to see another movie, and he could always ration his cigarettes or trade a nice Ruess watercolor for a pack.

The young people mulling around the streets of Bluff were a welcome sight for Everett. Finding love among one's peers was a schoolgirl's dream, not of interest to an explorer. Ruess had moved on to a spiritual plane that was beyond love or sex. Finding Dixon's Puebloan ruins was his nexus of focus for the foreseeable future. When fame finally found him—and Everett was convinced it would—the dark molasses of intimacy and its tentacles of pain could be tasted.

Fame would indeed find Everett in the future—but not in the way he imagined it. His journey was about to take a sinister turn.

CHAPTER 3

YABITOCH

The thought of two burros hitched to a lime-green lamppost across from the movie theater brought a grin to Everett's windblown face. It was a time warp he could appreciate. He removed the saddlebags, tied his two faithful companions to the pole, and gave them each a dried carrot. Then he brushed off his dusty slicker and entered the dark theater for almost two hours of abandonment. A comfortable seat and a bag of hot peanuts were his temporary camp for the afternoon, his saddlebags safely stowed by his side.

The young wanderer had attracted attention as he passed through town, burros in tow. A few boys gathered around Everett as he unpacked the animals' load. They wanted to know more about his travels, why he walked with burros rather than with horses, and where he was headed. Everett was surprised when two of the boys followed him into the theater and offered to help carry his packs; strangers like Everett were not an everyday occurrence in Bluff.

He welcomed the human interaction, even if he didn't want to admit that he could use a break from his self-imposed isolation. Simply talking—hearing his own voice and having someone respond in a like cadence—was soothing. Everett often sang when he was alone; an actual conversation was like speaking a different language.

Golden leaves filled the early November air. Everett had been on the trail for two months and had not seen a town since he left Kayenta. Cleanliness was not one of his priorities—although he did bathe when the rare water hole presented itself—but human and animal sweat was his parfum de jour; the odor permeated his clothes and couldn't be missed by his companions in the nearby seats.

Everett clapped loudly after the movie, alone in his exuberance. "Money well spent," he thought, the theme having a deeper meaning to the wanderer. One of the boys, intrigued by Everett's bravado and unparalleled need for soap and water, invited the stranger to come to his family's house, take an outdoor shower, and sleep in the barn for the night. "My mom will fix you a home-cooked meal of leftover mutton and biscuits and you can wash your clothes if you like."

Everett happily accepted the invitation. A roof was a treat as the occasional late fall rain or early snow was a real possibility—and no twenty-year-old ever turns down a free meal, especially mutton, something he loved. He wasn't interested in cleaning his clothes; they would be just as dirty in a day or two. But the shower felt good. Tangled hair encircled his head where the floppy hat had rested; no amount of brushing seemed to tame the unruly mats.

Smoke filled the valley of the Post ranch, Everett's adopted home for the next two days. Bryson Post, a red-haired, blue-eyed boy of sixteen, was enthralled by his wandering friend. Everett bedded down in a half-century-old barn with a fifteen-foot ceiling, brimming with recently cut hay and housing three milk cows. The homestead was well maintained, and Everett could see how one could be happy in such surroundings. Bryson had three siblings: two brothers who were five and three years younger, and an eighteen-year-old sister who was now raising her children at her own home down the valley.

Everett shared his adventures on the reservation with Bryson, telling the teenager how his favorite sleeping accommodations were the abandoned hogans that dotted the Navajo Nation.

"The Diné, as they call themselves, believe these empty structures are no longer homes but haunted places filled with *chindi*, spirits of past lives forever trapped in the dwelling. Some hogans have holes knocked out of the north side to release the ghosts," he said, "but they never scare me." In fact, the vagabond boasted that he had readily burned loose hogan logs as kindling, unconcerned about the serious implications of that act to the people on whose land he trespassed so freely.

"Those beliefs are about the Navajos' gods, Bryson—they are not my gods. My heavenly father is the trees and rocks I pass, the air I breathe, and the water I drink. Nature is my god."

Bryson was shocked by his friend's blasphemy and was sure that if his father heard this talk the invitation for food and bedding in the barn would be rescinded. Yet Bryson couldn't tear himself from this unique person who referred to himself either in the third person or as "Nemo," the captain of his own religion and fate. Everett had recently begun to assume the name of the protagonist in Jules Verne's *20,000 Leagues under the Sea.*

Telling stories of his life among the Indians led Everett to think more about his mixed feelings about the Navajo once he had bedded down to sleep.

Sometimes he wrote in his diary about how they acted like children and were a dirty and poor people who stole. Other entries contradicted this view, as when he wrote about how much he liked these happy people and listed the many Navajo phrases he had learned. In some odd way, he felt like he was a kindred spirit with these Athabascan people. They, too, had been explorers at one time, migrating from what they called their Third World to the Fourth. They had been brave and strong, feared by all until the whites starved them into submission and destroyed their homes in Canyon de Chelly. Everett could relate to hunger; he had experienced hunger and thirst on many of his trips, a pain deeper than love.

The Navajo felt a connection to the young man they called "Yabitoch," but also had some trepidation about him—"Yabitoch" loosely translated to "liar." Everett once participated in a three-day Enemy Way ceremony, a great honor for a white man, watching in amazement as the singer, or medicine man, created a beautiful sandpainting to help cure his patient. It worked, and the idea that art contained powers to heal resonated with him. In this way, Ruess was more Native than he liked to admit.

Part of Everett wanted to embrace the Diné world, marry a Navajo and disappear into the ecosphere, forever one with nature, never return to the white man's ways, but his rational mind fought this kind of thinking. He was a writer, philosopher, and painter; he was not a sheepherder, farmer, or silversmith.

Another compelling reason to stay in the white world was his love of ancient ruins. Finding an untouched cache of thousand-year-old artifacts—and being the first to handle a painted bowl last used for a precious meal or ritual—was the ultimate excitement. He often sent the relics he found to his parents in Los Angeles as a testament of his adventures—not as a trophy or a financial asset—to help him remember his adventures in his old age. To Everett, money's only purpose was to allow him to buy books, paint supplies, and food to support a journey. Cereal, peanut butter, chocolate, and cigarettes were the staples of life when he was in the backcountry.

To be a good Navajo meant shunning all prehistoric ruins to avoid the *chindi* that haunted the homes the Nasazi (as the Diné called the Anasazi) left behind. To the Navajo, these ancient structures were not ruins but abandoned homes, much like their own hogans.

Everett's quest was to rediscover the ruins Dixon had painted and collect some of the relics left behind, including the dinosaur-tooth marker. He couldn't relate to the Navajos' fear, but did honor beliefs that were an honest part of their religion. Overall, he respected the Navajo more than he liked to admit.

His real disdain was for many of the Indian traders who dotted the reservation. He looked at them as parasites feeding on the Native people, interested only in how they could make money off the backs of the poor Navajo. Unlike John Wetherill, who seemed to really care about the Navajo and loved to hike and explore their land, most trading-post owners had not ventured more than five miles past their rundown stores. Many had not even taken the time to visit Canyon de Chelly, the most sacred place on the reservation, one Everett had visited often and for weeks at a time.

"How could they not visit the magical canyon of the Anasazi, Hopi, and Navajo?" he wondered, not understanding how someone could live among a people but not care about what made them tick.

Sharing his upcoming adventure with Bryson Post helped reinforce Everett's resolve to travel the hundred miles to Combs Ridge on foot. The young boy wanted to come along and help—finding ruins lost long ago sounded like a great adventure, certainly much more exciting than working the ranch. But Everett assured him that this was a one-man job, although he did appreciate the food, which helped extend his depleted reserves. One more day of recovery, stories, and relaxation, and he would head off to Davis Gulch to make a semi-permanent camp, then head to Northern Arizona to find Dixon's guarded ruins.

Bryson warned Everett to keep his six-shooter handy as there were cattle rustlers working throughout the area. They were not nice people and wouldn't take kindly to some strange tenderfoot walking unannounced into their camp. "They'd just as soon shoot you and dump your body in the nearest ravine as take a fall for cattle rustling," Bryson warned. "We don't take kindly to those types around here.

We'd hang 'em high before turning them in. I know it's not very Christian, but they're taking food off our plates without askin'."

Everett promised he would keep his wits about him, but he wasn't worried about rustlers, or Indians for that matter. He was more concerned about slipping and falling into a cold river or running across a hibernating rattlesnake. He had never been afraid of the human animal—something he would soon come to regret.

CHAPTER 4

RUSTLERS AHEAD

Everett broke camp early, planning to leave his comfortable barn loft for the hardship of the backcountry. Putting ten miles behind him before noon was his goal—quite doable if he didn't stop too many times to write in his journal.

Next to the horse corral, eddies of steam floated above a small stock tank; a scraggly yellow-leafed cottonwood tree clung to its leaves nearby, a harbinger of an early fall. Everett documented his observations before he packed away his diary and went to earn a warm breakfast.

"A fine day to make miles," Everett said to Bryson as the teen methodically squeezed an old milk cow's teats, the milk hitting the pan with a rhythmic sound with each twist of the boy's wrist.

Everett tapped Bryson on the shoulder to signal him to take a break, grabbed the pail and took a warm gulp of sweet, creamy milk from the bucket. "Like candy," he said. "You should take a swig before it's all gone. Don't you know how good this would taste with a handful of warm peanuts?" he asked as his peeved host hoped he wouldn't lose much more of the morning's catch.

"Bryson, I will stop by when I come back through in three weeks. I'm planning to leave my burros at my base camp. Have you seen many lions around here lately?"

"Nah, no lions around much anymore. The shepherds cleaned them out for the most part about twenty years ago—but, like I said, there are rustlers in this neck of the woods, though I'm not sure they would want to bother with those two burros."

Everett felt a twinge of pain; he was fond of his animals even if they did cost less than $12 for the pair, including the saddle packs, and he would sell them at the end of his journey and move on. He brushed off the remark and asked Bryson if he thought it would be okay for him to bunk down here on his return trip. "I promise to fill you in on my latest adventure, show you the plunder I expect to find."

"Sure, can't wait," Bryson agreed. "You got to tell me all about it, and maybe we can go see a movie again. That was great fun, though the same picture may be on; the old man that owns that theater won't bring in nothin' new till he's got every last cent out of Bluff's citizens. Sometimes we go more than once just to push him to get a new flick."

Everett didn't quite understand Bryson's humor. He had recently graduated from high school in Los Angeles, where newly released films played on every corner. Small-town life had its downsides, as did traveling in the wilderness for months at a time—but unspoiled nature still trumped it all.

"Okay, it's a deal!" Everett spat on his hand and stuck his mitt out; Bryson spat too and they shook hard on the deal.

With his hotel accommodations set for his return visit, Everett packed up the last of his gear and slowly made his way up the canyon toward the hundred miles or so it would take to get to Hole-in-the-Rock, which Bryson's Mormon relatives had discovered in 1880 while migrating to new lands to spread the word of the Latter-day Saints.

The San Juan Expedition wagon train stopped at the natural impediment and spent the next six weeks pecking through the sheer sandstone walls from the mesa top to the river's floor, a feat of pioneer spirit that would test even the bravest in the group—something that had not changed over time. The crossing was still dangerous and herding two burros, no matter how sure-footed, down the one thousand-two-hundred-foot embankment loaded with gear tested all of Everett Ruess's resolve.

Everett liked Bryson more than he thought he should. The boy had touched his heart with his unflagging generosity and good looks. As Everett crested the mesa top, he stopped and pivoted for one last glance. In the distance Bryson was wildly waving a red handkerchief and yelling something undecipherable, but the message was obvious: good-bye and come back soon. Everett smiled, returning the sentiment by using his floppy hat to salute his new friend, then turned his attention to the trail ahead. His destiny lay north.

Ruess did not know he would never see the boy with the bright eyes and friendly smile again.

✴ ✴ ✴ ✴

A sweat-stained shirt confirmed that Everett had met his ten-mile goal at a breakneck pace. A sheltered white rock outcropping was the perfect stop for a late lunch—a bite of hard tack and some beef jerky. The heat radiating from the stones felt good on his sore legs. The fifty-degree weather and calm winds were ideal for hiking. So far, his luck was holding. "Ten more to go before sundown," he thought.

Energy restored, Everett revisited his breakfast treat as he stretched his legs for the second stage of the journey. "Ah, for a drink of that sweet milk to dip my stale biscuit," he thought.

An ever-growing bruise on his right leg had started to throb; it was painful, but not yet debilitating. Everett had struggled with pernicious anemia in the past, its recent return giving him pause to worry. He had battled "tired blood" for much of his life and there wasn't much he could do about it. Cool weather and exercise were his only therapy; the doctors were useless.

This red rock country was new territory to Everett, but he was sure he was on the right trail. He briefly considered a quick detour to 16 Room Ruin, a large Mesa Verdean-style ruin not far from Mexican Hat. A defensive construction plastered into a larger alcove, it had been well-known since it received its name in 1896. Everett had seen pictures of it, and it was indeed impressive.

The San Juan River Basin had dozens of unexplored sites, but Everett's attention was on Dixon's remote find; dinosaur teeth and pots stacked to the roof exerted the greater magnetic pull. Ruess wanted to please his mentor, and finding the ruin was a sure-fire way to do that.

John Wetherill had drawn a map to Hole-in-the-Rock for Everett, and Bryson confirmed the route. Using a red and a blue crayon, Bryson highlighted the best spots for safe water and grazing for his burros, adding little notes as a reminder. He recommended Davis Gulch for a semi-permanent camp, saying, "There's a lot of brush there to make corrals, along with water and knee-high grass for the animals to eat." It was Ruess's only map of Southern Utah.

Everett's mind was focused where the blue sky intersected the edge of a red mesa as he lay on a comfortable bed of dry buffalo grass memorizing his map. Bliss washed over him, and his ever-churning thoughts had slowed when an unexpected sign appeared—a thin line of brown smoke was blowing over the knife-edged mesa, coming from the direction in which he was headed.

His calm vanished and Everett instinctively stood up, detecting a faint whiff of singed leather in the air. He heard Bryson's sweet voice saying, "Rustlers, be careful," and lunch was over.

Everett retrieved his loaded revolver from his pack. The safety was now off and a slow go would be necessary. There was no sense in challenging his gods. He might be a great explorer but no man was immune to a bullet's wrath if his presence wasn't appreciated. The country's ever-deepening Depression had changed men's hearts. They were desperate to feed hungry mouths and "dead men don't talk."

A smile appeared on Everett's face and his pulse slowed as he retrieved his diary and settled back down in the crumpled grass. Using his revolver as a table, he began furiously writing in his precious book:

"What a great adventure! I am Everett Ruess, gun loaded, safety off, rustlers ahead!"

CHAPTER 5

A NEW YEAR COMING

A dusting of fresh snow capped the tips of the famous Two Grey Hills just northeast of the Toadlena Trading Post. Rays of intermittent light bounced back and forth, illuminating each formation as Charles Bloom meditatively swept the trading post's front porch.

He loved looking at the obelisks that encircled his life. Nothing in Santa Fe could compare, not even the daily clamor of the gallery's resident white-neck ravens. Toadlena brought him a deeply organic source of calm. He couldn't explain it, but didn't deny its presence either. Maybe he had found the proverbial *hózhó* and this bliss needed to be embraced; these new feelings of peace were real and he respected them.

Bloom's trance was broken by Marvin Manycoats' arrival for his daily ice cream bar. Like the Chuska Mountains, Marvin had become a fixture in Bloom's life. The two had become close over the last four months and bonded after Marvin had saved Preston Yellowhorse,

Bloom's wife Rachael's son, only a month earlier. Preston had been held captive by a deranged pawnshop owner turned gunrunner, and would have been killed had it not been for the ex-Marine's bravery. After that, Manycoats was part of the family and Rachael had taken to inviting him for dinner every night.

"You got anything planned for dinner tonight?" Marvin asked, only half joking.

"Leftovers, I would guess—same ones you had last night," Bloom kidded back.

"Mmmm… sounds great. I can't wait to have some more fry bread and chicken potpie. Usual time?"

"I'm sure we can muster another chair at the table. Seven-fifteen probably. You can catch a ride with me if you want after I close down. It's been busy lately with Christmas and all, so we might not get out of here right on time."

"That's okay. I've got no schedule, being retired and all. Besides, you know we Navajo don't care about time; that's a bilagáana's hang up."

Bloom smiled, knowing Marvin was right. Most of the locals could wait for hours and not be the least bit disturbed. After all, it was just time—nothing more. For Bloom, who looked at time and money as the same entity, wasted time meant lost money. He was working on that part of his Navajo sensibility, but so far was not having much luck: Ben Franklin still had a strong pull.

"Marvin, let me ask you a question. Why is it that Christmas is such a big deal out here? Seems like the Diné wouldn't care so much...."

"Yeah, it's kind of weird I guess, but the fact is we like to cover all our bases, just in case you guys happen to be right." Marvin laughed at the absurdity, knowing that while he, too, celebrated Christmas, he was also firm in his Navajo beliefs.

"Every year I've been in retail," Bloom said, "I've made some of my best buys in Santa Fe around this time. Ten days out people start to realize they don't have enough money for gifts so they bring in some wonderful heirloom to sell to buy a bike or a TV that's broken in a year."

"The smart ones pawn it in Gallup," Marvin countered, "then get it back later when their government check comes in, so they don't lose it to the white man by selling. You get anything good yet?"

"Nah, not yet, but we're just at that time. The same folks that wait to get rid of some great old piece also wait until the last minute to do their shopping—or at least that was what happened in Santa Fe. We'll see if it's the same here."

"Hope it does, and hope it don't," Marvin replied thoughtfully. Bloom understood that the Navajo hated to see prized pieces getting sold, but also wanted his friend to do well.

"I hear Rachael started a rug. Is that true?"

"Yes. I helped her warp her loom over the weekend. She thinks her wrists and arms are up to it now, so she's starting on a medium-size piece. You know that Indian Market in Santa Fe is a big deal for our family. It's a great time for us to make money and it's only eight months away—so if Rachael wants to have anything significant for the market she has get going now."

"You going back to Santa Fe soon?" Marvin was hoping Bloom would take over Sal Lito's place and become the full-time trader. Sal and his wife Linda would be back from their around-the-world trip right after the first of the year, and things would go back to the way they were pre-Bloom. Marvin loved Sal and Linda, but Bloom was the future, and he hoped his friend would somehow work out a deal with Sal to take over the post—assuming Bloom wanted this responsibility.

"Not sure exactly," Bloom replied. "I promised Rachael that we would stay put until after the school year and then make a joint decision.

I've got a good business there; my gallery has been part of the Santa Fe fabric for over twenty-five years, and I own my buildings—or at least the mortgage on them.

"I promise I'll let you know once I decide. I know you're worried about losing an easy mark for free ice cream and dinner at the best café north of Gallup, so I can't blame you for your concern." Bloom smiled and put his hand on Marvin's broad shoulder, letting him know he cared.

"Yeah, that's right, Mr. Bloom. You got me figured out. What can I say? I have a sweet tooth and you are the cheapest way to keep it satisfied."

Both men smiled, knowing that no sweets could fill the void if Bloom decided to leave.

CHAPTER 6

IT'S THE PRESENTS, DUMMY

Marvin's questions were swirling about in Bloom's mind. The gallerist had already been thinking seriously about talking to Sal about succeeding him as the post owner if they could come to a fair agreement. Sal had a lot of capital tied up in those little brown and gray rugs so, even if the trader wanted to sell, Bloom simply might not have the money to swing it—unless, of course, he sold his buildings on Canyon Road.

Bloom's Santa Fe digs consisted of one large home that served as the gallery, and the annex, which was a small adobe casita. The casita might, in fact, be the oldest house in Santa Fe. There was enough land to split the small building from the main house and sell it as an independent structure, although he had been hoping the city would take over the place and turn it into a museum. Even if he didn't make much money on the sale of the building, a city-owned museum would draw customers to the gallery and Bloom could bank some of the money from the sale and not have to worry about the extra expense of maintaining the old structure—a win/win proposition.

If he could finagle the casita sale, Bloom would have a sizable down payment toward the Toadlena Trading Post lease and its inventory—assuming this was the direction he decided to follow. The Navajo Nation owned the building, but old Sal owned all the inventory and good will. Without Sal's blessing, it wouldn't be feasible to take over the lease.

After dinner, Bloom would discuss his feelings with Rachael; her input was critical to his decision. She was smart and had a good business sense, but he wasn't completely sure about her reaction to the idea. Knowing the real work and money required to succeed, Rachael initially had been less than enthusiastic about him running the post in Sal's absence.

Fresh, chunky chicken gravy graced the leftover potpie, adding a flavorful new twist to last night's leftovers. Marvin had gained two pounds in the month since he started having "occasional" meals at the Bloom house. He had begun walking more miles each day, but the family meals were winning the race.

Marvin recognized he was barging in on the Blooms' home life, but Willy and Sam were the grandchildren he never had, and they filled a void he had never known existed. Marvin had grown attached to the kids and they to him.

"Rachael, looks like you're going to have a nice rug for market this year," Marvin observed.

"I hope so. Not a lot of progress, slow going. My right wrist is hurting like I'm seventy."

"Watch it...." Marvin warned jokingly.

"Sorry, no disrespect. I forget you're almost that old, but you're so youthful it doesn't occur to me you're a senior citizen." Rachael smiled, poking back.

"Well, I think that's a compliment...."

Rachael blushed, not knowing if Marvin was being serious or not. Bloom rescued her.

"So, Rachael, we have a Christmas tree and presents—but I have to ask why."

"What? You don't like Christmas? I thought all white people paid homage to their god this time of year."

"Well, I may have forgot to mention it, but Bloom is a Jewish name, so Christmas isn't that big a deal for me—but you are a traditional, practicing Navajo for the most part, yet you LOVE Christmas. What gives?"

"Presents, dummy. What else?" Rachael gave him a wicked grin.

Bloom took her at face value. "Well, this year maybe we should dust off the menorah and celebrate Hanukkah, and then Christmas, along with whatever Navajo rituals seem appropriate."

"We call those rituals giving your wife great presents, and I'm sure cool with that. You actually have a menorah?"

"No, I didn't figure you would call my bluff, but if you want I can get my dad to send me one from Las Cruces. I doubt he uses it much since mom passed."

"What's a menorah?" Marvin asked.

"It's a lampstand made of nine branches and represents the idea of universal enlightenment in the Jewish faith.

"Well, Bloom you may need some enlightenment; it's only two weeks to Christmas and I think Hanukkah starts this week," Rachael said.

"Damn... you're right. I guess I'm not much of a Christmas or a Hanukkah guy. But this year we should do it up big, a real celebration of the season."

"Now you're getting it," Marvin said. "That's the Christmas spirit."

All three laughed, knowing Christmas was a different animal on the rez.

✱ ✱ ✱ ✱

Bloom drove Marvin home. Even though the Navajo insisted he wanted to walk, Bloom wouldn't have it: a five-mile hike at night—even for a seasoned walker like Marvin—was a risk not worth taking just to lose a couple of pounds.

Charles Bloom had never been the outdoors type. Other than the occasional overnight camping trip with his dad to archeological sites, he had little experience out in nature, and he just couldn't imagine walking in the cold dark for five miles without the least bit of trepidation.

"Marvin, don't you worry about walking like that at night? It's dark, cold, and hell—you don't know what's out there. Aren't there lots of drinkers this time of year?"

"Skinwalkers are what I worry about, not slaneys," Marvin said, "but they are rare, and I'm in balance. It's not so cold or dark that I have to worry too much about it right now. But the drinkers are a problem every night."

"True, but still—five miles?"

"Bloom, what I figure is knowing you are one with nature and understanding her protects you. I'm aware of a change in the wind or the smell of an animal, all those things. I trust my instincts because I was raised in nature's isolation, and she embraces me as one of her own."

"Still, you must have had some close calls being out alone on so many nights...."

"I have, but it's never nature that's the danger; it's nature's enemy— man. Man can cause problems. That drunk who could run me down? That's why I always have a red bandana and white shoes and never walk too close to the road. The bad man who's looking for money to steal? Well, I have $5 in my pocket and it's his for the taking. Those angry fools who want to fight for no reason? The military trained me well, so I don't worry about them either.

"In Vietnam, when we did night ops, I was acutely aware of my surroundings and channeled my fear into pinpoint alertness. I saw many men die because they were never one with nature. They would step on our friend the snake and die of a bite. Or trip a wire because they couldn't tell a root from a monofilament line. Nature has kept me alive, so how can I be afraid of her?"

"So you really would rather have walked home?"

"No way. I'm playing you. It's cold and five miles with a belly full of your wife's fine cooking is not easy. Driving is much better. I'll work off those pounds during the day!"

Marvin's sense of humor was every bit as sharp as his awareness of the natural world that surrounded him.

CHAPTER 7

KEEP THAT RECEIPT!

The house was quiet by the time Bloom returned from dropping off Marvin. Willy and Sam were sound asleep. Bloom kissed their foreheads good night and went into the kitchen to help with the dishes, most of which Rachael had luckily already finished.

"Marvin got home safely, I'm assuming? No mountain lion attacks?" she teased.

"No mountain lions, not this time at least, but your friend the bootlegger was out walking."

"Tommy Jackson was out walking?"

"Stumbling was more like it. I offered him a ride home on the way back from Marvin's. He was completely tanked; he's going to die from exposure one of these nights."

"I'm afraid you're right. He has had a problem with alcohol for a very long time. I feel sorry for him. He's not a bad person, but he comes from a long line of drunks. He's the last member of his family left."

"What will happen to his place? He has no siblings or kids, does he?"

"No, he's all alone, which probably adds to his drinking. One of his cousins will take it over. It's not much of a place anyway. He's run it down, but he does have a nice view of Tsinigine and Tsingine Yaz, our beloved Two Grey Hills. He's lucky to at least have the gifts of nature."

"Speaking of nature and the beauty of Toadlena, you know summer will be here before we know it and I need to get back to Santa Fe to harvest some Texas wealth. Any thoughts?"

"I don't know, Bloom. I'm happy here for sure. I really wanted to live in Santa Fe, but when I hurt my arms and couldn't weave, I had nothing there but you. I guess we can play it by ear and see how things work out."

"When you say work out, what do you mean exactly?"

"Well, maybe you want to take over from Sal, if he wants to sell. We've talked about that possibility in the past, though not seriously. It could be time to have that discussion," Rachael said thoughtfully.

"The first question is whether you can live on the reservation and give up your gallery. You're kind of a big deal in Santa Fe—in a small town kind of way."

Rachael knew how to rib her husband. He smiled, but she could tell he was listening carefully to her words.

"It's a big decision," Bloom acknowledged. "Once I give up Bloom's, there is no turning back—and you were the first one to tell me Sal has been at it for fifty years and really doesn't make much of a living."

"It's true, and as good a businessman as you are, Charles Bloom, you shouldn't consider making a profit from the trading post—a given under your reign. People need money out here. There is no Salvation Army or any other freebies. Many people have to struggle to survive and the post helps them do that.

"This is your decision, Bloom," Rachael continued. "As much as I want to say it's ours, in the long run this one is your call. I can weave rugs anywhere, as long as I have grazing for my sheep, but if you're not happy and regret giving up what you built and love, none of us will be happy."

Bloom pondered his wife's sage advice.

"You're right. It's a big decision, but maybe not one I have to make right now. Sal isn't dead yet; he could run the place for at least ten more years before his wife kills him or forces him to retire."

Rachael nodded her head in agreement, knowing his words were true.

"I'll give it some deep thought," Bloom continued, "maybe go to Santa Fe soon and check in on the place and see how I feel when I'm there. I love it here—I really do—but Santa Fe has its own pull, and when I'm there I fall back into my $7 lattes and my green-chile enchiladas at The Shed. And, for all I might complain, we do make a good living there. We also have our children to think of; college for two kids will cost a lot of money."

"Yeah, and three will cost even more," Rachael shot back, watching for Bloom's reaction.

"What do you mean by three?"

"Well, I was planning to discuss this with you tonight, but I missed my period—so it's possible you will be a father again."

"WOW! That's incredible. I can't believe you're just now telling me! Let's go pick up a pregnancy test and find out!"

"You're on the rez, my love. The pregnancy test will have to wait. Nothing will change between now and tomorrow, but I think we're safe to proceed as if we are pregnant. How about we work out our excitement in bed?"

Rachael moved her right thigh against her husband's leg and smiled wickedly, thrilled by Bloom's response to the possibility of a third mouth to feed.

"You're right. There's plenty of time to pick up a test tomorrow. For now, it looks like we need to have an intimate conversation about our future."

The couple moved to their bedroom to explore life and love: at the moment, the possibilities seemed endless.

CHAPTER 8

SANTANA CLAUS

Shiprock's City Market opened at 6 a.m. and Bloom was first in the door. The timing for the trip was perfect; he needed a few supplies for the post along with the two pregnancy test kits. Bloom was not a man to take chances; he wanted to be prepared in case the first test run was ambiguous.

When he was checking out, Gloria, the young Navajo cashier, smiled and said, "Nice to see you again Mr. Bloom. Post groceries today?"

Bloom blushed. He didn't think he was that well-known at the City Market. He didn't usually buy his groceries for the post there but at the Grocery Warehouse in Farmington. He hadn't even thought about the ramifications of his purchase. The word would spread before he even got home—that was life on the rez.

"Yeah. We're hoping for a little surprise, so please keep this quiet until we know for sure. Would you do that, Gloria?"

The cashier nodded her head yes in rhythm with the gum she was chewing. "No problem. If you saw what I see here, you wouldn't worry. I know the whole rez's shopping list—it's pretty scary."

"I'm sure. Thanks." Bloom smiled and made a mental note that living on the rez meant even in Shiprock your personal business was open for discussion.

"You know we don't sell many of those tests here; usually they expire first. I'm surprised management hasn't noticed and stopped carrying them."

"Why is that?" Bloom asked, trying to understand another piece of Navajo culture.

"Well, I guess we Navajo figure why spend good money on something that's beyond our control? The test results don't change nothing, except we would have $20 less in our pockets. The gods have already decided."

Bloom somehow understood this, and, in an odd way, he liked the concept: don't try to overthink things; just let life flow on as it has for generations. There was still a lot to learn, but Bloom rushed home before stopping to restock the post's shelves. He trusted in science and didn't want to wait for the Holy People to make their decision.

The warped metal screen door hit the side of the hogan with a loud clank as Bloom rushed in, the cold winter air filling the living room as he left both doors wide open.

"I got them!" he shouted, waving a test in each hand.

Rachael came out of the bedroom dressed only in a raggedy, oversized NMSU T-shirt from Bloom's side of the closet.

"Charles James Bloom, shut those doors. Firewood costs money and you're letting out all our heat. You went to Shiprock already?"

"Yeah. I've got the post groceries in the truck and your pregnancy tests in my hands."

Just then Willy popped his head out of his room.

"What's a peg Nancy test?"

Rachael frowned. "Way to go, Bloom. This one's yours to handle."

Bloom quickly changed the topic, a trick he had learned from his late mother.

"Hey, Willy... I got groceries. You want to come to the post with me and help me unload? If you do, I'll let you pick out a piece of candy."

"Charles! He hasn't had breakfast yet."

Bloom smiled sheepishly. "Go get your sister dressed and we'll head over to the post. It's cold out there."

Bloom looked at Rachael and clicked the two boxes, which he had put behind his back when Willy appeared, together like castanets.

"Here you go, my love."

"Oh, my god, Bloom. You really are something else. Two tests? Really? Isn't that like $50?"

"Nah, more like $40."

"I've thrown up twice today, so I hope you kept your receipt because you will be returning one of those kits for sure."

Bloom had a lot to learn when it came to being married to a Navajo.

"No problem. If it's a strong positive, I'll return the unopened one next week."

"Make sure it isn't going to expire; these things aren't used much out here."

Rachael went into the bathroom. When she returned, her face said it all.

"We're pregnant?" Bloom asked, already knowing the answer to his question.

"Yep, very much so. You're going to be a dad again. I hope we can get Dr. Riddley to deliver us." Rachael was beaming as she worked out the plans in her head.

"Oh, my god!" Bloom sat down and started counting on his fingers. "July! You will be a mother before August—you have the absolute best timing!"

Bloom the businessman knew if Rachael's rug was finished at the same time as their new child came, and it was before Indian Market, they would be assured of both some extra money for the family and a boost to Rachael's career. This intense business awareness was a side of Bloom Rachael didn't care for, but she hoped to change him over time. In her mind, money and career were second to the importance of the family unit.

"We will see, Charles Bloom. Things happen in life, so don't be counting on a rug by August. I have to say special prayers so I can weave—many weavers won't even make rugs while they're pregnant. The only thing you can be assured of is that I will be with our child—so don't count on me unless I'm up for it."

Bloom quickly realized his goals and cultural understanding were different from those of an expectant Navajo.

"Of course, you and the baby come first. I'm just trying to plan moneywise; that's something I have to take seriously. Which brings us to our next major decision: after the baby, do I go back to Santa Fe or try to make a go of it here when Sal and Linda come back?"

Rachael felt a twinge of guilt. Her husband was right to be worried. Major decisions did have to be made.

"Talk to Sal. He's back right after the first of the year. Get an idea if he wants to sell or will make it worth your while to stay and work with him. Meanwhile, you and I can crunch numbers to see what makes sense. I know you love that gallery and an extra child does cost more money, but it's cheap out here—and Santa Fe? Well, you know—it's Santa Fe."

Bloom decided not to bring up the fact they would need to add an extra room to their home if they stayed in Toadlena. This would become apparent to Rachael soon enough.

"I've got an idea. Let's go up to Santa Fe for Christmas, stay a week and see which location draws us the most. I can make good extra money over the Canyon Road walk on Christmas Eve. You and the kids can serve fry bread and cider, and I'll serve up some salesmanship, lots of stocking stuffers filled with bracelets and such; we can make enough in one night to cover the baby clothes. You like Christmas, and there is nothing like Christmas in Santa Fe!"

"Excellent idea, Charles Bloom. Preston can come and help out, and maybe even make you a bracelet by then. Will your buddy Brad Shriver let us stay at his guesthouse? He's not there now is he?"

"Guesthouse? He's in Europe most of the time now. He will give us the whole house—especially when I tell him I have a kid on the way and 'Brad' is on the short list for potential baby names."

"That's not true, is it?"

"Of course not, but it never hurts to grease the wheels with Brad and stroke that oversized ego of his."

Rachael smiled in relief. Bloom didn't tell her Shriver's middle name was Eugene, although he went by Santana after the band both men loved. He would float this idea by Rachael at a later date. There was plenty of time for naming. Santana, Sam, and Willy all had a nice melodic sound, and Santana would work as either a boy's or a girl's name. Bloom knew how to close a deal—even if this one would take some finesse.

41

CHAPTER 9

ONE FOR MY SISTER

Bloom's world was turning into the big bang of fatherhood. In five short years he had morphed from a confirmed bachelor to a soon-to-be father of three. And his professional life was no less turbulent as he transformed from a Santa Fe gallerist to a Navajo reservation trader, from selling modern art to focusing on traditional Native art.

As an older father, the math was not in his favor. There was no way Bloom could have imagined this crazy scenario. If this kind of change was possible, what could the future bring? He needed some time to think about his high-wire act.

Should he retire his Santa Fe gallery? Once it was gone, there would be no returning to the art business. Bloom's had been his lifeblood, and he could hardly imagine not having his cherished Canyon Road space. To walk away, sell the building, and become a permanent trader at Toadlena seemed unrealistic, yet he had found some inner peace on the rez, a calmness he had never experienced in town. Santa Fe was the City Different—but nothing was as different as the Navajo Nation.

Could his *hózhó* be more important than money, world-class restaurants, and erudite friends?

At the moment, a veil of uncertainty cloaked his imagination. Maybe a happy medium was possible; maybe he could somehow manage both worlds. Supporting three children as an Indian trader—even one receiving free medical care and housing—might not be enough. Giving up an established gallery was a big risk. Once out of the game you didn't come back: like a crack dealer, once you stopped dealing you lost your edge and your client base to the competition. So-called colleagues would be happy to rid themselves of Bloom's—there would be one more piece of the art pie to swallow up—"Goodbye, sorry to see you go, such a loss." Bloom could hear their voices as they scrambled to pick up potential clients and orphaned artists.

Succeeding as a gallerist takes ten years of constant work. Bloom had put in way more than the ten thousand hours Malcolm Gladwell recommends to learn a trade, and in the last few years he had been reaping the rewards of his labor. It still was not easy, but it was not nearly as hard—and now he was considering blowing it all up.

There had been tough times before he had a family to support. He had survived three recessions and other obstacles. During lean years, the one thing most people don't need to spend money on is art; supporting creativity is not a necessary part of their lives. Bloom wanted to be prepared when the financial world went through its next rhythmic swing. When the economy dropped lower, he would need to be in the strongest position possible—and he wasn't sure working as a trading-post operator was a position of strength.

The Two Grey Hills were chameleons of light on this particular day, and Bloom's eyes were fixed on the two stark obelisks as they shifted from one color to another in the blink of an eye. Their mesmerizing beauty was definitely one factor to consider staying at Toadlena. The other was the people—two of whom were sitting patiently in a beat-up truck, waiting for the post's proprietor to open up.

"Another rug to buy," Bloom thought. "Is this my role in life? Helping support my wife's community? Is this what I'm supposed to be doing?"

With his hands full of groceries, he nodded his head toward the visitors as he fumbled with the keys. It had been a cold, dry winter so far. A couple of decent snows in November, but nothing since. The thermometer read fifteen degrees, although it felt more like zero with the sharp wind blowing off the Chuska Mountains.

"Yá át ééh," Bloom said as the grandmothers struggled to open their truck door. Once free of their bonds they started their penguin walk up the slick, hard-packed ground, just as they had done a hundred times before.

"Yá át ééh, Mr. Bloom. I got a nice rug for you. Need to get a good price because it's Christmas in ten days."

"Okay, we'll take a look. Come on up. I'm going to get the fire stoked and make some coffee. Help yourself to a donut—they're still soft."

The grandmas had come on a good day. The fresh groceries wouldn't last and free food was always popular on the rez.

Christmas was a double-edged sword for the trader. Lots of folks were bringing in rugs and jewelry to sell to raise cash for presents, but everyone wanted a little extra money for their goods. Bloom was used to buying during this time of year—it was a Santa Fe ritual, too—but he hadn't been prepared for the hordes of weavings that were all coming off the loom at the same time. Obviously, this was no accident. Bloom halfway expected this was why Sal was waiting until after the New Year to come back home. After fifty years of running the post, he understood the rhythms of the rez.

The rug was a nice 3- by 5-foot weaving with a wonderful design. Well executed and tight, it was better than Violet Yazzie's usual productions, and Bloom was pleased that he would be able to pay the grandmother more than usual for it.

He and the two women headed back to the rug room and settled in on the rickety couch as Bloom pulled up the records of Sal's past sales on the computer and compared notes. The grandmothers watched Bloom intently as they polished off their chocolate donuts, wiping their hands against the old couch adding to its deep, rich color.

"Nice weaving, Violet. It looks like you outdid yourself," Bloom said proudly, waiting for a positive response to his compliment.

"How much you gonna give me for such a nice work?"

"Well, your last rug was only 2 by 4, and not as intricate in its design. Sal paid you $500 for that one. This one is going to be double—$1,000!" Bloom said happily, expecting a big thanks. But that's not what he got.

"Kind of low, don't you think? I spent more than double the time making this one, so I should get paid more than double the usual price, don't you think? I got lots of grandkids that need gifts."

"I'm reading Sal's notes and he says not to expect anything before Christmas from you because you went to see your sister in San Diego for two months. Were you weaving in California?"

"No, I can't weave without a loom."

"So the extra time was more a function of being off the rez and away from your loom than of putting in more work, wouldn't you say?"

"I never said it wasn't. All I said was this one took me more than double the time to make, and it did. So are you going to give me more?"

"Well, I think $1,000 is very fair. You know there are lots of rugs and jewelry coming in right now."

"OK, I'll settle for $1,100 cash and $50 in groceries."

Bloom pondered the offer. It was more than he should pay but it was Christmas and the rug was magnificent. "How about we do the $1,000, which is a fair price, and I give you $100 in credit toward your bill?"

The grandmothers conversed in their native language, and Violet said, "Okay. One hundred dollars off the bill, $50 in credit for food, and I'll take the $1,000. That's close enough. Merry Christmas."

Bloom knew she had made up her mind and it wasn't worth the $50 to make a big deal over it. Besides, he was going to take back the unopened pregnancy test so he had a little found money in his mind.

Bloom stuck out his hand to do a limp handshake, signifying he was in agreement. "I'll get Ronda to write you a check, and you can go pick out $50 worth of groceries. I've got lots to choose from."

"Okay, that sounds good. Can I get another free donut for my other sister? She can't weave no more, but she still likes donuts."

How could Bloom say no? "Sure, it's on the house. Keep up the great work. That's a really nice rug, Violet."

The grandmother could tell Bloom's words had weight. She gave him a heartfelt hug and the two women shuffled from the back room to get their groceries from Ronda, Bloom's part-time helper from the Toadlena community. Twelve dollars was spent on two tins of tobacco to feed Violet's dipping habit. Bloom hated tobacco in all forms and cringed every time he sold a tin, but he had learned enough about the culture to understand he wasn't going to change an eighty-year-old-grandmother's tobacco habit—although he might be able to persuade her to keep making exceptionally fine rugs.

Bloom's concern over a weaver's rug quality and wanting her to do better was an insight for him, and he made another notch on his newly formed mental column: "One more for staying in Toadlena."

He really did care.

CHAPTER 10

YOU'RE IN CHARGE

At 8:50 a.m., Bloom peered out of the rug room window. Marvin Manycoats was on the last leg of his walk down the winding dirt road to the post. Bloom hated the fact that he hadn't been able to wean himself from wearing a watch. He had tried going without it few times at Rachael's behest, but he functioned better on a schedule, as did Marvin. It was a common thread that connected the two, though Marvin kept time with an internal clock by watching the sun's position.

Bloom was fond of Marvin and happily anticipated his arrival. The Navajo had become part of the fabric of Bloom's life. Each day the routine was the same: Marvin would plop down in the barber's chair and pontificate about life's meaning—but today Bloom had a surprise offer he hoped his friend couldn't refuse.

"Hastiin Manycoats, it seems you're a bit late. Did you notice that my fire is hot and the coffee is already brewed?"

"I believe I'm not late, but that you were early. You must think it's April first by the way you make stuff up. The sun hasn't changed its location on your behalf—or has it, my almighty Bloom?"

A large smile spread over Bloom's face. He knew there was no way to trick a man whose survival depended on the careful observation of his surroundings.

"You are correct, my all-knowing Manycoats. I was early—something as revolutionary as changing the rotation of the sun."

"True words, my friend. You don't like to get here one minute before 9 a.m., so what gives?"

"I've got big news and it may affect you, too."

"I'm listening. Does it start with a free ice cream bar?"

"In fact it does, so help yourself. It's on you, so to speak."

"Okay, now I'm interested. How is it on me?"

"Well, first off, I'm going to be a dad again, and you're the first person I've told. Rachael is nearly one month along!"

"You're blessed, Charles Bloom. Many mouths mean lots of blessings, so you are very lucky indeed."

"I know. I fought the idea of having three kids for a long time. It seemed crazy considering I had never held a baby in my arms until five years ago. But somehow it feels right now, as if this is the way my life was supposed to be."

"I never had the honor of being a father," Marvin replied. "I would have enjoyed it, I'm sure, but I'm happy to be Grandpa Manycoats to your growing pack. Hope it's a boy—Marvin Bloom has a nice ring, don't you think?"

"Let's hope it's a girl. Now go get your ice cream and I'll fill you in on my plan."

Marvin looked through the ice cream freezer as if he were picking out a prime cut of meat before selecting just the right flavor—the most expensive one, of course. Then he climbed back on his throne and waited for the rest of the story.

"Rachael and I are going to take a week off to go to Santa Fe to check on the gallery, a kind of retreat before the new baby reality sets in. I would like you to be in charge of the post while I'm gone. You'll have Ronda three days a week to help out; she knows what needs to be done book-wise. The truth is that you've spent more hours in this store than I have, and know the people better. The major difference is that you will need to move from in front of the counter to behind it.

"I'll give you $600 in groceries for your trouble. I just bought enough supplies to get you through the time I'm gone, but if you do need something, you can use my credit card and go up to City Market to get it. I'll give you a key to open the store and lock up.

"What do you say? Care to be in charge of the ice cream freezer? It's fully stocked...."

"Sounds like a no-lose situation. I get free food and you aren't around to bother an old man. I'm in." Marvin flashed the wide-toothed smile that was his universal sign of happiness.

"Great! I'll let Ronda know. She's in the rug room tiding up now. You will meet and greet, help fill grocery orders and be in charge of buying rugs and anything else that walks into the store. Ronda can write the checks for your purchases."

"I've watched old Sal do it for so many years I don't even need the log to figure out the prices. I just know. The good thing is the grandmothers know I'm not going to negotiate from the set price, so it should be pretty easy all around. I do have a question though...."

"What's that Marvin?"

"Well, what do I do if someone brings in something to sell that I don't know anything about—which is everything besides rugs and jewelry. I've seen old Sal buy all sorts of things—kachinas, saddles, tack, furniture, even the occasional painting."

"You can tell a Navajo kachina from a Hopi one, right?"

"Sure. The Hopi doll means something to the people and is well made; the Navajo kachina is beer money, made in some Gallup sweatshop."

"That's right. If it's a Hopi carver, he will tell you what he needs on the piece and you can pay half his retail price if it seems fair. If there is something else you have a question about, you can have Ronda shoot me some phone pics and I'll let you know what I think and how much to pay, if anything. Not many carvers come in and most of the rest of the stuff that shows up is usually worn-out junk that's not worth much, so I doubt it will be a problem."

"What if something weird comes in that I don't have a clue about, and Ronda doesn't know either, and we can't get a hold of you, but I think it's pretty good?"

"If it looks great, ask them what they want for it. If it's under $200, and you can't reach me, just buy it. And make sure Ronda has them fill out a bill of sale. If they want more than $200, get their names and contact information and I'll take a look when I get back.

"More than likely, anything you buy will be fine. I'm not going to get mad if you overpay a little; it will be my problem not yours. When in doubt, be cheap. I'm sure you can tell quality, so go by your gut. I'm available by phone for the most part, and chances are there won't be much besides rugs and the occasional bracelet coming in."

"Okay, boss. When you going to leave?"

"Willy gets out of school in four days, and we'll take off the next day, so you have a few days to shadow me in case you have any other questions."

Marvin couldn't help but let out a laugh.

"What's so funny, Marvin?"

"Bloom, what do you think I do every day? I know your patterns better than you do. And remember, I got that crazy memory thing...."

Bloom realized telling Marvin Manycoats to watch him was ridiculous; the Navajo had a near-photographic memory for people, places, events, and times.

"You're right, Marvin. Hell, you probably know me better than I know myself."

"I do, in fact, know that in about five minutes you're going to head to the bathroom."

Bloom turned red, then his stomach growled. "Wrong! Looks like you don't know everything. I'm heading there now."

Bloom left the room as Marvin finished his ice cream, secure in the knowledge that the post would be in good hands while he was gone.

CHAPTER 11

HONEY BUN

Rachael was in nesting mode, the nursery particulars finalized in her mind. The baby would sleep in their room; it was a two-bedroom hogan, so there were no other options. She would repaint the room blue; her instincts told her this was the correct color.

If Toadlena ended up as home base, a construction project would be necessary as the baby could only sleep in their room for about a year. That gave her twenty months to get a new addition built, find another place on the rez (which would never happen), or move back to Santa Fe and find an appropriate house that would allow her to graze her sheep.

Santa Fe was on the calendar for next week—a family vacation and Christmas. If they came home by the first of the year, a tentative decision would hopefully have been made. There were lots of pros and cons to consider, and a fresh look at Bloom's stomping ground would help.

Her first choice for herself would be to stay in her family home, but this didn't seem responsible if they wanted to continue to build Bloom's Santa Fe gallery. Bloom's was successful—not an easy feat in a city where galleries closed as fast as they opened.

The Toadlena Trading Post was fraught with issues. Rachael knew firsthand it was a money pit most of the time, and if they took on the responsibility for the community that commitment would never end. It would be a lifelong job and she wasn't sure either she or Bloom could deal with the consequences.

Trading-post life looked romantic from afar, but she had watched old Sal at close range when she was growing up: he was often strapped for money and always on call. Bloom seemed more enthralled with the idea of taking over the post than she was, which surprised her. Maybe he saw something bigger for the business than she could envision?

Spending time in Santa Fe over Christmas could be a good litmus test. Shriver was indeed out of town, so his house was theirs, and Dr. J, Bloom's only employee, was thrilled not to have to man the store on his own during the holidays. Too many visitors and not enough eyes meant losing inventory to shoplifters over Christmas—an event as common to the season as carolers singing "Silent Night," and plastic farolitos topping homes and hotels.

The northern route to Santa Fe was about four hours long and went through some of the most desolate land in America. The moonscape terrain of the Bisti Badlands was for the most part uninhabitable, even by the Navajo. U.S. highway 550 and N.M. 96 shifted from barren desert to ponderosa and juniper, finally emerging at picturesque Abiquiú, a route Rachael never tired of, even in the winter when the roads could be treacherous. Interstate 40 was safer, but the drive through Gallup and Albuquerque didn't give her the real flavor of the Land of Enchantment. The northern route was dotted with the churches of Regina, Gallina, and Coyote—all now decorated to the hilt in their Christmas finery.

The temperature was well below freezing, with crystal-clear blue skies and a hint of orange across the horizon as the Bloom family dropped into Santa Fe.

"Well, Mr. Bloom, is this our home?" Rachael asked, as the kids were yelling, "We're home! We're home!" from the back seat of the pickup.

"I guess for me it is, but I'm torn. I love the solitude of Toadlena and its natural raw beauty—but this town has so much to offer, including the best enchilada sauce in North America. How about we stop at DeVargas Center and get a bowl of green-chile stew at Atrisco?"

"I'm with you. I'll have a stuffed sopapilla and lots of honey."

Again the kids screamed, "Sop a pilas! Sop a pilas!"

"Can you have honey in your condition?" Bloom asked.

"What condition is that, Charles Bloom?"

"P-R-E-G-N-A-N-T condition. What did you think I meant?" Bloom smiled as he spelled out the word.

"I don't know, maybe you were hinting about someone who is about to grow by thirty pounds over the next eight months."

"Rachael, you know I'm not worried about your weight. Your problem is you never gain enough—even Doc Riddley tells you to eat more. What I was referring to was that I had heard honey was a no-no for babies."

"Oh, man you got a lot to learn. This is number three kiddo, right?"

Bloom's face flushed.

"It's fine while I'm P-R-E-G-N-A-N-T, although you are right that newborns cannot have honey. So I will be having sopapillas with LOTS of honey."

Willy and Sam chanted, "Honey, honey," as the Bloom family headed directly to the DeVargas Center on the north side of town. A cluster of independently owned shops and restaurants, the mall had not yet gotten the word from the outside world that its brand of local retail and food was dying out; in Santa Fe, the combination thrived.

The restaurant was packed, as usual, and it was too cold to wait outside so twenty customers huddled in a space made for ten. Servers were clearing tables as quickly as one family left and the next family sat down—the fast service and excellent food were two of the reasons Bloom loved this so-called hole in the wall.

Once they were seated, the Bloom family ordered without a menu and gobbled up last summer's chiles and steaming hot sopapillas. Once their hunger was satisfied, it was time to make room for the next Santa Fe family and check on the gallery before they headed to Shriver's house.

Rachael's pickup snaked through the Santa Fe Plaza crawling with tourists. The ground was whitish-brown with snow, and leafless elm trees twinkled with an array of colored lights. Bloom double-parked next to the Starbucks on West San Francisco Street so the kids could get a good look at the Cathedral Basilica of St Francis of Assisi, its large pines transformed into humongous Christmas trees.

"I want one that big," Willy screamed in Bloom's ear, as his father was wishing he had bypassed the plaza at that moment.

"We will see what we can find, Willy. We need to get a menorah, too"

"A mi-what?" Willy asked.

"It's for the Jewish faith; you are a part of the Jewish tribe, too."

"Mommy is Diné, so what about her? She needs a Christmas, too."

"Don't worry about me," Rachael laughed. "I got lots of Christmas to go around for all of us—Navajo, Christian, and Jewish."

Bloom cranked up the truck and increased the volume on his favorite Santa Fe radio station. His faith was not something he wore on his sleeve, so it was time to change subjects again.

"Hey, kids... when we go to the gallery you can build a snowman in front of it. There should be enough snow, so what do you say?" Bloom offered.

"Snowmen are cool," Willie screamed. "I'm going to make a Navajo snowman with a big feather bonnet."

Bloom would explain to Willy later that Navajos didn't wear bonnets—it was the Plains Indians that did that—but for now he would keep his mouth shut and drive. By this time next year, a crying baby would add to the cacophony of kid noise.

He could hardly wait.

CHAPTER 12

POINTS ADDING UP

The entrance to Bloom's gallery was awash in twinkle lights, while the plastic farolitos lining the driveway gave off a yellow hue that resembled an airport runway in a fog bank. Two sets of tire tracks and a few footprints were visible in the new snow, an indicator of today's slow sales; next week would be different.

Bloom was observant. The "snow sign," as he had begun calling it ten years ago, had become an indicator of slow sales over years of long winters in Santa Fe. The "trash can sign" was another negative indicator: fewer than normal trash cans lining the street on Tuesday meant there had not been much packing or unpacking by the businesses along the road.

As soon as the Bloom family truck came to a halt, Willy bolted for the casita's back yard and Sam started screaming to be let out of her kid's seat, kicking her feet wildly.

"Dad, the gate's locked. Open this thing so I can start the Navajo snowman!" Willy joined Sam in the chaos.

"Sam, you're free. Please stop screaming! My hearing is bad enough," Bloom pleaded.

"Willy and Samantha, get back over here. You two have to put on your gloves and hats; it's freezing." A white cloud emerged from Rachael's mouth as she yelled to her children.

Willy ran back to get the gloves lying on the floorboard of the truck as Sam trailed behind.

Charles rummaged through a dozen keys before he found the right one for the gate. Once it was open, both children were off and running, the sound of their laughter filling the chilled air.

Bloom opened the front door of the gallery, turned off the alarm, and switched on the lights. The thermostat read a balmy seventy-six degrees inside: Dr. J had forgotten to turn down the thermostat. Bloom's sole employee was getting older, and Bloom had begun wondering how much longer he could leave the day-to-day business of running the gallery to him. His arrangement with the heretofore responsible employee might be reaching its expiration date.

Two lights had burned out, but Bloom could see the walls looked great. His winter group show, an exhibit he had hung in late October, was in place. A red dot on one painting's tag indicated his negative sales signs were not holding totally true. Dr. J had not told him about the sale, which meant the piece was still listed on the website as available. Bloom would correct that when he got to Shriver's house. The exhibit was scheduled to run through the end of December; Bloom would rehang the gallery walls before he returned to Toadlena.

Bloom plopped down in an oversized green chair that he had owned for twenty years, his body neatly fitting into the foam's permanent indentations.

"Well, what do you think? Santa Fe contemporary with a bit of Santa Fe funk OR the rez and all that comes with it?"

"I don't know, Bloom. It's so easy here sometimes; a $4,000 painting sold and you didn't have to make it or buy it."

"That's true enough. Sometimes it's a lot easier to sell an expensive painting than a $250 rug."

"And, if you want your morning coffee and don't want to wait on my magnificent cowboy brew, you can walk to the bookstore on Garcia Street—or, if you're ambitious and want some exercise, you can walk to the plaza and window shop along the way," Rachael said, adding, "The only window shopping back home is for panes of glass to replace the ones that have broken."

"You're a funny woman, my love, but in a lot of ways your words couldn't be truer—life is different here and I'm used to my Santa Fe routine. But maybe that's the problem. Maybe I could use a midlife change. Hell, I'm going to have three kids, so how bad could it be?"

It didn't sound like Bloom was accentuating the positive of his present life circumstances.

"I don't know—how bad could it be?" Rachael frowned.

"No, I don't mean it like that. It's just I had struggled so long with the idea of having another kid, the same way I did with number two, but when you told me I was going to be a dad again, it felt wonderful—zero struggle. So what I was so ineptly trying to say is change can be good. I can handle that bumpy, unpaved rez road if we decide to take it."

Rachael's shoulders relaxed and she smiled.

"Okay, Charlie Bloom. How about you and I crunch the hard numbers over the next few days, get my girlfriend from art school to watch the kids one night, and make a date to talk about how we should proceed. And, of course, after the date we can get some needed exercise if you know what I mean...."

"I do. That stationary bike at Shriver's house hasn't been used in a year."

"You're a butt, Charles James Bloom. You can get over here and warm me up—though it does seem kind of toasty right now doesn't it?"

Bloom squeezed his wife close and whispered, "Yes, it is very warm—hot in fact," as he nibbled at his wife's supple neck.

Rachael squealed with delight. "I love you, Charles Bloom."

✹ ✹ ✹ ✹

Rachael and Charles spent the next few days deep cleaning, paying bills, working on the grounds, and checking the general condition of their gallery and casita. Winter in Santa Fe takes a toll on a building; loose bricks can cause trips and tourists can sue, but that was never going to happen on Bloom's watch.

All was in order; the place was being well cared for by Dr. J in Bloom's absence, a reassuring thought. The Canyon Road Christmas Eve walk was in two days, with thousands of tourists and city's faithful making their way up the winding road caroling, laughing, and making last-minute purchases.

Bloom had brought a dozen small Toadlena/Two Grey Hills rugs, all priced below $500, to help defer the trip's expenses, and he was sure most of the monochromatic textiles would find new homes. He was starting to realize how many rugs the Toadlena/Two Grey Hills weavers actually produced, and knew there would be another dozen new rugs waiting for him when he got back to the post. He couldn't decide whether this was good or bad.

No points had been allotted to either the Santa Fe or the Toadlena columns yet.

Both Rachael and Charles were upbeat and generally agreed they were happy in Santa Fe and would be able to make a better living in the city than on the rez. The Santa Fe schools were marginal, though, unless they went the private route, which Rachael was against. They didn't teach Diné in Santa Fe either, but she could homeschool the kids in the evenings and make up for the weak curriculum of the public school system, which suffered from too many kids and not enough teachers.

No matter where you lived in the state, New Mexico always scored in the bottom tier of education in the U.S., a statistic that excluded Los Alamos. That city, nestled in the Jemez Mountains near Santa Fe, had one of the highest numbers of PhDs in a single town in America, a throwback to its origins with the Manhattan Project. Los Alamos recognized the importance of education, but it was too far away for Bloom to make it a comfortable daily commute.

Healthcare providers would not be an issue in Santa Fe either. There was an Indian hospital close enough for Rachael and the kids, and, even though Charles wasn't Native, he did qualify for services through Rachael's participation in the Indian Health Service.

Living on the rez meant an hour's trip each way for general medical care never seeing the same doctor twice; most left as soon as they had rotated through their placements to pay off medical school debts. The Indian Health Service's doctors in Santa Fe were at the top of the rung and were lifers. Who wouldn't want to have a duty station in Santa Fe for years at a time?

It seemed points for moving back to the City Different were racking up fast, and it would take a major upset for the trend line to change.

Unbeknownst to the expecting parents, great change was only a few months away: a pack of coyote spirits were on the prowl, and their hunger would not be denied.

CHAPTER 13

CALIFORNIA LOVE

Marvin Manycoats arrived an hour early to start his new position as head trader of the Toadlena Trading Post. He wanted the central potbelly stove hot to greet the day's clients, and to make sure all was in order by the time he opened the door at 9 a.m.

Unlocking the door with Bloom's key felt odd. Marvin had waited dozens of times in the last ten years for Sal to fish his ball of keys out of his pocket and struggle to find the right one to open up, but he had never considered the possibility he would be the keeper of the keys. He was proud of that responsibility—after all, he had led a platoon of Marines and made life and death choices for them in Vietnam, and he had often been in charge of construction crews when he worked in Los Angeles. But this was different; this was his home turf. Marvin had been thinking of himself as retired and, to some extent, past his prime; he certainly wasn't expecting to take on anything of substance.

Instinctively, Marvin headed over to the refrigerator to retrieve an ice cream bar. As he slid the door open and reached in, he realized he, and only he, would decide if the treat was on the house or part of his $600 credit. As Marvin selected this morning's choice and went to the credit sheet to write down his purchase, he started to chuckle out loud.

"Bloom, I see why you hired me. You just want me to pay for all these ice cream bars that are usually on the house, you white devil!"

Marvin straightened cans, rearranged the ice cream bars so he knew exactly what was available, and did a quick count of the money in the cash drawer. He was ready for Ronda and some customers.

Ronda arrived on time and the two conversed in Diné about their strategy for running the post in Bloom's absence. They both laughed that this was the first time Navajos had been in charge of their own supplies since Kit Carson rounded them up for the Long Walk in 1864.

Ronda was fine with Marvin being in charge. This was a part-time job for her, not a long-term position. Ronda preferred to weave to earn a living, but the extra money helped pay the bills and the post was close to her home. If a problem occurred, it would fall on Marvin's shoulders rather than hers.

The first visitor of the day was Elma Yellowhair, who brought in a small Kokopelli-inspired rug, her trademark. Marvin had known her family for sixty years, so the negotiation was nothing more than having coffee and talking about grandkids for an hour before paying the $375 she always received. But this time he threw in a candy bar.

The simple act of giving away food felt great and Marvin planned on doing it every time he bought something from the locals, even if it had to come out of his credit. Marvin marked the giveaways down on a separate sheet so Bloom would know what he had done in case it was a problem, though he doubted it would be an issue.

A winter storm was bearing down on the Chuskas, only the second wet blast of the season. The mountains were lost in snow flurries, the post's ground a cover of white. Locals stocking up on provisions provided a steady flow until noon; by 2 p.m., most residents were tucked into their homes and Ronda left early.

Marvin worked the broom in areas that had been neglected since summer, ferreting out a variety of dust bunnies, gum wrappers, and dead insects. After sweeping, he got out the mop and spent an hour on the floor until there was a clean shine to the boards. The big Navajo smiled; a neat workspace pleased him.

The sun had set and the snow had completely stopped—another hope for needed moisture foiled. It was 5 p.m.—closing time, Marvin thought—when he heard the creak of the heavy plank door opening. He turned his good ear toward the sound and saw a Navajo in his mid-twenties, woolen hat pulled down to his eyes, wearing a worn army jacket and a large black backpack slung over his right shoulder. The young man stopped at the door to give a cursory tap of his boot tips against the outside wall before entering. A small amount of snow fell off as he shuffled in.

Marvin watched as the man left a snail track of snow and red mud on his freshly cleaned floor before he stopped at the counter, removed his pack, and rested it next to Marvin. Manycoats' happy demeanor soured as he looked at the wet floor.

"Yá' át' ééh," the stranger said.

"Yá' át' ééh. Cold day to be walking. You catch a ride up here?"

Marvin was aware he had heard no engine sounds and assumed the man hadn't come by horse, as he didn't recognize him as a local.

"Yeah. Tough to hitch a ride today. Cost me $4 to get someone to stop and I had to walk the last quarter mile. You guys must not be used to snow; everyone's hiding like bunnies from the coyote's jaw."

"Where you from?"

"I live up by the Utah border, outside of Mexican Hat. We get a lot of ice, so this is nothing much to worry about unless you got worn tires."

"Well, that's about every other truck." Marvin's smile reappeared.

The young man caught the joke and nodded his head in agreement but did not break a smile.

"You visiting relatives?"

"Nah, no clan here. A girlfriend in Shiprock. Most of my family is up around the Utah/Arizona border. I came down to see a man named Bloom. You're not him, are you?"

"No, I'm more Manycoats than *mensch*," Marvin chuckled.

Still no change in expression from the young man.

"Can you get him? I was told in Bluff he would be the guy for what I got to sell."

Marvin's interest peaked at the mention of something Bloom might want.

"I'm Mr. Bloom's buyer when he's not around. I can listen to offers in his absence. If it's something we might want, I can write a check."

Marvin liked the sound of "we might want" coming out of his mouth; he was important again.

The man hesitated and stared at Marvin as he sized up his offer.

"Okay. I was told this Bloom guy likes paintings and he's got some big gallery in Santa Fe. I got a painting he might like and I want to sell it today."

"That's all true. You got the painting with you?"

The man opened his pack and pulled out a badly stained, cream-colored muslin cloth secured with a rattlesnake skin, rattle intact. Marvin inched away from the package. Rattlesnakes were sacred in the Navajo world, not something to be messed with unless they were to be used in witching.

"You're traditional, huh?" the man asked, watching Marvin's reaction.

"Yes, I know the power of the snake firsthand. It's not something you want to mess with unless you want to challenge the Holy People."

"Yeah, my grandfather said the same thing." The man smiled for the first time.

"Smart man. Is he a medicine man?"

"Not exactly. People say he is powerful, but I don't believe in that stuff. Sorry, but we modern Navajo need to move past those old ways."

Marvin did not like this man; he was asking for trouble.

The man untied the skin and opened the package. The painting was of an Anasazi ruin in the high desert framed in cheap pine. The subject matter was another negative sign for Marvin.

"Okay. Looks like a bunch of Nasazi homes. Can you bring the painting closer?"

"It's not a snake," the young Navajo scoffed. "You can hold the painting if you want; it's on a board so it won't break."

Marvin picked it up and examined the piece. It seemed old and was dated July 1922, with "Ariz" written in the paint. He didn't recognize the name of the artist—someone called Maynard Dixon. The back of the board also had some words on it, maybe a title, a San Francisco address, and some other writing that meant nothing to Marvin.

"Looks pretty nice. What you asking for it?"

"I was hoping you could tell me, that's why I came to you. I had some guy offer me $500, but that didn't seem fair. I don't know nothing about art or if this painting is any good, but the other guy seemed real interested. I know it's old—see, it has a date, 1922."

"How do you know that's the date it was made?"

"It's been in my family for three generations. I need as much money as I can get. If you don't want it, I know someone will pay me more. It's the real deal.

"Give me a minute and let me see what I can find out."

Marvin walked away, keeping the man in his range of vision, and called Bloom. He watched the stranger help himself to one of his favorite ice cream bars and sit in his barber chair, looking around. His inner voice was saying, "Watch this kid closely; he may be up to something."

The phone went directly to voice mail, so Marvin left Bloom a message to call him back as soon as he got the call.

"Well, I tried to get Bloom but he's not answering. If you want to come back tomorrow I can see what he might offer."

The young man considered his options, then said, "Nah. I need to sell it today. How about $2,000? I know it's worth that much."

Marvin had never bought a painting in his life. The only art in his house was an old Ford calendar of running horses—and that had been thrown in with his truck purchase.

"I can't authorize that, I'm afraid. But I can do $500 like the other man." Marvin gulped at his bold offer, but the painting looked well done and old.

"Shit man, that won't help me. I told you I was offered $500 and I need more. I'm selling it today, to you or someone else if I have to.

"How about $1,500 cash?" the man said, trying to make a quick sale.

"Give me a minute." Marvin tried Bloom's cell again; still no answer.

Marvin decided to do the deal anyway. He would put in half his money and half his boss's money. If Bloom didn't like the deal, he would only be out $750—not the whole $1,500. Marvin could live with that risk and he was sure Bloom could too. The worst-case scenario was that Marvin would never be given the post keys again.

"Okay. I'll agree to $1,500. You will need to fill out a bill of sale that says you are the rightful owner of the painting. Is that going to be a problem?"

"Nope, not a problem. It's a family piece. Cash money, right?"

Marvin went to the cashbox and checked. He had the money; it would wipe out his petty cash, but he had enough. Tomorrow he would replenish the post's half of the purchase from his own stash.

"Correct; $1,500 cash."

Marvin pulled out a bill of sale and recorded: "Dixon painting 1922 purchased for $1,500 cash."

"I'll need an ID for the bill of sale."

"Don't have one, no car, but I'll sign your paper."

Marvin thought about it, and decided a photo would be as good. "Okay, sign the paper, but I want a photo of you, the money, and the painting as documentation that I bought the piece."

"Whatever. Doesn't matter none to me. Like I said, it's a family piece. No one's gonna need any bill of sale or ID anyway. Once it's yours, it's yours."

"Well, you never know about that. Better to be careful than regretful," Marvin said, knowing just how important a receipt could be.*

Marvin pulled out Sal's Polaroid camera and took a photo of the kid holding the cash. The young man posed gangster-style and stuck out his tongue with the Dixon propped up next to him. Marvin shook his head at the ridiculous image that slid out of the camera.

Marvin handed the young Navajo a pen and the bill of sale, which the man filled out in a crablike position, his body covering up what his left hand wrote. When he finished, he gave the document to Marvin.

> Name: E. T. Tsosie
>
> Address: Mexican Hat, Arizona
>
> Phone: blank
>
> Email: blank

"No phone?" Marvin asked.

"Nah, too expensive," Tsosie shrugged.

"No P.O. box?"

"Everyone knows me in Mexican Hat. I don't have a regular place right now. Me and Grandpa are having our differences, so I'm kind of between homes."

Marvin couldn't help but make a jab. "Maybe get rid of that rattlesnake skin."

---

*Read Marvin's backstory in the sixth Bloom book, *Indian School Days*.

Tsosie ignored the taunt and recounted the cash in front of Marvin, as if he had shortchanged him in the deal.

"Okay; $1,500, and you're getting a bargain."

Then Tsosie grabbed an oversized handful of gum off the counter and shoved it into his pocket with the wad of cash. Two Double Bubbles rolled under the barber chair. Marvin figured he would leave the gum there as a secret stash for later down the road.

"You don't mind, do you, since you're getting such a smoking deal?" Tsosie asked. Marvin did care and made a note on the bill of sale of "handful of bubble gum" and the earlier "ice cream bar."

"You know, Mr. Tsosie, our post has to pay for the groceries just as you would at City Market."

"You don't have to be such an old grump; it's just a handful of cheap gum. Here take this—it came with the painting anyway."

Tsosie fished a stone from his pants pocket and slid it along the glass counter. Like a bar beer, it skipped across the surface, pinging each time it hit an uneven area of the bubble-filled glass top. Marvin winced, hoping the rock hadn't scratched the antique surface.

"What is that?" Marvin asked.

"Suppose to be a dinosaur tooth, but it could just be a triangle-shaped rock that looks like one. I don't really know for sure. We have stuff like that all over our property, but my grandfather Roanhorse says it's a tooth and it came with the painting."

"Anything else come with it?"

"Yeah, that old rattlesnake skin you love so much, and the beat-up cloth covering the painting. Maybe you need to embrace the skin, stop worrying about witches and skinwalkers, and enter the real world of the modern Diné—a world of alcohol, drugs, and poverty mixed with rap music. The rest of that stuff is made up."

"I'll take the cloth, but the skin is your problem. Please take that with you. I would recommend you bury the snake's spirit near a juniper— and soon—then get a cleansing sing. It's not good to handle a snake unless you're witching someone. Otherwise, you're witching yourself. Ask your grandfather; he will tell you that's not made-up, but part of the reality of our complex world."

The young man broke out in laughter.

"You and my grandfather are both old school, man. You're right. I should keep the snakeskin 'cause it's bad-ass looking. I don't believe in witches, and the only old-school sing I'll do is "California Love" by 2Pac and Dr. Dre."

Tsosie balled up the muslin cloth and tossed it to Marvin. "Here you go, one old painting sack."

The young Navajo then laid out the thin, worn snakeskin and fashioned a loop, then slid the circle around his knit hat, the tail draping back off his neck.

"How do I look? Pretty bad-ass, huh?" Tsosie jumped up and down trying to make the rattle sound its warning.

"No, Mr. Tsosie, not bad-ass—just a lost Navajo desperately in need of a sing. Wearing a snakeskin like that can make you crippled. That noise you hear means caution and it's ringing for you," Marvin said, his face deadpan.

Tsosie ignored Marvin's warnings. Taunting the older Navajo's traditional beliefs, he turned his head side to side in a Warholian style—then stopped his idiotic behavior when he realized that he had what he came for and it was time to go.

"You're closing soon, aren't you? Can you give me a ride down to that Shell station on 491? It's cold out tonight, not safe to be walking this time of day."

"Yeah, I will give you a ride, but first I need to walk home and get my truck. You can walk with me if you want; it's about a five-mile hike to my hogan. I'll lock up in a few minutes."

"How about you walk home to get your ride and I'll sit out on the porch and have a couple of smokes. I'm not feeling the urge to walk any more than I already have today—got a bad foot."

Marvin thought to himself the only thing wrong with this kid was that he needed a boot in the butt. He was lazy, rude, and had lost his way as a Navajo. His *hózhó* was in shambles. Marvin would help him tonight, but he saw bad things in the man's future if Tsosie didn't drastically change his ways.

"Okay, go have a smoke—just make sure you put the butts in the can next to the bench; we don't want any building fires."

Tsosie nodded his head "yes" and settled in on the porch. He retrieved a set of earphones from his backpack and started bouncing his head and chewing his gum to the beat.

"No phone, huh?" Marvin thought, then let it slide.

Marvin had indeed seen the kid's future and it was all bad—for Tsosie and for anyone that came in contact with him.

CHAPTER 14

THE RUSTLER'S SONG

When the burros were safely tied to a massive juniper whose branches provided ample shade, Everett traversed the edge of a steep sandstone mesa to determine the origin of smoke filtering down the valley. Once at his vantage point, it didn't take long for him to pinpoint the source.

About a half-mile away, six scraggly cattle in the process of being branded were pinned against a cliff face. Three men's voices were discernable; two had western twangs, the third a Native cadence. Their words were hard to understand, but they appeared to be the rustlers that Bryson had warned him about.

There was no apparent way around the roadblock of cattle, and to try to guide the burros to the top of the mesa was dicey at best. The rock's fragility could mean losing a burro and being discovered. Moving them would be a huge risk, one Everett wasn't willing to take. He had no schedule; Dixon's ruins weren't going anywhere. The prudent action was to wait out the rustlers and let them finish branding their stolen cattle so they would move on.

Everett wanted a closer look so he could decipher what kind of men he was dealing with in case they came his way. The advantage was his. They would never guess another human was within twenty miles, as demonstrated by their boisterous conversation. He methodically picked his way through the waist-high sage until he reached a point where he could make out the men's words. The Indian appeared to be Ute or Navajo; the men, in their thirties, were hardened by the elements and all business.

One man slit the throat of a steer. The Indian held its horns as it struggled for life, showing no emotion other than "hold her tight." They butchered strips of bloody meat off the rump and laid them against a makeshift wooden drying rack. The smell was intoxicating — fresh hot beef on the grill.

Everett wanted to walk into camp and say, "Hi, I'm Everett Ruess, explorer and nature lover. How about a strip of one of those rustled cows?" The absurdity of his thoughts gave him an idea. If he had to spend the next half-day waiting for these hombres to move on, he might actually try to sneak a few pieces of meat once they went to bed. Stealing from the stealers would make a great story for his diary!

The wanderer wedged his thin body into a crack in a nearby mesa wall who's entrance was obscured by a huge clump of Apache Plume. The natural camouflage allowed him to observe the men and wait for them to retire. A four-pole willow drying rack ran nearly ten feet, with the desiccating meat lining the entire length. Puddles of drippings looked like raindrops on the dusty red sand below.

A late half-moon illuminated the camp an hour after the three men went to bed, and Everett crept out of his hidey-hole. Using his knife, he fashioned a long pole from a tender sapling limber enough to have some give. Like a fisherman noodling catfish, he dislodged strips of meat using his rod as an extension of his hand. The meat had adhered to the poles and the limber rod made it hard to free the tasty treats, but once a strip had been flipped to the ground, Everett used his sapling rod to drag the meat home. He dusted off the dirt and gobbled it down. The beef was delicious, dirt and all.

By the time he had stolen eight pieces, his technique had improved and he called it a night, afraid he was pushing his luck. He secured the small sack of meat next to the painting in his pack and headed back. Finding the small path took a couple of minutes; the trail was not as obvious in the night sky.

Everett climbed, worked his way along the mesa, and then started the descent to his camp. Once he was two-thirds of the way down the steep trail, he started a low hum in his throat. He was not singing or speaking out loud—his usual way of talking to himself—but humming. The sound gave him the sense of being one with his world. Soon he felt out of danger and began composing a new song for his most recent adventure.

> *"Rustlers and meat, I'm not afraid to repeat, I'll grab what I see and eat what they seek.*
>
> *"I'm no rustler, bandit, or thief; I'm a man of nature on a mission of peace.*
>
> *"But given a stick, I'm able to pick a tasty dinner, courtesy the rustler's retreat.*
>
> *"Yes, I'm a man of nature and peace, but don't underestimate Everett Ruess and the risks he will take."*

Everett began singing his tune in a low voice as he headed toward the bottom of the steep ravine, memorizing the words as he hiked along in the cool November breeze. He couldn't wait to draw an image of the meat rack and rustlers asleep and put a copy of the new song right underneath it. Everett's final entry into his diary before retiring to his cold woolen blanket read: "No fire tonight, rustlers a mile away, procured some fine strip steak that will make two nice meals. Hope to move on tomorrow, will wait to see what transpires."

✳ ✳ ✳ ✳

The morning light was like an alarm clock ringing in Everett's brain as the sun's rays bounced off his tanned face. It was 7 a.m. and his blanket was frosted with the season's first heavy crust of ice. As his eyes cleared, he noticed two ravens heading north.

"Were the rustlers gone?" he wondered to himself, wishing for a fire and some warm coffee—a luxury he shouldn't allow himself. Everett listened for any signs of human life and looked more closely at the sky: "No smoke."

He decided to risk a very small fire that he started with a match, dry moss, and a few juniper sticks. He poured some coffee grounds into a tin cup filled with two-day-old water and waited for the steam to announce it was ready. Then he laid a strip of meat on a semi-flat granite rock he had placed in the fire; the sizzling fat smelled wonderful. He devoured the meat in a few seconds, nursing the aromatic coffee as he extinguished the fire. Once again he would head up to the rustlers camp to verify their presence. He hoped they had headed back home with their loot.

The walk up the narrow road to the mesa top was not nearly as taxing as it had been the day before. His legs felt better today, the swelling and bruising that he had been experiencing for the last week had eased, giving him more energy for hiking.

The three men were indeed gone, having taken down their meat poles and hidden them. From his vantage point, Everett couldn't see the racks, so he crept nearer to inspect the abandoned camp. The men had been careful, sweeping the dirt so no grease droppings were visible. This wasn't their first rodeo; they were professionals.

Everett thought he could see a small cloud of dust in the distance, formed by the remaining cattle and the men. Feeling better about his situation, he lingered at the camp until he found the drying poles in the same crack he had hidden himself in the day before. That ground was also swept clean. Suddenly a streak of terror raced up his spine: they must have seen his tracks! What to do? He looked around wondering if this could be a trap. Could they be watching him?

Everett started to panic; he hurried back up to the mesa top and down the trail, looking behind himself constantly. Nothing. An hour passed while he did nothing but listen and watch for movement. This was a first for the man who loved nature; his only concern was the men. With his nerves now in check, the proverbial bullet dodged, he planned to give a wide birth to these rustlers and their plunder—no more bravado songs today.

He sat under the eaves of a large overhanging rock and pulled out *20,000 Leagues Under the Sea*, a book his mom had sent to Wetherill's post. For the next three hours Everett was Captain Nemo, battling the forces of evil. He could relate to the man, especially with rustlers close by. His stomach started to churn: lunchtime. He put the book away and took out some hardtack to nibble on while he reviewed his situation. He was sure he would recognize the men; he had been close enough to see the details of their faces. He hoped he didn't accidently run into them in Bluff, especially when he returned to see Bryson in a month or so.

Honesty is a virtue, his mother used to say, but turning local thieves into the law was risky business in a small Mormon town. He was pretty sure if he squealed on these banditos, only the Indian would be arrested; the other men would be free to take care of loose ends.

In a few days he would be at Hole in-the-Wall Gulch where he could set up a camp for his animals and hustle back down to Dixon's ruins, leaving the rustlers in the past. The adventure was heating up even as the weather was cooling down.

CHAPTER 15

NEMO

It took three days to reach Hole-in-the-Wall Gulch. As promised, there was ample grazing and water. Everett knew he could safely leave his burros there for two months if needed, and immediately began construction on a large brush corral.

The math was simple enough: two weeks to hike down to northern Arizona and find Dixon's ruins, then a few days to paint and explore before returning to his gulch base camp. This was assuming the weather held, and in mid-November nothing was certain. If all went as planned, he would make a two-day stop on his way back up to retrieve his burros and spend some time filling Bryson in on the adventure.

Once back at camp, he would go through the Hole-in-the-Wall and explore the canyon country of Utah. In late December, he'd head back to Wetherill's post to present the trader with a watercolor of the elusive ruins, sell or board his burros, and hitchhike home to Los Angeles for the winter.

Of course, any of these plans could be delayed a month or more depending on food, his findings, or poor health. "Tired blood" caused unremitting fatigue some days, and he knew he might have to rest before making long hikes. All this went through his mind as he constructed the corral.

Everett admired his handiwork. He had never constructed such an elaborate structure before; it was two days in the making. He would spend one more day with the burros to make sure the corral was sound, and use the time to finish Jules Verne's book. The young explorer identified with the fearless captain Nemo and decided that for the rest of this adventure—or maybe even longer—he would be Nemo, not Everett Ruess. To mark his commitment to his new identity, Everett/Nemo climbed to the top of a small cave and carved "NEMO" on the wall.

A cold wind woke Everett with intermittent snowflakes. Winter was coming—a good day to start south, he thought. The burros had stayed put, even after he tried to scare them. They would be safe as long as no rustler or mountain lion came by. He worried less about the latter as Bryson had assured him the big cats had been cleaned out.

Nemo reduced his backpack to the bare essentials to keep its weight under forty pounds—matches, food, canteen, one change of underwear, shirt, two pairs of socks, a large wool blanket, painting gear, diary, two pencils, camera, pocket knife, compass, cooking pot, fork, first aid kit, revolver, one box of bullets, and Maynard Dixon's painting wrapped in muslin. His one extravagance was Jules Verne's book; he had enjoyed it so much he planned to read it again.

His supplies provided sustenance for two weeks to a month, assuming his journey progressed according to plan. Nemo would need to restock food at some point during the trip; he couldn't pack too much because of the weight. He carried the lighter food items and stowed the cans in a tall, bear-proofed juniper tree. His rations were peanuts, dried fruit, hardtack, broken cookies, and a two-day supply of water. With any luck he might run across an old apple grove or slow rabbit, but for the most part he had to follow a strict regimen. He would love to have a plate of fresh vegetables; his diet had been bare of any green-leafed items for over a month, and his body was craving them, even if they weren't his favorite food group.

Nemo double-checked his gear and hauled the burro packs and the extra food, minus the cans, into a small cave he had discovered. These supplies would be critical for his survival when he returned from his search for the ruin. The saddles were too cumbersome to hide, and he figured if anyone ran across his burros they might as well have the saddles too. The outfit would bring in $20, and Everett knew it would be hard to resist free money in these tough economic times. He was fine with this potential loss. He knew he was luckier than most, with understanding parents who regularly provided food money for his extended trips and supported his painting.

Everett recognized man was sometimes evil and there was nothing he could do to change that—just avoid the dark side whenever possible. In Everett's case, though, encountering evil was about to become unavoidable.

✳ ✳ ✳ ✳

The first two days of the journey back down toward Mexican Hat were uneventful. The storm that had threatened snow never materialized, though the temperature changed significantly. There were no more pesky mosquitoes; it was winter regardless of what the calendar might say.

Everett followed the same route he had used when he came across the rustlers' butchering area. Now there were fresh tracks. The men were back, but how long ago had they been there? As much as he loved nature and the outdoors, when it came to tracking or hunting, Everett was not very adept, surprising considering the amount of time he had spent in the backcountry. For the painter, killing animals had no joy.

The drying sticks had not been touched, but the area was not the same as he had left it a week earlier. Maybe the rancher who had lost cattle was on their scent, or maybe the tracks were from some shepherds passing through. He had talked to a couple of peaceful sheep wranglers with their flocks on his first day out of Bluff. They were moving slowly, so it was possible, though he didn't see any tracks that seemed to belong to sheep.

Everett decided to leave the area quickly and not take any chances with whomever might be in the area. Human tracks in this place could only mean trouble. He would go down to where he had camped the last time and snoop around. If all looked safe, he would make a cold camp, then head west in the morning to circle around this area before heading back south.

He snaked his way down the ravine and finally found his old camp—more tracks, and these looked even fresher! He said it out loud, then quickly covered his mouth when he realized his stupidity. Everett scanned the sky and closed his eyes to sharpen his senses. He thought he heard movement and turned toward it. That was the last thing he remembered before the lights went out.

The rustlers had been waiting.

CHAPTER 16

THE GODS ARE ANGRY

A sharp pounding in his left temple was the only feeling Everett could identify as he fought to open his eyes. Blinking rapidly, he tried to focus. The sky was dark, though it had been light the last time he remembered.

He tried to sit up but something prevented him from moving—ropes.

"The kid's coming to," the tallest of the three men said.

"What's your name, boy?"—a question from the short, blond cowboy.

"Who are you? Why am I in ropes?" Everett asked.

"You didn't answer my buddy's question, cowboy. What's your name and why are you out here in the backcountry?"

"They call me Nemo. I'm an explorer, artist, and nature lover, just enjoying what god provided, nothing more."

"Nature lover, explorer, and artist—now ain't that something. Ed, you ever hear of such a thing?" the short man asked.

"Nope, sure haven't," Ed replied.

"How about you, Joe. You ever heard of a white man by the name of Nemo who explores God's backyard painting for fun when half America is starving to death and struggling to find work?

"No," the Indian replied.

"Okay, Señor Nemo. We done went through your belongings and some of what you say seems to fit with your cockamamie story. I found your little box of paints and a diary. Since only Ed, the good Christian, can read, I'll let him fill in what we learned."

"Well, thank you, Roy," Ed said to the short man.

"I see here in an entry, it looks like you procured some meat, just like we used to do from the Jerrys back in the big war, and guess what? We found meat in your backpack and you know, it looks like the same jerk that me, Roy, and Joe made ourselves just a week ago. Care to know how I know this?"

Nemo was scared; these were the cattle rustlers.

"Sure, how do you know it's your jerky?" Nemo asked.

"I like to use molasses on my jerk, and the stuff you have here is my mom's old recipe. I can even taste the bite of rock salt she always taught us to include. Would you like to explain why you have my mom's jerk in your backpack?"

Nemo was in trouble and he knew it. He would need to be careful; lying might get him killed, if he wasn't already dead.

"Well, I admit I took a few pieces off your drying racks a week ago. I was hungry. You can understand that, can't you, in these times?"

"Sure, I got two rail-thin kids that are hungry, the whole damned country is hungry. But what you're telling me don't add up. You got plenty of tack, fruit, peanuts—hell, even cookies in your pack! How damned hungry are you?"

"Well, you're correct. I have ample food, but it's got to last me weeks. And I must admit your mom's recipe smelled so good, and I hadn't had any fresh meat in forever. I confess I took it, but I didn't take much, then I moved on."

The men considered their positions. Nemo who was trembling and lightheaded in the cold night air, waited for their verdict. None was forthcoming.

"Well, first of all, you didn't take it—you stole it," Roy said.

"Yes, I'm sorry. You're right, I stole it."

"Damned right you did. Well, I guess you ain't no hero or rancher's son or you would have bushwhacked us, but you are a problem. We can't afford to be linked to no rustling. They hang rustlers high in this country and I don't plan on getting lynched over some kid's craving for a hot meal."

Roy was thinking out loud. "Tell you what, kid. You give me your gun as payment for our food and we'll call it an even trade. You can have the rest of your pack, but if we see you ever again or our faces end up on any wanted billboards, I will assume you are the cause and I will kill you—and not in a good way. Understand, Nemo?"

"Yes, sir. Fair trade indeed. Take the bullets, too; it's all yours."

"Don't worry, I already did." Ed laughed as he untied the kid. Nemo rubbed his wrists, his head throbbing as he tried to figure out his position.

"You go over there and bed down. You can leave in the morning. I don't want to hear nothing out of you unless you are spoken to—*comprende*, boy?"

Roy and the other two men stared hard at the kid.

"Yes, sir, I do."

"One more thing, Nemo. Tell me where you hail from. I can see by your skin and hair you been out in the elements for a good bit, but you're not from around here. I can tell that by how you speak, so no Mormon school, that right?"

"I'm from Los Angeles, California."

"I'll be damned. I always wanted to go to Los Angeles. How about you, Ed? You want to go to California, pick oranges off trees, and swim in that big salty ocean?"

"I like it here, Roy. I don't care for city slickers; they all think they're better than us country folks—just like this kid does, I guarantee you."

"Nemo, you better than us?" Roy asked, pushing his hat up on the top of his head and watching Everett's eyes for a true or false answer.

"No sir, I'm just like you. I love the West. Being out in the desert is part of me. My folks are from Los Angeles, but as far as I'm concerned, this is where I belong."

"Okay, then. I like that. What you think, Joe? You're awful quiet. You think this white man belongs out here on your people's land?"

"No, he's not my clan. And this bilagáana is the worst kind of thief, one who steals from other thieves. I don't trust that kind of man; there's no honor among thieves."

"Nemo, if I were you I would stay clear of our buddy Joe tonight. He can be kind of mean sometimes, and really handy with a butcher knife—but I guess you already know that."

Roy laughed as he smiled at Joe, whose unchanging face was staring into Nemo's eyes.

"I will keep to myself and leave first thing in the morning. You will never see me here or near your land again, Joe. I'm heading back to California anyway before the snow comes."

"Okay, boy. Go get your stuff and don't cause me to regret my kindness. I've lightened your load a bit to make it easier hiking. I took your extra clothes; I figure you won't need them since you're leaving town. That camera is heavy, too, so I figured you would be happy to see it gone. Am I right?"

"You are correct, Roy. Thanks. That pack was heavy and the camera works fine; be nice for you to have a token of my appreciation after you let me off for stealing from you and all."

Roy smiled and the other two men said nothing.

Nemo wobbled to his feet, then drunk-walked over to his backpack, which he dropped in a far corner of the camp illuminated by a roaring fire. A metallic taste in his mouth made him reach for his head, where he felt a line of dried blood plastering his hair and temple. Tomorrow he would leave at first daylight, as soon as he was given the go-ahead.

He slept in fits before waking from a nightmare of falling down a deep ravine. His body was shivering and he felt nauseated. Turning his head to the side, he dry-heaved for a minute and a thick green mucus found its way out of his mouth. He searched in vain for his canteen—gone!

At that moment, Nemo realized these men weren't going to let him go. He would need to sneak away tonight. That dream had been a precursor of bad things to come. He'd have to pack light and make a run for Mexican Hat. His enemies had horses and guns, so his chances weren't good, but it was better than staying put and waiting for Joe to come slit his throat.

He would leave their horses. Maybe they would relent when they found him gone; if he took a horse, he was dead for sure. He would leave his bedroll fluffed up over Jules Verne's book, his favorite floppy hat perched on top of the decoy. He took his favorite snakeskin band, which he wrapped around his neck. He hoped the subterfuge bought him extra time. He would miss his hat and book, but his head hurt and he reasoned that removing the hat would help the pain a bit.

Nemo found a knife and compass the thieves had missed tucked away in a special pouch his mom had sewn under the flap of the backpack. Most importantly, he retrieved the Dixon painting, his diary, and the little food that had not been taken and slipped out of camp. Time— something he usually cared nothing about—suddenly took on great importance. The sun would be up in four hours and they would come looking for him.

Snow started falling as he breathlessly crested the mesa. The gods were angry and Nemo wasn't sure why—but he knew their jaws were tightening.

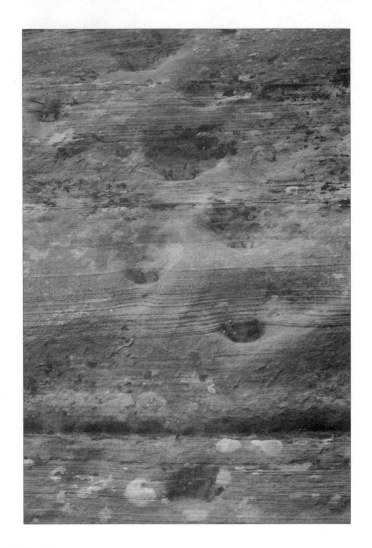

CHAPTER 17

HAND- AND TOEHOLDS NO MORE

Joe Kirk rose before the sun cracked the snowy horizon; there was a young pig needing slaughtering, no loose ends. After all, he was Indian and white men would kill him for stealing their precious cattle if they caught him. He had lived around the white eyes long enough to know his fellow thieves would turn on him and feign innocence. With a murder they, too, would have skin in the game, be it white or brown.

He would attack from behind and slit Nemo's throat, hold him until he bled out, then wrap the human refuse in his blanket and dump the evidence in a nearby crevice. By the time the skeletal remains were discovered, they would be miles from the scene; it could take years to find the boy explorer.

Joe jumped on the blanket, knife slashing at the neck area, but making contact only with the leather-bound book, which fell to the ground; the snow-covered blanket revealed nothing but dirty clothes.

"What the hell!" Joe yelled out in confusion as he looked under the blanket.

"Hey, what's going on? Joe, what you yelling about, goddammit!" Roy shouted back.

"The kid—he's gone, lit off."

"Shit, I told you, Roy, we should have taken care of that problem yesterday. Now we have a bigger issue on our hands," Ed exclaimed.

"He couldn't have gotten too far on foot with minimal water, little food, and an apple-sized bruise on his noggin. Let's break camp. We'll find that kid; he can't be more than a few miles away."

The men quickly got their gear and horses together, not even taking the time to put out the fire. Nemo's tracks were easy to follow in the fresh snow; it was only a matter of time before the men on horseback caught up with their prey. The sun peeked through the clouds at the horizon, lighting a path for the men to follow.

The last three hours of snowfall offered an easy roadmap for the three seasoned rustlers following Nemo; they would find him fast unless the young man could find an equalizer. Then an opportunity presented itself to him. A river far below in a deep gorge lay in his immediate path—but angled to the right, a few hundred feet overhead, was what interested Nemo: a small Anasazi outcropping perched high above the cliff, only faintly visible in the morning light.

The thousand-year-old handholds used by the cliff dwellers were recognizable only to the most seasoned archaeologists. Everett had spent two weeks in 1928 working as a hired hand for an archaeologist excavating Woodchuck Cave, a place that uncovered beheaded Anasazi corpses. He had learned more about the ancient ones and their religion in those weeks than he could ever have learned in class.

Everett understood the intelligence of the people who made faux routes up the cliffs to keep their enemies at bay long enough to escape to safety. He could see the correct line of handholds and toe-trails that would take him to the ruin, but there was one significant problem. The sandstone steps were precipitously steep and Mother Time had added erosion to the equation—but there were no other options. Everett loved risk, and this would be the biggest one he had taken to date.

Nemo removed the Dixon painting, his diary, and the pack of cigarettes he kept under his hat and wrapped them tightly in the muslin cloth, binding them with the snakeskin hatband and tying the light load to his belt. He left the majority of his food in the pack to give it weight, then heaved his old leather friend as hard as he could, aiming for the river bottom. It was a perfect throw, near enough to the water to be believable.

The pack was visible from the mesa top but gave no clue as to where Nemo had gone. He rolled a few rocks down the side of the slope as if he had gone that way, with one landing on the pack. With the false trail set, he hopscotched from boulder to boulder, leaving no tracks while heading toward the cliff face he would need to scale.

Nemo hoped the rustlers would assume he went down to the river to make a last-ditch effort to escape the horses. Or maybe they would think he had lightened his load at the bottom of the cliff before trying to climb out on the other side. Or that he had simply slid down the cliff, taken off his pack, and was hiding, his head too hurt to travel further.

In reality, Nemo had stayed on the same side of the chasm where the nearby cliff face held his hidey-hole. If he could ascend, the chances were good he could wait out the men; if he fell, he hoped the fall would kill him so he wouldn't have to face their wrath with a broken body.

As he looked up the cliff, he heard the sound of rocks slipping under horses' feet. There was no time to think, so Nemo methodically pushed himself upward, focusing his gaze above his goal. Halfway through the climb, one of his toeholds gave way and he nearly plummeted to his death. It was only by pure strength that he held his ground and pushed higher. He finally reached the top, pulled himself over the cliff lip, and slid onto a fine dirt floor that had been untouched for a millennium.

A horse's neigh broke the silence. The men were below him, and it was now up to the gods to decide if his plan would work. When Nemo peered over the small square window at the scene below, he could hear his tormentors talking.

"He stopped here," Joe said, scanning the surrounding area.

"There, his pack, he went down that way," Ed chimed in.

"Or maybe that's just his pack; the kid's no dummy," Roy said, surveying the immediate area for evidence Nemo was nearby.

"Joe, why don't you go down and check out the river bottom. See if his tracks are there. Maybe he fell, maybe he didn't, but this is a stopping point for the moment."

Ed nodded his head in agreement. Joe handed the reigns to his compadres and headed down the cliff, a large Bowie knife in one hand, the other helping him balance on the steep trail.

Once on the bottom, he carefully lifted the pack and looked inside, then cupped his hands around his mouth and shouted, "His food is in here, nothing much else. Don't see any tracks but the rockfall is new. He may have come down here, can't say for sure. Maybe he's downstream."

Roy shouted to Joe: "Go down river to see if you find anything. I'll look around here and Ed will go upstream on his horse. That kid has to be close!"

The men took their duty stations, each looking for their prey. After two hours and no signs of the kid, Joe came back up and Ed followed suit. There was nothing to report; the young man had disappeared.

"Now you tell me how a kid can simply vanish like that," Roy said to no one in particular. They sat down and pulled out a smoke to consider their next move.

Nemo had watched the drama play out. The ruin had an old doorway of rocks in which he laid his body, so he was encapsulated with a small viewing window where one of the rocks had been displaced. Like a lizard pulling the heat from the ground, Nemo kept his body glued to the dirt floor.

Joe started to blow a smoke ring and watch its ascent when he recognized what looked like an Indian ruin.

"Hey, you see that?" He pointed his lips in Navajo fashion toward the upper ruin. "It's a Nasazi house. Maybe he climbed up there and is hiding."

"You got to be shitting me, Joe. You think anyone could climb up that steep grade? Hell, that's suicide, and if he was stupid enough to do it, what do you think the chances are he can make it down?"

"I don't know; all I know is that it's possible," Joe retorted.

"You want to go up there and find out, go ahead, be my guest. I know I'm not doing it. How about you, Ed—you want to climb that death trap?"

"The way I see it, Roy, is there's only one Indian in this here group and that's Joe. He's got a lot more experience climbing sheer ledges than us. Joe, you found it; you climb it."

Joe considered the possibility, then said, "My people don't go into the Ancient Ones' *chindi*-filled homes. The Nasazi are our enemy. But we can do what the Spaniards did to my people in Canyon de Chelly."

"What would that be?" Roy asked.

"A Spaniard garrison trapped a hundred of our elderly, children, and women in a cave in Cañon del Muerto. When they couldn't get to them, the soldiers shot their muskets into the cave and killed them all. We can do the same and knock out a few of those handholds, too, for good measure."

"Hmm... I like this idea. If we do it, though, we will need to skedaddle 'cause that many rounds of ammunition going off will surely catch attention if there is anyone in earshot. People don't go around wasting valuable bullets unless it's for good reason."

The men checked their rifles and took aim at the entrance to the cliff dwelling.

Bullets started flying inside the cave. Nemo quickly grabbed a large flat rock and positioned it over his head as a shield. The noise was deafening, bullets pinging off the large stone, a large cooking pot shattering. Dust clogged the room's air until the shooting finally stopped. One bullet had grazed Nemo's butt; a searing pain filled him, but he didn't let out a sound. Then the bullets began again in earnest as the men shot up the first few hand- and toeholds.

"Okay, Nemo. If you're up there you're screwed. You can't get down without a ladder or rope. If you happen to survive and do escape, you better go a long way away. We will track you down and kill you if we ever hear about you in the area. We have a lot of kinfolk so you better take heed!"

Everett heard everything, even with the ringing in his head and the pain in his ass. His heart started to slow, knowing he had survived part one, the test of courage; part two would require even more fortitude and ingenuity. He would need to channel the fictional Nemo to survive.

CHAPTER 18

KING OF HIS DOMAIN

Everett's body shivered uncontrollably, his ears ringing from the shots fired. His tactical position was uncomfortable under the best of circumstances; he was in pain, mixed with fear—but he didn't move. One hour went by and there were no more sounds; the three riders appeared to have left him for dead. The explorer's composure improved slowly, but his head and butt throbbed with each thump of his heart.

He decided it was time to sit up. Lightheadedness overtook him and his face flushed. He managed to put his feet on the ground, then stood up precariously. The upright position intensified the pain in the injured areas, but he pushed through.

Blood oozed in tiny rivulets along the side of his temple. A trembling index finger examined the sticky goo; it was only a small scalp laceration, but his already-impressive bruise had grown larger. He checked out the wound in his butt next, pulling down blood-soaked pants and underwear. A deep flesh wound presented itself, although it appeared to be limited to muscle. His poor blood clotting condition was not helping his cause. Stitches were needed, but the injury was not life-threatening if the bleeding stopped. His finger said the wound was a half-inch deep, but he could feel no bone.

The blood coming from his butt was brighter in color than that coming from his scalp. Instinctively, the artist wiped his red-stained finger on the adjacent cave wall, forming a line, then adding two more strokes to make an "N." Additional dips in his blood made an "E," then an "M," and finally an "O." He would leave a record for the ages, he thought.

He was alive, but was his Dixon painting as fortunate? Nemo limped over to the wrapped piece and picked it up; it had been spared. His thick leather diary had a couple of deep tears in the cover, deflecting the rustlers' hail of bullets and preserving the precious painting. The cloth satchel had a faint blood-tinged handprint where the overflow from his bloody pants had seeped into the muslin. He laid the cloth and snakeskin out on the cave floor to dry.

It was approximately 2 p.m. and about thirty-five degrees. The lack of wind was a reassuring sign. Everett would not stick his head out until sunrise on the off chance the men had doubled back to look for an easy headshot. Tomorrow he would make an escape plan; for the next few hours he could examine the ruin while he still had some light. He smiled as he looked around, knowing he was the only human to visit the site in a thousand years, and recalling the unbelievable sequence of events that allowed him to gain access. He understood his odds of leaving were not good, but for the moment he felt a surge of happiness.

The dirt floor had accumulated a foot or more of fine powder, centuries of detritus, with recent chunks of rock from the barrage of bullets scattered like checkers. There were numerous stone implements, broken pots, and one large twenty-inch storage vessel shattered by the rustlers' fury. Inside the remains of the pot, Nemo found gifts from the Anasazi—a long rope made out of human hair and a rabbit cape. The rope was the longest he had ever seen, at least twenty feet in length. The cape was immediately put to good use on his shoulders, the warmth helping his body maintain the heat that was desperately needed to counteract his state of shock.

Another hour of searching turned up a shallow grave with two adults, their knees flexed to their chests, leather-wrapped femurs adjacent to the bony cavity. The remains appeared to be those of adult males; when he compared their long white bones to his own leg, they were equal. Everett couldn't help but wonder if these mummies were part of a cosmic puzzle playing out after centuries, waiting for him to be summoned to their burial ground by the gods. The realization of his predicament made him think of Bryson, and he wondered if he would ever see the boy's angelic face again, or find someone with whom he could share his life. He had been so consumed with exploring nature that the rest of life's fruits seemed superfluous. But in this moment of reflection he couldn't help wonder if this was what the gods had in store for him—skeleton partners in a macabre dance of life and death.

The ruin was a two-story complex, small by most Anasazi standards. It had probably served as a defensive structure rather than as a day-to-day dwelling. It clearly performed that protective function well, both then and now.

Nemo found a safe place to sit and watch the setting sun illuminate some low-hanging clouds. Soon he began to sing in a low hum and consider his options. All the scenarios he could think of were fraught with danger. His only hope of escape lay with his skeleton partners. If he could just channel their empty minds for help, he might have a chance.

✳ ✳ ✳ ✳

Surprisingly, Nemo slept well and awoke an hour after the sun rose. His joints were swollen and stiff, but the bleeding had ceased. A puddle of gelatinous mud lay under his side, attesting to the seriousness of the wounds. He considered eating the bloody mass, but couldn't bring himself to do it. Instead, he pulled out a hardtack cracker and nibbled at the edges as he took measure of his supplies.

The day was partly cloudy, the temperature barely below freezing, and the wind about five miles per hour—a decent day for an escape. Behind the south-facing wall he found a couple of handfuls of crusty snow, which he ate. It tasted as good as any rye whiskey, refreshing his parched mouth.

For the next half-hour he gathered all the accumulated snow and finished off his last two crackers. His stomach growled with hunger, but lack of food was not new in the backcountry; he could brook with this discomfort for quite a few days. The men were gone, there were no signs of smoke or sound, and the day was looking better every minute. It would be a wonderful day for a hike if he could just figure out how to get off his perch. He missed his faithful companions and wondered if the burros were also doomed. Someone would find them and they would be worth good money for the lucky soul. This thought reassured him, though he hoped it wasn't the cattle rustlers who discovered the animals.

The closest handholds leading to the top of the structure were toast. With the first fifteen feet nonexistent, Everett's chances of survival were narrowing fast. Then the bones whispered a plan to Nemo's subconscious mind: he could wedge the skeletons' femurs into an adjacent rock window that seemed structurally sound. Using the human-hair rope as a pulley looped around the long bones, he would be able to lower himself down to a level where he could find a hand- or toehold. At worst, he could lessen the distance he would fall by fifteen feet, improving the odds he would survive the drop. The landing area at the bottom of the cliff was an uninviting, bone-shattering rock rubble. A clump of dense mountain mahogany bushes a few feet further out offered a much better possibility of survival if he could maneuver his way into the thick hedges.

Miraculously, a pottery food bowl had survived the barrage of bullets. A red human handprint decorated the deep interior. Nemo, who until yesterday generally wasn't superstitious, couldn't help but see this as a cosmic connection to his own "NEMO" handiwork staining the adjacent wall.

"Am I supposed to be here? Are the ancient gods working on my behalf?" A shiver went down his spine and the throbbing in his head eased. The bones were magic, a sign that the *chindi* were helping him leave their home.

"How could it be?" he said out loud as he went over to his makeshift bed and examined his Dixon painting. Everett craned his head out of the small stone window. From his elevated vantage point, he could see some dense junipers at the edge of ferrous water lines. These might not be the exact ruins Dixon had painted, but they were similar enough for him to make the connection. There must be an even more obscure ruin nearby. Everett's heart raced; he had found the sacred place or, more accurately, it had found him.

His painting kit was on the river floor, assuming the men hadn't taken his pack, which was likely. Only a pencil remained in his possession. Nemo sat down and started feverishly drawing his surroundings— the pots, a group of a dozen broken shards once stacked neatly nearly to the ceiling, and their current location. His Nemo wall was included in the image. Everett ripped the pages out of his diary and shoved them deep inside his damp pocket.

"No wonder Wetherill had not found the place," he thought. "It was further north than Dixon had thought; painting and riding for two days can make one forget about time and space." Nemo knew that somewhere below him there was a dinosaur tooth cairn, and another ruin to explore. Adrenaline again began pumping through his body.

"Time to escape," he said to the remaining intact bowl as he placed its hand-printed interior on top of his head and severed fifteen inches of the human-hair rope so he could secure the new helmet to his head. The bowl would protect his bruised noggin; another fall might kill him if he hit the same area—even a small bump could be fatal. The ceramic bowl might give him the extra protection he needed to survive another blow to his head.

What to do about his painting and diary? He could easily throw the book to the bottom of the cliff, but, if he died on the descent, his writings would be lost forever. The book represented his inner thoughts and a personal vision of nature, one he hoped would last long after his passing. The painting was his connection to Dixon, his mentor. As a map, it had achieved its purpose; the painting was now singularly important as a link to the past.

Three years ago, when Nemo was exploring Cañon del Muerto, he discovered a remote cave in which he cached an Anasazi cradle and a worn burro saddle—a personal statement for future archaeologists, and Everett/Nemo's artifacts for the ages. He would do the same with the diary in case his descent was his undoing.

He dug a hole in the sand underneath his bloody inscription until he reached the floor a foot below. On the front of the diary, he scribbled in a shaky hand:

"The adventures of Nemo, Everett Ruess, 1934"

The large protective head stone, which had saved his life while he was under attack, was positioned in the bottom of the diary's shallow grave. Then he prayed to the gods: "Protect my writings, listen to the earth's beat, and, when the time beckons, bring it forth for all men to hear."

It was a watershed moment. Everett's life would likely be extinguished minutes from now. He had accomplished more than most, and was satisfied with his life's journey. Now he just hoped he would somehow be remembered.

Nemo cut another few feet of the precious hair rope, leaving him with less than fifteen feet, a risk he considered worth taking. Using his knife, he cut his snakeskin belt in half. He used the new section of skin as a tie for the muslin to secure the painting and diary as a single unit. He fashioned a loop with the small section of hair rope and attached the remaining part of the rope to the package. The looped end would be exposed to the outside elements. When and if he could return, a grappling hook would be needed to catch the loop and pull the package down to the bottom of the cliff. It would be too dangerous to make the ascent again, but the painting was safe in the isolated ruin, which only a raven or the most athletic of mountain lions could access.

On his return—hook in tow, practice under his belt, and Lady Luck by his side—he would retrieve the precious package before it floated to earth. If he died in the descent, the rope would disintegrate over time but the diary and painting would be safe under the ledge until Mother Earth's slow erosion covered them up for eternity.

Nemo surveyed his surroundings from the edge of the ledge, feet dangling toward the inevitable as he gauged what skill might be needed to survive. Instinctively, he pulled the next-to-last cigarette out of its white paper carton and lit the remaining precious match in a blaze of sacrificial glory. He sucked hard to ignite the crumpled end in an atavistic ritual of strength. "Well worth the cost," he declared as the pungent odor of phosphorous filled the morning air.

A deep warmth circulated through his lungs as he exhaled, and a thin line of blue smoke threaded its way up the precipitous canyon wall. He readied his nerves for his great escape—or death—whichever it might be.

"Everett Ruess has accomplished much on this earth," he told the crumbling structure. A distant smile lighted his face as he envisioned the idiocy of the moment. Here was an Anasazi hair rope secured to a makeshift ladder by human bones, an ancient ceramic crown, and a 1,000-year-old rabbit cape secured by a rattlesnake skin belt—and here he was, puffing on an old Viceroy cigarette.

He was indeed the king of his domain, though abdicating his throne with a suicidal plunge was a real possibility. The thread of his lineage would either perish in the red dust of the desert or miraculously survive a jump. The time had come to find out.

CHAPTER 19

THE TRICKSTER

Marvin shivered on the walk home—a combination of cold and concern. He couldn't help wondering if Tsosie was legit. By mile four, Marvin was considering the real possibility he had been taken. The painting was probably newly made. How would he know? He was no art dealer. So what if the date said 1922?

The muslin cover that the kid threw in after the deal was completed did appear old; there were stains imbedded in the cloth and, for that matter, the painting on board also looked old; the writing on the reverse side was worn in places.

Panic set in—not the kind he experienced in 'Nam, but an adrenaline surge all the same. Maybe he could back out of the deal, demand his $1,500 back, give the kid $20 for his time, and drop him off at the Shell station. Then the young man would be someone else's problem.

Having watched it at close range for many years, Marvin knew about the post's day-to-day operations, but that was not the same as being the proprietor. His respect for the professional art dealer increased. He had watched Bloom make quick buying decisions, often for big money, and the man made it look easy. Marvin, on the other hand, was in panic mode.

"What if that oil painting of old Indian ruins is truly from 1922," he thought. "A piece that old and with such compelling imagery had to be interesting to tourists. Even if this Dixon fellow wasn't famous, the piece was well done and seemed worth that much money, even to an untrained eye." Marvin vacillated back and forth. Should he back out or stay the course? He had good arguments for each option—and he wished Bloom were here.

Snow filled the air as Marvin finally reached his truck; the five-mile walk from the post had helped focus his mind. The sacred Two Grey Hills were shrouded in an eerie gray glow.

"The kid was right about one thing," Marvin said to the Two Grey Hills peering through his hogan window. "It is too dangerous to be walking alone on a snowy night." Marvin didn't particularly like the kid, but he was glad he had offered to give the young Navajo a ride to the Shell station; it was no night for walking if you didn't know the territory.

He retrieved his truck keys from their deer-horn peg and started a fire in the iron cook stove before venturing back outside to warm up his truck. Marvin liked warm weather and often wondered why he didn't move down south to Phoenix or Tucson for the winter.

He decided a cookie and glass of milk were also in order before driving back to the post and rescuing the kid. "No sense in a hungry stomach," he thought. "The kid can wait. He should have walked me home. My feet always hurt, and I still walk ten miles a day," Marvin complained to his boots as he rubbed his lower calves and simultaneously polished off most of his cookie in one bite. "That kid is full of bull, lazy and rude. I sure hope he isn't also a forger," he said to the half-empty milk glass.

Swallowing his last gulp of milk, Marvin made up his mind: he would grill the kid more in-depth about his grandfather, Roanhorse, and demand a more complete history of how the painting came into his possession—questions he should have asked before parting with so much money. He was getting cold feet on the deal and it wasn't because of the weather.

When he arrived at the post all Marvin could see was a yellow light flickering in a strobe-like fashion under a gentle fall of snow. The front porch was inadequately lit, but there didn't appear to be any sign of Tsosie there.

"Damn that kid, where'd he go?" Marvin rudely honked his horn and waited. No answer. Marvin laid on the horn again. Still no answer. So he got out of the cab, put his hands deep into his coat pockets and looked around. He found the answer to his question in the fresh snow—tire tracks and two sets of footprints, neither of which was his. Apparently Tsosie had found a ride, which was surprising. It was long past the trading post's regular hours and it was snowing at a fast clip. Only an outsider who didn't know better would come by. No locals would appear unless they were in trouble or looking for someone.

Marvin's inner voice rang out: "I wonder if I got taken. Is that so-called painting all a scam—or worse, is it stolen?"

He replayed the earlier conversation in his head. The kid seemed legitimate; he needed a ride, he wasn't that bright, and he was no actor. If this wasn't a set up, then who would have come by to give Tsosie a ride on such a snowy night? A total stranger? The kid had the money to negotiate a ride. Marvin could see him offering a passing car a few bucks to go down to the Shell station, but who would be driving by the post? Maybe his grandfather came looking for him....

Marvin decided to drive slowly down the road toward the gas station to see if he could get a better picture of what had happened. The highway was deserted, which was nothing out of the ordinary. Then a coyote crossed the road, running full tilt in front of his truck. Marvin nearly hit the trickster.

His right foot was pushing hard on the brake pedal as he parked in the middle of the narrow road, idling, and considering the implications of what had just happened. A bad spirit was warning him. If he were to continue on his journey, he might be in serious trouble, even killed. Marvin dug deeply into his front pocket, retrieved a buckskin pouch filled with fine corn pollen, and sprinkled some into his palm. He placed a small amount on his tongue, put a pinch on the top of his head, tossed the rest into the air in front of his eyes, and said a prayer to the Holy People.

Marvin made a U-turn and retraced his tracks back to the post. This time he walked around the post's entire perimeter. Maybe there was something he had missed.

The two sets of footprints were already partially covered. That was nothing unusual, but then he spotted a small symmetrical stick, a toothpick. Marvin picked it up and examined the fibrous object. It smelled like cinnamon! The scent of one of his favorite sweets permeated the moist, snowy air. The toothpick was soft from being chewed on—another clue. It had been in a person's mouth long enough to reduce the hard spike to a wooden mush.

The faint fragrance transported him back to childhood and a small glass vial with a white tin screw top, a cherished object he had carried in his front pocket for nearly a year. At age twelve, the vial was everything to him. He slept with the precious cargo and never let it leave his possession. Marvin sometimes wondered if his lifelong relationship with sweets had developed from this early connection with treats.

The vial had appeared during irrigation class in his second semester at Indian boarding school. A burst of rain filled the lines of the red dirt rows he was hoeing and the miniature glass tube floated down the reservation waterway past his worn boots. The hoe's dull edge grazed the jar, tossing it into the air as if a frog were jumping from the mouth of a predator. Amazed it hadn't broken, Marvin picked up the jar and stashed it in his pocket, where it stayed for the rest of the semester—a new storage unit for tasty beetle larvae.

A week passed before the container revealed its true purpose, not as an entomologic prison, but as a container for delicious treats: cinnamon-dipped toothpicks. At the time he assumed this was a unique confectionery invention. Apparently not, he discovered later, as many children love toothpicks and cinnamon and small vials filled with sweet, hot, burning juices—a seemingly universal craving that often follows a child into adulthood.

On Tuesday afternoons, the boarding school served hotdogs, and the kitchen staff attached one sliced pickle to a flash-fried wiener, an Indian school gourmet meal. Marvin collected all the used pickle sticks from his fellow students, then modified each pick by discarding the yellow fringe and breaking it in half: eight picks to one half-ounce of thick syrup. The fibrous wood acted as a sponge soaking up the sweet, hot treat. A single pick could provide an hour of delight before the thin stick began to disintegrate.

Mrs. Patemeway, the school's head cook, was a middle-aged Hopi woman whose kindness was outsized only by her enormous, strong hands. She let Marvin fill up his small vial every week from her stash of cinnamon extract. Her deal was he wasn't to let anyone know where he got his scrumptious juice; any slip of the tongue meant treat time would be canceled forever. Marvin heeded her words as if she were his mother, and the juice flowed the entire school semester. His fondness for Mrs. Patemeway persisted, and he often wondered what had happened to his school-lunch savior. He owed her much for that taste of happiness in a not-so-happy place.

Most of Marvin's memories of Indian boarding school were negative, with the exception of his dispenser of delight. Each time the spicy syrup touched his taste buds, his sad thoughts melted away, even if only for a brief moment. One of his favorite treats was still Blue Bunny cinnamon ice cream, each bite bringing him full circle. Mrs. Patemeway must have seen the change the treat made in Marvin, and it was her way of fighting the unjust system.

But Tsosie didn't have anything in his mouth, and Marvin would have recognized the aroma of cinnamon. Whoever had the toothpick had been sucking on it for its flavor, not to remove food. But if it wasn't the kid's pick, whose was it? Marvin figured it must belong to the person who gave Tsosie the ride.

Marvin made the mental note and decided there was nothing else he could do tonight. The trickster had spoken and he would not go against the spirit talking to him. Tonight he would be in his own hogan with the door locked. He retrieved the Dixon painting from the post's safe and took it home. There was no sense in taking chances; the Holy People were watching and he was paying close attention.

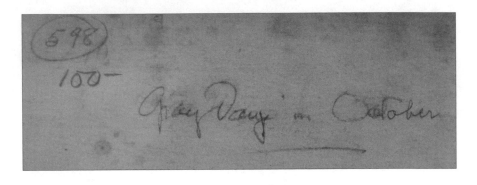

CHAPTER 20

SAY THAT AGAIN

A blast of hot air greeted Marvin's cold, chapped face as he opened the hogan's front door. He had secured the painting under his army jacket to keep it dry. Once home, he propped the board against a flat pillow on his World War II cot, where it could be viewed from across the room.

The wooden floor squealed as Marvin dragged his $5 metal chair across the room. The day had been long and he was feeling all of his sixty-eight years at that moment. Boots and socks were removed and tossed near the hot stove. After sitting for a moment, he gathered enough energy to consider dinner. A can of Hormel chili and extra beans, courtesy of the Toadlena Trading Post store, would be just fine. When you're alone, not much matters in the manners department. Scratched floors and smelly toots were all part of the isolation equation.

Finally, he gathered the strength to open the can with a pocketknife and pour the contents into the oversized skillet sitting on the top of the second-generation iron stove. The sizzling chili's aroma filled the room as Marvin contemplated the Dixon painting.

The picture was well done, though the subject matter did not appeal to his Diné sensibilities. The ancient Nasazi ruins took up most of the space on the canvas—*chindi* homes that were taboo to traditional

Navajos. Marvin couldn't understand the whites' obsession with exploring these abandoned enemy strongholds. These remnants of a long-gone world were nothing but trouble in his mind; maybe those lost civilizations could lead to self-realization for those without a beacon of purpose. He assumed the artist must have felt some connection to these lost people to make the effort to paint their homes.

Marvin didn't recognize the land in the painting. The red earth indicated it was in Navajo territory, as did the type of ruin, one he had seen often—Kayenta type he reasoned.

The popping of the chili bubbles brought Marvin's mind back to his dinner. He stood up and stirred the thick soup while his subconscious worked out the possible origins of the only real painting to decorate the Manycoats' homestead.

Satisfied the Hormel chili wasn't burning, Marvin took down the 1986 calendar of running horses that hung over his bed. Spider skins floated free from their bondage and Marvin carefully picked them up and laid them on his desk to dispose of tomorrow in proper fashion.

The Dixon painting didn't have a back wire, but there was a well-worn groove in the frame on which the painting balanced nicely. He stepped back to see what fine art should look like. The wall popped. There was an added dimension to the room he never knew was missing—real art. Marvin was surprised by how much he responded to the change in the way the wall looked. Too bad the painting wasn't of a red cliff or a distant mesa he recognized instead of Nasazi homes filled with dangerous *chindi*.

He would not want to own this particular piece, but if it turned out to be fake and Bloom got mad, he would reimburse the art dealer for his part and keep the painting regardless of the subject matter. It was time to upgrade the house. Maybe he would even start eating chili without beans. Time to find a mate was running out, and making funny butt sounds wouldn't be high on the list of desirable traits in a husband.

Marvin singed his tongue on the first scoop of meat and beans. He was too hungry for his own good, but the pain didn't diminish the flavor of the beans. One can of chili turned out not to be enough, so he heated up a second course, surprised by how working at the post gave him an appetite.

He took his time eating the next bowl of chili, his tongue smarting. With his stomach full, there was more time to inspect the art. Rich, thick colors enveloped the board; a professional artist had to have made the piece. Next to the date, in nearly invisible red paint, Marvin noted an additional inscription, a location: Mexican Hat. He was surprised he had only noticed the date earlier. The location made sense; there were lots of red dirt canyons and Nasazi homesites near there.

He removed the painting from its precarious hook and examined the back. In the upper left corner there was a number circled—#240—and below that "Lost Canyon." In the right upper corner was another number, 300. Marvin positioned the back of the board under his one floor lamp for closer inspection. The pencil was faint, but then he saw something that made his heart sink. It was a dollar sign, a $300 price tag!

The painting's value was $300 and he had paid $1,500 for it. The kid had made a $1,200 profit on an old painting of *chindi*.

"Oh, well, Marvin," he said to himself. "You learn under fire. Remember 'Nam? Those first few weeks were brutal, and you almost died twice before you figured it out, thanks in great part to Captain Smiley—he had experience you didn't. Same thing, this is only money. Maybe Bloom will take it off my food credit." Marvin pondered the possible ways he could repay the man and a smarting tongue and bruised ego weren't helping.

He returned the calendar to its rightful place and laid the Dixon on the oak table. Tomorrow he would make contact with Bloom. It was Christmastime; hopefully the dealer would be in the holiday spirit and not a Grinch.

CHAPTER 21

DUMPSTER DIVING

The sky was bright blue and a stiff wind rushing off the Chuska Mountains was purifying the Toadlena basin—a postcard from the rez.

Marvin rose early, finished his chores, and decided to open the post ahead of schedule so he could try to reach Charles Bloom and break the bad news. But first he would visit the Shell station to see if anyone had any information about Tsosie. Maybe he could find the kid and talk him into taking the painting back. Marvin hated the idea of losing money he didn't have.

The Shell station was lively at 7:30 a.m., with working folk filling up on cheap gas and hot breakfast burritos before heading to their 8 to 5 jobs. The young woman running the checkout line had a sweet smile, but she hadn't seen Tsosie. She would have noticed a handsome stranger, she said, but she was not on duty last night; her shift just started at 6 a.m. The person he needed to talk to was Wanda Yazzie, the clerk she replaced. Yazzie lived in public housing with her mom and worked the night shift. She would be up now, having breakfast with her mom after she saw her children off to school.

Marvin asked a few other people at the gas pumps if they knew the Tsosie kid, but none did, so he bought a sugar-covered bear claw and headed back to Toadlena. He would stop at the public housing development on the way to see what Wanda might know.

Public housing provided good homes with little personality, although true to Navajo tradition, they did face east. The buildings were on the north side of the road, halfway between the trading post and Highway 491. All the homes looked alike, with toys scattered over dirt yards and plenty of lawn furniture, each plot inhabited by at least two collarless dogs. Marvin understood that for most of the people there, this was a nice place to raise a family, with a solid roof and good neighbors. But there were too many people living too close together for Marvin's taste. He needed an unobstructed vista, without a clothesline, crying baby, or barking dog in sight or earshot.

Wanda Yazzie answered the door, her untucked shirt and lopsided nametag saying, "I'm off duty." Marvin hated barging in on family time.

"Yá' át' ééh. I'm Marvin Manycoats. I know your mom, Milly. We're about the same age."

"Yá' át' ééh, Marvin. Nice to meet you. My mom's here if you want to come in."

The cold wind and smell of coffee brewing were an attractive invitation—Milly was a bonus.

"Hey, Mom. Marvin Manycoats is here. Come on out and say hi," Wanda yelled, her booming voice ricocheting off the paper-thin walls. Working at the Shell station had permanently raised her voice a few decibels.

"Marvin Manycoats! How have you been? I haven't seen you in years— where you been?" Milly asked in a pleasant voice as she straightened her hair.

"Hi, Milly. Nice to see you. You haven't changed a bit."

"Thanks, but I know I'm an old woman now. I guess we're all on the downhill slide."

"No, I mean it. You look like the same girl I used to know in high school. I worked construction, California mostly, but I finally retired and now I'm home for good. I'm running the Toadlena post right now."

"Running the post? My daughter told me that Rachael Yellowhorse's bilagáana husband was taking over for old Sal for now. I don't go to the post anymore, not since Sal and me had a run-in a few years ago."

"Sorry to hear that. I'm there every day."

"That's good to know. So are you in charge?"

"No. I'm just filling in for Bloom. He has a gallery in Santa Fe that he needed to check on, so he asked me to run it for him while he was gone. I'll be in charge for the next week. If you come up to the post, I'll give you a free ice cream bar and we can catch up."

Marvin smiled widely, then blushed, realizing he had as much as made a date with the widow.

"I'll do that as long as Sal's not around. The years have treated you well, too, Marvin—the Holy People must be shining their light on you."

Marvin continued smiling, not knowing how to answer. So he turned his attention to Wanda, who was shaping her nails with a sandpaper file, oblivious to her mom's flirting.

"Wanda, did you see anybody come by last night? A kid maybe 25 years old named Tsosie who lives up by Mexican Hat? He probably would have been in around 7 p.m., just about when the snow started coming down hard."

Wanda thought for a moment, stopped filing her nails, then began again as she answered. "Nope, don't think so. It was dead so I would have noticed. I do remember a nice car pulling in for gas not long before 7. It was a fancy car, pretty sure it was a black Lincoln sedan. The man didn't come in, but I could tell he was a bilagáana. He was in good shape, maybe forty, but I have a hard time figuring out bilágaanas' ages—they all look older than they should. I remember wondering why he was out on the rez getting gas in a snowstorm, but tourists going up to Monument Valley come through pretty regularly. I saw a limo once with a driver wearing a little hat, suit, and black gloves. Can you believe that?"

Marvin kept Wanda on task. "Anyone with the man in the sedan?"

"Don't think so, just the one guy. He came through around 6:45 and filled up, looking at his phone the whole time. Maybe he was smoking a cigarette or sucking on a lollipop. There's nothing else I can remember, except...."

Wanda was thinking. "It's probably not important, but he did throw out a big black plastic bag in the south-side trash can. I remember that because I had just emptied the can and thought, 'How rude. If you're so rich, use your own trash can, not mine.'

"Why you so interested in this kid, Tsosie?"

"Well, nothing important—just trying to do a little reconnaisance. The kid sold me something. I wanted to get a bit more information about the piece but he left the trading post before I could — that's all."

"Huh? What did you buy, a gun or something?"

"No, nothing like that—just an old painting of some Nasazi ruins."

"Why would you buy a picture of a Nasazi ruin?"

Wanda wrinkled her noise, clearly disapproving. Her mother, who had been listening to the conversation but not talking, chimed in on this bit of information.

"Yeah, Marvin. That doesn't seem like a picture a traditional Navajo would want."

Marvin could feel some Navajo morality coming his way. "It's not for me, ladies. It's for the store inventory, for Bloom, business only. I'm with you guys. I'm not a fan of the ancient ones."

Both woman seemed to accept this explanation and nodded their heads in agreement.

"Well, Wanda, if you happen to hear anything about this Tsosie kid from Mexican Hat could you let me know?"

"Of course. I'll leave word at the post."

"One last question, Wanda: when do they usually pick up the morning trash?"

"Supposed to be at 7 a.m., but it always gets busy so they never get to it until about 9. Why?"

"Oh, no reason—just curious."

Marvin thanked the women and headed directly from their house to the Shell station. It was time to do some dumpster diving.

✳ ✳ ✳ ✳

The two trash receptacles at the Shell Station were overflowing when Marvin arrived, the steady stream of red-caked trucks heading to work filling the dumpsters as they passed through. Digging through trash was not Marvin's idea of a fun morning. Fortunately for him, the good times were limited to just one bin.

As he began emptying the bin, Marvin wondered what his neighbors would think—that old Marvin had fallen on hard times? But, if he wanted to find any clues about what had happened to Tsosie, he would have to hold his nose and do what was necessary. He regretted not insisting on getting the kid's phone number.

An overflow of trash had begun piling up volcano-style around the sides of the dumpster; there was no room left inside. But Marvin knew his payload was at the bottom of the bin, so he could avoid the excess garbage. Excavating to the bottom of the honey hole required him to pull out sticky Coke cups, a dirty baby diaper, and an assortment of the refuse of modern Navajo life. But there, at the bottom, was a large black sack with a red tie, just as Wanda had recalled.

The bag was light and gave off no noxious orders, so it was probably just paper debris. But a sticky orange liquid clinging to the bottom of the bag dripped onto Marvin's boots. He gave the bag a shake and tossed it into the back of his pickup.

"Why did I agree to work for Bloom?" Marvin muttered to himself as a neighbor gave him a concerned smile. "This is not what I signed up for." He put the trash he had pulled out back into the can, tossing one of the overflow bags in as well. At least the space was cleaner than when he started his work. Marvin smiled weakly. He felt more in balance when he could control his environment, even if that meant organizing a dumpster in a gas station.

Marvin borrowed the restroom key, washed his hands, and purchased a large cup of coffee with two packs of sugar. The same young woman who had sent him to Wanda's checked him out, asking, "Find all you needed?" Her eyebrows told the story; she must have seen him dumpster diving.

"Yes, I did. Thanks again, Lidia, for your help earlier," Marvin said, reading the young woman's tag and flashing his trademark smile.

Her concern lessened and she smiled back. "Hope it all works out for you, Hastiin."

"Me too—some days you wonder if it will."

Lidia didn't answer. She had moved on and was now helping the man behind Marvin. He returned to his truck, sipping the hot coffee. He had more dirty work to attend to.

CHAPTER 22

DIXON?

Santa Fe's charm had sucked Bloom and Rachael in—as it does most people, no matter how many times they've visited.

Twinkling lights and the scent of burning piñon was an aphrodisiac Bloom knew all too well. In good times, there was no better place than The City Different—but Bloom also remembered the recessions and summer fires when tourism fell off a cliff but the bills didn't. Those were the times he had to guard against: if only he had a good-sized nest egg instead of a second mortgage to call on when he was in need of credit.

Bloom had turned off his cell phone so he would have no distractions while he was in paradise. It had been off for nearly a day and he needed to get back to the real world. He switched off the airplane mode and a voice mail and two missed calls popped up, both with the trading post's number.

"Well, the post couldn't have burned up," he thought. "The phone is still working, so how bad could it be?"

It was 10 a.m. and the post had been open for an hour. Bloom tried to read the voice mail transcription on his phone, but the message was incomplete—something about Dixon and call me. Easier to call, he thought as he deleted the message and rang the post number.

Marvin picked up after one ring. "Toadlena Trading Post, Marvin here."

"Marvin, how goes it? I see you tried calling me yesterday—what's up?" Bloom asked as he finished his last bite of an organic apple, his first in months.

"You got my message, right?"

There was a pause as Bloom finished his last bite—another point for Santa Fe, where natural produce was always at the ready.

"Saw the message but didn't listen to it. Something about Dixon?"

Marvin told Bloom the story of Tsosie, the painting he purchased, and how he knew $200 was the limit but he put in his own money and was happy to be a part owner of the painting if he had screwed up—even if it was only was worth $300, the way it said on a tag on the back.

"So this is a Maynard Dixon painting, 1922. Is that correct? Does it look old?"

"Yes, I'm sorry if I paid too much. I didn't see the price tag until I got home that night. I was going to get our money back, but the kid caught a ride and vanished and he didn't give me a phone number to call. I probably should have gotten more information or waited, but the kid said it was now or never, so I took a chance," Marvin said in a conciliatory tone.

"Marvin, I have never had a Maynard Dixon painting, but I know they are very valuable. In fact, I think there is a museum that shows just that artist's work in Arizona."

"Really, a museum? But what about the $300 price tag? How could it be that valuable?"

Bloom laughed out loud. "Well, you've got a little to learn about the old stuff. Now I haven't seen the back yet, but my guess is that the price is in 1922 dollars—so do the math...."

There was silence on the other end as Marvin realized that $300 dollars in the 1920s would be thousands of dollars today.

"So I did real good on this buy, didn't I?"

"Yes, if it's real, it could be worth thousands of dollars. I've never priced a Dixon so I honestly don't have a clue. And, after twenty years dealing in paintings, I also know it could just be a copy. I won't know for sure until I show it to an expert who specializes in Western art, but if it's real we did very well."

"We?" Marvin asked.

"Yes, Marvin. I would have never gotten the piece without your help. You risked your money, and I appreciate that. It takes guts to put your wealth on the line, especially on something so speculative. I'm guessing you've never bought a painting before."

"You would be right. I never bought any art before yesterday."

"Well, Marvin, I'm assuming you're willing to take a little more risk as my partner, right?"

"You bet I am."

"Then you, my friend, may have just experienced what they call beginner's luck down at Fire Rock Casino. Apparently, when it happens your first time gambling, you're hooked for life. You feeling hooked, Marvin?"

"I'm not a fisherman, but, if I were, I'm sure this fish wouldn't get away. I'm all in."

Marvin was beaming on the other end of the phone. He began giggling, thinking about how he had dug through a disgusting trash can trying to find a lead so he could get his money back from the kid. He wouldn't share this part of the story with Bloom. The Hefty bag could stay in his truck bed until the next time he went to the dump.

The day had just gotten a lot better. He couldn't wait for Bloom to get back to see if he had won the lottery. The two men were in an upbeat mood, chatting and laughing about the possibility of such a fortuitous windfall.

★ ★ ★ ★

The rest of the day Marvin felt wonderful. Maybe the painting was worth $5,000. If true, his take would be $2,500—a lifetime supply of ice cream bars. It wasn't until later that evening that Marvin began to wonder about Tsosie. The kid had wanted $2,000 and said the painting was real. Marvin didn't pay him that, and his earlier joy started to feel more like he had done something wrong. He would need to discuss the ethics of this with Bloom; he wasn't an art dealer and didn't know what the protocol was. For now, he would hope the painting was real and deal with the consequences when there was actually something to worry about.

Bloom, on the other hand, seemed to be less concerned for the moment. He hadn't bought the piece; if he had, he wouldn't have made such a low offer. He would have found out the value and paid the kid a reasonable price. But Marvin had handled the sale and had not given Tsosie the $2,000 the kid wanted for the painting. Bloom figured the Dixon could easily be a fake and that the partners may have lost everything. He had been down this road before and saw no sense in spending any mental energy on the problem until there was a reason to do so.

Bloom hated being in this position; he wanted to be as honest as possible. Once he found out what they had bought, he would deal with Tsosie. If the painting were real, he needed to make a profit; if it were extremely valuable, it would change the dynamics. He would be home in less than a week and the fallout could wait. He wanted Marvin to feel the thrill of the buy, something Bloom had known all his adult life.

CHAPTER 23

DECEMBER 24

Two days had passed since Marvin's amazing purchase, and Bloom's preliminary research on Dixon was promising, to say the least. A paragon of the Southwest and a unique character whose career spanned the first half of the twentieth century, the painter was also an acclaimed muralist and illustrator who worked in San Francisco and New York City. His acquaintances included Frederic Remington and Charles Russell, and he was married for fifteen years to the celebrated photographer Dorothea Lange.

The piece Marvin had purchased from Tsosie—assuming it was genuine—was painted at a time when Dixon was on a fertile multi-month trip to Kayenta, Arizona, where he and Dorothea stayed with the famed Indian trading post owner John Wetherill. Dixon's trademark clouds and interest in traditional Navajo life began in earnest during this trip: the painter was enthralled with the Southwest, its inhabitants, and their lands.

Dixon knew Lorenzo Hubbell, the owner of the historic trading post in Ganado, Arizona, for almost 30 years. Hubbell was a mentor to Dixon, and when the painter's San Francisco studio burned to the ground during the great earthquake of 1906, Dixon famously grabbed weavings Hubbell had consigned to him, letting his own art perish. You can replace paintings but not blankets, Dixon had reasoned.

If the painting were real, the auction prices Bloom found online made the piece very valuable. It also meant the partners had ripped off Tsosie, paying him just cents on the dollar. A 16- by 20-inch painting—the size Marvin had purchased—with compelling subject matter from the 1922 timeframe could easily fetch $100,000.

Bloom understood from experience that many dealers would simply say tough luck: the kid asked for $2,000, we paid $1,500, which was a stretch, and we took a chance not knowing the work's value or authenticity. We won and he lost—too bad! A verdict would almost surely be in Bloom's favor if the case went to trial, but the court of law was not as important to him as the court of ethical responsibility. He hoped Marvin, who had half-ownership, felt the same way.

Bloom realized selling the artwork would have to wait until this ethical hurtle was handled. In a few days he would be home and could examine the piece. If it looked genuine, he would take the painting to an expert to determine its value. The dealer in Tucson who owned the Maynard Dixon Museum seemed the logical place to start. But for now, Bloom was not going to clutter his mind with "ifs" and "maybes," and he wasn't going to burden Rachael with the problem either.

It was Christmas and Santa Fe's beauty commanded his full attention.

✳ ✳ ✳ ✳

Bloom felt that those who have not had the chance to experience a Christmas Eve walk in Santa Fe had missed a true bucket-list experience. A large portion of the town turns out for the event. Canyon Road is closed to traffic and is lit from top to bottom and along every side street with bags of sand holding a single candle—the region's famed farolitos, an atavistic Spanish tradition that brings the modern world back to a time when electricity and commercialization of the Christmas season did not exist. Somehow it all worked for Bloom, the Jew; Rachael, the Indian; and all those in between. The event was as much about one's fellow man as it was about the birth of Jesus, and this was what Charles Bloom loved about the Christmas Eve walk.

Charles wanted his children to feel the same love for the walk that he had for so many years. Most gallery owners on Canyon Road had hot apple cider and treats for the kids as well as a full sales staff on hand. Bloom's was almost always open. Being halfway up Canyon Road was a great advantage: no matter which way people started walking, they almost all made it to the mid-point. His gallery was a perfect landing spot, something that hadn't been lost on Bloom when he first set up shop in Santa Fe.

Tonight's weather was average, for which he was grateful; keeping his heating bill down with all the opening and closing of his front door was almost as important as selling art. Twenty-two degrees at 7 p.m., no snow, and lots of good cheer. Bloom liked a big snow for Christmas, but was pragmatic enough to realize it hurt sales and made getting around a nightmare.

Bloom and Dr. J positioned their vehicles in front of the gallery parking lot and put orange cones in his additional parking area for special clients. Knowing the back route allowed a quick escape down Camino Escondido once the crowds thinned out around 9 p.m. Escondido was a small paved road of adobe homes, many still owned by the original Hispanic families. The short outlet dead-ended onto a rutted dirt road paralleling the Santa Fe River that allowed traffic in both directions—important local knowledge as Canyon Road was largely a one-way street, even if most tourists never seemed to learn this important fact.

Rachael, Willy, and Sam filled their cups with hot cider—Sam spilling as much on herself and the ground beneath her as stayed in her cup. Bloom winced seeing the sticky mess on his perfectly clean oak flooring, but it was Christmas and he knew Rachael would take care of it on her watch—another reason to love this woman.

A half-dozen rugs had been sold in less than three hours, making Bloom think of Toadlena. In the month of December he might not see a single tourist at the post in two days. This kind of hard-core retail action could not be denied: Santa Fe earned another point.

By the end of the night, a stack of Dixie cups overflowed the large plastic tub and Bloom had settled into his green chair for a rest.

"Merry Christmas," he said for the umpteenth time to a group of Texans breezing through the shop looking for something "pretty." Rachael had shown the sisters everything in the shop, but nothing took their fancy. Bloom hadn't bothered trying to sell them anything; his dogs were hurting and he had seen the pair before. "Looky-loos," he called them.

"I told you, Rach, those gals come every year, half polluted by the time they get to our place, and they never buy, just look. Waste of time in my opinion. You're better off giving them some food and sending them on their way."

"Huh—so that's your take on your clients?"

"Yes, ma'am, it is indeed," Bloom said, smiling.

"Then how come this one 'gal' handed me her business card. Looks like she's a CEO, too. Told me she wanted this necklace for $1,200 but didn't want her sister to know, so she asked me to invoice her tomorrow."

"Are you kidding me, Rachael Yellowhorse?"

"No, I'm not, Charles James Bloom. You simply needed to understand the woman's perspective. You probably try to hard-sell her every year instead of spending a little time with her. I told her I thought she looked so pretty in the piece and that it brought out the blue in her eyes—apparently she agreed."

"My god, woman. I need you on the floor every day. Maybe you're missing your calling. Hang up the loom and hit the floor—we will be rich!"

Rachael frowned at Bloom.

Bloom backtracked. "I'm kidding, my love. What I meant is that you can do anything you set your mind to. We both know Spider Woman's gifts are your destiny in the world."

Rachael's smile returned and she moved closer to her husband, kissing him on the cheek.

"OK—as long as we both realize I can do anything I set my mind to—and now I'm setting my mind to sitting down. You do realize I'm pregnant and that I'm an older mother...."

Rachael's condition had slipped Bloom's mind for the moment, and he jumped out of his chair, realizing he was a fool.

"I'm sorry, hon. I'm here complaining about my feet hurting and you just worked an eight-hour day while you were holding up two. Last I saw, Dr. J had tucked our kids into the backroom to play with my phone."

"Bloom, you know I hate that. Those things are for communication, not babysitting. Let's call it a night and close this place down before someone else tromps more dirt in."

Bloom ran for the door and closed it, smiling at a couple that had hiked up the gravel driveway. "Sorry, we're closed. Merry Christmas!"

The couple was clearly perturbed, but that was retail. Sometimes you had to have a life too.

CHAPTER 24

TWENTY-FIVE TO ELEVEN

Bloom's Christmas high was waning—a week of intense retail sales made sure of that. Suddenly he was looking forward to the slower winter pace at Toadlena. He appreciated the frenzied activity that Santa Fe's Christmas season brought for the bank account, and he knew that after January 3rd there would be a buying crash that would last until Memorial Day.

Bloom was well aware of the lean times, a natural rhythm of life in Santa Fe, and he understood a gallery had to have enough dry powder to take care of any problems that arose during these times—which they always did. Rachael's pregnancy reminded him that life had ways of throwing you a curveball when you were expecting a fastball.

The latest pitch was a slow ball down the middle, with a potentially valuable Maynard Dixon painting sitting in his vault back at the post.

A day from now, he would have a pretty good idea if he had hit a homerun or struck out. The possibility of an infusion of money at this sluggish time in the season was a gift from the Holy People, at least for him and Marvin—but what about the Navajo kid?

Bloom and Rachael had decided to celebrate the New Year in Toadlena, where the occasional Black Cat firecracker was the thrill of the night. Santa Fe's way of bringing in the New Year was sometimes lethal, as many in the town found that the best way to mark the occasion was to shoot aimlessly into the air at the stroke of midnight, neither considering nor caring where the lead might land. It was not uncommon for an accidental death to occur in Santa Fe on January 1st: no one was immune to wayward bullets falling back to earth. On the rez, the houses for the most part were so far apart it was almost an impossibility for that problem to occur.

Tonight there would be a dinner to celebrate surviving another Christmas season in Santa Fe, and to compare notes on where they both stood on their plans for the upcoming year. Would Bloom ask Sal to let him take over the post—or stay on the path that had been so successful for him the last twenty-plus years?

The Shed is a Santa Fe institution, serving spicy, fresh New Mexican food at a fair price in an idyllic setting. Located in the heart of downtown, the restaurant was an easy walk from Bloom's. There was always a line and it was always loud, but Bloom had never had a bad meal there, and they made some of the best sopapillas in town, not to mention excellent blue corn enchiladas. This would be their last big-city meal for the next five months if you don't count Taco Bell, McDonald's, or the Blake's Lotaburger in Gallup as a real meal—and, for Bloom, Lotaburger did count as fine dining.

The scent of burning piñon and tortillas fresh from the grill enveloped the restaurant's inner sanctum. Bloom had snagged a highly desirable two-seat table in the far back of the room, against the thick adobe wall, a natural noise block. He had to duck down twice going to his seat. His six-foot, one-inch frame was not made for the low door jams of the 1800-vintage building that housed the restaurant.

"Bloom, do you miss all this?" Rachael was intently watching for his reaction.

"Honestly, yes. How could I not? It's The Shed."

Rachael dipped a blue tortilla chip into the spicy salsa and plunged it into her mouth before replying. "I know; it's great and all that, but is it enough to add a point for Santa Fe?"

Bloom smiled. "Yes, definitely!"

"I'm glad. I hoped it wasn't just me being shallow. I'd give it one too!" She matched Bloom's smile as their chips dueled in the salsa bowl.

"Rachael, so what do the books look like? We now need to save for three colleges."

"Our kids will be like their father and mother and get scholarships— and never have to worry about paying for their education," Rachael replied optimistically.

"We both know we can't count on that. If we have to, I can always sell the painting Willard gave me. That would pay for a couple of years of state school for all the kids."

Rachael's brother Willard Yellowhorse, a great contemporary Native painter, had been murdered years ago by a deranged art dealer. The price of his paintings had risen astronomically, and Charles had hung onto one small but tasty piece.

"No way, Bloom. We both know that has to stay in the family. That painting has a strong connection to us both and no amount of money makes it worth selling—not even for an education."

Bloom knew that Rachael was attached to the piece, but had no idea how deeply her emotions ran.

"Okay, I'll take that off the table, value zero. So what's the total point count? Do we live in Toadlena or Santa Fe?" Bloom asked, already knowing the answer.

"Well, the point count so far is twenty-five for Santa Fe, eleven for Toadlena. It's not even close, I'm afraid." Rachael said sadly.

"You know, Rachael, we don't have to do this right now; we can wait until Brad Bloom is born and then discuss it."

"Brad!?!"

"Yeah. I forgot to tell you Brad Shriver and I made a deal: we get the house free for Christmas and he gets naming rights, like a wing in a museum. Is that a problem? I thought it was a good trade...." Bloom smiled.

"No, not at all, as long as you don't mind me throwing in Sal as the middle name. Since he let you work at the post, it seems only fair."

"Let's hope for a girl," Bloom laughed.

The waitress brought two bubbling plates of blue corn enchiladas Christmas-style to the table, with a plastic bowl of fresh sopapillas on the side.

"Hot plates!" the waitress barked as she expertly slid a metal dish in front of Bloom, protected by a blue napkin for safety. A cloud of steam and savory aromas rose off the delicious meal as the second burning plate made its way next to Rachael's hands. Dinnertime!

The couple simultaneously broke off opposite ends of a single sopa as if it were a Santa Fe ritual, soaked the crust in the bubbling red chile on the side of the plate, and judiciously popped the treat into their open mouths.

"MY GOD, THAT'S GOOD!" Bloom said, the food visible in his mouth as he talked. "I think we need to award two points for New Mexican food, don't you?"

Rachael nodded her head in agreement, her lips open to let air flow through as she tried not to burn the roof of her mouth.

"It's hard to deny this is great New Mexican food—on the other hand, my fry bread and mutton stew are pretty damn good too." After swallowing the first incendiary bite, Rachael was now able to talk.

"Yeah, they are good, no doubt, but maybe you should take away a point because you have to cook the meal instead of just walking down the street, eating, and walking away from the dirty plates for under $30," Bloom said.

"Point well taken. Okay, Charles Bloom—do your magic and figure out some housing for us after the kids are out on summer break. We can give Santa Fe another go and see if we can't make enough money here to move back to Toadlena when old Sal really gets old."

"I'm in, but you will need to get an obstetrician set up—the baby comes in July," Bloom mumbled, his mouth again full of food.

"I'll call Carson Riddley tomorrow for recommendations. I wish he still worked for the Indian Health Service. Do you think he would deliver me if I traded him a medium-sized rug?"

"He might. He has that great Daisy Taugelchee rug; a killer Rachael Yellowhorse weaving to keep it company would be pretty cool. Call him—if anyone could convince him to do it, it's you."

"Okay, I'll call Carson. We'll need to find a place for my sheep—you know that—so you better start looking sooner than later."

"Well, Rachael, as it turns out I took the liberty of talking to our old landlord in La Cienega, and he said we can have our rental house back at end of May. His tenant is leaving then, so we're all set: all I have to do is tell him it's a go."

Rachael put her fork down, making a clink on the metal plate, and looked at the man she loved. It was a big decision: she would be leaving her precious family home and committing herself to come back to Santa Fe for an unknown period.

"I love you, Charles Bloom, and we need to make as much money as possible for our children's and our own welfare. Toadlena will always be my home, but for now I have to agree with you: Santa Fe wins. Let him know we would love to take him up on his offer for the La Cienega rental—and I promise to stay put this time."

Charles and Rachael soaked in the possibilities and ordered another round of sopapillas. An important decision had been made—one that would be life changing for both of them.

CHAPTER 25

DOOR KNOCKER

Richard Bass's world revolved around things. Whether objects he bought and sold for a profit, or the accessories of a lifestyle that made him feel important—fine clothes, wines, a beautiful woman, and a nice, slightly used car were the medicine he needed to treat his low self-esteem. Art and antiques were only a means to an end for him.

Bass was not an art dealer per se. More on the picker end of the spectrum, he hoped to open a gallery someday, but for now he picked his way through life. Picking was a lifestyle choice as well as a job. It was never easy, but it did have its perks: no boss and no regular work hours. He submitted an annual income tax return, but rarely paid much as his was a cash business for the most part.

He did get hit with a big tax bill once when he had scored a small but very tasty Thomas Moran watercolor that had been incorrectly sold as a print. He flipped his $10 investment to a New York gallery for $150,000. There was no way around the taxman this time; the big-time art dealer insisted on a receipt and paid with a check. Since the dealer had paid up front, the taxes Bass owed were easily covered—they would not have been had he sold the piece at a discount to a more unscrupulous cash-and-carry type dealer.

The last fifteen years had been tough, with monumental changes in the art world. In pre-internet days, Bass would travel the antique circuit. One stop was particularly lucrative: the Brimfield Antique Show in Massachusetts. The one-week fest was about buying and selling as fast as humanly possible, a showcase for the art of the flip. Usually Bass could clear $50,000, all cash, with no paper trail and enough funds to not have to work for at least a few months.

Bass was a generalist; he was well versed in most fields of art—just not deeply in any of them. His strongest areas of knowledge were Native American and Western art. Growing up in Lubbock, Texas, contributed to his interest in Western material. Though he was not a fan of formal education, Bass loved to read, was smart, and had a good memory.

He realized early in his career that a person could make a decent living by walking the cluttered rows of antique stores, looking for back-road barns filled with junk, and having the balls to knock on doors. It wasn't as glamorous as the shows on television portrayed, but for the most part picking was fun—especially when he made a big score.

There are lots of techniques for being a successful picker, or a scout, as Bass preferred to refer to himself, but his favorite and most successful tactic was going door-to-door hunting once-affluent neighborhoods that were now on a slow downward slide. The contents of these inherited homes were in various stages of liquidation thanks to unemployed kids burning through hard-earned family assets.

Once the money petered out, the heirs turned to selling the art and furnishings, often leaving the best pieces in the house as their last-ditch sources of income. Homes in disrepair, with long grass and weeds, were a flag for a door knocker: the potential financial distress of the residents could mean free money for a man who knew how to harvest the tender shoots left.

"Bass the Mouth," as he was known to his colleagues, was a man who could talk to anyone about anything. His enemies just called him "Dick"—and didn't need to elaborate any further.

Once a neighborhood had been chosen, Richard Bass would canvas the entire place, carrying two pockets filled with rolls of cash, a .38 revolver in his boot, and a pencil and paper to write a quick bill of sale.

The hard part wasn't the knocking—it was getting in the front door. Once through the door, he was golden: the "Mouth" would take over, explaining how he was an antique and art dealer and had been told that they might have something he would be interested in buying. Who "they" were and what the "something of interest" was were never clarified. Bass claimed he paid top dollar and said he owned a small but very exclusive gallery in Fort Worth: Bass was a prestigious name in Fort Worth, as the Bass brothers were some of the richest men in the country.

But Richard Bass's name came from an Italian great-grandfather, Francisco Bassimonte, an undocumented immigrant who arrived in New York in 1900 and became Frank Bass, respected businessman. Richard's father moved to Lubbock looking for easy money in the oil fields soon after Richard was born—so his Texas accent was legitimate, even if his pedigree was a bit more West Texas then Fort Worth.

Once Bass entered the mark's house, he scanned the walls and floors and quickly moved the conversation into the living room, knowing anything of value would probably be found there. If he located something he wanted, his pitch of wealth and connections was followed by an offer of ten cents on the dollar to the unsuspecting sellers. Nothing was off limits: he once bought a man's antique bed, took it apart and left the bedding and mattress on the floor. Paying $125 dollars to the seller, the rare Gustav Stickley bed frame brought Bass $2,500 dollars from a dealer in Santa Monica before the bottom dropped out of the Arts and Crafts furniture market.

Trends come and go in the antiques world; not long after Barbra Streisand sold her Mission furniture collection, tastes changed and Mid-century Modern became the rage, with Richard Bass adapting his pricing accordingly. Bass didn't care about what was in; he only cared that he could buy something at the right price and flip it fast: turning product was the name of the game.

His understanding of the Indian and Western art market gave him an advantage over his fellow pickers, as knowledge is always king. But even there the internet changed the balance. YouTube videos filled the airwaves, with turncoat dealers sharing information that would make buying low that much harder. Antique shops were dead for the most part. With eBay and Etsy it was easier to buy and sell in the comfort of your own home. You didn't need some dinosaur knocking on your door; a good internet connection would do the job.

Unfortunately, the internet revolution had passed Bass by. He had no laptop computer, and the tiny "Always Buying" notices in the nickel-and-dime papers that once worked for him were now relics of the past. Although he had invested in a smartphone and was struggling to adapt, in Bass's opinion the phone didn't seem all that smart—it was just an expensive toy.

The tsunami of online selling platforms had washed over his mindset and his lifestyle, and having the ability to buy nice things had become a struggle. Bass still relied on good, old-fashioned detective work to ferret out collections that were undervalued so he could use his golden tongue to close a deal.

For the last ten years, Albuquerque, New Mexico, had been home. The amount of Indian art there was immense for a populace of about one million. But Bass was forced to expand his picking circuit; he could no longer depend on Albuquerque and Santa Fe alone to provide enough finds to live well. So, for two weeks out of each month, he would scavenge the Navajo reservation, hitting every pawnshop and even occasionally knocking on a hogan door to find material. Rarely did any valuable old pieces turn up—it was mainly pawn jewelry from the 1960s through the '80s—but if the prices were low enough, he could resell to a dealer or partner with a buddy who understood eBay.

A year had passed since Bass's last big score, an 1860s child's blanket that he had found in a contemporary Indian art store in Albuquerque, where it had been misidentified as a new revival. He made $15,000 that day, flipping the weaving to one of the fancy Santa Fe galleries that tripled the price. Bass couldn't care less what the other dealer sold it for as long as he made his hit and moved on, cash in hand.

The blanket windfall encouraged Bass to splurge on a pair of white and black Tom Ford shoes that had gone on sale, and he wore them everywhere. "People notice a man with great taste in shoes," he told himself. The real reason he loved them was that the fancy footwear helped shore up a fragile ego, but the shoes were wearing thin and Bass needed another cash infusion. The answer to his prayers came from a call from, of all places, Bluff, Utah.

Bass had greased the palms of most of the pawnshop owners and worker bees around the rez. He received a message from Bertha Young, a fixture in Bluff's pawnshop environment for forty years. A Navajo kid had come in looking to raise money early that morning. He had a painting to sell and Bertha had seen the piece, a nice looking

1922 desert scene. Bertha had forgotten the name of the artist, but remembered he was one of those "important early guys." Her memory was slipping fast, and Bass knew Bertha's days as a reliable source for material wouldn't last another year.

The ignorant old curmudgeon who owned the shop ran the kid off, thinking he was full of crap. But Bertha followed the Navajo out the door and got a phone number. The kid was ready to sell. He needed money for something—drugs being her guess. His name was Everett Tsosie, and he was out of Mexican Hat. Bertha gave Bass the Navajo's phone number, suggesting he might want to check it out sooner than later. "You know when they're ready to sell, it don't take very long and this kid is in the selling mode. It's a race as to who gets to him first."

Bass knew her words rang true, and he promised Bertha a steak dinner and a slow dance the next time he was in Bluff. The old lady was thrilled; her mind was going, but not her heart.

The picker was on the hunt for a small fry with something he might want, and he wouldn't be waiting. He picked up the phone and called Tsosie.

"It's time to knock on a couple of hogan doors and pay for this damn phone," he said to himself as he waited for the kid to answer.

CHAPTER 26

I'M THE INDIAN

Tsosie picked up on the second ring. He sounded loaded to Bass. This was looking like the perfect pick, a young, drugged-out seller in need of money—an easy target.

"Yá' át' ééh," Tsosie said.

"Yá' át' ééh, Mr. Tsosie. My name is Richard Bass out of Albuquerque. I'm a painting dealer and a Mrs. Bertha Young in Bluff who you talked with this morning said you might have a painting I would be interested in purchasing. Do you still have the piece?"

Tsosie, who had recently finished two boxes of Nitro poppers, was feeling lightheaded and needed a moment to put Bass's sentences together.

"Yeah, that's right. I have a painting."

"Who's the artist?"

Again Tsosie had to concentrate; the nitrous gas was making his head spin.

"Dixon, an old one."

"Maynard Dixon, an original oil painting?"

Bass began salivating on the other end, knowing this could be something great.

"Yep, that's right. Maynard Dixon, oil painting, the real deal."

"If you don't mind me asking, how do you know it's an original and not a poster or print?"

"Been in my family for three generations. It's real, can see the brush strokes, thick paint. It's no print, guaranteed."

"How big is the piece?"

"Mmmm... about one foot by two, I would say, picture of old Nasazi ruins up by Kayenta, dated 1922."

Tsosie's high was starting to wane, his thinking and speech clearing. He wanted money, but hated having a good high interrupted.

"Mr. Tsosie, I would have interest in the piece. What are you asking for it?"

Dealers and pickers always hope to get sellers to set the price to help gauge their expectations and maybe get the piece on the cheap.

"Hell, I don't know. You're the painting dealer, right? You tell me."

Bass frowned on the other end of the line, knowing setting the price was up to him and that he had just irritated his mark. He would low-ball the kid and see if he could steal it. He didn't want to scare him off with a big number. But he tried another tactic first, to get additional information before making his offer.

"Can you take a photo of the painting with your phone and text it to me so I can see what I'm dealing with?"

"Wish I could, but I don't have a good enough phone. It's a flip phone with no Wi-Fi connection."

Bass was seething on the other end of the line. He had stepped up to buy a smartphone and had even learned how to use it—and he got the only millennial in the country who couldn't send him a picture. He would have to work blind, never a good thing for Bass.

"I think I could pay $500 for the piece assuming it's in good condition and real. Cash money. And I can be out there today."

Tsosie went quiet, soaking up Bass's price. Even semi-lucid, the kid knew it must be more valuable with such a fast offer—probably double what the man with the Texas accent was proposing. He was interested even without seeing the piece.

Bass's hands were sweating on the other end, knowing he had rolled the dice.

"I'll think about it, Mr. Bass. Let me get back to you. Thanks, I got to go."

Before Bass could counter, the kid hung up. He had another carton of whippets waiting to be inhaled. Tsosie turned off his phone. He had spent most of his money, but planned on replenishing it soon. He had a lead on a painting dealer in Toadlena who was supposed to be fair.

Bass tried to call back, dialing frantically, not wanting to lose the piece. No answer. He tried twice more and again an hour later. Nothing. Nothing. He had rolled snake eyes.

Mexican Hat was now on his radar. He would go find the kid. Tsosie was going to sell that painting to him one way or another. There was a new set of Tom Ford shoes that Bass had his eye on, and they weren't the kind that went on sale. A Maynard Dixon painting would pay for them and much, much more.

✳ ✳ ✳ ✳

Bass loaded up his sedan for the impromptu road trip. Occasional snow flurries were in the air, not a good sign when traveling north. Two thousand dollars in hundreds were neatly tucked into a belly pouch. Tsosie would be lucky to get a thousand; there were not many ATMs around the rez.

The drive to Bluff was almost five hours in good weather; today it might be longer. Bass would try to make contact with Tsosie on the road. In the worst-case scenario, he would simply show up and go find the kid. He had to roll the art dice; important paintings like this didn't come around but once in a lifetime.

Bass checked his gun; the cylinder was loaded. He stuffed a half box of ammo into his money pouch. There was no way to know how this deal might play out. He had never considered killing a man for a piece of art, but he was pretty sure this painting was a $75,000 hit, and that could make a man do a lot of things he had never planned on doing. For now, he would play it safe—but if Tsosie didn't want to play ball, he might have to use means other than money to get the painting.

Bass decided to take I-40 instead of going north through Cuba. The snow flurries were increasing by the minute and the billowing black clouds looked ominous. If he hadn't heard from the kid by the time he reached Gallup, he would stop to eat and make a final decision about continuing to push further north.

The snow was accumulating as Bass passed Grants; by Gallup it was nearing whiteout conditions. Apparently the storm had swung south, and his best-laid plans had backfired. He pulled off I-40 onto NM 491 and stopped at his favorite Lotaburger, whose sign was now obstructed by signage from other national fast food restaurants.

Continuing on to Bluff was a nonstarter. "It's too bad outside; the kid wouldn't go anywhere, not in this weather," Bass said to himself.

Not one to waste a day, the picker decided to run his regular traps in Gallup—trading posts and pawnshops that often would hold lower end material for him. His goal was to make enough to cover tonight's bill before he checked into any fleabag motel off old Route 66—and to keep trying to talk with the kid.

The weather was perfect for picking as the storeowners were more than happy to make a deal on a slow day, and they had lots of new inventory from people selling family heirlooms for Christmas cash. Bass found a nice 1960s squash blossom necklace with natural stones for $400. He could turn it around in Santa Fe for $600—lodging, gas, and food paid for. A 1940s Chinle rug in gold colors had not been an easy sell since the mid-1970s; price $125, a double. Now in the black, he stopped picking to save his cash for the Dixon. His current capital reserves were $1,475, triple what he offered on the first go around. He was sure Tsosie would take it if Bass could only make contact with him.

A neon teepee motel sign blinking "pee"—the "tee" having burned out long ago—offered a reassuring welcome mat. A sandwich sign under the neon promised rooms starting at $50; Bass offered $35 cash and they took it without a fight, no registration necessary. The place was a favorite for the down and out, but he didn't need anything but a bed and a place to park his sedan. The room did not meet his criteria for quality, but he needed to save his cash: a Dixon painting was in the crosshairs.

Still no word from Tsosie at 6:15 p.m. Bass gave it one more try before calling it a night—and payday! Tsosie picked up.

"What's up, man?"

"Hi. It's Richard Bass here. We had discussed me buying your painting. Any more thoughts about that? I'm in Gallup for the night, not that far from Bluff."

"Gallup, huh? I'm at the Toadlena Trading Post. Any chance you can come get me now so we can talk?"

"Sure, happy to do it. I'll leave now. Where are exactly are you?"

"I'm on the front steps of the post." Bass decided to not ask if he had the painting with him. He could be there in less than hour, and it would be better to ask in person.

"Okay, I'm on my way. How will I recognize you?"

"Really? How many people you think are hanging around out here on a cold, snowy night. Just look for the Indian." Tsosie hung up.

Bass didn't like this kid, but it was worth putting up with his attitude for a big score. He left the TV blaring as security, took his possessions, and headed out to make his fortune.

CHAPTER 27

TWO CONDITIONS

Empty roads and minimal snow accumulation were a green light to make good time on Highway 491. Toadlena Trading Post, a place Bass knew well, was an hour away from Gallup. Sal Lito was fair, selling him well-priced jewelry over the years. The old trader never made him wait an hour to get seen, treating him as an equal, not some lowly picker. Bass appreciated this. He wondered if the kid had sold Sal the Dixon painting. If so, Sal might flip it at the right price.

A lifetime of sifting through garage sales and storage units didn't leave many art dealers with a positive image of pickers. Lito saw Bass for what he was—a man with a lot of knowledge who didn't want or need to work for anyone. The trader understood that a good picker could make a lot of money and, on occasion, make a great find and maybe bring it to him. Respecting pickers made good business sense. Bass hoped this was one of those times as he barreled north on the lonely road, his gas gauge reading empty. The Shell station was deserted; he filled up and deposited the trash sack he had brought with him from Albuquerque.

For the last ten minutes before he reached the post, Bass rehearsed his lines, not wanting to seem too interested in the painting—which, of course, by picking the kid up he obviously was.

The flickering yellow light shone its beacon for a half a mile— Toadlena. Bass checked his pistol; he didn't know this man and trouble had a way of coming out at the darkest moments, even under a faint yellow light. A young Navajo man was perched on the post's porch, extinguishing the butt end of a cigarette. Tsosie, Bass assumed.

Tsosie got up and headed over to his sedan. Bass unlocked his leather holster as a precaution.

"Yá' át' ééh. You Mr. Tsosie?"

"Yeah, that's me. You must be Richard Bass," Tsosie said matter-of-factly.

"That's correct. You can call me Bass—everyone else does. I hear you need a ride...."

"My friends call me E.T. Thanks for the ride. It's cold out here and no one is going to be coming by anytime soon. I need to get up to Shiprock. If you can give me a ride there, I'll fill up your tank for taking me."

Bass had worked the rez long enough to know that offering to pay more than a dollar or two for gas was highly unusual—especially $30 worth of gas from a kid who didn't look like he had a credit card. Bass's antennae went up.

"Not necessary, E.T. I just filled up, but thanks anyway. I'm happy to give you a ride up to Shiprock. Is that where the Dixon painting is?" Bass just couldn't help asking.

"Nah, just a close friend. That's great. I got nothing but this pack, so I'm ready to go now if you are," Tsosie said, changing the topic.

"You see old Sal?"

"Nah. The post's closed."

A good omen in Bass's mind, and enough questions for the moment. He would drive slower than usual forty-five-minute trip north to Shiprock—a perfect time for small talk and to tease out information about the painting. Tsosie hopped in and laid the seat back as if it were naptime—something Bass wasn't going to let happen.

"That dinging noise won't go away till you put your seatbelt on, E.T."

"Sorry. Usually I'm in the back of a truck, no seatbelts there."

Another marker of poverty in Bass's mind. Maybe Bertha in Bluff didn't know shit about art or her mind was finally blown. After the sedan turned north on Highway 491, Bass concentrated on extracting information. He nudged E.T. to remove his earphones so he could start a conversation.

"So, did you consider my offer of $500 for that painting?"

"Yeah, I considered it." A long pause. Tsosie didn't elaborate.

"Well, what you think? A pretty good offer sight unseen I would think?"

"Yeah, I guess so, considering you never saw it." Tsosie gazed out the window.

"So you want to sell me the Dixon and I can give you $500 in cash money?"

"Well, that's too little I'm afraid. I want lots more than that," Tsosie said, leaning back in the seat once more and closing his eyes. But before he could put his headphones back on, Bass asked, "How much more?"

Tsosie considered the possibilities. "Probably about $2,000. You got that much cash for a painting you haven't seen?"

146

Bass considered the proposal, not wanting to answer too quickly.

"Well, I'll tell you what. I could go $1,500 and throw in a sweet squash blossom necklace, an old one, got to be worth $1,000. Now that's a deal!"

"You got the necklace with you?" Bass now had Tsosie's full attention.

"I do indeed. Open the glove box; it's underneath that pile of papers."

Tsosie peered inside the unlit glove box, found the necklace, and brought it out.

"Emma Begay," Tsosie said recognizing the silversmith's hallmark. "She was a good one with the metal. My dad knew her."

"Yep, that's real quality. You might be able to get even more than $1,500 for it, or give it to your sweetie." Bass could see the last option resonated with the man.

"I don't have the painting with me. It's put safely away. If you give me a week, I'll bring it to Gallup and we can do our deal, but I want the necklace now. Christmas is in couple of days and my girl would love that necklace."

Now it was Bass's turn to consider the possibilities. It was never a good idea to give money or merchandise to someone you didn't know, much less some kid whose painting he had never seen. Bass would give Bertha more than a dance if this piece turned out to be a fake or, even worse, a copy.

"Okay, I'm in, but on two conditions: first condition, the painting has to be an original Maynard Dixon, not a print or a fake. If I don't think it's the real McCoy, our deal is off. And second, I want the piece this year, before January 1st."

"No problem, man. It's real and I'll get square by then."

"One last thing: you have to sign a piece of paper, a bill of sale that says I gave you the necklace as advance payment for the Dixon."

"Cool, write it up. You just bought yourself an old painting."

Tsosie shoved the squash blossom deeply into his backpack and put the headphones back in his ears. A mop of long black hair began grooving to a steady, unheard beat. Bass couldn't stop smiling. He was rich!

✳ ✳ ✳ ✳

Before going much further down the road, Bass decided to pull over. He wanted to close this deal officially so he composed a bill of sale for Tsosie to sign before the kid changed his mind or got out in Shiprock and disappeared with the necklace.

Bill of Sale

$1,500 cash on receipt of the painting.

A 1960s Emma Begay squash blossom necklace as half-payment to secure the Dixon painting.

This transaction is nullified if the painting is fake or not an original oil.

Bass had E.T. sign and date the paper. Deal closed, the men shook hands and for the remaining thirty minutes of the trip neither one talked, each happy in his own world of acquisition.

Shiprock's volcanic wings filled the dark sky as Bass pulled up to a dilapidated trailer on the far west side of town—million dollar views in the midst of extreme poverty. Kids' toys and broken furniture dotted the dirt front yard. Music and a haze of marijuana smoke filtered out of the trailer, where a pretty young Navajo woman holding a small child was visible through the undraped window; she was talking on a cell phone, oblivious to the sedan engine's whine.

Bass's mind went into overdrive. Had he made a terrible mistake? This kind of abject poverty and a Maynard Dixon painting simply didn't mesh. His inner voice was screaming, "You're getting screwed," but the greed factor was too strong to fight. The deal was in play, winner take all.

The black car rolled to a stop and Tsosie cracked the door open to leave. Bass grabbed his left arm forcefully, stopping him from exiting the car, his powerful grip speaking volumes about the man Tsosie was dealing with.

"Remember, E.T., next week I'll give you the $1,500 in cash and you'll bring MY Dixon to Gallup. You have my number and I've got yours, so we can set a time and date."

Tsosie jerked his arm free, his rattlesnake headband sounding danger.

"Yeah, I got it. Any other conditions, Bassman?" Tsosie asked indignantly.

"Nope, that's it. By the way, is this your girlfriend's house?"

"Yes, why?"

"Nothing, just curious. Hope she likes the necklace. It should look great on her."

The picker smiled and pulled out of the yard, gravel flying as the neighborhood dogs responded to his presence. Bass could be a hard man. He was raised in a broken home where a punch in the stomach and a kick in the ass from the old man was part of everyday life, and he reciprocated in like fashion to those who showed him disrespect or, worse, ripped him off.

He wasn't a man to be double-crossed. For now, he would play it straight, no rough stuff, but if the Navajo tried to screw him, he wouldn't like the outcome and neither would his girlfriend.

No one was safe if Richard Bass was pissed off and bent on revenge.

CHAPTER 28

ALBUQUERQUE

Marvin's thoughts were occupied with the endless possibilities of his purchase as he rubbed down the 1900-era grocery counter for the third time.

Ronda touched his arm: "You trying to refinish that wood, Hastiin Manycoats?"

"Never hurts to put a good shine on it," he replied sheepishly.

The Dixon painting was safely stored in Sal's gun vault. And it could be worth thousands of dollars! Bloom's voice echoed in his head, and he, Marvin Manycoats, was half owner. What good fortune!

Marvin was considering what to do with the money—maybe take a trip overseas. He had always wanted to visit Japan, although he knew keeping the financial windfall was the best plan of action considering he had zero savings and only a meager pension along with some government money. But, like so many Navajos, the future was not a concern for Marvin. Why save for something you couldn't predict? For better or worse, Marvin's life was lived in the moment, and right now traveling to Japan was an idea that appealed to him. Visiting prehistoric Athabascan relatives might be worth blowing his share of the windfall.

Bloom would be home in a few days and the dealer would let him know what they had purchased. Maybe Marvin could take his own trip around the world, like Sal and Linda, the Toadlena Trading Post owners. Marvin would quiz Sal about what it was like, and then he could decide.

This potential conversation made Marvin begin to wonder if Sal would want part of the painting. After all, Sal was the trading post owner even if Bloom was in charge. He remembered Sal telling Bloom he could buy anything that walked in the door and it would be his for the taking during his absence. But would a very valuable painting count? Sal was probably thinking about rugs or jewelry when he made that statement.... The fact a painting could be more valuable than most Navajo rugs was a concept foreign to Marvin, but he was glad that world existed, at least for now.

Marvin ate lunch in the back closet that held the Dixon. Propping up the painting, he stared deeply into the image and wondered why was this piece so valuable. Yes, it was pretty, but the subject matter was of little interest and it was small. It wasn't even as large as his running horse calendar, and he had paid $1,500 for it! Marvin chuckled at the absurdity of taking such a risk.

The Navajo continued his examination of the work. The board was a dark honey hue. Using an uneven fingernail, he scratched a line on the back of the painting. The furrow revealed that the wood underneath was a lighter creamy color, a sure sign of oxidation. It was indeed old. The price of $300 on the back represented a lot of money in 1922; he had not considered that it was the original sticker; it had to be worth a couple of thousand in today's money.

Marvin's daydream was broken by the sound of a tinkling bell; someone had entered the post's front door. He stashed the painting back in the large safe, shut the heavy old door, and went to help the third patron of the day.

A white man in his forties wearing a black baseball cap that said "You Don't Want to Pick on Me" was standing next to the large glass pickle jar by the old-fashioned register. The visitor was staring at the ceiling, examining the tools hanging from the rafters. Marvin had seen this man at the post before, but hadn't talked to him; he was a trader of some sorts, like old Sal.

"How you doing. Can I help you?"

"Hi. I was looking for Sal. He around?"

"No, Sal's on vacation. He won't be back until after the first of the year. Maybe I can help you?"

Bass looked skeptical; the old Navajo didn't seem like he would be running the place.

"You in charge here?"

"Right now I am the boss, filling in this week for Charles Bloom. Sal put Bloom in charge while he's gone."

Bass didn't know anybody named Bloom. Last night's trip from Shiprock back to his hotel room had given Bass plenty of time to rethink the deal he had made. He had considered the possibility that Tsosie had come to Toadlena for more than food or to meet an old friend. Maybe the kid had sold the painting to old Sal. The post wasn't closed. Thus the morning reconnaisance mission—but with no Sal and a Navajo in charge, that seemed highly unlikely.

Bass was irritated that he hadn't asked Tsosie more about why he was in Toadlena, but he figured it was to score drugs. It didn't matter. If the kid had sold the painting, his dated receipt would prove his ownership and he would retrieve the piece one way or another.

"My name is Richard Bass. Sal knows me. I come by on occasion looking for pawn jewelry or anything that might be old or have value so I can resell it."

Marvin remembered this man now; he had bought Indian material from Sal in the past.

"Yes, I have seen you here before. Well, I have some nice old Fred Harvey bracelets in the case, but no new pawn has come in since the last time you were here. That was five months ago, right?"

Bass was taken aback. It had indeed been five months, nearly to the day, when he had been shopping for Indian Market, buying well-priced jewelry and off-loading it to the overpriced stores around Santa Fe's plaza. A man with this kind of recall was to be taken seriously.

"You've got an excellent memory. Have we met?"

"Yeah, I've been told that before, but I don't remember when."

Marvin smiled, waiting for Bass to react to his joke—which he didn't. After an awkward pause, Marvin continued: "We never met, but I spend a lot of time at the post, that chair is kind of my Navajo throne, so I see what goes on."

Bass didn't laugh at the throne joke either. Marvin was leery of individuals who didn't have a sense of humor, so he changed the subject. "I do have lots of new rugs, Mr. Bass, if you're interested in seeing those."

Bass concentrated on the jewelry, looking through the old, upright glass case. It was mostly the same merchandise he had seen on his last visit, nothing exceptional. But he wasn't there to buy bracelets or rugs; he was making sure HIS painting wasn't there and he, too, had an excellent memory.

"You're right. I've seen these bracelets. It's a nice selection, but there's not enough room for me to make any money flipping them, and I don't have clients for new rugs. How about paintings? I also deal in those. You got anything like that in the back?"

Marvin momentarily froze. He didn't know how to answer that question. His Dixon wasn't available for sale yet. It was half Bloom's and until his partner looked at the piece there was no way to know what the price would be, or even if it were real.

"Nope, nothing like that right now."

Bass noticed the pause. He wasn't sure if this was a language disconnect, as Marvin was clearly a Native speaker, or whether it was something more. He decided to push the Navajo further.

"You ever get any old paintings, maybe by Maynard Dixon? With your memory you would know...."

Bass watched Marvin's face intently. The Navajo remained stoic in his response, realizing this bilagáana was fishing for information about his Dixon painting.

"No, not that I can remember, but we do get sandpaintings in. Do those count?"

"I'm looking for fine art pieces, oil on canvas types of things, especially older pieces. Nothing like that, huh? Ever heard of Maynard Dixon?"

"No, I'm afraid not, but maybe Bloom has gotten something like that or knows about this Dixon guy. I can have him call you when he gets home in a couple of days."

Marvin's reaction made Bass doubt his truthfulness.

"I'll just call back in a couple of days. I don't carry my phone with me much," Bass said

"Is this Dixon fellow worth a great deal? Is that why you're interested, Mr. Bass?" Marvin couldn't suppress his curiosity.

"Yes, he can be, and I'm a real fan of Maynard Dixon's work."

"I'm making a mental note and will let you know if anything turns up, but I guess I need a phone number."

Bass didn't like giving his number out, especially not to this man.

"I'll check in from time to time. Thanks for keeping an eye open for me."

"No problem. You live around here?" Marvin pressed.

"Albuquerque," Bass said—more information than he wanted to give Marvin. Sal might have his phone number and address, but for now he didn't want this Navajo to know them.

Each man ended the conversation with concerns about the other.

CHAPTER 29

CRACK, SNAPPLE, POP

When Everett Ruess flicked the remnants of his cigarette toward his bloody Nemo inscription, the cartwheeling butt bounced off the back wall—"juxtaposed evidence of man's evolution; enjoy, my next generation of archaeologists," he thought, smiling at the irony. Having worked as a hired hand at the Woodchuck Cave ruins under the thumb of an archaeologist as a kid, it seemed like a fair payback.

Ruess tested the strength of the human-hair belt encompassing his waist by giving it a good tug, then did the same for the femur bones positioned in two nearby windows—all seemed solid. Luck would also need to be on his side; the bones, hair, and ancient windows must hold firm to avoid disaster—and even at one hundred-forty pounds the proposition was dicey. There was only one way to find out what the gods intended for him. Ruess stepped outside the ruin, his painting safe. If he could survive the descent, he could retrieve the painting at a later time and continue his journey.

He wrapped the excess rope into a loop and held it in his right hand. He would ease off the edge of the cliff and let line out as needed on the way down. His knife was close by, just in case.

Nemo looked skyward and prayed to the heavens.

"Nature is my religion. I call on your power to help my descent. If I survive, my life will be given to protecting your bounty." He then said his goodbyes to his brother, father, and dear mother. With one last look at the precious Dixon package, his back positioned to the ground, he slid off the edge.

The first two steps went as planned—then his injured gluteal muscles went into severe spasm and his right leg crumpled. Nemo lost his grip on the rope and found himself in a twelve-foot free fall. Amazingly, the hair rope retained the elasticity in its thousand-year-old fibers and he bounced a foot upward. After the initial terror of the double bounce, he realized that this could be fun if done properly—but not while attached to the end of a rope made of human hair and bones.

His left foot was just short of the first toehold when the muscle spasm eased. One half-destroyed handhold was intact and Nemo made contact with it. He would have to cut the rope with one hand, support his entire body weight with the other, and somehow find an adjacent foothold. The bottom was forty feet below, its jagged rocks looming ominously. He readjusted his ceramic helmet and, holding his breath, started to make his move when a sudden crack reverberated through the air. One of the bones had given way!

Nemo knew the other section of the lifeline would also break in short order; there was too much weight for one ancient femur to hold him. He pulled his body close to the iron-stained wall and flexed his knees. A lightning bolt of pain shot through his injured buttocks as he positioned his feet against the wall and kicked off with all his might—a trick he used to perform at the public pool, this time, unfortunately, without the water. The great thrust finished off the remaining brittle bone brace, the rope, bone fragments, and a few stones followed Nemo on his rapid descent to the bottom of the cliff.

Nemo's push propelled him past the dragon-tooth rock outcropping and toward the thicket of trees branches, just as he had hoped. The center of his back made the first contact with the ground. His head struck a limb, breaking his helmet in two pieces, but the rope wrapped around his head somehow maintained the pot's position.

A searing pain similar to that from the bullet that had hit him the day before jolted his entire body and he screamed in pain, his voice and the sound of breaking bones echoing against the canyon wall. Then the pain in his butt and lower back vanished. His spine was severed and his lower legs were paralyzed, but he was alive—at least for now. His head hurt. A trickle of fresh blood rolled down his face, but his cranium was intact. The bowl had saved his life; the question was whether that was a good thing.

Even with a severed spine and the possibility of many other broken bones, relief washed over Nemo; he had survived what should have been a mortal fall. Then a new thought crossed his mind: the rustlers—or worse, a hungry mountain lion—could have heard his cries, and all he had for protection was a pocketknife. His lower body was useless. He had to drag himself to safety or die. Two real dangers loomed before him: the first was intruders, man or beast; the second was the elements. Nature can be brutal whether it is your religion or not. The next few hours would be critical to his survival.

❋ ❋ ❋ ❋

Arms strengthened by carrying wood and packing burros freed Nemo from the mat of branches. Below him was a deep gorge with a river running through it. To survive would ultimately require water. Snow would suffice for now, but a more immediate problem was the approaching darkness. The night temperature could drop way below freezing and he had no cover.

Nemo was regretting not keeping the muslin cloth. If he hadn't used it to protect the Dixon painting, it would have made a wonderful head insulator. He needed a fire, a big one. The idea of the rustlers returning began to seem more palatable; they might kill him, but it could be more merciful than freezing, starving, or being food for wild animals. He was also regretting wasting his last match on a cigarette. He would have to find another way to produce heat.

His snakeskin belt, a twig, and a piece of old, dry cottonwood lying nearby were all he needed to start a fire. The snakeskin sling could rotate the twig in a notch in the cottonwood root. Some human hair would make great kindling and there were enough dead branches nearby to make it all feasible. He had often made fires in this primitive fashion to test his abilities; today he was doing it not for his ego but for his survival. After a couple of failed attempts, an ember emerged, though it was nearly extinguished by the large drops of sweat flowing off Nemo's face.

Within twenty minutes a small fire was burning brightly. It was now noon. There was no real cover for Nemo to drag himself to, and the only wood source was where he lay. Tonight he would make a bonfire and not worry about its consequences. He would sing as loudly as he could and hope the rustlers were nearby.

His physical condition was precarious. He was lightheaded, his temple throbbed, and he couldn't feel anything below his belly button. Thoughts of what happened to invalids were daunting. He had seen plenty of polio victims dragging themselves around pools and figured this was his best-case scenario. No trips into nature's wilderness would remain on the table. Nemo's usual upbeat disposition flipped over to despair.

He would pray for rustlers. If they didn't come, he would consider slitting his wrist tomorrow rather than face the other, unthinkable consequences. Nemo—the great explorer, archaeologist, and naturalist—was no more.

CHAPTER 30

THE LAST SMOKE

The fire was blazing; small pops and smoke filled the brisk air. Night would fall shortly. Nemo pulled out his last cigarette, lighting the end with a bit of the remaining hair rope. The odd aroma of burning hair and nicotine infiltrated his imagination. He inhaled deeply, contemplating his dim prospects.

The smoke tasted wonderful. "My last human pleasure on this earth," he thought, instinctively reaching for the diary that was now high above him, buried in the sand for eternity. "I don't even have a way to capture this moment," he thought. "I am lost, but my body will at least be a wonderful meal for the ravens. Nature, if you truly are my savior, it's time for some help."

Nemo began to sing a deeply felt spiritual song whose meaning no longer mattered; it was the music and the intention that he hoped would somehow be rewarded. The song continued for an hour, sound shifting with the wind like that of a great jazz performer. To die alone is not the worst thing that can happen to a man; to die without a song would truly be a travesty.

As Nemo sang and the old growth fuel released its stored heat for the last time, a man on the other side of the mesa top looked and listened in amazement. He had been patiently waiting and watching for more than a day and a half.

The ancestral Roanhorse land had no close neighbors, and trespassers of any race, especially those firing guns, were rare. Nemo's back flip into a bed of bushes was equally unbelievable, even to a man who had seen much during his thirty-eight years living in the isolated canyon. The Roanhorse clan liked its solitude and perceived their remoteness as a blessing from the Holy People rather than a hardship—and they were blessed in spades.

Not seeing neighbors for months at a time was not unusual. Tahoma was used to living alone, with his ten-year-old son Elton his only companion; his wife had died in childbirth. He maintained the flock of sheep as a daily reminder of a life extinguished too young—but now there was the singing bilagáana's life to consider. The two white men and an Indian had made their intention to kill this bilagáana clear; it was up to him to save the young man. No human should play god and take the life of another, regardless of his sins.

This was Roanhorse's third day away from his son Elton. He had told the young man to expect him back in two days. It was day three and soon the boy would start to panic, abandon the sheep, and come looking for his father. Time was running out; if he weren't home by nightfall, Elton would come looking for sure.

Winter was nearly upon the Roanhorse men, and backcountry living required ample supplies to survive the heavy snows. The ten bracelets, noodles of wool, and dried corn he had traded at the Kayenta trading post provided him with more than enough staples.

Roanhorse owned a few animals that lived deep in the canyon. He had happened on the rustlers' tracks and followed them. Bad men were out in force, he thought, since the white man's world had crashed. He had lost two precious steers a week before and figured these might be the men who took them. Maybe they were looking for more bounty—but no sheep would ever be lost on his watch.

The way the three men had methodically obliterated the handholds and shot into the ancient homes told the story about the person trapped above. Roanhorse was brave, but trying to climb the precarious cliff path to see who or what was up there would be a fool's errand; waiting to see what happened was the prudent move.

The men had moved on at a rapid pace—they were probably the same rustlers who had stolen his cattle, though they were empty handed at the moment—so he focused on the Anasazi stronghold. It was his land being violated, so he watched for half a day. Then the bilagáana appeared, cigarette smoke filled the air, and the crazy man jumped from the ruins, falling to his death—yet he lived. A large fire with a man lying flat on his back attested to this miracle. A lack of movement below the man's waist told another story, one of a broken back.

Roanhorse had seen many animals in this vulnerable state; it was not a good sign for the man who was presently singing a death song at the top of his lungs. His odd dress might be some sort of ritual wardrobe as he readied himself for the next world. A man in this precarious position could be highly unpredictable; he appeared unarmed, but one could not be too careful.

The time had come to find out who this man was, what he was doing on his land, and why he was being hunted. Roanhorse guided his palomino pony down the precariously steep canyon wall, crossed the river, and recovered some clothes strewn along the river's floor. He piled these into his own pack and headed up the steep incline to the other side. His pistol was loaded and the safety was off; he was ready for the unpredictable.

Nemo's off-pitch song still echoed off the canyon walls when Roanhorse broke the trance.

"What you doing here?" Roanhorse asked in a deep, booming voice, gun in hand.

"Oh, my god… you have answered my calls." For the first time, Nemo felt a sense of hope that he might survive after all, tears filling his eyes.

"You okay?" Roanhorse asked, holstering his gun when he realized this was a young man in trouble, not an evil spirit.

"No. Unfortunately, I'm not okay. I'm pretty sure I severed my spine. There are some bad hombres looking to hurt me. Can you help get me to safety?"

Roanhorse, whose English was passable courtesy of Indian boarding school, asked, "You can't walk or stand?"

"No, I'm afraid not. I'm hurt very badly and need to get out of here."

"I saw those men fire their guns at you. Why they want you dead?"

"They are cattle rustlers. I saw them steal some steers so they are not happy with me."

Then Nemo said something that changed the tone of the conversation.

In Navajo, Nemo said: "I'm trying to walk with beauty and need your help to save me. Will you save me?"

Roanhorse's demeanor shifted. This young man had spent time among his people, his Diné was good, and he could tell the young man was being truthful.

"Yes, I will help you. Your smoke is big and your voice is loud, so those men could come back. It will be dark soon and I don't want anyone following me back to my sheep or my family's hogan."

Roanhorse picked the young man up and laid his broken body on the flank of his pony, the rabbit-skin cloak and broken-pot helmet still intact. The Indian strapped Nemo in with a rope. A lower leg was broken, but the young man didn't flinch when he repositioned his oddly angled foot into the stirrup. He was indeed seriously, if not fatally, injured. The best medicine man could not help him; a miracle was needed.

"You got everything you need? We ready to go?"

Nemo thought for a moment and said, "Where the men fired at me there is a package, a painting. I would like to get that if possible...."

Roanhorse had seen paintings while attending Indian school, and had been good at drawing, but he couldn't imagine a painting worth the precious time it would take to retrieve it. This man was indeed odd, or the cracked bowl on his head had scrambled his brain.

"Where is this painting?"

"It's on the ledge I jumped from. There is a rope and a small loop is showing. If you have anything that can grab the loop, you can pull it off the ledge."

Nemo pointed toward the ledge with his lips in Navajo fashion.

"What you mean by loop?"

Nemo formed a circle with his hands. Roanhorse understood the picture. He blocked the setting sun's glare with his hands and squinted, scanning for the loop. When he was satisfied, Roanhorse went to his saddle and pulled out a fine braided rope with an egg-sized iron ball attached to one end. A Navajo-speaking white man deserved the chance to regain his belongings, if it could be accomplished quickly. Men who stole cattle and devastated another human could easily wipe out a father and son and enjoy butchering precious wool sheep for meat while never losing a night's sleep.

The horse carrying Nemo and Roanhorse was stationed under the ledge. It would take an expert hunter's throw to get the ball through the loop. On his third attempt, Roanhorse hit his mark and the ball passed through the loop. Roanhorse gently pulled the rope back until the ball caught the edge of the rope. With a slight tug, the painting fell downward, like a kite floating to and fro, which Roanhorse easily caught.

"Here is your painting, mister. Can we leave now?"

"I'm Nemo, and thank you so much! Yes, let's get the hell out of here."

The two men headed toward their destiny—one that would keep them forever intertwined.

CHAPTER 31

GOOD NEWS, BAD NEWS

A new start: it was the last day of the year and Bloom had seen this movie before. Twinkling dots of light reflected in his truck's rear-view mirror, early-morning Santa Fe disappearing as he crested over La Bajada Hill. He would soon be back on rez time.

It was déjà vu all over again. How many years had it been since he last saw this same picture, wondering at the time in which direction his life might flow. Six years? It seemed longer. Sometimes it felt as if he had always been married—but so much had changed over those years. On the first go around, he was single, with no kids, only a gallery to worry about. The rez brought him Rachael, who changed his course in life. As he left Santa Fe today, he was not alone. His companion for life was sleeping next to him, and in the back seat of the truck were two wonderful children. Bloom knew that finding the way back home would be easier now, and that finding the right partner made life an adventure.

He had gotten an early start because he couldn't wait to see the painting he had invested in. Would it be an authentic Maynard Dixon or something to chalk up to a learning experience for both himself and Marvin? There were lots of questions to be answered; if the piece was real, they had moral issues to deal with. Paying $1,500 for a Dixon—even when the buyer has priced it low—comes with its own set of problems.

The kids began to stir as Bloom slowed down at the turnoff from I-40 to U.S. Highway 491, heading north toward Toadlena.

"I'm hungry," Willy said, struggling to open his eyes

"Bloom, let's take a break, get the kids some food, and hit the restrooms before going home."

"We will be home in less than an hour...." Bloom countered. He was anxious to see the painting.

"Are you pregnant?"

"Hey kids, you hungry for some eggs?" Bloom replied without missing a beat.

After a less-than-satisfying McDonald's break and a quick stop at Safeway for groceries, the Bloom family pulled up to their house. The sky was a crystal blue and the temperature twenty-five degrees—a wonderful last day to the year.

"I know you want to get going to see your find, but can you get the stove going first? I want to get a pot of pintos and this ham hock I bought going for dinner."

"Make you a deal, my love: I'll get the stove going and even put on the beans if you can unpack and let me bug out for a while. I'm dying to see whether I wasted $750. If I did, Marvin is going to be upset on more than one level."

"Marvin will be fine; it's you I have to worry about."

Rachael knew her husband well. She also knew that the Navajo way of looking at life's obstacles was not the same as that of her bilagáana husband. When your family history starts with starvation and a four-year internment, your priorities around loss become very clear.

Bloom smiled. The neatly stacked firewood touching the roof's rafters would provide more than enough fuel for the worst of winters. It was a job well done, even if he hadn't cut the wood himself. He knocked off a dusting of snow and brought in an armful of split juniper wood. When the kitchen stove was crackling hot, he decided a run to the post was in order. The blue skies wouldn't last many days this time of year and the adrenaline kick would help clear his mind.

Running allowed Bloom to observe the small details of the land that he ignored while driving. Individual homes, debris, and abandoned structures were interspersed with the living forces of the reservation. A flock of sheep flanked by two mixed Australian shepherds trailed Bloom, voicing their concerns in no uncertain way: "Keep your distance, stranger."

When he reached the top of the hill, the two flat mesas that tourists referred to as the Two Grey Hills came into focus. Today's light tinted the mesas a bright tan. Their color could change hourly and this hue seemed unique—or maybe it was just the flood of adrenaline that made it seem that way.

Ronda's truck took up space for two vehicles directly in front of the post. Marvin would certainly have walked to work on a day this nice. Smoke was billowing into the air; the post would be toasty warm.

Bloom stopped and rested his hands on his bent knees. He was struggling for air, the high altitude and Rachael's cooking taking its toll. Staring up at the old stone building, he couldn't help but smile;

history was staring back at him, and he knew he had played a small part in it. He felt a twinge of guilt as he realized he would probably not be the next caretaker of rez life—at least not for the foreseeable future.

The bulletin board adjacent to the post's front door—a pipeline for the Toadlena basin and Four Corners region—had added one new wanted sign while he was in Santa Fe. Bloom had learned to always check the board if he wanted to know what was happening in his back yard.

The new advertiser was looking for empty flour sacks. The notice, scrawled in a mishmash of capital letters, spoke of a person whose first language was not English. A scrap of last week's *Navajo Times* supplemented the writing paper. Bloom could envision a large format art piece made up of hundreds of these small "wanted" signs patched together. It could be a big seller in Santa Fe or New York City, worth tens of thousands of dollars depending on the artist hype, but in Toadlena it only represented a need for flour sacks—nothing more.

Bloom could only imagine what the sacks would be used for. Clothing? To fill cracks? To make sandbags? All were possible scenarios. A Blue Bird flour bag had as much value as the grain inside. No weaver would consider bringing in her latest creation without first storing it in a protective flour sack. Bloom would miss this unpretentious part of daily rez life.

The door opened before Bloom could touch the handle. Marvin had been waiting for him anxiously. Rachael's analysis notwithstanding, Marvin was fully invested in their joint acquisition.

"Yá' át' ééh, Marvin. We buy any more masterpieces today?" Bloom joked.

"Well, depends on if you consider a bundle of wool noodles the start of one...."

"In Rachael's hands, I would think it could be pretty even."

Bloom walked in, glancing around the post: it had never looked better. He wondered why Marvin hadn't been the one put in charge of the store; he might have been a better choice than the art dealer. The floors were spotless, the groceries fully stocked and organized.

"Other than no ice cream bars in the refrigerator," Bloom teased, "how about the rug room? I got a feeling it's never looked better."

"Yeah. Ronda was a little miffed that I wanted to redo the stacks of rugs. She told me that the first tourist to come in was going to mess them up again, but we redid them anyway." Marvin flashed his famous grin as Bloom followed him into the back for a look.

"Wow, I can see why Ronda was ticked. It must have taken a whole day to get it looking like this," Bloom said as he looked around in amazement.

"Nah, only half a day—but on two different days." Marvin directed a fresh show of teeth at Bloom.

"Marvin, this looks great. Now let's see what kind of an eye you have for art."

Marvin gulped, knowing the answer could go either way. They walked back to the safe room and he turned on the overhead lights. The Dixon was propped up against a stack of Navajo tapestry weavings. He had positioned one of the spotlights on the painting as if it were a private showing at a high-end art gallery—something he had learned about from Bloom.

Bloom knew the answer to the question without picking up the painting. It was magnificent, the real McCoy. A wonderful payback opportunity presented itself: up until now, Marvin had always gotten the better of Bloom when it came to pulling his leg—but not today.

"Hmm, hmm...." Bloom murmured as he reached for the painting, trying his best to show serious concern. He glanced over at Marvin, who responded with a doomed look.

"Not good, huh?" Marvin asked in a low voice.

"Well, I'm afraid you could say that, Marvin. How much did WE pay for this?"

"Fifteen hundred dollars, split down the middle. I take responsibility if it's bad. I'm willing to work some to help pay it off," Marvin said sincerely.

"You see Marvin, it's not good—it's GREAT!" Bloom's face broke into a broad smile.

"Bloom, you got me! I guess I had that one coming, but you can't tell Rachael. She will tease me unmercifully."

"I won't tell if you don't."

"So, boss how good did I do?" Marvin asked, beaming with pride.

"The good news is I think this painting has to be worth at least $75,000."

"NOT POSSIBLE! REALLY?"

"I'm afraid you are going to have to deal with having money in the bank, Marvin—no more credit for you."

"So is there any bad news?"

"Unfortunately there is, and I'm not kidding about it. We only paid this kid $1,500, so anyway you look at it we are taking advantage of him, even if he priced it low himself."

Marvin hadn't let his mind go there. His great mood flipped as he realized the consequences of Bloom's words.

"So do we give it back or what?"

"Marvin, I'm not planning to give anything back, but I've never been in this position before, even though plenty of other dealers have been. I'm sure the courts would rule in our favor: we have a bill of sale, the kid set a low price to begin with, and you paid what you thought was fair. You sure didn't have a clue about its real value or even if the painting was real. But this is a community and if we just say, 'tough luck kid,' I think the ill will would be sizable. Besides, it's the right thing to do."

"Bloom, I didn't mention what now seems like an important detail. A bilagáana trader came into the post the day after I bought the painting. He was looking for Sal and wanted to know if we ever got any old paintings, like by Maynard Dixon."

"He asked that? 'Do you get any Maynard Dixon paintings?'"

"Well, he first started by asking for old Indian material. I have seen him before; he's what you guys call a picker, out of Albuquerque I think. He looked at the jewelry but I could tell that wasn't what he was really interested in. It was the Dixon."

"What did you tell him?"

"He asked if I was in charge and it seemed to me he was one of those guys who thinks no Navajo can be the boss, so he wasn't surprised when I told him no, we hadn't seen a Dixon, but he could ask you or Sal."

"Did he know who I was?"

"I know this will hurt, but no." Marvin smiled, trying to break the dark turn in the conversation. But Bloom wasn't biting.

"Okay," the dealer asked. "Is there anything else I should know about the painting?"

Marvin considered the question.

"Well, the kid brought the piece in wrapped in an old muslin cloth tied with a rattlesnake skin. I told him to go bury the snakeskin, but he is not traditional and laughed my warning off."

"You have the muslin cloth?"

Marvin stuck his hand into the post's safe where he had placed the neatly folded fabric and handed it to Bloom.

"Here you go...."

Bloom unfolded the cloth and laid it next to a light. The fabric was obviously old and dotted with sienna-colored stains—possibly blood.

"Anything else?"

Marvin replayed the Tsosie interaction in his mind, then reached into the safe and retrieved the triangular stone.

"Yes, he threw in a rock after I bought the panting. He said it was a dinosaur tooth that came with the painting. The kid didn't seem to care about it too much and skidded it across my counter. Luckily he didn't damage the glass."

Marvin wanted Bloom to know he took care of the place in his absence.

Bloom looked at the strange object. "It looks legit; it probably is a tooth from some prehistoric beast. Tsosie didn't elaborate on why this odd artifact came with the painting?"

"I didn't ask, sorry. I'm not used to this dealer stuff. It didn't seem important at the time. Does an old stone like that even have value for our painting?"

"There are collectors for everything. I doubt a single tooth would bring much money unless it was from some rare animal like a T-Rex. That's not my field, but we do need to find out."

Marvin nodded his head in agreement.

"If there's anything else, I know you will remember it." Bloom smiled, respecting Marvin's never-failing memory.

Marvin then told him about how, when he came back to give Tsosie a ride, the kid was gone, but he found the remnants of a cinnamon-

173

flavored toothpick in the snow that he assumed belonged to the person who had picked Tsosie up. Marvin explained how he dumpster-dived at the Shell Station the next morning and dug out a trash bag that he figured belonged to the person who gave the kid a ride. The trash was still in his truck, covered in two inches of snow.

"So whoever gave Tsosie the ride left his trash behind and you have it?"

"Yes, I do." Marvin was happy he hadn't tossed a possibly critical clue.

The two men left Ronda in charge of the post, grabbed the Dixon and its trappings, and headed to Marvin's house to go through the trash.

They spread the contents out on the back of Marvin's Ford truck bed and started searching for clues as to who had probably picked up Tsosie. It didn't take long to piece a reasonable scenario together: there was a small, empty bottle of cinnamon extract and a letter to Richard Bass that included an address.

"Damn it, Marvin. I'm afraid this takes on a much more serious tone. We don't know for sure that this painting wasn't stolen, or if Bass was just a little late to the buy. Whatever the case, this is not going to be a simple deal. I smell trouble, big trouble."

"So what's the next step?"

"We need to find out what we bought and who actually has ownership of it. For now we will assume the Dixon was Tsosie's to sell and that Bass is trying to horn in on our deal. The old cloth and tooth have some importance, but I'm not sure why.

"I found a Dixon expert who lives in Tucson on the internet. I'll give him a call tonight to see if we can shed some more light on this painting before we talk to Bass or Tsosie. And I'll make a few more phone calls to see if I can find out what kind of dealer Richard Bass is."

Both men stared quietly at the Dixon painting in its tailgate showroom, now strewn with trash. The painting was beginning to take on a new, more ominous light. There were serious issues to be dealt with and a plan of action would soon be needed. Rachael would not be happy.

Marvin and Bloom would have to take a trip to Tucson as soon as Sal got back. What they hadn't factored into their plan was that Richard Bass was also formulating a course of action—and he would not take kindly to either losing the painting or having people looking into his affairs.

CHAPTER 32

OUTSIDE THE BOX

Sal Lito dropped his bags at the front counter of the trading post to announce his official return. He had come back a day early, knowing this time of year could be busy, and he was ready to get back to making some money. He was happy to be home and was anxious for a complete update on post happenings during his three-month absence.

Sal made it clear that traveling the world was for retirees, and that nothing he had witnessed in the big world compared to his beloved Toadlena/Two Grey Hills formations. Retirement was off the table, which helped solidify Rachael and Bloom's decision to return to Santa Fe in May. The couple realized Sal would probably die in the saddle, which might be best for the local families. Sal was part of the glue that held the rez fabric together.

A time would come when another opportunity would arise, but this was not that time. Bloom felt a twinge of sadness when he realized he would no longer be making a difference in the community, but the discovery of the Dixon painting helped fill that hole. Depending how the Dixon deal played out, he might have one more way to be of use to at least one more Navajo.

Marvin would go along with whatever Bloom thought was best for all involved. The Navajo had never had any money and didn't expect his fortunes to change—maybe it was for the best. Secretly, though, Marvin hoped for some small payout; the trip to Japan was still an inviting proposition.

Rachael insisted that Bloom immediately tell Sal about the Dixon deal to make sure the trader didn't feel cheated if a windfall did happen to come their way. Surprisingly, Sal wasn't at all concerned with getting a piece of the Dixon action. The painting had been bought while he was gone, and their deal was whatever Bloom purchased while Sal was on vacation was his to do with as he pleased.

Bloom innately understood that there were many possible problems when it came to a valuable painting that had been bought too cheap. If he had found the piece at an estate sale or in another dealer's shop, it wouldn't be an issue. They were experts who should know better, a point of view confirmed by the courts. One famous case occurred in Tucson, when a Martin Johnson Heade painting was bought for a hundred dollars at an estate sale, and a picker turned it into a million-dollar payday at Christie's.

Both Marvin Manycoats and Tsosie were novices, and that was where the rub began. Marvin had negotiated on Bloom's behalf as the expert, a gray area no doubt. Bloom hoped to avoid getting a lawyer involved, as that would be a sure money drain. The more they stirred the greed pot, the more the issues—and billable hours—would accumulate.

Bloom's plan was simple enough: find Tsosie, explain the Dixon's potential value, and try to make a three-way partnership where all owned part of the painting and split the profits when it sold. The dealer figured he and Marvin might have to take only half of the painting, but he would try for an equal one-third ownership each. If Tsosie refused the partnership and wanted the painting returned, then Bloom would ask to sell it on consignment and retain a percentage that he and Marvin could split after it sold.

The possible resolutions seemed fair and simple enough to Bloom, but this was a new and unexplored world for Tsosie, and anything could seem appropriate, including taking the piece back for himself. Bloom was afraid Tsosie would want the piece returned and that receiving a refund was not a given: no doubt the $1,500 was long gone. Doing what was right and fair could become unmanageable. For now, the reality was that they owned the painting, with a bill of sale to prove the fact.

Marvin followed Bloom's reasoning and understood why the art dealer was so successful. Tricky situations required thinking outside the proverbial box, in this case a 20- by 16-inch rectangular box covered in old oil paint.

The New Year brought fresh challenges for Charles Bloom. A baby on the way, no more duties as trading post manager, and a potentially valuable Dixon painting with significant baggage were on the table—but for tonight, it was family that mattered most.

Rachael and Charles spent New Year's Eve with their phones and computers turned off. Playing Monopoly and Go Fish with the kids, while drinking homemade apple cider, was on the schedule. Bloom tried not to let his subconscious dwell on the implications of Bass's visit to the post looking for Dixon paintings. Twenty-five years in the art business said coincidences like that didn't exist: Bass was on the hunt. Breaking the news to Rachael that he was going to Tucson tomorrow could wait until next year.

Bloom's Santa Fe New Year's Eve tradition had been iced Modelo beer and green-chile nachos. Rachael was not a fan of alcohol, which was illegal on the rez and, in her mind, an evil spirit that robbed her people of their dignity and future success. There would be no alcohol in her home.

Bloom considered making a quick visit to the bootlegger down the road. Old English—or OE beer as the locals call it—with its high alcohol content and its cheap $5 price, would be an adequate substitute, but he knew better than to cross his wife on this issue. Besides, driving on a wintery night was risky on the rez; between the ice, hitchhikers in dark clothes, grazing cows and horses, and drunk drivers, New Year's Eve was a dangerous proposition past sundown. Nachos with extra chile and warm apple cider would suffice for this year's celebration.

Maynard Dixon Museum

CHAPTER 33

N-E-M-O

A variety of methods go into determining a fair price for an antique painting. Most collectors use appraisers who research auction records and search for comparables sold through art shows or dealers. There are, however, unscrupulous appraisers that suggest a price, then try to buy or otherwise handle the pieces they just evaluated. Bloom had decided long ago not to do appraisals to avoid these kinds of conflicts of interest.

Art dealers are closed-mouth about releasing sales information to appraisers in fear of giving away trade secrets—or worse, losing a painting to the appraiser or another dealer should their private information be shared. A competing dealer could use this data to undercut future sales or go to the client and to try to pry loose a piece to resell.

Bloom was often asked to help with the pricing and authentication of Willard Yellowhorse paintings, as he was the expert in a field where little material was available and fakes had flooded the market. It is not unusual in the art world to find fake paintings by contemporary artists with astronomical prices, so some de facto expert or estate must become the arbitrator. For Yellowhorse, this duty had fallen onto Bloom's shoulders because he had exclusively handled Willard's work during the artist's early career.

Willard's sister Rachael Yellowhorse understood her deceased brother's work nearly as well as her husband. Bloom would never appraise Willard Yellowhorse's paintings, instead he would give his "opinion," knowing that it was a fine semantic line to walk as the unhappy owner of a fake could easily come back for monetary reparation. It helped to have Rachael's opinion to tip the balance of doubt and litigation.

Researching the work of Maynard Dixon, Bloom found the de facto Dixon expert in Mort Shandling, an apparently quirky recluse who owned and operated the Maynard Dixon Museum in Tucson, Arizona—Dixon's last home.

Dixon had lived in Tucson for the last six years of his life, dying in 1946 at the age of seventy-one from lung disease, producing some of his best work at the very end. Dozens of important pieces had been scattered among southern Arizona collectors, and many of these paintings had found their way into the collection of Shandling's very wealthy grandparents, who had moved to Tucson in the 1920s to combat consumption, now recognized as tuberculosis. Before the advent of drug therapy, Tucson's hot, dry climate was the best treatment for lung ailments.

Like Dixon, Shandling's parents grew up in Tucson. Both his grandparents and his father knew Dixon and acquired numerous pieces both while the artist was alive and after his passing, creating a large and important family art collection. Mort's father, like his grandfather, was a demanding man, a stickler for perfection. He collected only the best examples of an artist's work; anything less was failure.

The genetic propensity to collect was passed on to Mort, their only child, who inherited both the family's art and fortune. Mort had been interested in Dixon's work since childhood, so he sold off the majority of the other artwork to raise funds to purchase additional Dixon paintings and to help support his Dixon museum. Rounding up quality Dixon artworks and ephemera to add to his ever-expanding museum was Mort's mission in life. He was determined to outdo both his father's and grandfather's accomplishments—a single-minded obsession with no tolerance for second-rate pieces.

The Maynard Dixon Museum was nestled in the Catalina foothills, not far from Dixon's old home at 2255 East Prince Road. At one time, Dixon's humble adobe house sat in an isolated area of Tucson; now the Sonoran Desert was filled with thousands of snowbirds living in high-end secondary homes to escape the brutality of a Midwest winter—yet somehow the artist's home was still intact.

According to what Bloom found on maynarddixonmuseum.com, Shandling was working on a catalogue raisonné of Dixon's work, and was always looking for new pieces to add to his collection—highest prices paid. A catalogue raisonné represented as complete as possible a record of an artist's body of work, mostly paintings, but in some comprehensive books, this could also include drawings, illustrations, pastels, sculptures, and watercolors.

Bloom figured anyone crazy enough to attempt a raisonné on a man like Dixon, who had documented close to one thousand five hundred paintings, would be happy to take a look at a painting fresh to the market and render his opinion. The painting had apparently been in a Navajo home for a very long time and it was doubtful that the art world knew of its existence—a tantalizing opportunity for a Dixon expert.

Bloom gave the museum a call and Shandling picked up after one ring.

"Maynard Dixon Museum, this is Mort Shandling. How can I help you?"

"Hi, Mr. Shandling. This is Charles Bloom. I've turned up what I believe is a Maynard Dixon painting, one I doubt you have seen."

Shandling was wary; most of these so-called works were not by Maynard Dixon at all, but by other artists who signed with that name.

"Really? You know I have seen a lot of what's been produced. There are not too many paintings out there that I haven't at least received a picture of. Why do you think this one is a piece I don't know about?" Shandling asked skeptically.

Bloom gave Shandling an abbreviated history of the piece, leaving out the owner's name and no mention of Bass on the trail. The tenor of the conversation changed as Bloom described the circumstances.

"So tell me, Mr. Bloom, your name sounds familiar.... Do you have a gallery in Santa Fe?"

"Please call me Charles."

"Okay, Charles. Is Bloom's yours?"

"Yes, that's my gallery. I specialize in Native American art, primarily contemporary, but lately I've moved into the more traditional realm. My wife is a Navajo weaver."

"I thought I recognized your gallery's name. I've been in the shop before. It's up on Canyon Road, correct?"

"That's right, halfway up on the right side."

"Lovely place. You might find this interesting if you don't know much about Dixon. In 1900, when he was twenty-five, Dixon traveled by train and wagon to the Navajo Nation and Santa Fe. Dixon loved the Navajo and their blankets and visited the reservation often. I have some great pieces that depict this imagery I'm happy to share if you ever get down to Tucson. I'd love to see what you've turned up, too."

"Well, I may just take you up on that, Mort. I need to find out what I have and, quite frankly, I would rather have you see it in person than by sending photos. I'm sure you can understand...."

"Completely! Those photos might get out into the art world ecosphere and before you know it some hooligan has reproduced it as a poster and is selling it on eBay."

"Something like that. You just never know where images can end up, and to my knowledge this painting has never been outside of a Navajo hogan."

"Dixon had lots of friends on the reservation, including Lorenzo Hubbell, whom he referred to as his *patrón*. They were friends for nearly thirty years. In fact, Dixon acted as Hubbell's agent and sold rugs for the trading post to help supplement his art sales. In 1906, when the great earthquake of San Francisco hit, Dixon abandoned all his paintings so he could save the beautiful Navajo weavings, which in his mind were irreplaceable," Shandling said with authority.

"I'm liking your Maynard Dixon even more," Bloom said.

"Charles, is there any writing on the back of the painting? Dixon was very good about record keeping."

"There is an address."

"Let me guess: 728 Montgomery Street, San Francisco."

"Yes, that's correct."

"How about a number. It would be a three-digit number in the upper left corner that was usually circled."

"Yes, there is one. It's 240."

"That sounds like my boy. It's a good number for 1922 and fits with the date on the front of the painting. Do you see something that sounds like a title on the back, probably underlined near the number?"

"Yes, there is. It says Wetherill's."

"Interesting. I'm not sure I know that title. Can you see anything else?"

"There is an price that I'm assuming is an original value: $300."

"Yes, that was a standard Dixon price for 16- by 20-inch piece. It's all looking good for it be authentic. Anything else?"

Shandling was now fully engaged in the conversation, knowing this was an authentic painting and the title and imagery of Anasazi ruins that Bloom described were nothing he had seen before.

"Well, Mort, there is some writing on the back that doesn't appear to be in the same fluid handwriting as the title and address. It's more childlike and looks like it was written with a different type of pencil. It says Nemo."

Shandling was quiet for a few seconds, trying to process that name, which he knew was Everett Ruess's alias.

"N-E-M-O? Is that correct?"

"Yep. Does it mean anything to you?"

To Shandling, finding a Dixon piece that was once in the possession of Everett Ruess was like finding the Holy Grail—it was a piece his father would have killed for to add to his collection. But Mort wasn't about to let on about its importance, at least not yet.

"I'm not sure. Sometimes kids get ahold of pieces and draw or write on them. I will need to see the piece and dig a little bit. When can you bring the painting down?" Shandling asked nervously.

"How about sometime this week, Mort. It's as cold as a witch's behind up here in Toadlena, and I could use a mini-break."

"Great. You can come down tomorrow if you like. I'm free and I believe this could be quite the find."

"It will probably take me most of the day to get to Tucson, so maybe we can plan on the day after tomorrow. When does your museum open?"

"If you could come around 9 a.m., Charles, we won't be bothered with visitors."

"That's fine. I have a partner in the painting and he will be accompanying me. I hope that's okay."

"Sure, the more the merrier. Since you have a partner, it sounds like this is something you are interested in selling...."

"Potentially, yes. There are few kinks to be worked out, but yes, I would like to see what you think it's worth and make sure it's authentic."

"Well, Charles, you have come to the right place on both counts. Can I use the number that's popping up on my caller ID to communicate with you?"

"Sure, this is my cell. I look forward to seeing you in two days, 9 a.m."

"Wonderful! I can't wait, Mr. Bloom. You will enjoy seeing my little museum; it's a three-generation collection of Dixon's lifework."

Shandling knew this was an important painting. He hung up the phone and headed directly to his vault, where the Dixon log resided. This master list represented nearly all of Dixon's painting production over a forty-year period and was the museum's most important document. Painting number 240 was listed as "Dream Shadow," not "Wetherill's," as it was called on Bloom's painting. Next to the title on the log "discarded" was written in Dixon's hand. Apparently the artist had scraped the original painting to reuse the board and painted "Wetherill's" in its place. He had not retitled and added this new work to the log, which meant it was special to Dixon.

Perhaps Dixon had made the piece especially for Everett Ruess. There was no other explanation, assuming the Nemo inscription was real. This was indeed a pivotal painting, possibly the Rosetta Stone to understanding Ruess's disappearance, and just maybe the most important clue about what had happened to the vagabond wanderer to surface since 1934.

Shandling remembered the big deal *National Geographic* had made a few years earlier upon finding the bones of a young man buried on the Navajo Nation, near the last sighting of Ruess; the local Navajo lore said a white boy had been killed by bilágaanas and his body hidden in a crevice. The made-for-TV special was national news as the preliminary genetic testing of bones found in the desert identified them as belonging to someone related to Ruess. But the documentary was soon engulfed in scandal as an archaeologist disputed the finding; his research indicated the skull was Native in origin, not Caucasian. Under public pressure, genetic retesting of the bones revealed that the skeleton was most likely of Navajo origin.

Bloom's find, a Maynard Dixon painting that carried Nemo's name, originating from a Navajo source, pointed to the fact that Ruess had indeed somehow survived and lived with the Navajos. Or, alternatively, that he had been murdered by Navajos, with the painting pointing to a possible killer.

There had always been talk of Ruess living out his life on the Navajo Nation, and even having children. If the truth was revealed, answers would be forthcoming and there would be a new and even more intriguing story ready for prime time. Shandling realized he would be center stage and his Dixon Museum would finally get the attention it deserved. No more would his great collection be languishing away in some strip mall in the Catalina foothills. National recognition would be his, besting all his father's accomplishments.

Shandling would acquire this painting. He would not let an important piece of history escape, no matter how much it might cost. It would become part of the museum's holdings at any cost—and the true story of Everett Ruess's disappearance would finally be told.

CHAPTER 34

BURN, BABY, BURN

Bass had received no communications from Tsosie—even after making multiple attempts to reach the kid by text and voicemail. The New Year had arrived and Tsosie had gone radio silent.

Richard Bass was not happy. The deal was the kid had seven days to produce the painting and Tsosie was late. Bass didn't want to push too hard, but he also understood time was of the essence. Every day that passed without locking down his painting made it more likely the flaky Navajo kid would take it elsewhere or get cold feet. Regardless of the paperwork, in the West, possession was still nine-tenths of the law. Bass had already given Tsosie an expensive squash blossom necklace, and the thought of also losing a valuable painting was grinding hard on his disposition.

Bass wasn't going to sit around waiting for Tsosie to return his calls; he had property to recover and today looked like a good day to go hunting. There were two paths he could follow: on the one hand, he could start with the girlfriend; she was an easy target and would have valuable information. Bass figured he would scare her if need be to make his point about the seriousness of the situation. He didn't like men who hit girls—his mom had been in one of those relationships— but a lot of money was at stake. The second possibility was to go back up to Bluff to track down the kid. Bertha at the pawnshop was his contact (assuming she remembered any of their conversation), but that choice would take more time and require some luck. The girlfriend was the surer bet, so he decided on option one.

Rosemary Franklin lived in rented a trailer with her two-year-old son. She had no husband, no education, and no family to speak of except Tsosie, who was the father of their child. The young Navajo helped her with bills, but lately he had become erratic in his moods and visits. Rosemary's own father had left the family for greener pastures when she was five, drugs taking him before he was forty. Tsosie was on the same path, and she knew there was nothing she could do to stop the scourge of addiction but reassure him of her love. The expensive squash blossom necklace around her neck proved Tsosie loved her too.

Their child was smart and healthy. Rosemary had given up drinking when she found out she was pregnant. Her only occasional vice was marijuana, which opened a window to a happier world. She was on a wait list for a cashier's job at the Food Mart, but needed to find decent childcare to make that plan work. She had asked Tsosie to move in with her and be a househusband to their child so she could work for the family, but he had resisted. He was going through his own issues at home and she hadn't seen him since Christmas. She feared he was on a bender huffing nitro, something he did when confronted with a difficult decision.

There were no good options. A poor single mother raising a child alone with few job opportunities was a recipe for disaster, and Rosemary recognized the gravity of the situation. She was stretched out on her paisley couch when she heard a hard knock on the aluminum door.

"It must be Tsosie!" she said out loud, as her son's call of "Daddy!" chimed in the background. Rosemary unlocked the door and opened it with a wide grin—her smile turning to disappointment when she saw the out-of-place bilagáana on her stoop.

"Yá' át' ééh. My name is Bass, Richard Bass. I'm a friend of Everett Tsosie. I've been trying to get him and he's not answering his phone," Bass said in the most friendly and unassuming voice he could muster. But Rosemary's antennae were on high alert.

"How do you know my E.T.?"

"Well, it's an interesting story. I have some money to give E.T. I'm happy to discuss it with you, because it might affect you too."

The man seemed to know her Tsosie and he didn't look like a cop or social worker. Money was the magic word, so she reluctantly let him in.

"Okay, come in. Have a seat at the table. I'm going to need to rock my son; you woke him with your knock."

"Sorry about that," Bass said with a wide grin.

"So tell me Mr. Bass, why do you want to give my Tsosie money?"

Bass's squash blossom necklace was dangling from Rosemary's neck and he thought that if he were mad enough it wouldn't take much to strangle this woman. The picker tried not to let such thoughts enter his mind, but he had a great deal of pent up anger toward Tsosie. Bass, ever the professional, assessed the environment: there were no photos on the shelves, no paintings on the wall, nothing of value in the trailer. She appeared to be the lone adult occupant and was dirt poor.

"Nice place, plenty of room for two," Bass fished.

"Yes, it's big enough, but I think calling this dump 'nice' is a bit of a stretch. I'm okay with it. It's what I can afford for now, but it's not my future, and I don't plan to always live on the outskirts of Shiprock."

Bass was impressed. Rosemary seemed smart and was quite attractive; he could see why Tsosie wanted to be with this girl.

"Well, you have made it a nice home, though a couple of paintings would add some color, don't you think?"

"Paintings? Maybe a sandpainting or when my kid is old enough to make some art, but I can't afford anything like that."

"How about Tsosie? Maybe he could give you something to hang?" Bass continued to fish.

"I love my E.T., but he's not that kind of man. He's more into posters of his favorite band. I doubt he would even notice if I hung a painting over my couch. It's just not his thing."

"Huh? I thought he was trying to sell a painting." Bass waited for a response to see which way he would pivot with regards to Rosemary's welfare.

"Sell a painting? That's hilarious—maybe some homegrown weed, but art is not something he would ever consider. We are talking about the same Everett Tsosie out of Mexican Hat, right?"

"Yeah, I'm sure he's the same one. Well, you see, Rosemary, your E.T. actually did come up with a painting, something I collect. I offered him quite a bit of money for the piece and he in fact sold it to me. That lovely necklace around your neck you got for Christmas was part of the deal he made with me. I bought that in Bluff, Utah. It's a very nice necklace—in fact, it's worth $1,500 retail."

Rosemary's mouth hung open "Are you kidding me? E.T. gave me something worth $1,500, and he's never even given me an engagement ring!"

"Yes, that's the honest truth. Any Santa Fe gallery would have something with those natural Kingman stones priced at least that, maybe higher. Not only did I trade him that prized piece of jewelry, but I also promised him $1,500 cash when I got the painting."

Bass pulled out his dated receipt and showed it to Rosemary.

"Yep, that's my boy's signature, but he didn't say nothing to me about any painting or money due to him."

"Well, he didn't say anything about trading me for the necklace either, did he?"

"No, he said it was an old family piece and he wanted me to have it...." her voice trailed off as she tried to put the pieces together.

"So, Mr. Bass, what do you want from me? I don't know where he is. My guess is he's on a bender; he's hooked on whippets."

"Whippets?"

"It's nitrous oxide. It comes in small metal canisters that you inhale. It's bad for your brain and your lungs, but he can't stop. He's tried a bunch of times, but it helps kill the pain of life. He's probably too stoned to bring you the painting—until he runs out of money and needs more drugs."

"So he needs help. I can understand that; my own dad was a bad alcoholic, and it can be rough to watch someone you care about destroy himself. How about this: you help me get what's mine, and I'll make sure you get $200 for the effort."

"I'm happy to help and, honestly, the money would change my world. I'm tired of washing dirty diapers. I'd love to be able to buy some throwaway ones for once.

"What do you want to know, Mr. Bass?"

"Well, for starters, where can I find E.T.?"

"He's near Mexican Hat. I'll draw you a map. That's the only way you'll find him. Google doesn't map where E.T. lives. He's got an old family hogan near his grandfather's place. E.T. doesn't care about the Holy People, so he moved into the abandoned place after a big fight with his grandfather. Most Navajos would avoid a place like that."

"I know, bad *chindi*," Bass said, reinforcing the idea that he was not ignorant of the ways of the traditional Navajo.

"*Chindi* are real, and I wasn't about to move in with him. This is part of our problem: even though he argues with his grandfather, he won't leave his family farm, so there is no place for us to be together."

"That makes it tough. Isn't there some way for E.T. to make up with his grandfather and move back in?" Bass asked, trying to sound as sympathetic as possible.

"Hastiin Roanhorse, E.T.'s grandfather, has been trying to get him to have a cleansing sing and move back into his hogan so he can retrieve his lost *hózhó*, but that boy is stubborn and won't listen when it comes to the traditional stuff unless it's his idea. I'm with his grandfather."

"You think he will be holed up doing drugs at the old hogan?"

"Yeah, he's most likely there. If not, go to the next dirt road north and ask his grandfather where he is. Hastiin Roanhorse is old and not much for leaving his home, so he will know if E.T. has been around. He's a nice man and really loves his grandson."

"Thanks, Rosemary. I'll let you know what I find out. I wish you the best of luck, so I'm going to go ahead and pay you $100 of the promised $200. If E.T. shows up here, please give me a call. The number is on my card.

"You mind if I use your bathroom before I go?"

"Go ahead. There's one in the back. I'm sorry it's kind of a mess—and thank you for the money. I need to get food for my baby and this is a huge help."

"I'm glad I can help, and don't worry—my house is always a mess."

Rosemary smiled. She hoped this man got his painting and that E.T. hadn't done something stupid.

Bass worked his way back toward the master bedroom, carefully searching to see if there were any firearms. If he had to make another trip to Rosemary's home, it would be under less than happy circumstances. You never knew when a trailer might catch fire. They can be death traps, especially if your boyfriend reneged on a deal.

CHAPTER 35

ON DUTY

Tsosie's energy and money were spent. The last of his whippet canisters were piled in a stack with some Coors beer cans—a true pile of despair. A fog of dystopia persisted. No food and only a few cups of water over the past two days had pushed E.T. to the bottom of his addiction. He never heard the whine of Bass's car engine or the subsequent knock on the heavy plank door. He thought it was all in his head.

Bass could see Tsosie's body curled in a fetal position in the center of a dirt floor, and he wondered what kind of mess he had walked into. His own anger began a fast boil and he kicked open the door, breaking the small wooden security latch. The door swung to the side and stuck in an open position, pinned against the door jam.

"What the hell, man?" Tsosie said, his dry mouth slurring his words.

"Tsosie, you're a fricking mess—and two days late on delivering my painting, I might add. You've got some explaining to do."

The Navajo's mind was struggling to make a complete sentence. The cold air was helping sober him up, but what was the deal? As he came back to reality, E.T. realized serious trouble was standing inches away. Too strung out and weak to put up a fight, he began shaking uncontrollably, the withdrawal, cold, hunger, and fear all kicking in at once in a giant speedball of endorphins.

"Sorry, I'm pretty screwed up right now. I've got a problem and time isn't real, you know. What day is this?"

"This is Thursday, a new year. What planet are you living on?"

Tsosie tried to stand up, wobbled and fell back on the ground. Bass grabbed his arm and helped the young man to the couch.

"Okay, let me ask you: do you have my painting?" Bass's nose was nearly touching Tsosie's. The Navajo was panicking, his eyes darting away from any contact with the angry dealer.

"Hey, give me minute would you, man? I'm pretty messed up right now."

Bass pushed him away roughly and took a quick inventory of the hogan's sparse interior. There was no painting, just an old stick in the corner, a bed, couch, bureau, and kerosene lamp. He riffled through the drawers but found no money, guns, or paintings. The place was not a real home, just a flophouse for a drug addict.

"I don't see my painting. Where is the goddamn painting?"

"So, here's what happened. The night I met up with you I had already sold it, but I'm sure I can get it back."

"YOU SOLD IT? I've got to tell you, E.T., that I'm not very happy right now. You notice I know your friends call you E.T.? You know how I know this?"

"Uh-uh...."

"Your sweet girlfriend Rosemary and I had a nice little visit—that's how I found you. You remember her, don't you, and that cute baby boy?"

"Hey, you gotta leave them out of this; she's not involved."

"On the contrary, she is most definitely involved. I saw a nice necklace—my necklace—around her neck, the one you took as part of our deal. I have a written receipt for that which you signed.

"Now where is the painting?"

"I sold it to that old Navajo guy at Toadlena. He paid me $1,500 cash."

"Did you sign a receipt?"

"I don't know, man. I honestly can't remember. I think so but I'm not sure; my mind is a jumble."

Bass set down on the couch trying to figure out his next move. Manycoats had lied to him. The old Navajo did have the painting and probably figured out that Bass was after it. Manycoats was sharper than the picker had given him credit for. He could take care of the drug addict, but what would that get him? For now he needed Tsosie, and maybe he could get the piece back.

"You have any of Manycoat's money left?"

"Nah, it's gone."

"Fifteen-hundred dollars, right?"

"Yeah, cash."

"Okay, you're coming with me, and we're going to get my painting back. You're going to do whatever it takes to get that damned Dixon returned to me, you understand?"

"Sure, whatever I can do."

"I'll give you the $1,500 so you can pay Manycoats back. Here's the plan: first off, you tell Manycoats you have seller's remorse. If he refuses to give your painting back, you say the painting wasn't yours to sell and the owner wants it back—so he can return it now and get his money back or the owner is going to sue him. That's the storyline; do not deviate from it."

"What's 'deviate' mean?"

"It means, E.T., that you keep to the story, add nothing else and do not elaborate or come up with any of your own ideas. You want it back, have seller's remorse, and it's not yours to sell."

"I can do that: seller's remorse, not mine."

"That's remorse—it means you changed your mind, got cold feet."

"I got—sorry my mind's kind of hazy."

"Get some clean underwear and socks and find a goddamned shoe for that other foot. We're heading south. One more question E.T., and you need to be straight with me: you got any weapons on you?"

"No weapons, man."

"I believe you, but you're going to need to put both hands against that wall and spread your legs."

E.T. did as ordered and Bass gave him a cursory frisk; he was clean.

"Get your shit and let's go before the weather gets any worse."

With snow flurries filling the air, Tsosie and Bass left the hogan, leaving the front door wide open—so the picker never saw the portrait of Elton Roanhorse that Dixon had painted on its backside.

Bass had checked into a Farmington hotel on the way up to Mexican Hat in case he needed to bring in the Shiprock girlfriend to apply more pressure. He had used an assumed name and paid cash in case things went south. Fortunately, he had found his prey; once E.T. was fit for travel, they would head down to Toadlena and retrieve what he considered his rightful property.

The dirty black sedan left the isolated hogan in a puff of dirt, but it was not unseen. On a nearby mesa top, the guardian was on duty and saw what had transpired. The witness had different plans; after all, it was HIS Dixon painting, not Tsosie's, at the heart of it all.

CHAPTER 36

GUARDIAN OF THE CORNFIELDS

Hastiin (Perry) Roanhorse had salt and pepper hair, rich chocolate-brown skin, and a muscular physique that belied his age of seventy-three. The true marker of longevity could be seen in the dark circles under his eyes, indicators of years of lost sleep and painful nights. The Roanhorse clan lived long or died young; there was no in-between.

Perry's father, Elton Roanhorse, had hoed his corn crops into his late eighties, when a rogue lightning bolt from a clear blue sky felled the old man—a fateful sign from the heavens that his time was up.

Mortally wounded, but with his warrior's heart unwilling to surrender, the octogenarian stumbled back home, his faithful Puebloan dibble locked in a death grip. The prehistoric hoe, which had planted fields for untold centuries, followed Elton into his next journey.

The old man collapsed on his bed, gasping for breath as the last cells of his heart fired in a giant burst of energy. Elton struggled to rise so he could abandon his family's home, knowing that if he died inside it the dwelling would be lost, but the next world came calling before he could get through the door. Perry concluded that this was another dark sign that must be respected, and left the ancient hoe in place, a warning of the *chindi* that filled the home.

E.T. lambasted his grandfather's warnings of witches, spirits, and other signs to be respected and feared. The dibble, with its sharp edge and slick handle, was no icon of death. It was nothing more than a window prop on a hot afternoon, or a back scratcher for a hard-to-reach itch.

Perry's aunt, Sally Tsosie, his father's younger sister, died at thirty-five from leukemia, a casualty of a life lived near the uranium mines. Sally's only child Jacob moved back to live with Perry Roanhorse, and was like a son to him. Jacob followed his mom's road and died young, but from another evil—alcohol. Jacob's only child, E.T., then became Perry's responsibility and default grandson, though the rebellious youngster fought Perry at every turn.

The family's traditional isolated lifestyle was a burden to E.T.—a daily reminder of his father Jacob's alcoholic world. But Tsosie was good at farming and in this capacity was of great help to his grandfather, managing the large fields. Then came the drugs, occasional at first, then quickly overwhelming the young man until he and his grandfather fought constantly. In a final act of defiance, E.T. retreated to the one place he knew his grandfather would never follow him—his great-grandfather's hogan-crypt.

The Roanhorse property was vast and remote, even by Navajo standards. There was no running water and, until solar panels were recently installed, no electricity. Neighbors were few and far between, which was fine by Perry. The towering red cliffs dotted with fertile patches of soil balanced on a Mesozoic seabed were his home.

The region had been more populated in 1200 CE when the Nasazi ruled the region, their numerous artifacts and homes a testament to their skills as farmers and survivors. The exceptional agricultural lands blessed with annual springs of bubbling, cool water were, for the most part, inaccessible except by animal or on foot. No barbed wire fences were needed; deep natural canyons acted as pens for all that could find the entrance.

Caring for the cornfields and their secrets had been a way of life for the Roanhorse clan. E.T. was now the same age as Perry had been when his father had revealed the commitments of the fields to him. Perry understood the ramifications; fifty years earlier he had accepted the responsibilities and followed his father's example.

Perry blamed himself for E.T.'s shortcomings, and tried to keep a vigilant eye on the young man, pushing him gently toward the light of responsibility and the Holy People—but to no avail. E.T.'s cell phone was his only source of solace for the unbearable isolation, music his only escape until drugs filled the void.

Perry decided to explain the significance of the painting and the secrets of the fields to the young man. He hoped these revelations might help tie E.T. to the lands Perry loved above all else. E.T. understood that, as his grandfather's only heir, he would one day inherit the land and the responsibility that came with it—and it drove him more deeply into himself.

The Dixon painting was an incidental fixture of E.T.s life, hung on a single hand-forged nail in the family outhouse. For Perry, though, the painting represented a Navajo art gallery and retreat; he never failed to be transfixed by god's beauty. The outhouse's missing door latch offered the opportunity for reflection on body and soul with an unobstructed view of a valley compressed between two iron-rich cliffs dotted with Nasazi ruins.

The Dixon painting was a snapshot, a sliver of the land, a reminder of the importance of Mother Earth. That moment in time captured in oils bore witness to what Perry experienced in a way he could not articulate. He respected this artist he had never met. He wished that, like his grandfather and father, he could have met the man behind the paint.

The story his father told was that Dixon had visited their valley on horseback a hundred years ago, lost and in desperate need of food and directions. The vagabond artist bonded immediately with his kind hosts, who shared fresh venison steaks and a corn soup with him before guiding the painter to a special formation of ancient houses.

Dixon thanked Perry's grandfather for his generosity in the only way he could—by painting a quick study of his only son Elton standing draped in a colorful red blanket with blue stripes on the back of the hogan's entrance door—the same hogan in which Elton had passed from this earth, E.T.'s current home.

Perry's father remembered the tall, lanky artist with a black Stetson hat riding low on his friendly tanned face, a cigarette in his hand, and a silver Colt pistol laced to his flank. One artist stumbling on the Roanhorse property would be a rare occurrence, yet it had happened twice—once with Maynard Dixon and again, thirteen years later, with Everett Ruess.

The appearance of Maynard Dixon and Everett Ruess at the homestead was more than a coincidence in Perry Roanhorse's mind. The events were preordained, in the hands of the Holy People, and, as such, the painting was treated with reverence. The portrait of his father in the abandoned hogan was a dark sign better left to the *chindi*.

At the first snow of each year, Perry performed a blessing ritual for the painting, as his father and grandfather had done before him. Perry included a special prayer to the snake for its skin sacrifice to help guard the painting through the upcoming cold winter months, as if it were hibernating in a warm, comfortable den. Once properly prepared in its muslin covering and snakeskin belt, the triangular stone tooth secured on top like a fetish, the package would be stored in a nearby deep, dry cache, a stone door placed in front of it for good measure. It would remain there until the spring rains arrived in April.

Although E.T. recognized the pattern, he never wondered why the painting cycled in and out of the outhouse. Clouded by youth, he had assumed it was simply part of the seasonal rotation in the Roanhorse family. Perry decided the time had come to tell the story of how his father had found the broken Everett Ruess and brought him to his home, and how Ruess's gift of the painting to his grandfather had been handed down for two generations. Someday, Perry said, it would be E.T.'s responsibility. The story had interested E.T.—but he was more curious about the work's potential value than its spiritual significance or its place in the family's lineage.

Perry explained that the painting did have worth, as Dixon was a known artist, and the man who had given the family the painting had become a mythological hero in the white man's environmental movement. But he emphasized that because the painting would never be sold, its monetary value was of no relevance.

Even though E.T. seemed less than interested in the concept of stewardship, Perry included the young man for the first time in the ritual blessing and placing of the painting in its winter home. E.T. was underwhelmed by the entire process, and his lack of interest in anything beyond the painting's value was upsetting to his grandfather, so Perry decided it was not time to divulge the entire story or tell E.T. anything about the importance of the stone fetish or Ruess's presence on the land. If the kid couldn't be trusted to be a guardian of the painting, he could never be trusted to guard the secrets of the fields. Roanhorse would wait for his grandson to mature and get off drugs before he revealed the rest of the story.

Seeing the black sedan's arrival confirmed he had made the right decision; his grandson was traveling a dead-end road. The bilagáana appeared to be a hard man, and the rough treatment was a testament to the man's anger. E.T was nothing more to him than vermin to be disposed of without a second thought.

Perry Roanhorse prayed this was not the case. This was a serious problem he would need to explore; the situation had become dire and it was up to him to stop his grandson's destructive behavior—otherwise there could be deadly consequences.

Was the Dixon painting now part of this equation? Roanhorse feared the worst. The bilagáana had taken his grandson to parts unknown. After the sedan had vanished on the horizon, Roanhorse hiked up to the painting's hidey-hole, which was not far from where Dixon had painted the piece. A deep thicket obscured the entry into the box canyon, so retrieving the cached painting took work. It was all part of the ritual, one that wasn't due to take place till spring.

Climbing the slick wall face in winter was dangerous for an old man, even one with a hundred trips behind him. A bad sign appeared on the ascent: the small rectangular sandstone door that covered the crack's entrance had been tossed carelessly to the side, and the painting was nowhere to be found inside the vault.

E.T. had taken the piece and would most likely be selling the heirloom for drugs. The fraternal trust that had held strong for nearly a hundred years was fractured, and a cascade of dangerous events was inevitable, unless the old man could recover his family's patrimony.

The field's secrets were at risk—and Perry Roanhorse would never allow their truth to be discovered.

CHAPTER 37

NO PHOTOS, PLEASE

E.T. fixed his gaze on the horizon and remained silent during the two-hour trip to Farmington. This was serious trouble. He wished he could talk to his grandfather, explain his predicament, and promise to be a better human—but that time had passed.

The young man innately understood that Bass was as dangerous as a wounded animal and not to be taken lightly. The man's anger was visible in his eyes. E.T. would retrieve the Dixon; Hastiin Manycoats was nowhere near the threat Bass represented.

No words were spoken until Bass pulled into the rear of the Farmington Holiday Inn. The car rolled to a stop in a secluded space next to the motel dumpster. The smell of onions and stale beer began to fill the car as Bass leaned into E.T.

"You sober yet?"

"I'm better."

"Let's get a few things straight: you sold MY painting. I want it back and if I don't get it, I'm going to make you pay—and not in dollars. Do you understand me?"

"Yes, I do," E.T. said, nodding his head in the affirmative.

"Good. I've got us a room. You go get cleaned up and we'll see if we can make a plan to return the painting to its rightful owner—ME."

The room had two queen beds, and Bass motioned to E.T. to sit on the unmade one.

"You need a shower; you smell worse than that dumpster. Empty all the contents of your pockets onto the bed and then take your pants off in front of me. I need to frisk you down again to make sure you don't have any weapons. This is nothing personal, I'm just taking care of business."

Bass had cursorily frisked E.T at the hogan, but they were in close quarters now and he didn't want any surprises.

"Good; you told the truth. Now head to the shower and feel free to use lots of soap. We'll talk when you're done."

Cold water penetrated the last of E.T.'s haze and his mind started clearing. His son and girlfriend were important, and they were counting on him. It was time to grow up and start anew. If he could retrieve the painting and rid himself of this demon man, at least he would come away with a nice squash blossom necklace for his girlfriend.

The painting had a special place in his grandfather's world and he was the rightful owner. E.T. didn't see him going to the law, but anything was possible; stealing the piece would cut deeply into that old man's heart.

Bass was ready to declare war on whoever stepped into his path. This would be his biggest payday ever, and it was well within his reach. The plan was simple: go down to the trading post and ask for the painting back. If Manycoats and his partner Bloom didn't play ball, he and E.T. would threaten a lawsuit and bad press. If that bluff didn't produce results, he would ratchet up his methods. All he needed was the painting; he had the invoice and, if E.T. disappeared, the piece was his. Possession was still nine-tenths of the law in the West—the old finder's keepers.

It was getting late and Bass hated to wait one more day, but the kid was simply not ready and he needed E.T. to have his head on straight as possible. They would leave early in the morning and be at the trading post by 9 a.m.

✽ ✽ ✽ ✽

That night Bloom broke the news to Rachael he would be leaving town in the morning because he had an appointment in Tucson to authenticate the Dixon. He was afraid Rachael might push back against his taking off so soon after returning home, so he waited to tell her until they snuggled in bed—but, to Bloom's surprise, his pregnant wife understood and encouraged the trip.

His term as the Toadlena Trading Post manager had ended and if the Dixon painting were real and a deal could be worked out, it would mean a great paycheck coming in the lean winter months. Rachael worried about the bilagáana picker Bass, but knew Bloom had dealt with worse so she didn't offer any suggestions about how to handle the situation—at least not yet.

✽ ✽ ✽ ✽

As the almost-out-of-range *Voice of the Navajo Nation* crackled on the radio, Marvin felt a twinge of insecurity. He had traveled to many places, including a stint in Vietnam, but for the last ten years he had been firmly planted in the Toadlena basin. The last time he had left the state of New Mexico was on a trip to Chinle, Arizona—

not exactly Japan. He had no idea what to expect. He was in Bloom's hands and would follow his lead, letting the Holy People decide if he needed a passport.

Bloom enjoyed KTNN 660 AM. The radio station gave him insight into the world in which he lived, and he figured the familiar Diné voices would be soothing for Marvin. He could tell his partner was nervous.

As the radio airwaves turned to full static, Bloom switched to his phone's playlist. A medley of Eagles hits filled his truck. When "Take it Easy," his favorite song, came on and "Standing on a corner in Winslow, Arizona," blared out, Bloom started singing along and pointed Marvin toward the obvious—a roadside sign that read "Winslow, Arizona 40 miles."

"How did you plan the timing of that song so perfectly?" Marvin asked amazement.

"Old bilagáana family recipe," Bloom laughed.

"I hope you're as good as an art dealer as you are at song timing."

Bloom understood Marvin's concerns and knew the song's spot-on appearance was partially luck; he usually had good timing and he always followed his instincts.

Bloom deflected the question: "According to my internet searches, Shandling is the guy when it comes to Dixon. He apparently comes from money and has managed to amass a significant holding of Dixon works. The website says he is also a buyer."

"So maybe we can sell the piece and let him deal with Tsosie," Marvin said hopefully.

"No, it won't be that easy. We have to get it right or you and I could be stuck in legal hell. Tsosie is part of this equation, but I don't have a clue how to structure the deal without knowing more about a few critical pieces of that pie.

"Is this painting real and does Tsosie actually have ownership? If the answers to the first two questions are yes, then comes the more important question: 'What's it worth?'"

"What about Bass? He seems to be an important part of this too, don't you think?"

"No doubt, but he's a complete wild card. I don't want my mind to go there until I get more info, but you're correct: he somehow fits into this puzzle. And from what I hear on the street about the guy's reputation, he's smart and has been in the business a long time—but he's not always the straightest of shooters."

"None of you white men are. It takes an Indian's aim," Marvin said, flashing his trademark wide-tooth smile. Bloom loved Marvin's sense of humor.

"I've splurged a bit, I'm afraid. We're staying at Loews Ventana Canyon Resort in the Catalina foothills. I'll pay for it, Marvin—and if we end up selling the painting we can take the costs out of our profits. If for some reason this deal goes south, then I'm responsible for the bill if that's cool with you."

"Sure, how much could it be? $150?"

"More like $300, I'm afraid."

"WOW, that's a month's groceries. You're kidding me now, right?" Marvin's smile was nowhere to be seen.

"Afraid not. I know it's a lot, but Tucson is gearing up for its yearly Gem and Mineral Show and all the cheaper hotels are booked. Besides, we can almost walk to Shandling's museum from there."

"How far is it—eight miles or so?"

Bloom chuckled, knowing that for Marvin it was nothing. "A mile."

"We are definitely walking." Marvin's smile returned as he recognized the cultural chasm between himself and Bloom.

✳ ✳ ✳ ✳

The last of the sun's rays filled Bloom's rearview mirror as the unlikely pair of art dealers turned east off I-10 and headed into Tucson. The late light filtering through the Santa Catalina Mountains was a deep orange hue, exposing fingerling canyons. The majestic mountain's foothills still retained a patchwork of saguaro cacti scattered among a glut of Southwest-style homes.

Bloom hadn't visited Tucson in twenty years and was amazed at the amount of human detritus filling the once pristine Sonoran Desert. In the course of his research on Dixon, he had found numerous old photos of Dixon's home off Prince Road. The Catalinas were bare of homes then, Dixon's and Gilbert Ronstadt's adobe structures the only signs of civilization.

It was easy to see why Dixon found Tucson so compelling. The city fathers had done a decent job of protecting the natural environment, leaving numerous swaths of untouched desert in place. Unlike Phoenix, with its high-rise structures, grass, and concrete parking lots, Tucson had somehow managed to retain its sense of time as an Old West city. Bloom assumed Dixon would be pleased his adopted city was a place he could still recognize.

"How about we swing by the Dixon Museum before we check in?" Bloom asked.

"It's past 5 o'clock. I wouldn't think it would be open. Do you, Bloom?"

"I doubt it, but at least we can look through the windows and get a sense of what Shandling is all about. The more information we have, the better."

"Okay by me. According to your phone's Google map thingie, there's a Bashas' market right next door."

"Great. That will save us some money. Let's go over there and get some water and snacks. Ventana will probably charge us $5 a bottle."

"Do they do that?" Marvin asked with genuine concern.

Bloom realized Marvin didn't get out much and was certainly not familiar with five-star hotels.

"I'm afraid so. It could even be more. You don't want to know what they charge for a package of cookies."

"Well, I wanted to get an ice cream bar, but now I want to get dinner and breakfast supplies too. They don't charge us for putting it in their refrigerator, do they?"

"Actually they don't have a refrigerator. There's just a mini-bar for drinks, snacks, and alcohol."

"Bloom, I'm definitely out of touch. Liquor at the tips of your fingers… how do you think that would play out if we had that at the post? 'Yeah, help yourself; we'll bill you later.'"

"You mean kind of like I do with the groceries and ice cream?" Marvin laughed at Bloom's picture of his world.

"Here it is." Bloom pointed with his lips to the flickering neon Maynard Dixon Museum sign.

"The sign's nice." Marvin tried to put an upbeat spin on the museum's otherwise unremarkable strip mall location.

"Yes, neon is expensive, believe it or not. I'm sure the rents here are not cheap. This is apparently Tucson's most coveted area, the Catalina foothills. If I remember correctly, the Sabino Canyon Recreation Area is a mile east of here. If we have time, we can go take a nice hike there."

"Ten miles?" Marvin teased.

"Something like that—but I'll take the tram up and meet you on the way down."

The two parked in front of Shandling's museum and peered through the decorative iron bars. The walls were covered floor to ceiling with paintings—all Dixon. In the rear of the building, a hunched figure was slumped in an overstuffed chair reading a book.

"That has to be Shandling; maybe we got lucky," Bloom said as he started knocking on the window. After a few loud raps, the man looked up and waved the pair off, pointing to his watch as if to say, "We're closed."

Bloom returned back to his truck, unwrapped the Dixon, placed it against the glass and knocked again—this time with authority. Shandling peered up from his roost again and spied the Dixon. The pencil he was using to underline the book fell from his grip and bounced off the wooden floor. Shandling stood and headed directly toward the front door, a broad grin on his face. Bloom was a day early.

"Well, well, Mr. Bloom. You are early."

Marvin was used to being marginalized, but what this bilagáana would soon find out was that the Navajo was half-owner of the painting.

"Hi, Mr. Shandling. This is Marvin Manycoats—he's my partner in the Dixon painting."

A quizzical look on Shandling's face betrayed an underlying, subtle prejudice toward those who didn't fit his idea of art owners.

"Oh, so sorry, Mr. Manycoats. It's a pleasure to meet you."

"Call me Marvin."

"And I'm Charles."

"Well, that's grand. We can all be on a first name basis. I'm Mort. Come in and let's take a look at what you have to show me."

Bloom went back to the truck and retrieved the muslin cloth and rock fetish. A good art dealer knows that you can learn a great deal not only from the painting itself, but also from the frame and the wrappings—anything that is original to the work and tells a story. But not all dealers and buyers are smart enough to look.

"So the painting came in this package and it has been in an old Navajo collection?"

"Correct," Bloom said.

"Was it in your family, Mr. Manycoats?"—Shandling again showing his racial stereotyping.

"No, not my clan. The piece was brought into the trading post and I bought it."

"Nice. I'm sure you got a good deal." Shandling fished for an idea of what Marvin had paid for it.

Manycoats' facial expression didn't change and he did not reply to the rude question.

Bloom smiled at his friend's savvy, then shifted the subject to his own advantage: "So, Mort, how about you tell us what the hell we have here—you're obviously the expert."

Shandling realized he was dealing with a professional and that he had to tread carefully if he didn't want to lose the painting.

"Of course. We can go to my office and see what we have."

Shandling would let Bloom know only what he wanted him to know and no more. He was no fool; he hoped to buy the Dixon outright. He would not reveal the meaning and importance of the Nemo inscription unless he had to. The trio headed to a back office that was hung salon-style, with dozens of Dixons that looked much more impressive than what Bloom had brought in for evaluation.

Charles wondered if this piece would even be of interest to a man who seemed to like larger, more elaborate paintings.

"The painting came wrapped in this muslin cloth along with a rattlesnake skin that you don't have any more and this rock?"

"Yes, they all came together, minus the snakeskin, and the history, as I told you on the phone, this is from an original family collection," Bloom replied.

"I'm assuming, Charles, that you have black-lighted the painting?"

Bloom blushed, knowing he should have done that, but his black light was in Santa Fe. The ultraviolet light can help detect restoration or a signature not original to the painting. An unscrupulous dealer looking for a better payday might add an artist's signature to an unsigned study to ratchet up the price.

"Unfortunately, I did not, but my visual inspection of the painting looked clean."

Shandling knew this was a copout but let it slide. "You mind if we take a look, Charles?"

"Of course not, Mort. We need to see what's there."

Shandling switched off the overhead light and the three men's eyes struggled to adapt to the pitch-dark room. He then placed a magnifying glass headset on his brow to improve the resolution and slowly waved his long UV light over the entire painting as if he were a priest performing an ancient blessing. He repeated the process methodically, examining both the front and back of the piece. He stopped over the Nemo signature for a closer look. It was different paint, but it was clearly as old as that on the painting as it did not fluoresce, a critical clue for a possible Ruess connection.

"Looks clean, wouldn't you agree, Charles?"

Once again Shandling marginalized Marvin.

"Yes, it does. Did you see anything unusual under magnification?"

"Nothing; all is as expected. Now let's take a peek at the muslin."

Bloom realized he should have examined the cloth, but it hadn't entered his mind. Shandling was good.

"You see here, this coloration that lights up? My guess is that this is not paint, but organic."

"Organic?" Marvin asked.

"Possibly human or animal in nature."

"Like what?" Marvin asked.

"Could be lots of things. In ancient Peruvian textiles, which I also collect, this florescence would represent bodily fluids."

"You mean like after they die?" Bloom asked.

"Correct. They wrap the body in the textiles, and as it decomposes, there is some leakage."

"You think this is body fluids?" Bloom asked.

"Well, it wouldn't surprise me if it's some kind of blood. Again, it could be animal, but yes, it looks organic. Could be the snakeskin you no longer have was bloody when it was put on, but the stains seem more random—maybe something was killed and this was used as a rag to soak up the blood. I'm not sure it tells us anything yet, but we can investigate further if need be. Is there any way to retrieve the snakeskin?"

"I'm afraid not," Bloom replied. Marvin looked at his feet, hoping he had not let Bloom down.

"What about the rock? It's supposed to be a dinosaur tooth," Bloom said.

Shandling lowered his high-powered headset back over his eyes for a better look.

"It's not my field, but you are in luck; the gem and mineral show is gearing up and the expert in fossils has a part-time home in Pima Canyon, here in Tucson. He's the best. I'll see if he will take the time to examine your rock. He owes me one, so let me see what I can work out."

"Great, maybe it will tell us something." Marvin chimed in, wanting a seat at the table.

Shandling ignored him, pulled his cell phone from his pocket, scrolled through his contacts, and called Norbert Rosenstein.

"Norbert, it's Mort. A friend of mine, Charles Bloom, and his friend Marvin have a very interesting rock that appears to be a large dinosaur tooth. Any chance you could take a look at it today?"

Shandling nodded his head affirmatively toward Bloom and said, "Thanks. They'll be right over," and hung up.

"Okay, you're set; he will make time for you this evening. He's a busy guy, so you're lucky he will see you. I'm sure you're tired, but he's to dinosaur fossils what I'm to Dixon. He can let us know what you have."

"Wonderful. I appreciate your calling him. What's his address? I'll stick it into Google maps. If we will leave now, how long will it take us to get there?"

"It's close, fifteen minutes tops. He will leave your name at the gate. You will love his house—it's really over the top—must be a lot of money in dinosaur bones."

Marvin was amazed that someone sold bones for a living, that it paid well, and that the man didn't get a ghost sickness. Bones were not something Marvin liked, dinosaur or otherwise.

"Charles, would you mind leaving the Dixon so I can take a closer look? I promise no photographs, and when you get back from Norbert's we can discuss what you have. It's real—that much I can tell you now."

"That's great," Marvin piped up.

Bloom was less enthusiastic. "Well, I'm not a fan of leaving pieces, but if you promise no photos I can leave it for a couple of hours. I will need a receipt that says we are leaving it here for the next two hours for examination and that there are not to be any photos taken."

"Not a problem—that's a reasonable request, just good business on your part."

Shandling gave him a receipt on his fancy personal letterhead and signed and dated the document. Bloom did the same, then he and Marvin left to meet the bone whisperer. Shandling locked the front door behind them and headed directly to his back office where he grabbed his Nikon camera, which he used to take dozens of shots of the front and back of the painting.

"I promised not to take any photos for my own use—but no one said the museum couldn't document this piece for the raisonné," Shandling said to himself. He held up the Dixon as if it were a trophy catch; after all, his receipt wasn't on museum letterhead.

Mort Shandling wasn't about to lose an opportunity to record this piece for the art world history books. His word at this point was as flimsy as the paper he had signed. There was no way the Dixon painting wasn't going to be his; in Mort's mind he would soon own the rights to the image anyway.

An Everett Ruess Dixon with a Navajo reservation provenance was priceless in an expert's hands—and nothing would get in the way of his quest to own it. He had finally uncovered the Rosetta Stone that could explain Dixon's previously undiscovered work and Ruess's disappearance.

CHAPTER 38

T-REX

Pima Canyon—home to Tucson's most privileged residents—was nestled deeply in the Catalina foothills. Full-time guards judicially monitored visitors' whereabouts once they came through the ornate copper gate. Bloom's name had been left with Burt, the guard, but Marvin Manycoats' name was missing. The burly man with an East Coast accent took Marvin's information before opening the six-foot-high gate. Marvin took the slight in stride, but it bothered Bloom.

Norbert's home was in the most exclusive part of the community, past a large, decorative waterfall and through another set of protective, decorative gates. Bloom's truck was buzzed in without any verbal communication from Rosenstein. Bloom was used to dealing with the ultra-rich, and both he and Marvin understood that the lesser classes were lumped into one category, regardless of race. Marvin smiled, knowing he was not alone in the world of have-nots.

"Welcome to my world," Marvin said. Both men grinned, realizing this was probably a fool's errand.

The house was the size of a castle—easily ten thousand square feet—built into the hillside at the end of a cul-de-sac. There were no neighbors; this was the premium house in a community of premium homes. The house was composed of what appeared to be fossilized bricks. The doorbell was a single round object, most likely a dinosaur artifact. Bloom pressed the button and the roar of a T-Rex greeted the visitors. Both Bloom and Marvin jumped. The massive mesquite door pivoted open and Rosenstein's voice rang out.

"Come on in. I'm in the back, just past the Giganotosaurus skull, next to the pool."

Bloom and Marvin exchanged a quizzical look, both wondering what a Giganotosaurus might be, their eyes transfixed by the magnificent surroundings. A T-Rex skeleton filled the front foyer, which was forty feet high. Another full-sized dinosaur hovered in a flying position toward the rear of the room. The house was a museum, and Bloom cringed at the thought of showing this man his miniscule tooth. Marvin, on the other hand, was thrilled. He stood there with his mouth wide open. He had never been in mansion before, much less one decorated with dinosaurs.

Norbert Rosenstein was splayed out under an oversized umbrella, an intricate headset perched on his oversized forehead as he examined a small pile of rocks. The view behind the man included a multi-tier waterfall straight out of a Hawaiian Four Seasons hotel.

"Sorry about not answering the buzzer; I was right in the middle of an exciting find," Rosenstein said, putting down his rocks and raising his magnifying glasses so he could see his guests. Bloom felt better about his own rock, which looked similar to the pile of stones in the plastic tub.

"I'm Norbert. Mort told me you might have something interesting for me to look at?"

"Yes, I'm Charles Bloom and this is Marvin Manycoats." The men stuck out their hands to exchange greetings. Marvin was surprised when Norbert gave him a weak Navajo handshake. Marvin was even more surprised when Norbert spoke to him before addressing Bloom.

"So, Mr. Manycoats, where is your clan from?"

"I'm of the Bitter Water people on my father's side and the Bear People Clan on my mother's. I live near Toadlena."

"I love that area, so many great fossils on the reservation. Have you ever seen the Brown family sites in the Bisti Badlands? Those are some great dinosaur tracks."

"Yeah, I know that place. They make a good living on tips from walking tourists through the area with a jug of water. I always wondered about those."

Bloom was now the one with his mouth open. This man knew about the Navajos and seemed interested in them—he was definitely not what he expected.

"Oh, there are so many great fossil locations in the Four Corners. We must get together sometime so I can show you some of the more isolated places, places you can't get to on foot."

"So how do you get there—fly?" Marvin asked jokingly.

"Yes, exactly. I use my ultra-light Trikes, little single-engine airplanes that are great for getting into the most isolated areas. You would have great fun with it. Have you ever flown over your land?"

"Nope, but I'm in." This was sounding even better than Japan.

"Great, there is a decent air strip up by Kayenta. We can meet up there this spring and go out to some of the most unusual sites you will ever see. And you won't need a jug of water where I'll take you. Some great bones from these remote areas have ended up in mansions like mine."

Bloom, at a loss with what the water was all about, asked, "What's the jug of water for?"

Marvin smiled; the art dealer didn't know everything. "You take the water and fill up the prints so the beasts look like they were just walking down the canyon; it's big Navajo theater."

Bloom blushed, realizing he was the odd man out. He wanted to know how dinosaur bones leaving the reservation could end up in private collections. This just didn't seem kosher, but he wasn't up to asking another stupid question.

"So, Marvin, you have got this possible tooth? Can I take a look?"

Bloom pulled the stone out of his pants pocket and gave to it Marvin to hand to the expert.

Norbert sat down, felt the weight in his hand, and flipped the headset over his eyes. A wide grin appeared on his face.

"Damn it, boys—you do indeed do have a dinosaur artifact. This appears to be from an Allosaurus, a very rare subspecies. The only other specimen was found in southern Utah. Where in the hell did you find this?"

Bloom and Marvin sat down next to Norbert and explained the Dixon story, including how they ended up at his house, and how Tsosie was from near Bluff—even though they weren't sure if the tooth was from that area.

"Hell, now that's a story—good fossil-hunter fodder. The buyers will eat this tale up. Any chance we can meet Mr. Tsosie? I've got to see if he knows where the specimen came from—hopefully private property. In the United States, unlike most of the rest of the world, you are free to collect and sell fossils if they are not on government or Indian lands. Wherever this fossil came from, it's more than likely the rest of the cache is buried close by.

"My next week is pretty much free. Can you arrange this meeting?" Norbert added eagerly.

"Well, we are working on talking to Tsosie, so as soon as I hear something I will let you know and maybe we can get you guys together. It could happen in a week."

There was an opportunity here that Bloom hadn't expected.

"Perfect. My clients start showing up in two weeks. The annual Tucson Gem and Mineral Show kicks off early next month, but the real buyers come in before the official opening to snag the best stuff first. God, I would love to show my clients this piece and maybe be able to promise them the rest of the dinosaur. Any chance the fossil is for sale?"

"Well, I don't know its value and I'm not sure it's ours to sell quite yet. What would you offer for the tooth?" Bloom the salesman couldn't resist asking.

Norbert didn't correct Bloom, even though he knew it really wasn't a tooth, but one of the three large claws on each hand that the upper-tier carnivore used to tear into its prey's abdominal cavity. It was a great find, more rare than a tooth. It also indicated there was probably an arm somewhere close by.

"Hmm, well, if I could get first right of refusal for any other pieces that might be uncovered, top dollar of course. And if Tsosie would be on board for me excavating, then I'll pay $5,000 for the specimen, cash money."

Both Marvin's and Bloom's mouths dropped open.

"WOW—$5,000 for that stone?" Marvin asked.

"That's right Marvin. I know of a single T-Rex tooth that sold for $15,000. This of course is no T-Rex, but it's still not bad," Norbert replied.

"Well, Norbert," Bloom said, "I can tell from my partner's response that he is interested, and I would be lying if I said I wasn't as well. I promise not to sell the tooth to anyone else, but I need to make sure I have a clean title. Any idea how much an intact dinosaur would be worth?"

"It's hard to say. I'm sure you can understand, Charles, being an art dealer, that there are so many variables: condition, number of bones, type of bones, access, etc., but if the Allosaurus is, say, seventy-percent complete and in decent condition, I would think on a good day it might reach seven figures once prepped."

Bloom's pulse quickened as Marvin tried to understand what Norbert meant by seven figures. Then Norbert added, "It would have brought more a few years ago, but collectors are a bit skittish since Mongolia started repatriating their dinosaurs and the United States began tossing people into prison for black market activity, but that won't be a problem for us—unless it's on Indian land."

"So a million dollars payday, potentially, assuming it's legal to collect?" Bloom asked, skipping over the repatriation and prison questions that were also starting to swirl in his head.

"Yes, very possibly. Of course, there's lots of cost and time associated with getting it to that point of sale—the effort required to take the piece from the finding of the bones in the desert to a finished mount is immense—but, if handled correctly, it could be a big payday for all of us in a couple of years."

The three men were transfixed by the gray-black, reticulated artifact. The stakes had increased. No longer was it just the Dixon in play; an entire dinosaur had now entered the picture.

CHAPTER 39

NO RIDE NEEDED

E.T. slept poorly. Last week's drug binge had taken its toll. His mentation was better, but the rest of him felt like shit. His circumstances were precarious and he considered making a run for it, but Bass knew where his girlfriend and son lived and he was the kind of man who wouldn't have a second thought about using them for leverage. His best hope was to try to get Manycoats to return the painting. If the Navajo wouldn't do that, Bass would step in and make life hell for all involved.

Grandfather Roanhorse was the unknown variable in this Shakespearean tragedy: would he go along with his painting being sold?

Bass had eaten, showered, and dressed, his all-black attire accented with Versace boots—the color reflecting his somber mood. Today he would find out if the painting would be returned the easy way or if rougher tactics would be necessary.

Bass rousted E.T. at 7:15; he wanted to be in the Toadlena parking lot when the post opened at 9 a.m. The weather looked ominous; a front was building over the Chuskas and threatened to bring on the first big storm of the year. In Bass's mind, the gods were lining up against him.

"Eat your bagel. There's some cream cheese. I even heated it for you. How about some coffee to clear your head?" Bass said, trying to soften his confrontational stance. Now that he was sober, maybe the kid would work with him.

"Sure, thanks."

"Okay. I want us on the same page today. If this goes smoothly, we won't have to go to that next level, if you know what I mean."

E.T. nodded his head in the affirmative as he gulped down chunks of bagel, the first real food he had eaten in two days.

"There's another bagel if you want it." E.T. gave Bass a thumbs-up sign.

"When we get to the bend in the road right before the post, I'm going to let you out and you can walk up. I don't want anyone to know I'm there, not yet. See if you can find Manycoats. If he's there, tell him you have seller's remorse and try to get the painting back. If he won't give it back, tell him you didn't have the right to sell the painting and the owner is going sic the law on him.

"If Manycoats is not there, ask for Sal. He's the post owner and can find out where Manycoats might be. If Sal wants to know why you want to talk to Manycoats, let him know you sold the Navajo a painting—don't say a Dixon—and see how he responds. If Bloom is there without Manycoats, don't say anything and come back to me. If that's the case, I'll have to rethink my strategy. Bloom is a seasoned art dealer and won't be such a pushover. You understand?"

E.T.'s head was no longer pounding and he felt better. "Yes, I got it, seller's remorse, no talk of Dixon, get information if I can't get the painting."

"Remember, this is MY painting and I'm bailing you out to the tune of $1,500—and if you didn't know it before, you do now: I'm not screwing around."

When Bass slapped the receipt on the wooden table, the pistol holster under his black coat became visible. E.T. saw the gun, just as Bass had planned; he wanted this young man to know that there would be serious ramifications if he failed to retrieve the painting.

"I got it. Let's go—I want to get this over with."

The two men tossed back the remaining coffee and headed for the sedan. Bass scanned the distant horizon; dark clouds were building in the west, an omen of things to come, he thought.

❋ ❋ ❋ ❋

Bass backed his car into a parking spot so he could make a quick retreat. He partially hid the vehicle under a scraggly elm tree next to a dilapidated 1940s house a quarter-mile from the post. Clouds and a twenty-five degree temperature would make for a cold walk up the dirt road.

E.T. was still considering making a run for it, but the gun said, "Don't do it." There was only an old truck in the post parking lot and it looked as if it belonged to the owner. E.T. took one last look back, knowing that Bass was watching.

Sal, who had been back at work for two days, was busy stoking the fire. The room was a still chilly fifty degrees, but it felt warm to E.T. after his frigid walk.

"Yá' át' ééh," Sal said. "Sorry about the temp. I'm still screwed up from all that traveling I did and I woke up late. I'll have her toasty right quick."

"It's fine. It feels good. I hitched a ride here and walked the last little bit; looks like snow's coming."

"I sure hope so. It's not good for business, of course, but it's god-awful dry out there. What can I help you with, son?"

"I'm looking for Hastiin Manycoats. He was working here last time I was in. Is he around?"

"No, Marvin is in Tucson, Arizona, for a couple of days. He's smarter than both of us, heading south for nice warm weather just as a storm blows in."

"You know how long he's going to be there? He got family or something?"

"Nah, nothing like that. It's something about seeing a guy about a painting. I don't know the details, but he went with Bloom and Charles' wife won't want him gone long. My guess is they will be back tomorrow or maybe the next day. Is there anything you want me to pass on to him?"

E.T. considered the options and wasn't sure what to do. He decided it would be best to leave a number.

"Sure, if you don't mind. If you can lend me a paper and pencil I'll leave him my number so he can give me a call when he gets back."

"I'll bet Marvin has his cell with him. You want the number?"

"Sure, that would work, but do give him this message just in case I can't get to him. He seemed pretty old school, not sure he would have his phone on."

"You're right, he's traditional and often doesn't bother to carry his phone for days at a time. But going out of town is unusual for Marvin, so my guess is he at least brought it with him."

Sal handed E.T. a scratch pad and worn pencil. The young Navajo wrote his name, number, and a request to please call, saying, "We need to talk." E.T. folded up the note, wrote Hastiin Manycoats on the outside, and handed it to Sal.

Much to E.T.'s displeasure, Sal immediately opened the note and read it out loud to make sure he understood what was being asked.

"Okay, got it, I'll give it to him. You need anything else? Coke or cookies for the road?"

"I'm good, but thanks."

"You want to warm up before you go? It's a long walk down to the Shell station, not a lot of traffic today...."

"Thanks, but I need to hit the road. Just let Hastiin Manycoats know to call me. I need to talk with him as soon as possible."

E.T. walked out the door and headed back to Bass.

Sal wondered what the kid was up to. He wasn't from around Toadlena and passing up a warm stove before walking a few cold miles was not normal human behavior. The young Navajo also hadn't asked for a ride, which was equally unusual. There was an unshared a backstory there—and probably a friend waiting in a vehicle somewhere close by.

The trader cracked open the front door and peered out. The kid was walking at a fast clip, not the kind of pace one would set for a multi-mile hike: there had to be someone waiting. Sal would give Marvin a heads-up; his bullshit meter was saying, "This kid is trouble."

CHAPTER 40

A CLEAN PROVENANCE

Bass climbed up the small hill behind the dilapidated house and positioned himself so he could observe E.T. Using the hunting scope on his 30-06 rifle, he watched the entire interaction, which lasted eight minutes. He watched E.T. leave and saw old Sal poke his head out of the door—not a good sign. Bass had known Sal for a very long time, and knew it was a risk sending the kid in on his own. Sal was smart and had good intuition. Sal's face peering out meant the trader wanted to see where the kid was heading.

When E.T. rounded the bend on the dirt road, the sedan was ready to go. "Get in," Bass said in a firm monotone. As soon as E.T.'s door closed, Bass peeled out.

"Okay, play by play, and don't leave anything out—not even a pause in the conversation." E.T. replayed the entire event, Bass interrupting him half a dozen times to make sure he understood the exact tone and pace of the conversation.

"Shit, this ain't good...."

"Why you say that?" E.T. asked.

"Well, for starters you got Manycoats going to Tucson with Bloom. Manycoats probably hasn't left San Juan County in a couple of years. They're going see Mort Shandling. He's a big buyer and, trying to go around me, he's THE Dixon buyer."

Bass regretted his words as soon as they came out of his mouth.

"Big buyer of Dixon? How much is my painting worth?" E.T. was finally realizing that he was being played. The tables turned, and now Bass was on the defensive. This was a major problem.

229

Bass eased his large sedan off Navajo Route 19 and drove down a dirt road until it dead-ended at a dried-out cattle pond. There was no one else in sight, and E.T. started to panic. Was this bilagáana going to off him right here?

E.T. wondered if he could overpower this man, but he looked strong and mean. The kid's heart was racing: he was about to be eliminated. E.T. thought about trying to run, but knew Bass had a high-powered rifle; he would be picked off in the open grazing land.

Bass turned off the engine and looked into E.T.'s eyes, trying to decide what to do with him. "You scared of me, Tsosie?"

"I don't know... should I be?"

"Yes, you should be. I'm going to ask you one more time—you scared of me?"

"I am, very." Bass could see the fear in E.T.'s eyes and the perspiration running down his face in the cold winter air. The kid was indeed frightened. Bass smiled.

"Good, you should be my friend. Now I'm going to be straight with you. If you want to play ball, we don't have any problems. If you feel otherwise, I'm afraid I will need to rethink my offer. You ready to hear my offer?"

"Sure, I'm happy to play ball, Mr. Bass," E.T. said, meaning every word.

"Okay, E.T. Your painting is worth a shitload of money, way more than you sold it for to Manycoats or me. But hey, man, business is business and you were willing to sell it cheap, and when I offered you what I did, I honestly didn't know its real value. But I've been doing research on this painter, Dixon, and well, kid, he's legit and the reason Bloom and Manycoats are in Tucson is because they are showing the painting to an expert and collector of Dixon. If this guy Shandling gives them a price and gets involved, we're screwed."

E.T. tried to understand the situation. "How much you think it's really worth?"

"Well, from what I can tell, it might be worth $75,000, maybe more."

"Are you kidding me?" E.T.'s mind was spinning with joy and anger.

"I'm afraid not, it's big time."

"So what's your proposition?" E.T. asked, knowing his position was tenuous at best.

"Partnership. I wipe out your debt to me, you keep the squash blossom, and we split whatever it sells for. Remember, I have a legitimate bill of sale for the piece. I don't have to do a damn thing, it's my painting— but working as a team, with you understanding what's at stake, we have a much better shot at getting the piece. What do you say?"

E.T. sat looking out the window, gazing at the distant power lines, then turned to look at his new partner. "I'm all in, seems fair. You know that kind of money can change my son's and girlfriend's lives. What do we do now?"

"Great, E.T. I have one more question: is there anything else I need to know about this painting—and I mean anything. I can't have any surprises if we are going to pull this deal off."

E.T. once again fixed his eyes on the distant mesa and said, "Yes, there is a possible problem. The painting is not technically mine. It's a family piece. My grandfather Roanhorse owns it now, but it becomes mine once he passes, so it's kind of mine."

Bass was afraid there might be a hitch and this one could be big.

"Does your grandfather actually own the piece? He didn't steal it or anything weird like that? I need to know...."

"No, it was his father's before him, and it will be mine once he dies. I'm the only surviving relative other than my son."

"Does your grandfather know you have the painting?"

"I don't know, maybe. He's smart man, and I was pretty screwed up last week. He probably wondered where I got the drug money."

"Do you think your grandfather would be cool that you sold the painting, seeing it's going to be yours anyway, and that it will provide a windfall for your family?"

"I don't know. He loves that damned painting, but I'm pretty sure he loves me more, or at least he used to before I became such a loser."

"All right, we can deal with this. In my opinion, it's not a hurdle we can't get over. But right now we need to get our asses down to Tucson and find out what the hell is going on with OUR painting. You ready for a road trip? We can hash out our plans on the way. It will take us about six hours to get there if this threatening storm doesn't bum-rush us."

"You're right. Let's go get OUR painting. I'm tired of being poor and taken advantage of."

The two men laughed as Bass turned the car around and spun out of the pasture, heading for Tucson. Roanhorse wasn't an issue in Bass's mind. Once they had secured the painting, he would eliminate any problems; he wanted a clean provenance of ownership.

CHAPTER 41

HAPPY TO SIGN

The Dixon painting was the key that could finally unlock the almost century-old mystery of a young man lost in the Navajo Nation. Shandling was convinced he hit the mother lode and knew he must obtain the painting. It was critical to his museum, and once he unveiled the story to the world, there would be reporters camping on his doorstep to hear how Everett Ruess's painting came into his possession. He must figure out a way to pry it loose from Bloom and Marvin.

With an Everett Ruess history, the painting was easily worth $250,000. It could fetch as much as $500,000 if he decided to sell it, though he never would. With some due diligence on the provenance, he would have a cornerstone for his museum. The piece was irresistible to Shandling.

Auction records for a Dixon this size with a fairly simple Anasazi ruin imagery topped out at around $125,000 on a good day. Shandling never minded paying up for a great piece, but there was no sense in throwing money away—which meant keeping the Ruess backstory quiet for a while. Pay top dollar for a 1922 Arizona Dixon with no amazing history or figures, and a narrow focus on the architectural elements, and the owners would be thrilled.

Only Shandling understood the true meaning of the Nemo inscription and Dixon's painting log was in his possession: the "destroyed" entry in Dixon's hand would not be revealed until he had a major museum gallery unveiling for his "Everett Ruess's Dixon is discovered" event. He would make his play as soon as Manycoats and Bloom came back from the bone collector; the tooth seemed interesting and might add another element to the story.

❋ ❋ ❋ ❋

Bloom and Marvin made plans to have breakfast with Norbert before heading out of town the next day. Ventana's famous Sunday brunch was a must according to the bone whisperer, so they would meet there at 9 a.m.

Bloom was okay with Norbert visiting Tsosie to talk about the dinosaur tooth, but only after he had a chance to find out what kind of person Tsosie was. Finding the young Navajo became imperative. Bass was undoubtedly lurking nearby and would make contact soon. Bloom didn't believe in coincidences, and asking about a Dixon painting out of the blue meant Bass was on the hunt.

Bloom needed to firm up a fair deal with Tsosie before something got screwed up. A $5,000 offer was on the table for the tooth, found money. And he hadn't yet heard what Shandling had to report.

Marvin never stopped talking during the fifteen-minute ride back to the Dixon Museum.

"Five thousand dollars for a tooth? I hope we can figure out where that dinosaur is buried and discover that it had a smile like me!"

Marvin's grin showed all his teeth. "We could be rich, Bloom! Do you believe what the bilagáana is saying?"

"I believe him to a point, Marvin. He seems straightforward enough and you saw that house. If he's selling million-dollar dinosaur bones— and I believe he must be—then Tsosie could be rich and maybe we will get a bonus too."

"I hope we can work a deal, even some kind of finder's fee, like those fancy realtors get. Seems like a scam to me. Get paid to find a house? That wouldn't work out on the rez."

"Too much inventory," Bloom chuckled. Marvin didn't get the humor of the thousands of abandoned hogans that dotted the rez being considered possible leads for homes.

"If you put me in the Tsosie place, I can find those bones. I was always good at hunting mice, can't be too much different," Marvin added.

"Marvin, I wouldn't get my hopes up too much about finding dinosaur bones. I'm sure it's harder than it sounds and, honestly, I don't see us getting much out of this, maybe a small finders' fee and selling the tooth at best. In my experience, if something looks too good, then it probably is—so as much as we might like Norbert, it never hurts to keep our guard up. I recommend we focus on that Dixon painting. Don't get me wrong; when we find Tsosie I'll talk to him about the fossils, but I'm sure that Dixon is going to be worth a lot more than $5,000."

"Really, you think so?"

"You can ask Shandling yourself. After all, it's half your painting."

Marvin smiled, knowing his partner respected him even if he didn't understand the ins and outs of the negotiations.

Bloom pulled into Shandling's strip mall, which was empty except for a Model S Tesla parked in front of the museum. Shandling was sitting next to the door, painting in hand, waiting for their return. He was nervous, knowing what he said next could make or break getting the Dixon.

He opened the door before they could knock. "Well, what does my good friend Norbert have to say about the tooth? Is it from a dinosaur?"

Marvin took the lead: "Well, turns out it's from an Allosaurus, a very rare animal; only one other specimen has been found. Could be very valuable."

"Really? Did he say how much the beast's carcass might be worth?"

"If we can find the whole dinosaur, maybe as much as a million dollars!" Marvin said excitedly.

Shandling was surprised, but didn't show much emotion. His sights were set on the Dixon.

"You're right, that's big. Did he happen to say where it might have come from?" Shandling was more concerned about finding where Ruess's bones might be located than he was about the dinosaur's.

"Norbert said that only one other specimen of Allosaurus is known, and it was found around the Arizona-Utah border, near the Navajo Nation. He thinks this one must have come from that region," Marvin said.

"Well, that's interesting. The Navajo family you bought this Dixon from, are they from that same area?" Shandling was fishing for critical information.

Bloom chimed in, wanting to take charge of the conversation, and not wanting too much information to be shared.

"It's from southern Utah. That's what I'll put on the certificate once I sell the piece," the gallerist replied.

"Any family name with the painting?" Shandling pushed again.

"I would rather not say quite yet. I'm sure as an art dealer you can understand."

Shandling understood all too well that unscrupulous dealers would take this information and call the owners to see if there might be more pieces that hadn't been sold yet, poaching the lead. He had done it himself in the past. Bloom was protecting potential assets.

"Of course. If possible, I would like to get all that information if I end up buying the piece. You boys ready to hear my offer to buy your painting?"

"A million dollars?" Marvin blurted out.

Shandling frowned, then regained his composure. "No, I'm afraid not. This isn't a rare dinosaur, just a small, but very nice, Dixon painting."

He pointed to the walls behind him filled with similar-sized paintings to reinforce the idea that pieces like theirs were commonplace. "I wish it were, though. I would have a fortune on these walls if that were true." Shandling continued to smile.

"So, no million. What would you offer, Mr. Shandling?" Bloom asked, getting down to business.

"Well, Mr. Bloom, Mr. Manycoats, I'm willing to write you a check right now for $125,000. That is an extremely fair price. If you check auction records I'm sure you will see numerous landscape paintings this size and the prices they bring. I can assure you I'm being generous. I'm willing to pay up because I love the story and it fills a niche. I don't have a good representation of Dixon's 1922 Kayenta trip."

Shandling watched the two men closely, looking for any tell. He didn't have to wait long. Marvin flashed his teeth in an "I'm very happy" expression.

"That sounds great." Marvin said without hesitation.

Bloom was glad the painting price was high; otherwise he would have been very irritated with his friend Marvin.

"I agree with my partner. I have researched the auction records. This seems in line for a retail price and, honestly, it's on the higher end. Seems like you really like this painting. What makes it so good?" Now Bloom was fishing to find out how Shandling priced the Dixon and why—the offer seemed too high.

"Like I said, I don't have a very good painting from this 1922 trip. Dixon stayed with John Wetherill and it was the first time he really started working on his clouds, an important four months for Dixon, so it fills a hole for my collection."

Bloom considered this explanation. It seemed plausible, and the man clearly had an extreme interest in Dixon; the filled walls testified to this obsession.

"Okay, Mort. I think I speak for my partner. Assuming I can get clear title, I'll sell the painting to you, but there are a few loose ends I have to take care of. I won't show it to anyone else. You're in the driver's seat."

"That's great! Should I give you a check?" Shandling said, trying to close the deal.

"Like I said, I need a clear title. That should be accomplished this week, and then we can finish our transaction. I know you don't want any issues either."

"You're right about that. So how about this: I'll give you a check, you hang onto the check and I'll keep the painting. Once your title is clean, you can cash the check, and you don't have to drive down with the painting."

Bloom considered the offer. His gut was undecided. The man had money and the Dixons, and had been around a very long time. The check would no doubt be good, but if Tsosie balked, there could be trouble.

"Mort, let me lay my cards on the table." Shandling moved closer to Bloom, watching for any sign of deceit.

"We own the painting. I have a signed receipt from the Navajo seller and I have paid him in full, but we paid too little for what it's worth."

Marvin blushed.

"I know it sounds crazy for a dealer to worry about not paying enough, but I have to renegotiate my deal with the owner for a fairer deal on his behalf. My wife is Navajo and it would be very bad form for me and Marvin if we basically ripped off this person. So I have to talk with him and let him know the work's true value."

Shandling was shocked. Bloom really was a fool, an easy mark to be taken advantage of.

"Sure, I understand your position, as unorthodox as it might be. I can pay you or your original buyer, however it works out. The main thing, Charles, is that I would like to add this to my collection—and you do realize that if you go back with an extra big payday this guy might get squirrelly and want it back, and you wouldn't end up with anything for your trouble."

"I know it's a possibility, but unfortunately I have to go this route. I will let you hang onto the painting with the following caveats: the painting has to be insured for $125,000 for any kind of damage or loss; it can't be shown or photographed; and I retain ownership until I cash your check and give you a written go-ahead. If I can't make a deal with original owner, you have to FedEx the painting back to me next-day air, and I'll do the same with your check. All this has to be signed and dated on your letterhead before I leave the painting with you."

"Fine, this all acceptable. I have a vault in which I will place the painting while I wait for your instructions. If I need to talk to the owner, you can let him know who I am and where the painting will be going. That's fine too; you're in charge."

"Okay, let's write it up. I hope to have information in the next couple of days about which way this deal will go."

The three men shook on the deal and Bloom and Manycoats headed off to check into their hotel. A hot tub was waiting. Marvin had never been in one and was excited to feel how hot it really was.

As Shandling locked the door, he began laughing. He never said he wouldn't go to the original owner and cut his own deal if need be. He would see what Bloom could do, but the gallerist would never see the Dixon again, letterhead or not. That was why he kept a good lawyer on retainer.

CHAPTER 42

QUID PRO QUO

Bloom's stomach was churning as he left Shandling's office, his inner voice loudly wondering if he had just made a mistake.

Shandling was a well-established art dealer, and Bloom had given him clearly written, signed instructions for how to handle the transaction. In most circumstances, this would be standard operating procedure—but this wasn't your usual deal. Tsosie was a completely unknown entity, and Bass was no doubt also on the painting's trail. Bloom had thought that maybe the painting would be safer in Shandling's locked vault than it would be in Toadlena.

After breakfast tomorrow, he would check in with Rachael and then head north if the weather allowed. It was wonderful in Tucson, but the AccuWeather app said it could be difficult traveling in Indian Country.

Marvin, on the other hand, was thrilled by the procedure and asked to hold the check; he had never seen that much money in his life—and very possibly a good chunk of it was his. Japan was looking promising, and a plunge into his first hot tub was a bonus on the agenda.

Marvin had no gym shorts, so he decided to splurge at the hotel store for a pair of swim trunks. The price, on sale, was $55 dollars. He was shocked that he would buy something he could get for nearly free in any thrift store, but he was on his way to money and it somehow seemed okay.

The two men dipped their feet into the hot water.

Marvin's smile was omnipresent. "I boil food in this kind of water. You sure it's safe to get into it?"

"It's safe, Marvin. Just ease in; you will be in heaven once those jets hit your back."

"You're right; this must be what rich people do every night."

Bloom smiled at the innocence of his partner taking his first Jacuzzi. "Yeah, rich people like a clean butt."

"I hadn't thought about that. Maybe we should get out—this water has to be dirty," Marvin said.

"Smell the air—that's the chlorine they put in the water. It's fine. Relax and enjoy being rich, even if it may only be temporary."

"You think Tsosie will want his painting back?" Marvin asked.

"You tell me. You're the one who bought it.... What's your take?"

"He's got some serious problems and his *hózhó* is broken, but he didn't seem greedy to me. If free money is offered, I would have to think he would be fine with that deal."

"What about Bass? What was your take on that guy?"

"Hmm, he's different. He had an agenda, sneaky eyes. He's from your world—I'll let you figure him out."

"The word on the street is he will take advantage of a situation if he can. Let's hope we don't have to deal with Bass, Marvin, but my gut says he will appear sooner rather than later. We need to find Tsosie and fast. I want to come to an agreement and cash that check. Don't you agree?"

"Yes, I do, but I'm more interested right now in this jet massaging my lower back. I'm definitely taking my share and getting a hot tub; it'll be the only one on the rez!"

Both men laughed at the picture of a hot tub next to a hogan.

✻ ✻ ✻ ✻

Tucson was packed. January's warm weather was irresistible to the Midwest snowbirds. "No Vacancy" signs lit up the Miracle Mile. There were no rooms available. It was almost midnight, so Bass decided to spend $200 dollars for a single room with two double beds at the Windmill Inn in the Catalina foothills.

Bass had no problem spending top dollar on a designer T-shirt, but not on lodging for one night. However, this motel was close to the Maynard Dixon Museum. Bass had done his research on Shandling. He was old money, apparently with daddy issues, a big ego, and a great appetite for anything Dixon. Bloom had undoubtedly visited the man. The only question was who now had the painting. Every time the piece changed hands it became that much more difficult to assess how much pressure he would have to exert to regain control of his property.

Shandling was particularly problematic as he was a force in the Dixon world. If he became alienated, or worse, pissed off and bad-mouthed the painting, the price could drop precipitously—not an uncommon tactic in the art world. Unscrupulous dealers have no problem denigrating a painting owned by the competition to help push their own inventory. Bass understood the power game and would be respectful of Mort Shandling.

E.T.'s attitude and appetite had rebounded as had Bass's food bills. Bass told E.T. to order what he wanted—he would deduct the costs from the kid's share of the profits when they finally settled up— and the young Navajo obliged with an early breakfast of strip steak, potatoes, and scrambled eggs, with an additional order of French toast to go.

E.T. was already considering the possibilities of a financial windfall. He would give half of the money to his grandfather, as it was his painting, and use the rest for family responsibilities and maybe junior college. E.T. was tired of being unhappy and this newly found wealth could be his ticket to a new sense of self if he handled it well. Maybe his grandfather was right that he needed to regain his *hózhó* and get a fresh start.

Over breakfast, the newly minted partners worked out their unscheduled meeting with Shandling. E.T. would stay quiet until Bass gave him the sign to talk. Bass was pretty sure he would be able to read the dealer's emotions when he confronted him regarding the Dixon painting. Hopefully Bloom hadn't got along well with the rich art dealer. It may have been wishful thinking on Bass's part, but there was so much money at stake, along with the possibility of a better life for Bass, and he felt he was overdue for a life reboot.

The museum opened at 10 a.m. Bass arrived early to scope out the situation. He found an out-of-the-way parking place across the street from the museum and backed his sedan into the narrow spot. If things went poorly, he didn't want Shandling to see what he was driving; better to keep a low profile until more was known.

Bass sipped on his hotel coffee while E.T. munched on his still-warm French toast as they waited for the man to arrive. A royal blue Tesla quietly slid in front of the museum. Shandling unlocked the door, turned off an alarm, and disappeared. There was no sign of Manycoats or Bloom. Bass and Tsosie hurried over to the door when it was clear Shandling was alone, and Bass knocked loudly on the window's metal siding.

The gallerist stopped in his tracks, circled back, and cracked the door. "We open at 10 a.m. I need to get all the lights on—please come back in 15 minutes."

"How about if I have a nice Dixon painting for sale—are you open then?"

"Come right in, my friend; Dixon always gets an early pass."

As the men walked toward the back of the building, Shandling noticed that the young man with the white guy was Navajo, an unusual sight that had occurred two days in a row. Shandling's radar went into full alert.

"Hi, I'm Mort Shandling, and whom do I have the pleasure of meeting?"

"I'm Richard Bass and this is my good friend and partner, E.T."

"Partners? You're an art dealer by chance?"

Shandling raised his eyebrows. This was the second time in two days he had seen Navajo with a white partner and he smelled a rat.

"Well, not so much an art dealer. I deal in all sorts of material—antiques, Native art, paintings, cars, anything that's great."

"And Mr. E.T., are you also a dealer?"

Tsosie looked at Bass for direction; the picker smiled and the young man answered.

"No, I'm an owner and Mr. Bass is helping me sell my painting, a Maynard Dixon. It's a family heirloom."

E.T. stumbled over the word "heirloom" that Bass had coached him to use. Shandling's bullshit meter was now off the chart: either Bloom or Bass was full of crap—there were too many coincidences.

"So, do you have the painting with you, E.T?"

"Not exactly," Bass answered, before E.T. chimed in.

"I have a problem—a bad art dealer has taken possession of my painting and as soon as I find this thief I will be looking for a buyer."

Shandling knew E.T. was talking about his Dixon, and that Bloom was the dealer the kid was calling a thief. The question was who was lying....

"Can you tell me a little more about this Dixon that you don't have, but own? How did it come into your possession and how did you lose it?"

Bass told the story of how E.T. had been swindled out of the painting, that he had stepped in to make it right, and that he was going after Bloom and Manycoats. Only E.T., he said, had the right to sell the piece.

"Interesting story, Mr. Bass. I would like to hear it from your mute friend."

E.T. repeated a similar story, leaving out the fact that his grandfather owned the painting.

"Mr. E.T., how again did your family end up with this piece?"

"Well, my understanding is that this artist Dixon stayed with my great-grandfather near Mexican Hat. Dixon was grateful for food and housing and gave him the painting as a gift. It's been in our family since then."

"Is there any way to prove this?" Shandling asked.

E.T. thought for a moment, then gave an answer that shocked his partner: "Yes, I think I can prove that. There is another Dixon we still have."

Bass chimed in to cut off any more talk from his partner. "That's right, he has another one. If you want that information, then I think it's time for you to answer a few questions," he said boldly.

"Okay, what's your question?"

"Did Bloom and Manycoats come here peddling our Dixon?"

"Yes they did—quid pro quo, Mr. Bass. What's the other Dixon?"

"Fair enough. Give me a second to discuss it with my partner."

Bass and E.T. moved out of earshot and E.T. told him about the portrait of his great-grandfather that was on the back of his hogan door. Bass couldn't help but smile to think that he had been in the home and hadn't even noticed the piece.

"Okay, Mr. Shandling. We will share if you will."

"I'm listening."

"There is a full-size charcoal drawing of E.T.'s great-grandfather on the back of his hogan door, signed and dated by Dixon."

"Well, now you definitely have my attention. How is it signed and dated?"

E.T., who looked at the image every day while lying on his bed, answered, "MD. 1-9-22. To my good friend Roanhorse. Thanks for lunch."

Shandling knew this sounded right even without seeing the image.

"Okay, what else do you want to know, Mr. Bass?"

"Did Bloom sell you our painting?"

"Kind of. I gave him a check for $125,000. He wanted to talk to the original owner, who I guess must be Mr. E.T. here, to make see if he could get a better title. He wants to pay him more, didn't feel it was right that he didn't pay fairly for the piece."

Bass's face soured. "Do you have the painting?"

"Let's say I do, but I'm not giving it to anyone without more proof of ownership or other significant information. I get the feeling there is more to this story than you're telling me."

Now it was Bass's turn for a gut-check. He was afraid E.T. might dump him and go for greener pastures, so he need to put pressure on his unlikely partner.

"Yes, here's one small detail: E.T.'s grandfather is the owner of the painting until he passes. It was sold without his knowledge, but E.T. thinks he will be fine with him selling it. If you're offering $125,000 for the piece, I can't imagine Mr. Roanhorse wouldn't be happy with the sale."

Bass became a more important player, a man Shandling could do business with; selling paintings that weren't technically yours meant he could get a clear title from E.T.'s grandfather.

"Okay, I'm buying this now. How about we all go into partnership and say goodbye to Mr. Bloom and his friend Manycoats?"

"Mr. E.T., do you think you can get your grandfather to sign this painting over to me? I'm willing to pay the $125,000 for the oil and add a large bonus for that door if you want to sell that too."

"Yes, Grandfather Roanhorse will do that for me—he has to, it's a life changer."

"Well, it looks like I'm going to be closing the museum for an unexpected winter vacation trip to northern Arizona."

The men shook on the deal. Shandling retrieved the Dixon and Bass got to see what he had been chasing for the first time. He reveled in its imagery. It was his most important score, won with good instincts and big balls.

The trio agreed the painting would stay in Shandling's possession for now as Bass had to check out of the hotel, but the piece would come with them on the trip. The storm threatening the rez had stalled and there was a perfect window to visit Perry Roanhorse if they left right away. Bass and Shandling knew for sure the old man would sell: they wouldn't have it any other way.

Shandling immediately canceled Bloom's check after his new partners left the museum. There was a new sheriff in town—and it wasn't Bloom.

CHAPTER 43

KAYENTA BOUND

An exotic mixture of aromas greeted Bloom and Manycoats as they gazed on the array of jumbo shrimp, oysters on the half shell, and fresh roast beef.

"This all is for us?" Marvin asked.

"As much as you can eat; we can feast for hours if you want."

"Bloom, can you imagine what would happen if I brought a couple of hungry bootleggers to this spread? They would never leave. Crazy how the rest of the world lives."

The two men sat down by a panoramic view of the Catalina Mountains while they waited for Norbert.

"What's this going to set us back, partner?" Marvin asked Bloom as he looked around for the price of brunch.

A discreetly placed letter-sized chalkboard revealed a price of $89 per person, including mimosas.

"Take a guess, Marvin."

"Fifty dollars a person?"

"Close. It's $89 including mimosas and coffee or tea."

"My goodness, I hope they let me take two days' worth of leftovers, otherwise I can't spend that kind of money—even with free drinks. People really pay this?" Marvin asked in a state of disbelief.

"Apparently so. Look around; there are not many empty seats. I'll cover the cost for now; once we sell the Dixon we can have the partnership pay me back; it's the price for doing business in the big leagues.

"You know, Marvin, you might have to pay a nice chunk of tax this year, so you may need a write-off or two."

Marvin had never considered the implications of his newfound wealth. He had paid plenty of tax in his days working as a contractor in L.A., but that was years ago.

"Okay, so wasting money comes with the territory of being a 'good' businessman. I guess I have a lot to learn. You think we should we wait for our new friend?"

Before Bloom could answer, Norbert strolled in, greeting the manager and two couples near the door as he started making the rounds. He had command of the room; he was clearly a known entity in Tucson.

"Hey, guys—great buffet, isn't it? I don't know how they put on a spread like this for under a hundred dollars—what a deal."

Marvin giggled at Norbert's sense of value. Three mimosas arrived without asking, the waiter understanding a big tipper was in the house.

"You guys want one of these? It's a great way to start the day."

Bloom was more than happy to have a cocktail. Marvin begged off, knowing alcohol was a demon he had avoided so far—and he wouldn't start drinking today.

"Any news from your dinosaur landowner?"

"No, I'm going to have to go up to Utah to track him down. I've got a post office box number and I'm sure it won't take long. The rez is small when it comes to everyone knowing everyone—even if it's the size of Connecticut. I'm sure I'll have more information by tomorrow," Bloom replied.

"How about I come with you? I've got a plane we can fly into Kayenta to save time and get this ball rolling. Time is working against me with the big show coming to town, and I've got to be ready for the high-rollers next week."

"I've got to go home first," Bloom said, "to check on my pregnant wife and my kids. I can assure you she wouldn't want me flying in a small plane, especially with bad weather looming."

"How about you, Marvin? Care to stay behind? When we fly out to Kayenta, I can pass over your home so you can see it from a new angle."

"I'm in!" Marvin said without hesitation, disregarding the danger from inclement weather. "If that's okay with you, Bloom," he added.

"No problem. I'll go home, kiss the wife and kids, get our receipt and head up to Bluff tomorrow. Can you rent a car somewhere in Kayenta and meet me near Bluff?"

"Once you give me the location, Marvin, I can meet you. I have an SUV parked in Kayenta so that won't be a problem."

"You might as well know, Norbert, that the name of the guy the dinosaur tooth came from is Tsosie. He goes by E.T. and I've got a feeling he lives out in the boonies. You comfortable with that?"

"No problem. I'm a fossil hunter; I've been everywhere in the world, even Mongolia—besides, I've got a local to guide me if I get lost. Am I right, Marvin? Can you put us on point?"

"I won't get lost more than twice." Manycoats flashed his signature smile.

"Perfect!" I'll book a couple of rooms at the View Hotel thirty minutes outside of Kayenta. You must know the place—it's in the heart of Monument Valley. Great views of the Mittens to wake up to. This is sounding more and more like an adventure, my favorite pastime.

"Food is on me today, boys—no arguing over the check. I've already taken care of the bill; it's on my account. Now let's go eat!"

Bloom and Manycoats liked this gregarious fossil hunter. He seemed real, a man they could do business with—though a million dollar dinosaur payday might change things before the trip was over.

❉ ❉ ❉ ❉

Marvin and Bloom waddled back to their expensive room having taken full advantage of the buffet. The view of the Catalinas from their back window was almost as compelling as the view of the Toadlena/ Two Grey Hills. Bloom could understand why Dixon was enchanted with Tucson, a place he had called home in the 1940s.

"So, Marvin, you good with going on a small airplane in this weather?"

"I never told you about the time a helicopter picked me up in the dead of night as the Viet Cong were pounding our position?"

"No, you never have."

"Well, let's just say I'm not afraid to fly in this man's expensive airplane. I've seen much worse." Marvin smiled sadly, reflecting on how he won two Purple Hearts in 1968 during the Tet Offensive.

"Point well taken; at least I won't worry about you flying. Norbert appears to be a nice guy and probably is, and he's obviously generous—but you have to remember that a million dollar payday is a very tempting thing, no matter how rich you might be."

"I understand: don't be a patsy, and don't run my mouth off about the Dixon and Tsosie."

"Not exactly. I know you're highly intelligent Marvin, and I'm not suggesting otherwise, but men that buy and sell for a living sometimes have a problem not taking advantage of a situation if a big payday is nearby. They get on a scent like a hunting dog, and it's very hard to pull them off."

"Men like you?"

"Yes, even a man like me. I would try to glean as much information about the situation as I could and use it to my advantage."

"Thanks for your honesty, Bloom. I'll be careful. Even if I don't get a penny out of this deal, it's already been the best time of my life, rubbing shoulders with Tucson's big-time dealers and now flying on a private plane to Kayenta."

Bloom loved Marvin. The Navajo was straightforward in a way Bloom could never be, and money didn't seem to rule the man's life as it did his. He had to warn Marvin of the type of men art dealers could be and hoped he himself didn't fall into that category.

Bloom dropped Marvin off at the Pima Canyon mansion, and Norbert threw an arm over the Navajo, waving to Bloom as they strolled into his house. There was an adventure awaiting Marvin, but Bloom couldn't help worrying.

An expensive textured envelope had been pushed under his hotel room door. The resort was wonderful, and Bloom wished Rachael could have joined him to enjoy the luxurious stay, however brief. Still, he cringed when he reviewed the bill: $321.51 had been charged to his credit card, a sundry assortment of resort taxes pushing the total beyond his comfort range. Rachael wouldn't like this part of his trip, so he wouldn't tell her about his high-end hotel accommodations quite yet; better for her to find out on her own and then take the heat. Hopefully, the Dixon would have been sold by then and the expense would be a nonstarter.

Bloom headed toward Shandling's museum on his way out of town. He had a question regarding the Nemo inscription and had forgotten to ask Shandling if he knew what it meant. He was looking forward to a late dinner with Rachael, kissing the kids, and hitting the bed early. He had updated his wife in on his arrival, and she was making his favorite chicken potpie.

It was 11:30 a.m., and the parking lot was filling up. January in Tucson was a busy time and Bloom could see why Shandling put his museum in this location. He parked in front of the museum. Only the front lights were on and a sign on the front door read: "Closed for the next two days. Sorry for any inconvenience."

Bloom froze reading the sign.

"Closed? Why would Shandling be closed? He didn't mention anything about going anywhere…."

Bloom played out the possible scenarios in his head, then pulled out his cell phone and called Shandling's number, which went directly to voicemail. Bloom left a message for Shandling to call him, his mind awash in "what ifs." He didn't know where the dealer went, but he did know this was an unusual event, one that was not a good omen— especially when Shandling had possession of his painting.

As Bloom headed out of town, he ran through the possibilities, none good. Could Bass have made an appearance here? Sleep would be evasive tonight, no matter how filling the chicken potpie—unless Shandling reached out and returned his call, which Bloom doubted would happen.

CHAPTER 44

MEXICAN HAT

Shandling, Tsosie, and Bass decided to take two separate vehicles; the remote hogan on iffy dirt roads would be problematic in a snowstorm. E.T. and Bass would go to Gallup and park his car at a buddy's junkyard. Shandling would meet them in Gallup in his Land Rover for the final one-hundred-eighty-mile trip.

Bass was uneasy letting the Dixon out of his sight, so he suggested they travel in tandem in case there were any car troubles. Shandling understood Bass's concern; it was just good business. He would take this man seriously when it came to money.

Bass didn't trust partners as a general rule, but he had no problem working with Tsosie. He would have to keep Shandling at arm's length, though; after all, the man had betrayed Bloom.

Dark clouds raced across the sky as the caravan crossed the Salt River Canyon on the Apache reservation. The precipitous road was the worst impediment they would face on their three-hour journey. Light snow was falling when they reached Gallup. They filled their cars with gas, took a quick restroom break, and ordered two green chile and cheese Lotaburgers to go. Shandling had brought his own food in a black Tumi bag that also cradled the Dixon.

Bass eased his sedan into the back of a massive car-strewn lot north of Gallup, Shandling following closely behind. The picker exited the car and disappeared behind a stack of smashed cars. For a moment Shandling panicked, thinking of a scene out of *Pulp Fiction*. Might Bass kill him, take the painting, and dump his body in the junkyard's crusher?

Bass returned, key in hand, and opened the door of the faded green metal building he shared with his buddy. Shandling smiled, realizing he was overdramatizing the situation. This was a good place to keep vehicles that needed to be sold quietly. Inside the building were numerous stripped vehicle parts. The walls were covered with posters of nude women. Shandling recognized the way the building was used and made a note to himself that either this man or his buddy played outside the law.

"Nice wall art."

"It works for this place. You're welcome to put our Dixon on the wall if it's more to your liking," Bass said, recognizing a dig when he heard one.

"I think we are good."

Bass got into Shandling's front seat, Tsosie in the back, and the black Land Rover headed north to Mexican Hat. The smell of the hamburgers, chile, and onions filled the car. Shandling cracked his window, not wanting the stench to be a permanent reminder of the men he was associating with.

"So E.T., I know you told me that your great-grandfather got the painting from Maynard Dixon and that he painted his son's portrait on the door. Do you have any other family history to share?" Shandling asked, hoping to fill in some holes in the information about the family and the painting. He knew there had to be more to the story because the timelines didn't line up: Everett Ruess was in southern Utah in 1934, and the Dixon painting was dated 1922.

"Not really. We kept the painting in the outhouse and moved it each winter to a tiny canyon crevice. My grandfather would bless the piece, then pull it out when the male rains came and put it back on its nail."

"Fascinating! Do you know how long that's been going on?"

"As long as I can remember, and I'm twenty-five."

"The ritual makes it sound like the painting is very precious to your grandfather. You sure he will sell it?"

"I think so. We're talking about more money than he has made from his corn harvest in years. He could stop farming and let the fields go to seed. It's time; he's getting old, and I need money for my own family."

Bass listened, not saying anything as the conversation rolled down the river of speculation.

"What if he won't sell? Then what?" This question had Bass's full attention.

"I don't know. I hadn't even considered that possibility. Why wouldn't he? Who wants to farm corn?" E.T. replied.

"But let's say for argument that he says 'No.' Then what?" Shandling pressed.

"I guess we do what we have to do." E.T.'s words trailed off as he considered how far he had fallen.

That was the answer both art dealers wanted to hear, nothing else was needed. E.T. was all in, and the Dixon was theirs.

✳ ✳ ✳ ✳

The Hat Rock Inn near Tselakai Dezza was the best hotel available close to E.T.'s home, which was south of Mexican Hat, Utah. Bluff was closer and was where Shandling preferred to stay, but Bass insisted on The Hat Rock. He was not going to take the chance of being recognized in Bluff in case some shit went down at Roanhorse's place. It still wasn't clear in his mind how the deal would play out.

The trio would stay for one night. E.T. had never considered the place as a motel, but he knew it was a good watering hole. He knew the girl at the front desk, who was confused when he checked in with two white men—but it wasn't any of her business and she kept it professional. The men took two rooms. Shandling insisted on having his privacy, and Bass, who wanted to save money, bunked with E.T. Neither Bass nor Shandling wanted E.T. sneaking home without them; they would meet Grandfather Roanhorse as a single unit.

The clean, well-decorated rooms offered amazing views of the nearby San Juan River. Shandling checked his phone messages and email on the slow internet connection, and found Bloom had called because he had forgotten to ask about the Nemo inscription. It wouldn't take much of a Google search on Bloom's part to figure out it was a pseudonym for Everett Ruess. Shandling would not call Bloom back until he had possession of the painting. Bloom might want the painting returned once he understood the importance of the provenance.

Tomorrow they would settle up with Roanhorse one way or another. Shandling pulled a revolver out of his backpack and checked the cylinder. It was loaded. He would keep the gun within easy access in case it was needed.

Bloom was smart and starting to ask questions. Shandling could hear the concern in the dealer's voice, wondering why the museum owner had left town so suddenly. It was time to close the deal; the gun would provide some extra insurance if things went south.

CHAPTER 45

FORTY DOLLARS

Bloom rolled into his driveway ten minutes before 7 p.m. Two hyper children pounced on their father as he came through the front door, with screams of "What did you bring me?" echoing through the tiny house. Bloom dug deeply into his coat pockets and retrieved two malformed cookies that had been saved from the brunch buffet, one in each gloved hand. The gooey treats vanished before Rachael could complain.

"Charles James Bloom, these kids haven't eaten yet, and you're filling them with sugar and ruining their appetites."

Bloom smiled and, like a magician doing an encore, pulled another broken cookie out of his pocket and handed it to his wife—who returned his smile as she ate it.

"Okay, you're off the hook. I've missed you." Rachael wrapped her leg around her husband and kissed him on the neck. "How about we make some me-time once the kids go to bed. My hormones are going crazy, if you know what I mean," Rachael purred.

"Don't worry, I'm in, but I smell potpie and it's calling my name. I'm famished," Bloom said dampening the mood.

Rachael smacked Charles' butt with her wooden spoon. "I'm not done with you, Mr. big-shot art dealer. But if you must, let's eat while you tell me what's going on with this Dixon painting."

Rachael rounded up the kids and the family sat down to chunks of chicken and gravy. In between gulps, Bloom gave Rachael the details and waited for an analysis from his wife, his best sounding board.

"Huh. Sounds like this Norbert guy is interesting, and pretty friendly considering his wealth. I'm not sure what to make of that kind of generosity. Marvin will have a great time flying over the rez, but I'm glad you didn't get in that small plane. I need you around!"

Bloom smiled, knowing his wife's temperament well.

"This Shandling fellow hasn't returned your call and that was eight hours ago. You sure he's not just one of those eccentric rich guys who follow their own internal schedule?"

"Nothing, not a word. He's rich, but it seems out of character. I emailed him too, still no response. I don't really know the guy, and it's Sunday, so maybe he wanted a relaxing vacation to celebrate getting another Dixon for his wall. Hell, I don't know what's going on, but my gut is saying be careful. As far as Norbert's generosity goes, I just can't say."

"Well, except for your taste in hamburgers, your gut is usually right. I say you better get up early and get over to Mexican Hat and track Tsosie down. You sure he's from there?"

"All I have to go on is the bill of sale that Marvin had Tsosie fill out, and he left a post office box number with a Mexican Hat address, so my guess it's right. Someone local will know him. There can't be more than couple hundred Navajo families in that whole valley."

"You want me to come with you? I'm happy to go, and it never hurts to have a translator and a friendly face along."

"You don't like my happy face?" Bloom teased.

"It's your body I like...." Rachael winked.

"Thanks, honey—glad you like part of me. But I'll be fine. I'm going to meet up with Marvin and Norbert and, if I haven't located Tsosie's place by then, I'm sure Marvin can turn on the charm and find this kid. You take care of yourself; I hope to have everything settled by tomorrow night. With any luck we will soon have one-third of $125,000!"

"I hope you're right, but don't despair if Tsosie wants to renege on the deal. Remember that it's his painting, bill of sale or not," Rachael cautioned.

"I understand. I will be fair, but if he cuts us completely out of the deal and doesn't reimburse our money, I can assure you I'm not saying a word about the value of the dinosaur tooth."

"Well, that's your ethical dilemma, but how about you first see what you can work out before you start making rash decisions. Maybe instead of playing finders-keepers with the tooth, you can work out a deal on the whole dinosaur so everyone wins."

Rachael was once more cuddling next to her husband, whose full stomach was now open to his wife's emotional energy.

"How about we discuss the finer points in our bedroom," Bloom proposed.

"I thought you would never ask! Kids, it's time for bed."

✱ ✱ ✱ ✱

The weather service was predicting one to two inches of snow with light winds. The bulk of the storm had swung south, missing the parched Four Corners area—but just in case Mother Nature changed her fickle mind, Bloom made sure he had his snow chains, extra food, water, and clothing, and that his phone was fully charged; getting stuck out in the backcountry could be dangerous.

The San Juan Valley is largely high desert, with occasional pockets of trees and fertile valleys bisected by the meandering San Juan River. The Navajo Nation follows this natural watershed. Tsosie's place of residence boasted few people and much rugged beauty.

There was still no word from Shandling, and Bloom's concern-meter ratcheted up a notch. He decided to do a quick search on the word "Nemo," and what he found was disturbing. "Could this painting be related to Everett Ruess?" he wondered.

Bloom understood from the numerous articles, books, and documentaries listed on the internet related to the wunderkind lost in the 1930s, that if there were a connection it could increase the value of the painting. Bloom's first line of questions to Shandling would be related to Nemo, along with, "Why the f**k aren't you answering my calls?"

The sun greeted Bloom as he opened the front door. It was brutally cold, but there was no snow—a good day to travel. He bought a large cup of stale black coffee at the Shell station. He should have waited for Rachael's cowboy coffee, but he was in a hurry. Bloom awkwardly cradled the Styrofoam cup between his legs for warmth before heading north on Highway 491. He was on a mission and wouldn't bother to stop for breakfast until he got to Mexican Hat.

Bloom's search for lodging and restaurants the day before had found The Hat Rock Café, whose food reviews were quite good, especially considering the location. Marvin and Norbert would meet him at the cafe around 10:30 a.m., coming from the Kayenta airport using a truck Norbert stored there. Bloom hoped that by the time they showed up he would have gotten a lead on E.T.'s whereabouts.

Bloom scanned the dining room, but found no signs of his friend. The room was empty except for a middle-aged Navajo couple and two old men engrossed in talk at the bar. After a pit stop at a clean restroom, Bloom ordered his second cup of coffee of the morning, which was thankfully fresh, and figured a side of biscuits with homemade marmalade was in order. It was delicious, so he decided to eat breakfast without waiting for his friends.

When he ordered, Bloom asked his Navajo waitress if she knew a young man named Everett Tsosie who lived around there. She knew lots of Tsosies, but not one named Everett. She said she would ask around, and Bloom promised her a double tip if she could find out anything useful.

As he sopped up the last of his eggs, an attractive Navajo woman with a nametag that said "Mabel" pulled up a chair.

"I hear you're looking for Everett Tsosie...."

"I am. Do you know where I might find him?"

"Are you the law or something?"

"No, nothing like that. I live in Toadlena and work part-time at the post. He brought me something to buy. I don't have his phone number, so I drove over to ask him about the piece."

"Toadlena, huh?"

"Yes, my wife is Rachael Yellowhorse. You may have heard of her, she's a weaver."

"I know her. My grandmother is a weaver too. I met Rachael once when she was set up next to my grandmother at the Heard. She's good. I was a kid, but I remember her; she was nice."

"That's my wife."

"So I know Everett, but no one calls him that; he has always gone by E.T. He lives with his grandfather northwest of here, not far from the river. It's hard to get to. You got four-wheel drive?"

"Yes I do. Can you draw me a map?"

"Sure I can, but you know something funny is that I checked E.T. into this hotel last night. His fancy friends paid in cash for two nights."

"What friends?"

"A couple of older white guys. They must all have left early this morning, not sure when, but when I came on duty at 8 a.m. their expensive car was gone."

"What kind of car? Tesla, maybe?"

"Not sure what kind. It was one of those ones you see in the movies or in Phoenix. Rangerider, I think they call them. Cool-looking, real clean, not been on the rez."

Bloom pressed her: "So E.T. checked in to this hotel, but lives forty minutes away?"

"Yeah, that's what I thought—seems funny, huh? Honestly, I figured he was going to party down with them. Everyone around here knows he's got a problem with booze and drugs."

"Can you tell me what the guys looked like?"

"One was maybe sixty and the other maybe forty. The younger guy was good looking and well dressed; the older guy didn't say much other than asking if the room had a good bed. I told him it was new and all good."

"Anyway, can you look in your register for E.T.'s friends' names?"

"I'm not supposed to do that."

"I understand, but there is a possibility that E.T. might be in trouble and that he was with the men not because he wanted to be, but because he had no choice."

"I never thought about it that way. Okay, I'll give you what they wrote down, but don't tell anyone. I could get fired, and I need this job. I'm only doing this 'cause of your wife."

"I understand. I won't say a word, promise."

Mabel left and returned. The card had one name on it: R. Bass from Albuquerque, New Mexico, paid in cash.

"Thanks, Mabel—you've been a big help."

"Hope it works out for E.T. Make sure you give my friend a good tip; she's got two kids and is making it on her own."

"I promise."

Now Bloom was sure there was trouble. Bass and probably Shandling were heading for Tsosie's home—but why? He left forty dollars on the table and exited through the front door to wait for Marvin. He needed the cold air to help him think.

CHAPTER 46

COME FOR THE CORN, HAVE YOU?

The unlikely trio of art partners left the Hat Rock Inn by 7 a.m. after a cold breakfast of yogurt, nuts, and coffee. Shandling pressed his cohorts to get on the road; he wanted to head home by noon. Tsosie's mood was somber, knowing he was about to break his grandfather's heart. Bass tried to cheer him up, knowing a happy partner meant an easier day.

"What you going to do with your share, E.T.?"

"I've been giving it a lot of thought. The main thing I want is to give my girlfriend and son a safe place to live and a better life. This might be a chance for me to turn around my bad luck and stop killing my brain with drugs if I can."

"I've been there, had a bad cocaine habit in the '90s, wasted lots of money and destroyed a good relationship. I hope you can do it kid; we all need a chance at redemption."

Bass's voice trailed off, knowing there would be no redemption for him. He had visited the dark side too many times and the negative energy had engulfed his entire being.

The conversation cheered up E.T. and put Bass into his head.

"Okay, where do I turn?" Shandling asked E.T.

"Go past that broken-down tractor frame and turn left. It's up a steep grade five miles from here."

Bass shook his head affirmatively recognizing the landmarks. "Pretty country. All this property yours?" he asked.

"My grandfather's land. He and his dad plowed all the money they made from our corn and melon crops into purchasing land. We're on Indian land right now, my birthright, but more than half of what he owns is private property they bought up when nobody else wanted it. Good water rights and the corn here is chest high in places."

"Seems to me you would want to continue to build onto what your forefathers have accomplished. They've already done a lot of the heavy lifting," Shandling said, knowing all too well about the baggage that came along with inheriting great wealth from a father.

"I know. Maybe I'll see it differently when I don't have to struggle so much with my addiction. See that old dead cottonwood on the horizon? Behind that tree is my place and not far from there is my grandfather's hogan. You didn't see my grandfather's place when you rescued me from my drug-induced haze, did you Mr. Bass?"

"No, I was too angry, afraid you had sold off the Dixon. I didn't even see the second Dixon in your house. Anger has a way of blinding a man sometimes, like the reflection of this snow covering the ground," Bass said, trying to apologize in his own way for his rough treatment of the young man.

"Enough of this philosophical mumbo jumbo," Shandling cut in. "It's time for a paycheck for the two of you.

"E.T., like we went over, you have to let your grandfather know you have sold the painting to me and that he will be getting a huge paycheck, which you can split with him however you see fit. If your grandfather balks, Bass is willing to go to a third, aren't you Bass?"

"I don't want to, but if push comes to shove I will. I'm a much happier camper with half the money. After all, E.T., you wouldn't be getting anything if I hadn't been straight with you—and you have to remember you had already sold me the painting," Bass offered, hoping to keep E.T. on the same page.

A thin line of black smoke drifted out of the house's chimney. Perry Roanhorse had heard the vehicle approach and looked out the window; an expensive SUV was coming up the dirt drive. Three men, one of whom was his grandson, were in the truck. He expected bad news and went to the stove to make a second pot of coffee for the uninvited guests. The value of the vehicle meant they were most likely there about his missing Dixon painting.

E.T. opened the heavy plank door and walked in, his partners in tow.

"Yá' át' ééh, Grandfather. I'm home. These are my friends Mort Shandling and Richard Bass."

"I've seen Mr. Bass before. The last time he didn't seem so friendly." Perry Roanhorse closely eyed the man who had so rudely tossed his grandson out of the door. Bass broke eye contact immediately.

"I was on drugs, Grandfather—don't blame Mr. Bass. It was me. I'm feeling much better, been clean now for three days. Feeling like the old self."

Roanhorse nodded his head to acknowledge the good news. "What brings a fancy car and two white men out to the ends of the reservation? You don't look like you're here to buy some of my fine Indian corn—and my newspaper subscription is paid in full."

The old man smiled as he scrutinized the men in his home, looking for their hidden agenda. It didn't take long to find the answer.

Shandling took charge of the conversation: "Well, Mr. Roanhorse, I'm a big fan of Maynard Dixon, and your grandson came to my Dixon museum in Tucson to sell me your family heirloom, which I agreed to buy. We came out here to personally let you know the good news and to bring you a check. You're wealthy now!"

"Doesn't sound like good news to me. I'm pretty wealthy without selling my painting. Sounds to me like you bought something that was not for sale."

"I understand from E.T. that the piece is to be passed down to him soon, and I'm acquiring paintings and paying top dollar right now. Your grandson thought it would be an opportune time to sell as the market is strong for Maynard Dixons."

"Sounds like my grandson has become pretty smart when it comes to the art market—he's a fast learner, I guess."

Shandling could see things weren't going as he hoped and switched back to more talk about the money.

"Well, you see, sir, it's not like it's an inexpensive painting. I'm planning on paying you and E.T. $62,500 for the painting, and you don't have to declare the income unless you want to."

"You're right—that's a big paycheck if I were selling, but I'm not selling. I follow your world, even see the occasional TV program, so I understand money. Where is my painting, Mr. Shandling?"

"Well, it's possible that I could pay more—say $90,000 for you and your grandson—a real windfall."

"Indeed, that's more money than I have ever seen at one time. Of course, I could sell my land and get lots more, or dig up a bunch of those old dinosaur bones across the river and probably get even more—but then I wouldn't have nothing but money. So thanks for the offer, but I don't think I'm selling today. Do you have my painting?"

Shandling was flummoxed; the old man was smart and was not going to sell. Plan B would need to be implemented. He was not leaving the Dixon; it was going to hang in his museum no matter what Roanhorse wanted.

CHAPTER 47

SECRET REVEALED

"Mr. Roanhorse, I do understand this has been in your family for very long time. Do you mind if I ask how it came into your possession?"

"Why do you need to know about my painting and how I got it?"

"I have a museum that is dedicated to the lifework of Maynard Dixon. My father started collecting Dixon when he was still alive. I took over his collection and decided to take it to the next level. I have a great museum with over one hundred-fifty original works by the artist, and this would be a wonderful addition."

"If you have so many Dixons, why do you need mine? Seems like you're doing fine."

"Well, as I understand it, you got this painting from Dixon. That's a great history to have stayed in the same home for so long, and it's never been seen. It hasn't been seen, has it?"

"No it's hung on our wall since 1934, part of the family. That's why I don't want to let it go. It's not about money but about a family commitment," Roanhorse said, looking at his grandson.

Shandling's pulse quickened. The painting had been in the family since 1934, the year that Ruess disappeared—not 1922, when Dixon painted it. It was Nemo's painting!

"Yes, that is a very long time. How about Mr. Bass and I step out. I think your grandson might have something to discuss with you. Mr. Bass, care to join me for a look around outside?"

Bass took Shandling's cue and headed out to powwow about Plan B.

"Wasn't the painting done in 1922?" Bass asked.

"Yes, it was painted in 1922, during Dixon's trip to Kayenta to stay with John Wetherill. He brought his wife Dorothea Lange, the famous photographer, along and they stayed for four months."

"So why is he talking about 1934, and what did he mean by dinosaur bones?"

"Not sure on the bone comment; guess you would have to ask him. But he does live out here all alone, and it must be very isolating. He probably is just confused; he looks old and Indians don't show their age much."

"He seems pretty sharp to me, and he does not want to sell—so what's the next play? You've got the painting, and I still have my receipt," Bass said.

"All true, and I can assure you that old man's not getting this painting. Let's give E.T. a chance to change the old man's heart. If he can't, then I'm afraid we may have to stop his heart from beating," Shandling observed coldly.

The two had danced around the possibility that Roanhorse might have to be eliminated, but hearing the words come out of Shandling's mouth brought it home for Bass.

"Okay, so you're saying 'eliminate' the old man—but what if E.T. isn't cool with that? He says he is, but words are easy. Or what if he cracks afterwards? Then we have to deal with him. And Bloom and Manycoats aren't going to lie down either. From what you've told me about Bloom, there is no way he will play ball."

"All must go away that get in our way," Shandling said matter-of-factly.

A chill went down Bass's spine. This man was a stone-cold killer, something he had never been or even witnessed. The erudite man looked tame, but he was not to be underestimated.

Shandling looked through the window and could see E.T. in heated debate with his grandfather. He would give them time. Hopefully the kid could convince his grandfather to sell; if not, both men's lives were toast.

"You just don't understand," E.T. begged. "This painting means a new life for me and my family. What does it mean to you—bathroom art, rituals in the winter?"

"It's more than art. It's a commitment, a bond with my grandfather, father, and Everett Ruess, the man you are named after. Your father named you after Ruess in honor of the man. I never told you this?"

"Who is Everett Ruess, and what does he have to do with this painting?"

"Sit down, my grandson. I need to tell you the full story of this painting and why I can't and won't sell it."

E.T. sat down on the edge of the bed. His grandfather sat next to him and looked him in the eye to tell him about the secrets of the fields.

"Everett Ruess—we knew him as Nemo—was a friend my grandfather and father helped. He had been chased by cattle rustlers and broke his back and his leg trying to escape these bad men. This was in 1934. Back then we had no medical care and he needed more than a medicine man.

"My father was barely a man at that time, but he remembered every detail, which he told me and I'm telling you. Ruess was an unusual man; he was more like a spirit in a boy's form, and he was younger than you are now. He painted, wrote, and sang songs even when he was badly injured. Ruess knew many famous people, including Maynard Dixon, who gave him this painting as a gift. Ruess gave this painting to your great-great-grandfather. It has been handed down to me, and someday it will be passed along to you."

E.T. interrupted: "Something doesn't sound right. I thought Dixon gave the painting to us, along with that picture of your dad in the hogan. I don't understand...."

"Dixon did paint that door too. In 1922, he visited our land and my grandfather helped him, so he drew my father's image as thanks. Then the Holy People sent this young man Ruess to us back in 1934 with another Dixon painting. Ruess was looking for our ruins, the ones near our north cornfield; that is where he was nearly killed and ended up at our place.

"It was all meant to be, which is one of the reasons we can't sell the painting until we know we are supposed to do that—and this is not that time."

"How do you know? It seems right to me. My family lives in a crappy trailer, and I'm in an abandoned hogan doing drugs."

"Yes, this is true, but I've told you to come back and live with me. Bring your child and girlfriend; they are family and are welcome. I can build a house for you and help you get back your lost *hózhó*. The Holy People are talking to you right now; you must listen, or we will all pay the price."

"So what happened to this Ruess fellow? Why did he give my great-great-grandfather the painting? Did he die?"

"My father told me that Everett Ruess lived for nature, he was as one with the trees and plants, but he could never walk again. He was paralyzed and his leg had been destroyed. Blood kept seeping out from the wound no matter what my grandfather tried. Ruess slipped further and further from this world.

"My grandfather begged Ruess to let him take him to the white men, but it was winter, and Ruess had made up his mind: he wanted to die with no more suffering. He asked my grandfather to use his pistol to end his pain, but the old man refused. My father had heard Ruess's pleas to end his life, and one night my father took him up to the north cornfield, across from the river that looks onto the Anasazi homes that are in this painting so the young man could view them one last time as the sun rose. Then he gave my father the Dixon painting to watch over and cherish, and asked my father to honor his promise. My father took the family pistol, put it on Ruess's temple and killed him."

"He murdered him!"

"No, I didn't say that; I said he killed him, put him out of his misery, like you would a rabbit broken by the coyote's bite. My father buried him near those fields, those fields I watch. Nemo wanted to die. He was broken, and there was no way to escape his pain other than to starve or slowly bleed out. It was a merciful thing my father did."

"What did your grandfather do?"

"He was very mad at my father for a very long time. He knew that no one could ever know what had happened to Everett Ruess, or his only son would be taken away to prison or worse. The painting reminds us of the burden we must carry. It is our secret to bear, and our promise to Ruess to keep."

"Did Ruess leave anything else besides the painting?"

"He had the painting wrapped in a muslin cloth tied with a snakeskin. With my father's help, he added a rock tooth fetish to the bundle for protection before he died. The tooth had been left by Dixon as a marker of where that painting had been made. My father searched for a marker with the tooth on top; when he found it he returned it to the injured man. In Ruess's mind, the package was a single unit that needed to stay together.

"The only other remnants, besides Ruess's bones, are of few pieces of paper from a diary he once wrote in. I still have those."

Roanhorse walked over to an old veneered desk and fished out a yellowed, unsigned envelope. "It doesn't say much on the paper, but I guess it was a reminder of what Nemo had been doing before he was hurt. He gave this to my father too."

"Why did he go by Nemo?"

"That was how he referred to himself, like the way we use our Indian war names. We only found out later that his white man's birth name was Everett Ruess."

Roanhorse showed his grandson the papers, which had the same Nemo signature as the back of the painting.

"So this is why 'Nemo' is on the back of the painting—he marked his property."

"Yes, that is correct."

"Why do you think Nemo wanted to die with the Navajo and not with his own people?"

"Well, my dad told me Nemo saw himself as part of this land and its people. If he left, he knew he would never come back. He would once again just be Everett Ruess, but broken, and he would never be able to become one with the dirt. Like the corn that grows here, he wanted his soul to live through the plants that he could help nourish.

"Nemo saw his future past death. He realized white people would come looking, and he understood that my father's act of mercifully helping him to the next world also insured that the Roanhorse family would keep quiet and never tell the authorities about his remains.

Thus, his legend would grow over time, and somehow he might make a bigger difference than if he had lived, unable to ever travel the backwoods again.

"Nemo was right back then, and he's right now. His sprit fills this land in a celebration of Mother Earth. You and I are part of his legend; if we let the story unfold, our family will be dragged down and all the good will be lost. For what? Money?

"I think the Holy Spirits were talking through Nemo like they did with First Man and First Woman; we need to respect this at all cost, just as Nemo did. Do you now understand why I can't sell that Dixon?"

E.T. sat quietly, thinking before speaking. "Yes, Grandfather, I understand, but those men outside never will."

CHAPTER 48

RUN!

There was serious trouble outside Roanhorse's front door. The white men were not going to return his painting without a fight. Roanhorse's .30-06 rifle was hanging on his truck rack, and he was too old to take on Bass without a weapon, even with his grandson's help.

E.T.'s only hope was to make a run for safety and get the tribal police. Let the chips fall where they must. If the young man could escape, the dealers would be less likely to try to keep the painting. Otherwise, the Roanhorse men were toast; the dealers could simply keep the painting and dispose of their bodies, or make it look like a suicide-homicide. Either way, they would be dead.

The two Navajo hugged and Roanhorse spoke to his grandson before the younger man climbed through the tiny back window: "I love you, go and don't worry about me. I'm old and if I die I'm fine with that. I lived a good life and walk in beauty; you must now follow in my footsteps. Our wealth is the land and what it represents—never forget this."

Roanhorse help boost his grandson out the window to race for the one place the men might have difficulty finding him—the Nasazi ruins above the fields he watched. He hoped the gods would protect his only grandson from the evil *chindi*; these men would soon be bearing down on him.

✻ ✻ ✻ ✻

"Okay, Bass, if this kid can't convince his grandfather to sell you know we have no choice but to eliminate them both."

"How about we try muscle first? I can be very convincing; murder is big time. Besides, E.T. says he's on board, so it seems to me the old man is our problem. With E.T. in the game, we have the receipt and all is good: you get the Dixon and he and I split the money."

"You know damned well that's a bad idea; roughing them up won't keep their mouths shut, and that kid's a junkie. What's the difference between one or two murder charges? Both mean the death penalty if we get caught. We'll have fewer problems without any witnesses, don't you think?"

Bass knew Shandling was right and they headed into the house to see if E.T. had changed Roanhorse's mind. A breeze coming through the open window spelled trouble as they entered the front door.

"The goddamned kid is gone!" Shandling screamed.

"Where's your grandson, old man?" Bass asked. Before Roanhorse could answer, Shandling stepped in, slapped the man hard across the face, and pointed his revolver at him.

"I'm not screwing around here. Where did your grandson go?" Shandling demanded.

"He has fled the valley. You'll never find him; he knows this country too well."

The two white men knew he was right; there was only one way to get the information they needed and that involved pain.

"You know, Mr. Roanhorse, my family made a lot of money in World War II. They found out it didn't matter which side you were on as long as you didn't let on that you were the enemy. Our name wasn't always Shandling," the dealer said, his smile letting Roanhorse know he was indeed the enemy.

"You are going to feel a lot of pain, Mr. Roanhorse. I've endured pain before and know how quickly it can convert a 'no' to a 'yes.' You will tell me where your grandson has gone or pay in the currency of screams."

Bass flinched at the sight of his partner's evil side and pulled out his gun for protection—his own.

CHAPTER 49

CLEARING THE TABLES

Bloom texted Marvin again—still no response. Norbert and Marvin were probably caught in the no-service dead cellphone zone of northern Arizona and would not arrive at the restaurant for at least another forty-five minutes. Precious time was wasting, so Bloom decided to go to E.T.'s house alone, before it was too late. He wasn't sure what "it" and "too late" meant, but his inner voice was screaming, "major trouble ahead."

Bloom retreated to the warmth inside the café, borrowed a pencil and paper, blew on his cold blue hands, and wrote a note to Marvin. He considered texting Marvin one more time, but the note seemed more reliable when it came to the Navajo finding and reading it. A $20 bill, accompanying the handwritten message, was handed to Mabel. Bloom asked her to give the message to Marvin Manycoats, telling her he was afraid Tsosie might be in trouble and that he was heading directly to the young man's place.

He also told Mabel how to recognize the pair: Marvin was an older Navajo who would be arriving in the next hour or so accompanied by a tall, well-tanned white man.

"Speak only Navajo to Marvin and give him the note," Bloom requested. Mabel understood the unspoken meaning; the white man was not to be trusted. Norbert acted like a nice guy, but he could be a sociopath. Bloom had encountered this type of person before—they made the best salesmen. Better to let only Marvin read the note.

Mabel thanked Bloom for the money and promised to give the paper to his Navajo friend.

Bloom climbed into his truck. There was a chill in the air, even with the calm wind. He thought of Rachael and wondered if this was a sign of a storm waiting in the wings. He wondered what the other three men could be planning. Maybe he was overreacting to the situation, but he couldn't chance being wrong.

It was a mistake to have given the Dixon to Shandling. He should have known better, and he hoped his lapse of judgment wouldn't come back to haunt him. Bloom could envision all sorts of deception just waiting in the wings, including having his name disparaged in court as Shandling and Tsosie testified under oath.

"Manycoats and Bloom paid you what amount? Basically pennies on the dollar for your rare Dixon painting? And if hadn't been for that honest Mr. Bass's bringing it to your attention, your family would have been swindled out of a $125,000 heirloom—is that right, Mr. Tsosie?" the highly paid lawyer would ask. "Yes, the rich Santa Fe art dealer stole it from a poor Navajo; it had been in our family forever," the well-coached Tsosie would respond. And it would go on from there.

"How old are you, Mr. Tsosie?"

"I'm twenty-five."

"And how old is Mr. Bloom?"

"Objection your honor...."

"I'll allow it."

"Old! I heard he has been selling expensive art for thirty years."

"Have you ever sold a painting before?"

"No, sir."

"Did Mr. Manycoats or Mr. Bloom ask you how much you wanted for the work?"

"Yes. Manycoats kept asking me to give him a price even though I told him I didn't know nothing about art. Finally, I threw out a number, and then he paid me less than what I asked—and this was after he went to his phone and called his art expert, Mr. Bloom."

He was doomed.

Bloom's knuckles went white gripping the steering wheel as he headed toward his napkin-mapped destiny, periodically cringing as a crescendo of rapid-fire scenarios of career-ending questions fired through his imagination, each more terrifying than the next. According to Mabel, it would take forty minutes in good weather to get to the Tsosie place—and he refused to go down without a fight.

There were two vehicles in front of the hogan—an older Ford truck in typical rez condition and an expensive new Land Rover that was out of place. Bloom figured it must be Bass and Shandling's vehicle.

He pulled up slowly to the front of what appeared to be the Tsosie house and rolled down his window. Voices filtered into his truck; what they were saying wasn't clear, but they seemed to be raised.

What should be his next step now that he was here? Bloom hadn't thought this part through. He did still have the paperwork for the painting, so legally it was his—at least for now. He decided the best course was to find out what Bass was up to and why he and Shandling were at Tsosie's home. If he had to, Bloom would lay out all the chips and let the best man win.

But before he went in, he texted Marvin again: "Going into Tsosie's hogan. Not sure what's going on, but I hear loud voices. If you don't hear from me in ten minutes, assume there's trouble."

Bloom hesitantly opened his truck, stepped out, and walked to the front door stoop. Hearing loud voices, but unable to distinguish what was said, the voices abruptly stopped. Bloom froze, was it a mistake to confront these men head-on, had they heard him? His inner voice filled his racing mind—"Get out of here, fast." Just as he turned to make a hasty escape, the front door flew open hitting Bloom. A white man was in his face, and his eyes said he meant trouble. Bloom, knocked off balance, was trying not to fall, but it was too late; the man struck him on the head with his pistol. Bloom crumpled hard, hitting the frozen ground with an audible thud.

"What the hell is going on?" Shandling asked as he too backed out of the door, his gun trained on Roanhorse.

"We've got more company and now we do have a problem," Bass replied, eyeing his partner with contempt.

"Well, I guess Mr. Bloom has now become part of the elimination equation. It's no longer just a legal issue. He's got a partner, Manycoats—any sign of him?"

"I know Manycoats. I surprised Bloom as he was about to knock on the door and just reacted automatically, so we got lucky. He won't be out for long."

Bass bent down and took Bloom's phone and wallet. There was no sign of any weapons.

"Okay, I'll take care of Bloom. Go find that kid. Bring him back alive if you can, but bring him back!"

Bass went to the rear of the house and followed Tsosie's footprints; there was just enough snow to leave a decent trail.

Shandling barked at Roanhorse to strip to his skivvies, then ordered the old man to drag the unconscious Bloom into the hogan and place him on the bed, a snail's trail of blood and snow following Bloom's head to its resting place. Bloom's breathing was shallow; Bass may have fractured his skull. The picker was indeed good at the rough stuff; he might have killed Bloom with a single blow.

Shandling ordered Roanhorse to tie Bloom's hands to the bedframe using the worn leather belt, and watched as Roanhorse tightened the bonds.

"Now go sit in that corner and don't move!"

"You do all this for a painting? Kill people?"

"I haven't killed anyone yet."

"If you don't get this man to a doctor, you might as well have."

A large smile blossomed on Shandling's usually tight-lipped face as he stared into Roanhorse's inquiring eyes. He knew the old Indian was right. Like Dixon's Nemo, the museum owner had figured out how to handle the current predicament.

He had a receipt for the Dixon, for which he had paid Bloom in full the day before. Whether the art dealer had cashed the check or not was irrelevant; the transaction was complete and the courts would rule in his favor if pushed—which would be unlikely as the Bloom estate would be thrilled for the windfall regardless of what Manycoats might say, which was probably nothing.

All that was left to determine was how to clear the rest of the table and head home—alone!

CHAPTER 50

NEMO DISCOVERED

Marvin Manycoats' gaze never left the passenger window as Norbert's small single-engine plane glided over his beloved reservation. Norbert detoured over western New Mexico so Marvin could see his hogan from above—one item on his bucket list marked off. The flight to Kayenta took four hours, but time had stopped for Marvin, who oohed at the landmarks he recognized.

The Kayenta airport was not much to look at; it was more a cow pasture with storage than a transportation hub. Norbert parked the plane and walked over to his waiting, brand-new, cardinal-red Tahoe SUV. He fished under the wheel well and found the keys his man had left. The Tahoe was immaculate; and behind the vehicle was a trailer towing an ultralight Trike plane.

"What's the baby plane for?" Marvin asked.

"I thought if the weather was good once we meet Bloom, we might take it up for a spin and go look for dinosaur bones. This Trike has a four hundred-fifty mile range and can carry two full-grown men with no problem. What do you say—up for an adventure?"

"The last time I was asked that it was by a Marine recruiter and that turned out to be some adventure all right. But if you promise not to crash us, I'm up for the challenge."

"Perfect. We will head over to The View. It's the best hotel in Monument Valley and I've got two rooms set up for us. We can stop and get dinner here in town, which has a better selection of food. One of my favorites is the Blue Coffee Pot Restaurant—lots of food for the money."

"Sounds great. Bloom's not expecting us until tomorrow morning, so he will be surprised when he sees the little kite plane."

"Trike...."

"That's what I meant—it's an appropriate name. Hard to imagine two people can get on that thing."

"No problem for the two of us. If we were your average overweight Americans, then it could get dicey. Of course, after we eat at the Blue Coffee Pot we may need to reassess the payload," Norbert teased.

After a hearty dinner, the two men headed north on US-163 to Monument Valley. El Capitan—or Agathla Peak as the Navajo refer to the monolithic mountain—loomed on the horizon, where it had served as a geographic marker for generations of locals.

The View Hotel, a Navajo enterprise, was tastefully set into the side of the cliffs, the bar and café facing the Mittens, Monument Valley's most picturesque buttes. Marvin wondered how alcohol could be served on Navajoland, but figured it went along with the Hopi-style, Navajo-made kachinas in the gift shop. Just take the tourists' money and turn a blind eye to the cultural discrepancies. Norbert's and Marvin's rooms were the best in the hotel.

Marvin couldn't wait till tomorrow. He was looking forward to flying in a Trike, but if he knew what was to come, he would have checked out and headed directly home. The real adventure was about to begin—and it was not anything he could ever have envisioned.

✳ ✳ ✳ ✳

E.T. was no match for a man who had grown up tracking white-tailed deer in the hill country of Texas. The young Navajo had tried to cover his tracks, but Bass followed, the signs blatantly apparent in the early morning snow. The picker's eyes were focused straight ahead, taking in all movements; his prey was nearby.

Bass was an avid hunter who was deadly with a gun or bow; it was only a matter of time before he would find and overpower the drug addict. The trail passed through heavy Mountain Mahogany bushes, their leaves denuded of snow—a sure sign Tsosie had passed this way. Bass pushed his way through.

When the space opened up, he could see where the man had apparently vanished. A hidden slot canyon with steep walls lined with ferrous deposits from ancient springs appeared in front of him. The area was normally covered with foliage, but in the winter the cliff dwelling tucked into its side was visible. The footprints led to the bottom of the cliff; E.T. had been running. A small rockslide at the base of the cliffs pointed to a well-formed multilevel Anasazi home above; he had found the young man's hidey-hole.

The unspoiled condition of the ruin was not lost on Bass, who appreciated the history and aesthetics of the Southwest—but he focused on the task at hand and scanned the ruin for the easiest route up, one where he couldn't be bombarded with rocks by E.T. He wished he had a rifle as well as his revolver; he had a deadly aim at long distance and could outwait his victim, but there wasn't time. Bloom had shown up and Manycoats might be close behind.

Bass could see there was an easier access to the ruin, but it would require him to take a tightrope-like walk over a narrow ridge where a wall of the ruin had slid down. The wall would undoubtedly be unstable. The ancient rock slabs had no plant growth to hold them together, so this was a relatively recent slide.

After fifteen minutes of climbing while constantly scanning the large ruin for E.T., Bass reached the summit and pressed his left shoulder against the wall as he traversed the narrow walkway, then sighed with relief when the worst was over. As he entered the large, musty room he turned his camera light on, holding the phone in one hand and his revolver in the other. The ancient doorway was barely large enough to pass through. There were multiple rooms along the ruin line, but not many places to hide. There also were numerous intact pots scattered along the floor. No humans had entered this place—at least not any pothunters—since the original inhabitants had left.

"E.T., you might as well make it easier on both of us," Bass said. "I know you're in here and, if you don't show yourself, when I do find you I'm going to shoot you and leave your body for the *chindi*. You might claim you're not traditional, but no Navajos I've ever met want to have their souls caught for eternity in their enemies' home—do they?"

Silence filled the space, then E.T. yelled: "Okay, okay. Don't shoot. I'm coming out."

The young man stood from behind the low crumbled wall, his body covered in a fine dust that now began to fill the air, Bass's camera light bouncing in all directions.

"Why did you run? We can work together on this—just get your granddad to sign off. Hell, you're going to be rich. We all will!"

"He won't sign. He said he can't do it. That old man is never going to let that painting go."

"I understand. You and I need to go back to Shandling. He's holding your grandfather and I don't trust him. Unfortunately, Bloom showed up and, well, I knocked him out."

"You knocked him out?"

"Afraid so. It was a reflex; he's out cold."

The two men stood in the cold, damp air considering the options.

"Let's go E.T. No funny stuff. Go back to the hogan and we can figure this out. It's not too late. Otherwise...." Bass's words hung in the stale air.

"Okay, Mr. Bass. Let's go back and see what we can do. I'll try to talk to my grandfather again. Maybe Bloom's injury will make him understand how dangerous this whole situation has become. No funny stuff—I promise!

Bass looked closely into his captive's eyes; the kid was talking straight.

The men left the ruin and headed back down the trail with E.T. leading the way. Bass would shoot first and ask questions later if the young man didn't play by his rules.

Once he was safely back on terra firma, Bass felt more comfortable with the situation and asked E.T. to explain these untouched ruins; the young man told him what he knew.

"So you're telling me, E.T., that only Maynard Dixon has been here in all these years?"

"No white men. My grandfather and his father before him made sure of that."

"No other white man has ever been in this slot canyon?" Bass asked.

"Well, I thought that was the case until about an hour ago, when my grandfather told me another man had also come here. Nemo was a young explorer who came in the 1930s—I think he said 1934."

"Nemo—that's the name written on the back of the Dixon painting. I don't understand this."

As best he could remember, E.T. told Bass the entire history of the painting as his grandfather had explained it to him.

"That's goddamn unbelievable! You know, I have heard of Everett Ruess. He's well-known; there's a festival every year up at Escalante, Utah, to honor his legend. Hell, there was even a movie, *Into the Wild*, in which the main character talks about Ruess. It was a good movie," Bass added, his anger fading.

"I guess that's the same guy. You can see with my grandfather's history why he doesn't want to sell the painting; it opens up trouble for him and our family."

"His father killed the kid, huh?"

"Yeah, he said it was done at Ruess's request, out of mercy."

"I can see how that could open a big can of worms for your family," Bass said, thinking out loud. "You know, E.T., Shandling is screwing us here. He knows this Nemo stuff makes the painting even more rare, and he knows who Nemo is. He's been playing us."

"Do you think the painting is worth more than $125,000?"

"Yeah, it probably is. Nemo definitely makes the painting more interesting to Shandling. He wants it at any cost, and none of us are safe—including me. We need to work as a team. If you and me work together, maybe we can get some answers and rescue your grandfather."

"I'm in. Let's go," E.T. responded.

Bass holstered his gun and headed back to the hogan. A showdown was inevitable, and Bass hoped he had picked the right team—the one that didn't want anyone to die.

CHAPTER 51

DIBBLE DOWN

Bass and Tsosie decided the picker would bring the kid in at gunpoint and then see if they couldn't get to the bottom of the Dixon deal.

As they arrived at the hogan, Bass yelled out, "I got the kid," and kicked the door open with his foot. E.T. stepped through, with Bass's pistol on him.

"Good job, Mr. Bass. And you, Mr. Tsosie—what a disappointment."

"I tried to talk my grandfather into being reasonable but he wouldn't agree. Why don't you give him his clothes back? It's cold and he's old."

"Now, now, Mr. Tsosie. I don't believe either you or your grandfather are in any position to be making demands, do you?" Bass chimed in. "But I am—so what's the deal with the Nemo signature on the back of the painting, Mort?"

Shandling was taken aback. The kid must know something; maybe he even knew what had really happened to Everett Ruess.

"Nemo is a nickname for Everett Ruess, a young vagabond traveler that Dixon met in 1933 in San Francisco. It's possible that the inscription on the back is a reference to him. Maybe written by Dixon?"

"Or by Ruess himself?" Bass asked, already knowing the answer.

"Also a possibility," Shandling replied.

"I would think that attribution adds to the complexity of this deal, don't you, Mort?" Bass retorted, raising his voice.

"I guess it could, but mainly to me."

"I would think it could make a difference to many people, Mort. You and I need to renegotiate this deal. It seems a little light on the cash payout now."

Shandling knew the gig was up. If there were more information available about Ruess, he would be willing to pay more. Money was not the object of this deal; getting the painting was his only goal.

"Tell me everything you know about Ruess, and we will see how much more."

"My grandson, do not go into this with these men. They are the devils. No matter what you say, they are not going to let us live. We are nothing to them. The coyote spirits have gotten their souls."

"I know grandfather, but you need to realize we can also be okay if you give them the painting—and if you don't, I will."

Shandling smiled. E.T. was going to play ball even though his grandfather was completely correct: they would need to die. The young man went over to the desk, pulled out the envelope and handed it to Shandling, whose gun was pointed at him.

The museum owner opened it and looked at the pages. "Do you have more of these? They look like part of a diary. Ruess kept one for many years. His last diary, from 1934, is missing."

"That's all we have. My grandfather's father got these pages from Everett Ruess—isn't that right, grandfather?"

"Yes, that is correct. There are more in the haunted hogan, buried in a special place where the other Dixon drawing is located."

Shandling had completely forgotten about that other drawing; he had to see it and find the rest of the diary.

"Bass, tie our friend E.T. to the bed with Mr. Bloom. We need to find this diary. If we find it, the price I pay you will go up considerably."

Bass headed to the bed, took off his belt, and used it to tie E.T.'s hands to Bloom's bonds. Bloom was unconscious and blood continued to ooze from his head. Looking at the wound, Bass wondered how this was going to turn out; he might be a murderer after all.

As he lashed E.T. to Bloom, he whispered in the Navajo's ear: "I'm leaving you loose. Untie Bloom and go back and hide in the ruin. I'll deal with Shandling. If I don't come to find you, assume I'm dead."

"Are those bonds good and tight, Mr. Bass? We don't want Mr. Tsosie running off again; it's too cold to play hide and seek."

"Yes, very tight." Bass shook the straps to demonstrate the truth of his words.

"After you, Mr. Bass. It's time for our host to show us the rest of his art gallery."

Bass and Shandling, guns in hand, walked Roanhorse in his underwear to the abandoned hogan over the rise.

As the three entered the hogan, the old man said, "You shouldn't come in here. There are many bad *chindi* haunting this place, very powerful medicine. You should not mess with the Holy People. Let my grandson and me go, and I will sign the paper. I will sell you the painting." Roanhorse was trying to buy some time.

"Too late for that, I'm afraid. You should have been reasonable to begin with. Sit down on the bed."

Shandling turned and saw the life-size portrait on the back of the door. It was magnificent. A Navajo man with his hair in a tight bun, a red blanket wrapped tightly around him, was standing in profile. The regality of his stance showed him to be a man of importance in Dixon's eyes.

"My god, this is fantastic—and Dixon painted this in 1922?"

"Yes, that is what I was told. That's my father. He looks just like the one photo we have of him. It's yours—just take the door along with the painting."

"Where's the rest of the diary?" Bass asked. This was Roanhorse's only chance to make a play for his freedom.

"It's buried in the corner under the bed. Come over with your phone light and I'll try to find it for you."

Bass leaned over as the old man started to dig with his hands. Roanhorse's father's dibble—the one his own grandfather had been carrying when he died from the lighting strike—was nearby.

Roanhorse grabbed the ancient stick and with one fluid movement struck Bass hard on the side of the head. The picker's body fell hard onto the edge of the bed, his skull making a noticeable cracking sound as it bounced off the iron bedframe, knocking him out cold. Bass's revolver skittered along the hard-packed dirt floor. Unfortunately, it went toward Shandling, who picked it up and ordered Roanhorse to stop.

"I will kill you where you stand if you don't stop. Do you understand me, Mr. Roanhorse?"

The old man was out of breath, his heart was pounding, and he felt lightheaded. Before he could answer, he collapsed on the floor. He looked like he was having a heart attack—and he did not appear to be acting.

Shandling looked at the two unconscious men sprawled on the floor and began to laugh. "Two for the price of one, a reservation blue-plate special," he quipped before he headed over to the main house to eliminate his other two problems.

CHAPTER 52

AUTO-ICON

Marvin and Norbert pulled up to their prearranged meeting place with Bloom, the Top Hat Café. They were thirty minutes late, but since Marvin didn't wear a watch, in his mind he was on time.

He couldn't stop talking about seeing his house from above, and how tiny it had appeared. He was also taken with the Toadlena Trading Post's shimmering plastic covering, something he had never noticed. It was as if the land he had known and loved took on a new face, giving up long-held secrets. Marvin hoped to view the site again and soon—flying was his new passion in life. Japan might have to wait.

Norbert had explained the intricacies of using a Trike, and how it was like riding a bike. He showed Marvin how to use the handles to make the wings move, and said that it was fairly safe if you didn't encounter a downdraft or hit something on landing.

Bloom's car wasn't in the parking lot, so the two sat in the warm cab awhile, lost in deep conversation until Marvin's overindulgence in coffee finally required a break, and he excused himself to go into the café.

Mabel noticed the Navajo, even though he was not with any white man, and asked, "You Marvin?"

"Yes, I am. Do I know you?"

"A friend of yours, Bloom, left me this note to give you."

Marvin's felt an uneasiness wash over him as he read the note. "How long ago did he leave?"

"About an hour."

"He drew this map. Is this where Tsosie lives?"

"Yes, I helped draw one like this for him, He said he thought E.T. might be in trouble."

"E.T.?"

"That's Tsosie—he goes by E.T."

"Thanks. Where's the restroom?"

Mabel pointed the way with her lips. Marvin headed to the back of the restaurant, relieved himself, and tried to make sense of the situation. Then he remembered that his phone was turned off. He pulled it out and took a minute to power it up. Two messages popped up. Bloom sounded troubled. But when he tried calling Bloom, the art dealer's phone went directly to voice mail.

Marvin left Bloom a short message, saying he was on his way. But what should he tell his companion, Norbert?

Once Marvin got back into the SUV, he decided to let Norbert know there might be a problem. It would be better for them to be on the same page, though he kept some of the key details to himself. The timber of Marvin's voice changed the mood, something Norbert's perceptive salesman radar picked up immediately.

"Listen, Marvin, it will be fine. I have known Shandling for a very long time. He's a bit odd, but he's a good-enough guy. I wouldn't worry about him doing anything underhanded."

"How do you know him?"

"I actually met his family years ago in London. They had emigrated from Eastern Europe after World War II. They were quite wealthy—big-time art collectors. His father was lecturing at University College London, the school I was attending. Mort Shandling came with him that day. He was much older than me, but our love of art and history made for a bond even though we are very different people.

"When I got into the fossil business, I ended up in Tucson as the annual gem and mineral show is the big daddy of them all. Shandling actually helped finance a few of my first big deals. We see each other occasionally, but I'm rarely in town, and for the last few years he's been so engrossed with his museum that he doesn't do much else."

"You're an American. Why did you go to school in London?"

"Yes, I'm from Cleveland, Ohio—born and raised. But as a kid I was so interested in mummies and Egypt that my folks sent me to the Petrie Museum of Egyptian Archaeology at UCL. They figured it would be safer than going to Egypt, which is where I wanted to go. The funny thing is that it wasn't the mummies that made me interested in fossils; it was an eighteenth-century philosopher—a man named Jeremy Bentham—who got me interested in bones."

"How did that happen?" Marvin was relieved that the conversation was helping take his mind off the sound of Bloom's voice.

"Well, when Bentham died he had his body permanently preserved as an Auto-Icon."

"What's an Auto-Icon?"

"It's a preserved body that's clothed and displayed as if it were still living. Bentham had his body dissected. All the bones were pulled out and a physician named Thomas Southwood Smith built a new body around the real bones.

"Bentham wanted his body to be placed in the faculty room so he could be part of the meetings forever. This act of giving one's bones such meaning got me thinking about their importance to who we are and where we have come from—and I decided to make bones my life's work.

"Money is important to me," Norbert continued, "so my interest in bones led me to the fossil business; it's a very lucrative trade and I have never looked back. It's been a great ride so far, like today—who knows where this is going to take us? I'm looking for a dinosaur the world really doesn't know about, one that lived one hundred fifty million years ago and has been waiting, maybe for this very day, to be found. You can't tell me that's not an exciting proposition, an adventure that is worth putting everything you have worked for on the line to find."

"Well, I haven't ever thought about bones in those terms. We Navajo don't think of bones as being something we want to find or something valuable. We use them as powerful magic and are very careful around them—though I don't know about one hundred fifty million year-old dinosaur bones. I would have to ask a medicine man about that one." Marvin smiled at the ridiculousness of the thought.

"Same concept, Marvin. Magical or mystical, bones are special to every culture. I see them one way—as history, adventure, and lifestyle—and you see them another, as ritualistic magic. Both are powerful aphrodisiacs. Bones are the most important thing in my life, probably more important than people. They will last for the ages while humans, other than Bentham, just turn to dust."

Marvin wondered to himself what kind of man Norbert truly was. To be so consumed with the dead could not be healthy.

Both men sat in quiet reflection, looking for the turnoff to Tsosie's place, which soon appeared around a bend in the road, five miles off the blacktop. The dirt road with the proverbial used-tire marker had vehicle tracks heading into the property, but none coming back out, Marvin noted.

The hogan in the distance had smoke coming from the chimney and three trucks parked in front of it—one a typical rez vehicle and one a fancy SUV. Marvin recognized the third—Bloom's truck—as the pair inched their way up the driveway.

"That's Bloom's truck. Let me go in first and see what's going on. If I don't come out in five minutes, that means there's trouble, and you should leave and call the cops."

Marvin opened Roanhorse's front door and walked in. Charles Bloom was on the bed. Next to him, and looking very afraid, was E.T., who had just extricated himself from the loose bonds and was about to go hide.

"What's going on in here, Tsosie?"

301

"It's not what it looks like. I was tied up by Bass and was getting ready to escape. Bass and Shandling are over the ridge in my old hogan with my grandfather. We got to go—now!"

"You're not going anywhere until I find out what's going on. Why is Bloom's head bleeding?" Marvin walked over and put his hand on his friend's head to see how he was doing.

"Bass hit him with his gun and knocked him out. He's in pretty rough shape, and he's been that way for a couple of hours. We need to get him medical care, but I'm telling you, Shandling is going to come back. You got a gun?"

"NO, I don't have a gun. Does Shandling have one? Is he part of this?"

"YES, I told you he's got my grandfather. We need to go."

"Okay, help me with Bloom. Let's get him in the truck."

"Charles, can you hear me?" Marvin said in Bloom's ear. Bloom started to stir, opened his eyes and looked at his friend, then closed them again as he lapsed back into semi-consciousness.

"Let's go. We need to get him to a hospital and fast," Marvin said.

The two men struggled with Bloom's limp one hundred eighty-pound body as they dragged him to the front door—which opened just as they reached it. Shandling was standing there, Norbert next to him with a revolver in his hand.

"I see we have some new company. Mr. Manycoats, how nice of you to join our little party."

Marvin was trying to decipher the situation; it appeared that Norbert was part of the danger.

"Norbert, are you helping this man?"

"No, not exactly. I didn't plan for it to go down this way, but Shandling has an evil streak sometimes and, well, I owe him a big favor from the past. It appears that today is when he decided it was payback time— so to answer your question, yes, I am helping him."

"I don't understand why would you want to help him. Look at Bloom. And what's happened to Tsosie's grandfather and Bass?"

"I like you Marvin. You're a swell guy, but business is business and I'm in the business of bones, expensive bones. Shandling is in the art business and it happens both of our worlds collided today with yours. As you're finding out, dealing in antiquities can be a cutthroat profession—and it looks like your first big deal went south."

"Hurting people for bones and an old painting?"

"It's not just about the bones. Like I said, I'm paying back an old debt and, quite frankly, those bones are an important bonus. I've found a rare specimen that I covet. I'll regret your demise—you're a nice guy—but like I said, business is business.

"Mr. Tsosie, can you show me where the dinosaur bones are located? My understanding from my good friend Mort is that your late grandfather indicated they were north of here on private land your family owns."

"What you mean, 'late' grandfather?"

"Well, Mort informed me that your grandfather whacked Bass with an Anasazi hoe. The old man probably killed the guy, and got so worked up that he had a heart attack. I'm sorry to inform you that he died and you are now the sole owner of that Dixon painting. Crazy, huh?

"Now I'm asking you again if you know where the bones are located."

"There are lots of ancient bones not that far from here, but you can't get to them easily. It's a long, steep, hard hike. It will take some time to get there."

"Not a problem. You, me, and Marvin are going to take a little ride over to those bones on my Trike. You ever flown before?"

"No, never."

"Oh, you are in for a treat—and Marvin, you're going to get your Trike ride after all. I can use your help with the digging."

"Now let's go put Mr. Bloom back on his bed. He looks tired, and we have a few loose ends to take care of."

CHAPTER 53

I LOVE FOSSILS

Marvin and E.T. unloaded the red and gray Trike and were strapped face-to-face into the tiny back seat, a secure human package. Digging for bones was probably not the only holes they would be involved with, and Marvin knew he was in trouble.

"I thought you told me only two can fly safely on this thing," Marvin asked.

"Well it's not recommended for three, but E.T. is skinny, so you will be fine. It's time to go, boys. Just so you understand: if you screw with me in the air, I'm going to fly upside down and dump you both out to your deaths. So no funny stuff—and enjoy the ride"

Norbert fired up the small plane and took off. E.T. was supposed to yell out when they got over the bone field, where he said there was a flat place to land. It was a crystal-clear afternoon; the temperature was nearing freezing but the sun made it feel warmer.

Marvin was facing forward and, under normal circumstances, the flight would have been a wonderful experience. Instead, it filled him with dread. How could he handle the situation? He had completely misjudged this man who had seemed so nice but was in reality a monster. The bones must have witched him, Marvin thought.

E.T. yelled out and Norbert circled the area. Thousands of hours in the field told the bone whisperer the story: there were bones below. He pulled up the Trike and found a decent landing spot in the cornfield stubble. It was a bumpy landing as the wheels ricocheted off the remains of the corn stalks and pushed the Trike from side to side. It was nothing to worry about for Norbert, who was a skilled aviator, but the men in the back were terrified, waiting for the plane to flip.

Marvin's tour in Vietnam had honed his survival skills, and he hoped they would kick in at the appropriate time. It was two against one, but the Navajo men were unarmed; he was old and E.T. was skinny. Before they landed, Marvin whispered to E.T. to follow his commands at the right moment. He wasn't sure the young man understood; the kid seemed to be in a trance. Once they were on the ground and all three had all gotten out of the plane, Norbert began giving orders.

"Okay, gents. Take these shovels; we are going to do some digging. E.T., show me where the largest cache of bones is located."

E.T. walked toward the edge of a deep ravine and pointed his lips at the eroded side.

"Lots of bones here. Last year's male rains opened the area up, but you can find them bones pretty much anywhere. My grandfather says this used to be a sea and that's why the corn does so well."

"Your grandfather was wise, that's exactly right. And when the sea dried up it caught some of these dinosaurs in a muddy death grip. See that exposed round rock? I believe it's actually the femoral head of a very large leg bone—most likely from an Allosaurus, Marvin.

"E.T., go down, loosen it from the soil, and bring it back up to me."

Norbert's excitement was palatable. The sight of rare specimens free for the taking was almost unbearable.

Marvin and E.T. did as they were told. The frozen ground made for hard digging; a pick would have been better than a shovel. After thirty minutes of hard labor, a portion of the large bone broke loose and the men struggled to move it up the steep slope, the ground slick with yesterday's light snow.

"That's a beaut! This is from an Allosaurus, all right, but I don't think it's a fragilis. I'm not sure what the species is, but it's rare, that's for sure. That dinosaur must have weighed a good ton, gotten stuck in the mud, and laid there until now. My god, I love this job!" Norbert said, completely enthralled as he held the heavy fossilized bone in his hand.

"I'm glad you like it," Marvin said. Norbert's focus on the bone gave him the opportunity he had hoped for. The ex-Marine ran as hard as he could, hitting the man solidly in the chest with his shoulder. An audible whoosh of air came out of the unsuspecting Norbert, and the roly-poly men went down as a unit—but only Norbert completed the somersault off the ravine edge and tumbled down the slope. He was dazed as he hit the bottom and gasping for air, but he was not completely incapacitated.

"Now! E.T.—to the Trike!" Marvin shouted.

Marvin hobbled as fast as he could toward the Trike. E.T. reached the plane before him and was sitting in the back seat by the time Marvin made it to the ultralight plane.

Norbert's voice could be heard in the distance: "Big mistake, Marvin. You're going to wish you hadn't done that." Norbert struggled up the cliff, a pearl-gripped gun in his hand.

"Now what?" E.T. yelled frantically.

"Hang on. We're getting out of here."

Marvin climbed in the pilot's seat and turned on the motor with the key Norbert had left in the ignition. The Trike lurched forward as Marvin worked the stick. He had watched Norbert fly the machine, and he used his photographic memory to repeat the same maneuvers. This was their one chance to save themselves and Bloom—and Marvin would rather die trying to escape than be at the mercy of a psychopathic paleontologist.

The flat ground was disappearing fast, the end of the mesa coming into view, and it wasn't clear if Marvin would have enough lift once he went off the edge. Both men started to yell as they reached the end. The plane dipped down off the mesa, then caught an updraft and the motor propelled the Trike upward. Marvin turned around to see Norbert reaching the top of the ravine, shaking his fist at the unlikely aviators.

"Now what, Marvin?"

"We are heading back to your grandfather's hogan. I'm not leaving Bloom or your grandfather. We don't know if he's really dead. They may just be saying that. Norbert won't be able to walk out of that place for hours, and his phone won't work either.

"Shandling won't be expecting us. That's our advantage—he's only expecting Norbert."

CHAPTER 54

A FATHER'S LOVE

Each beat of Bloom's heart pulsated through his right temple. The world was fuzzy and his stomach churned. Marvin's face was the last thing he remembered before the lights went out.

"Was it a dream or reality? Where am I?" Bloom's scattered mind struggled to string the fragments of his memory—which was currently a giant, gelatinous mass of random images—into a recognizable thread.

What had happened? He remembered getting out of the truck and going up to the hogan door—then darkness. He tried to sit up, but couldn't. Something was holding him down. A rope? As his eyesight cleared, he craned his head around, trying to assess the situation. Pain told him he was alive.

An upside-down Shandling was rummaging through a drawer, a gun on top of the bureau; then the man looked his way. "Oh, Mr. Bloom, I see you are alive after all. I wondered if you might be a goner. This will make it a bit easier. If you're a good boy, I'll untie you. Do you understand me?"

"Yes, untie," Bloom stuttered.

Shandling gripped his pistol and headed to Bloom's side. He undid the belt restraining the dealer and said, "Okay, you can sit up now. Take your time; you took a nasty hit to your head."

Bloom struggled to get upright, bracing himself with one arm while he used the opposite hand to gingerly palpate his pulsating temple. It was moist; he inspected his fingers and tasted them—salty, coagulated blood. There was a matted racquetball-shaped knot where streaks of graying hair used to reside.

"What's going on, Shandling? Why was I tied up and who clocked me?"

"Well, that's an interesting story. Mr. Bass hit you with his gun butt—I see you found the point of contact—then I tied you up for your own safety."

"Why did he hit me and, more importantly, why did he use a gun?"

"You'd have to ask Mr. Bass that question."

"I would like to. Where is that asshole?"

Shandling didn't answer.

"How about Tsosie? Where is he?"

"Mr. Tsosie is off on an excursion at the moment, as is your friend Marvin. Norbert's taken them out for a little plane ride. How about you try standing and we can head outside for some fresh air."

Bloom could see a gun securely gripped in Shandling's right hand. He was a prisoner—something he understood even if it hadn't been verbalized.

"Okay, give me a minute." Bloom stood. His legs were wobbly, but he managed to take a step forward.

"That's the spirit, one foot in front of the other. You'll feel better outside. We can go over to see Mr. Bass. He also took a nasty hit to the head, I'm afraid. Last I saw, he was prone, just like you were."

The two men exited the door and slowly worked their way over the rise to Tsosie's hogan.

"I don't get it, Shandling. You know I was going to sell you the painting. Why go through all this?"

"Turns out you didn't actually own the painting. Tsosie's grandfather, a Mr. Roanhorse, does—or should I say did? Too bad about his passing, but luckily that work found the right home: my museum."

"Is that painting so important it's worth hurting, even killing, people?"

"Yes, in fact it is that important. This is Everett Ruess's painting given to him by Maynard Dixon. Soon the world will know the real story of Everett Ruess's death, or should I say murder. Turns out the Roanhorse family has some skeletons in its closet and fields."

Shandling chuckled at his gallows humor and added, "And now they too have met a tragic ending. Bad karma I would say."

311

Bloom stopped to rest. He was dizzy. Then he bent over and threw up, the heaves making the throbbing in his head more intense.

"You are badly hurt, aren't you Mr. Bloom? Let's go inside the hogan, get out of the cold. I want to show you this great drawing, exceptional in my opinion. Maybe some incredible art will cheer you up."

As Bloom entered the once-abandoned dwelling, the late afternoon sun illuminated the backside of the door, revealing the impressive drawing. The rest of the room remained dark. Bloom blinked, trying to adjust his eyes as he struggled to find his bearings.

"You see, this is one of Dixon's largest murals and we even know who the...." Shandling stopped in midsentence, his eyes darting around frantically.

"Where is he?"

Shandling realized Roanhorse was no longer lying dead on the ground. Bass had not moved, but Roanhorse was gone. He was not dead!

"Sit on that bed, Bloom, and don't move!" Shandling pointed his gun barrel at the mattress for emphasis.

Carefully, Shandling squatted and peered under the bed from a safe distance. No Roanhorse—he was not in the hogan.

"What happened to Bass?" Bloom asked.

"The old man knocked Bass out with his hoe, and then he had a heart attack—or at least that's what it looked like."

Shandling was trying to replay the events in his head. There were no signs of the dibble either. Roanhorse was indeed gone!

The museum owner went over to Bass and nudged him with his shoe. The picker moved slightly and mumbled a few incoherent words. Then the sound of an engine filled the air, the noise getting louder as it passed over the hogan.

"Norbert's back! Stay here and don't move, Bloom, or that head of yours will stop hurting forever."

Shandling scurried from the room and Bloom immediately went over to Bass.

"Bass, wake up, wake up!" Bloom said as he shook the other man as hard as he could without passing out himself.

Bass came to life. "What's going on, what's happened?" He looked at Bloom, his eyes unable to focus on Bloom's face.

"It's Charles Bloom. You got clobbered on the head. It doesn't feel too good, does it, asshole."

"No, it doesn't. Where's Shandling? He wants to kill you, probably me too."

"Yeah, I figured as much. He left us here. Norbert apparently is outside. You have a weapon?"

"I did...." Bass felt in his pants and looked around—nothing.

"Shandling must have taken it from me after that old man whacked me upside the head. Where is Roanhorse?"

"I don't know. He's on the run or maybe waiting for Shandling. Either way, it's a good diversion for us."

"Good for you if Roanhorse is out there, not so much for me. See this goose egg? That old man wants me dead; he thinks I'm part of this heist."

"Are you?"

"Honestly I was, but I freed E.T. and I don't want any part of killing people just for a painting. I'm not a nice person, but I'm also not evil. I'm on your side, I swear."

Bloom looked into the man's eyes; he was telling the truth.

"Okay, we're both head trauma cases, but maybe together we can figure something out. Two injured heads have to be better than one."

"I'm part of the reason you're in this fix, and I'm sorry about the head. I swear it was an automatic response to you suddenly opening the door."

"Bass, if you can help get me out of here alive and back in the arms of my pregnant wife, all will be forgiven."

"Deal. I'll go out first. I'm going to bum-rush the guy. You follow behind me; he can't take us both."

"It's better than no plan I guess, so let's roll."

As the men headed out the door, a loud crash resounded in the distance. They ran out the door, looking side to side. A large puff of dust and smoke was billowing up off the hard-packed ground. Shandling was running toward what appeared to be a wrecked plane, his gun flailing in the air. The two injured men ran after Shandling.

Marvin had not done as well landing the plane as taking off. He had come in too hot and was unable to figure out how to slow the plane. He bounced off an old tractor, destroying the plane and throwing both himself and E.T. out. They were alive, but neither man was getting up quickly, and Shandling was on top of the kid as he rose.

"Get up, Tsosie—and Marvin, don't move. Where's Norbert?" Shandling growled as he pulled E.T. up by the collar.

"With his precious bones," Marvin replied.

Shandling's mind was spinning. There were too many people to guard and not enough guns. He needed reinforcements.

Bass's voice rang out: "Give it up, Mort. There's too many of us. No one is dead yet, so you can just call it in."

"Call it in? You kidding me? Come over here and help me. We can take care of this, clean this mess up. We have to find Roanhorse— he's run off."

"I'm not helping you anymore. You're crazy, so just put your gun down," Bass said.

Roanhorse's voice piped in from a distance. "You put your gun down, Shandling, or I'll take you out. I'm a good shot and I won't miss, I promise."

Shandling used E.T. as a shield, and jammed his revolver against the back of the kid's skull.

"You better be a good shot, because even if you kill me my last shot will take your grandson's head off."

At that moment Bass realized that if Tsosie died, it would be his fault. He might as well have pulled the trigger himself. He started to walk calmly toward Shandling.

"We're done, Mort. Time to put the gun down. That old man is going to kill you. He damn near killed me with a stick, so what do you think he can do with a rifle?"

"He's right. I don't miss with my .30-06, so give up," Roanhorse said. "Let my grandson go free."

"Screw you, Roanhorse. No one is killing me in this field. I'm Mort Shandling. What are you? Nothing."

Shandling raised his gun and shot at Bass, who jumped, but not quickly enough; a bullet grazed his right arm. Then a second shot rang out, and a bullet zipped over E.T.'s left shoulder and entered Shandling's neck. The searing pain dropped the art dealer to his knees, and his gun fell on the ground.

Marvin ran to the downed man and used his medic training to put hard pressure over the spurting artery with his palm. A gush of sticky red blood pulsated through Marvin's fingers. The old man had hit the carotid artery—a kill shot.

"Why do you love this painting so much that you will die for it?" Marvin asked, trying to understand why a human would be willing to lose his life over an object.

"My father... he said I was not worthy of his collection, that I would never be anything but a second-rate collector," Shandling said. "I had to prove him wrong...." Shandling's eyes fluttered in his head.

Marvin held the man's hand and said a prayer to the Holy People, asking for peace for the father and son and that Shandling might find solace in the next world.

By the time Roanhorse came to Marvin's side, Shandling was unconscious and close to death. The old man looked at his grandson and said, "The painting is yours to do with as you like. I only care about you, nothing else matters."

"I know grandfather. I love you too."

Roanhorse wrapped his large arms around his grandson and led him away from the tragedy created by human greed.

CHAPTER 55

THE AFTERMATH

An act of self-defense was the prosecutor's determination of the events at the hogan; no charges would be brought against Perry Roanhorse in the shooting death of Mort Shandling.

Much to Bloom's consternation, Norbert Rosenstein had not been charged with any crimes. A high-priced lawyer argued his client had not had any knowledge of, nor interest in, the Dixon painting, and that he was a pawn in Shandling's plot as the other men. Norbert threatened retribution if civil suits were brought, and promised that his lawyer would be vigorous in his defense, including going after Marvin Manycoats and Everett Tsosie for stealing and destroying his Trike and leaving him to die in the desert. His proposition was simple: don't screw with me, and I won't screw with you.

Bloom wanted to use their home improvement loan to go after the fossil dealer, but Rachael convinced her husband that the Holy People would ultimately prevail. "Don't worry about Norbert, my love," she said. "Let the gods handle the one that worships bones."

Shandling had no heirs or will, so the state of Arizona confiscated the Maynard Dixon Museum and was searching for a suitable home for the collection. It looked as if Shandling's dream of his collection becoming a part of something more important might come true, despite himself.

E.T. decided to honor his family's wishes and keep the Dixon painting for as long as possible, the Everett Ruess history unrevealed for now. All those who knew the true story promised to remain silent. E.T. would consider donating the painting if a true Dixon museum ever became a reality. Then it might be time to tell the story of how the painting became part of a Navajo family's long-kept secret. Money no longer held the same power it once had for E.T, his family bond was his new wealth.

Perry Roanhorse convinced his grandson to bring his girlfriend and baby from Shiprock, move in with him, and become part of the family farm. Then he began work on an addition to his home for the new occupants.

Roanhorse, whose boyhood memories included looking at the portrait of his father on the back of the hogan door, decided it was time to sell that piece of his legacy. The Dixon portrait was scheduled for the spring American painting sale at Sotheby's. The large image and unique provenance led to a strong estimate of $75,000 to

$95,000, which the specialist assured the consignors was warranted and the piece would sell. Roanhorse decided the proceeds should be split three ways: one third to Manycoats and Bloom, one third to his grandson, and one third to the most unlikely recipient—Richard Bass, the man he had nearly killed with the dibble.

Bass felt he had been given a second chance at life and decided to make the most of the opportunity. He would take a year off, using the Dixon proceeds to write a book about his experiences as a fringe art dealer. A regional publisher had read the story of the Dixon museum owner's death in the *Albuquerque Journal* and contacted Bass, agreeing to help publish his finished manuscript.

Bloom kept his word and forgave Bass as promised. He also agreed to sit for an interview for the chapters on the Dixon that got away. Rachael had never been prouder of her husband and knew he was ready to be a father once more.

Marvin had stumbled upon love. The windfall from the Dixon drawing's sale would not be going to a visit to Japan. Instead, he would begin flying lessons in Farmington. A Trike was in his future, and he couldn't wait to work on his landings. With any luck he might also get Milly from public housing to join him for a ride. Maybe she was tired of living with neighbors. He hoped so, because he was tired of being alone.

All were amazed that Roanhorse had managed to fake a heart attack that ended up saving their lives. The Navajo attributed his inspiration to watching an old *Sanford and Son* episode at his doctor's office a week earlier—the one where Fred Sanford pretends to have a heart attack while camping. He figured it was crazy enough that it might work.

Roanhorse's life was complete. His family was back on track spiritually and emotionally, and his promises to his father remained intact. He would continue to care for the crops he loved and the legacy they represented. After all, he was the guardian of the cornfields.

The End

THE CANDY MAN

THE EIGHTH BOOK IN THE *CHARLES BLOOM MURDER MYSTERY* SERIES

BY MARK SUBLETTE

CHAPTER 1

MA

The mule's new F-10 pickup was a modified vehicle made for Mexican-U.S. border crossings. The side panels—constructed to secure loaves of uncut cocaine—were special-ordered from the factory for a select clientele. A pile of freshly harvested watermelons in the truck bed completed the ruse: five watermelons near the bottom were stuffed with bags of blow. The watermelon load was worth the risk. Mules by definition were expendable, and oblivious cops, often on the cartel's payroll, meant more money flowing into the borderland.

The hidden door compartments were expertly constructed. A modified truck had once been confiscated after border agents found fruit stuffed with sacks of cocaine in the bed, but the bounty-filled door compartments went undiscovered, the drug-sniffing canines unable to detect the load. The confiscated cocaine-laden truck was later repurchased by the cartel at a Las Cruces police auction at a bargain price—no risky border-crossing necessary.

Mules based in Mexico crossed minimally staffed entry points, the regular guards on both sides being friendly to the cartel's cash contributions. A favorite crossing was located not far from Mesilla, New Mexico—no invasive I-94 forms required. The newly constructed concrete barriers gracing the checkpoint were a Trojan horse, suggesting more security, more payouts, and the false appearance of safety. When the cartel was involved, no one was safe.

In the early 1990s, the cocaine hauls were substantial. Business flourished as white dust covered America's landscape, a booming economy making cocaine the drug of choice. Once cut for the market, the average load brought in $2.5 million; the mule was paid a handsome $5,000 for his efforts. After five border crossings in six months, a mule would likely be reevaluated and discarded at year's end: longevity was not a part of the job requirement.

Angel Molina Veracruz had been running transportation logistics for the cartel for the last five years. Under her guidance, the cartel's productivity and inventory had steadily increased. Products, once limited to drugs, had expanded to include such money-laundering goods as pre-Columbian artifacts, fruits, vegetables, electronics, counterfeit luxury purses—occasionally, even human chattel—all collected and sold in the name of the Veracruz family.

Angel was a graduate of New Mexico State University. Her degree, at her father's insistence, was in business. The major was not her choice; she leaned more toward the creative side of academia. But she understood her role well. Third in command in the family's male-dominated hierarchy, her ambitious nature and immense drive would never allow her to attain the top position: a woman's role was to coordinate the business, not control it.

Juan Gabriel Veracruz—a vicious man and her beloved father— had ascended to the number one position of the El Paso-Las Cruces drug cartel with the support of his wife. Descended from a family of well-heeled Colombians, she had provided Juan Gabriel access to the Medellin Cartel's cocaine production elites, a critical component of his rise as a drug lord. Connections, brutality, and intelligence provided the secret sauce for long-term success—and Juan Gabriel had equal portions of all three.

Converting the raw drugs into cash fell to the second-in-command, Angel's older brother Federico, whose lack of empathy and sadistic propensities were legendary.

Arriving cocaine bricks were unloaded into an unassuming adobe building with a nondescript flattop roof, speckled gray by the mourning doves and pigeons that gathered for the grain Juan Gabriel provided—a touch of local color. Located off a cottonwood-lined dirt road not far from the central Mesilla Plaza, the unassuming compound was now a center of commerce in the drug trade.

The old Hispanic home, constructed during the period of the Gadsden Purchase—a potential jewel for archaeologists—was now lost to time and corruption. It sat next to an enormous metal building, once a farm-machine hangar, whose spacious interior and electric doors offered easy access to vehicles delivering product.

The occasional tractor made guest appearances from the multitude of fields that surrounded the area, but for those who cared to look, the steady flow of dark Cadillacs told the real backstory. The Veracruzes were an old New Mexican family, generous to the community and church, which meant few questions were asked. In the community's eyes, they were simply chile, cotton, and pecan farmers—even if their crop production was sub-average year after year.

Through expert pharmacological manipulation, a single 4- x 6- x 12-inch block of pure cocaine quickly became four blocks judiciously doled out by Federico to a series of boots-on-the-ground dealers in Phoenix, El Paso, Tucson, and as far north as Albuquerque. Successful dealers were given more bricks, while those who reduced the guaranteed Veracruz buzz by stepping on the product, skimming profits, or missing their sale quotas, soon found themselves in a tragic combine accident on one of the Veracruz fields.

All monies generated by the sale of the cocaine went into the Veracruz family financial pool, destined for investment after laundering. Finding a bank to clean the money would have been the quickest route, but that had proved to be the riskiest. Juan Gabriel believed bankers were greedy by nature, and vast amounts of cash would tempt their so-called righteousness, so he preferred laundering his money himself. Cash-heavy enterprises proved to be the best way to do the job: half a dozen laundromats scattered throughout poor towns in southern New Mexico, topless bars, old Route 66 motels, cafés, and a marina at Elephant Butte, near Truth or Consequences, New Mexico, provided the bulk of outlets. Vehicles, cheap rental properties, and leased farmland were also desired assets: helping troubled sellers in need of cash was a Veracruz specialty.

Angel, who loved art and as a child dreamed of becoming an artist, not a drug dealer, had recently come up with another avenue for disposing of huge amounts of cash by investing in an appreciating asset—fine art—and convinced her dominating father to let her enroll at the University of Arizona for a fine art degree.

It wasn't the school's curriculum or professors that had piqued her interest: it was the story of the U. of A. museum's stolen Willem de Kooning painting.

In 1985, a middle-aged couple strolled into the University of Arizona Museum of Art, and, as the woman distracted the lone guard, her male accomplice neatly cut the masterpiece from its frame. The multimillion-dollar de Kooning painting was rolled up and smuggled out hastily under a rain jacket. By the time the empty frame was discovered, the thieves were long gone. With scant information, no video cameras, and a guard's shaky description, there was little to go on. Two decades passed with no sign of the painting or the culprits. All that remained in the museum was an empty frame with the canvas remnants of the once-spectacular painting left hanging on the museum wall, a reminder of the despicable act and a beacon of hope for its safe return.

The story of corruption, art, and millions of dollars tied up in one easily stolen painting was Angel's ticket to garner both her father's attention and cooperation, and to get back to her true love—art—by enrolling in the Master of Arts degree in Art History (MA). Juan Gabriel could relate to the well-executed heist, and realized that by learning more about art, Angel might be able to discover the whereabouts of the valuable painting and make a deal for it—an educational pursuit he could support. The business of art looked to be an excellent medium to launder big money or to use stolen masterpieces as a form of credit for the cartel.

Trading drug money for art was coming into fashion among the cartels, especially in Miami. In 1990, robbers dressed as police strolled into Boston's Isabella Stewart Gardner Museum and walked out with thirteen masterpieces worth hundreds of millions of dollars, and Angel was convinced these works were headed to the East Coast drug trade. Understanding the art market would allow her to advance from a dead-end transportation lackey to the head of a very lucrative trade in stolen art, where she could hopefully extricate herself from the world of drug kingpins and make her own mark. But the first step to success was to understand the foundation and nuances of this niche market.

Juan Gabriel gave his blessing, and Angel was off to get her second degree: Art History with a minor in painting. The one-time transportation expert who specialized in cocaine and human flesh would transform herself into an art expert. Her areas of interest—Western, Native American, and Hispanic art—were considered an old boy's club that excluded women, but those who crossed Angel would soon learn her name was a misnomer. Ruthless, and blessed with ample capital, she would become a force in the white-glove art profession. She wanted to be the boss of her own domain—and anyone who got in her crosshairs would feel her bullets' searing pain.

To be continued in THE CANDY MAN

GLOSSARY

Allosaurus: A carnivorous dinosaur that lived in the late Jurassic period; the "different lizard" weighed at least 40 tons, was close to 40 feet long and about 17 feet tall, the most common dinosaur fossil found in Utah

Anasazi/Old Ones: Ancestral Puebloans who occupied the Four Corners region of the United States; commonly defined as "ancient people," the Navajo word translates as "enemy ancestors"

Athabascan: Ethnologists believe the Athabascan people came from Asia about 35,000 years ago, migrating into what is now Canada and Alaska, arriving in the Southwest about 1350 CE; some believe the Navajo emerged from this group

Bilagáana/bilágaanas: White man/men or white woman/women

Bisti Badlands (Di-Na-Zin Wilderness Area): A desolate desert wilderness area located between Farmington and Crownpoint, New Mexico; once the site of a coastal swamp of an inland sea, it's now known for its unusual rock and sandstone formations

Bluff, Utah: The site of an Ancestral Puebloan settlement, Bluff was later settled by Mormon pioneers in the late 19th century; the 2000 census set the population at 320

Canyon de Chelly: A deep sandstone canyon on Navajo Nation land near Chinle, Arizona, inhabited first by prehistoric peoples, followed by the Ancestral Puebloans, and now the Navajo, who have lived and farmed in the water-rich canyon for more than 300 years

Cañon del Muerto: Canyon of the Dead, a prehistoric site rich in cliff dwelling and rock art on Navajo Tribal Trust Land; part of the Canyon de Chelly National Monument in Chinle, Arizona

Canyonlands: A national park near Moab, Utah

Canyon Road: A half-mile long art gallery- and boutique-lined street in Santa Fe that hosts an annual Christmas Eve farolito walk popular with both locals and visitors

Casita: The name for a small house in the Southwest

Catalinas/Santa Catalina Mountains: The most prominent mountain range in the Tucson area, named by a Jesuit priest in honor of St. Catherine

Catalogue raisonné: A comprehensive listing of all the known works of an artist—or all the works in a particular medium—that includes scholarly research and observations

Cerrillos turquoise: Turquoise from historic mines south of Santa Fe; an important source of stones for Ancient Puebloans

Chaco/Chacoan: Chaco Canyon was a major center of Ancient Puebloan (or Chacoan) culture between 850 and 1250 CE, when the site was abandoned. Now a National Historic Park located in northwestern New Mexico, it contains the largest collection of ancient pueblos in the American Southwest

Chinle: Located in Apache County, Arizona, the name, which means "flowing out" in Navajo, refers to where the water flows out of Canyon de Chelly; the population is more than 90 percent Native American

Chindi: The ghost left behind when a person dies; the Navajo believe *chindi* should be avoided because they are often "unbalanced," or malevolent, and can negatively affect the living

Chuska Mountains: A heavily forested mountain range towering almost 10,000 feet above the San Juan Basin, the Chuskas lie within the Navajo Nation near Gallup and Toadlena

Comprende: "You understand" in Spanish

Coyote/coyote spirit: A major figure in Navajo cosmology, the coyote is a Trickster, sometimes loved and sometimes feared

Dibble: A prehistoric Ancestral Puebloan hoe

Diné: Translating as "The People," it is the name the Navajo use to refer to themselves and their language

Farmington: The largest city in the Four Corners area; bordered by the Navajo Reservation on its west and southwest edges, Farmington is both a commercial hub and the traditional home of a number of Native American tribes

Farolitos: Small, sand-filled paper lanterns lit with a candle, often set along walls, rooftops, and sidewalks in the Christmas season; traditionally used to guide the spirit of the Christ child home

Four Corners: A remote region of the Southwest where four states—Arizona, Colorado, New Mexico, and Utah—intersect at one point

Gallup: A small town in McKinley County, New Mexico, on the edge of the Navajo Nation; according to the 2000 U.S. Census, more than 30 percent of the population is American Indian

Giganotosaurus: A meat-eating dinosaur, slightly bigger than the T-Rex, that lived in what is now Argentina between 98 and 97 million years ago; a 70-percent complete specimen was found in Patagonia in 1993

Hastiin: A title of respect for men, it's the Navajo equivalent of "Mr."

Historic Toadlena Trading Post: Founded in 1909, the Toadlena post is the historic home of the Two Grey Hills style of Navajo weaving; closed by its last owner in 1996, rug trader Mark Winter negotiated a lease with the tribe and reopened the carefully renovated post in 1997; it continues to provide goods and services to local families and Winter purchases their rugs, and sells them along with jewelry and other handcrafts to visitors

Hogan: A traditional eight-sided Navajo dwelling with a center hole to allow smoke from the fire at the center of the floor to escape and a doorway that faces east so the family can greet and be blessed by the morning sun

Holy People: Key figures in the Navajo creation story, the Holy People taught the Diné how to live in balance on the earth, and are believed to have the power to help or harm humans

Hopi kachina: Figures representing messengers between humans and the gods, kachinas (a.k.a. katsinas) are usually carved from the roots of cottonwood trees

Hóhzó: One of the most important concepts in the Navajo belief system, *hózhó* refers to the beauty, order, and balance that are at the core of a healthy and happy life

Kayenta, Arizona: A small town on the Navajo Nation 25 miles south of Monument Valley that provides lodging and services to valley visitors; the population in 2010 was just over 5,000

Kokopelli: A trickster and fertility god overseeing childbirth and agriculture, he is usually depicted as a humpbacked flute player

Long Walk: After systematic destruction of their Canyon de Chelly homeland by Kit Carson in 1864, surviving Navajo were force-marched more than 300 miles across New Mexico to the Bosque Redondo (Hwéeldi in Navajo) at Fort Sumner where more than 8,000 were imprisoned until May 1868, when they were allowed to return to their homeland

Male rain(s): Monsoons—heavy rains usually accompanied by thunderstorms—are considered male in traditional Navajo belief

Mensch: "Human" in German

Mexican Hat, Utah: A tiny village (population 31 in 2010) named for a sombrero-shaped rock outcropping on the edge of town, it sits on the northern boundaries of the Navajo reservation and Monument Valley

Monument Valley: A desolate desert region on the Arizona-Utah border studded with red-rock mesas and buttes; often used to film western movies, it lies entirely within the Navajo Nation

Nasazi: What the Navajo call the Anasazi, or Ancient Puebloans, who lived in the Four Corners region of the Southwest

Pawn jewelry: Personal or family Native American pieces exchanged for cash, which could be (but often were not) redeemed by the original owner; old pawn is highly collectible

Rez: Slang for a North American Indian reservation

Shiprock: Called Tsé Bit'a'í—winged rock or rock with wings—by the Navajo, the volcanic remnant is extremely important to the tribe's history, mythology, and religion; its Anglo name refers to its resemblance to a nineteenth-century clipper ship

Sings: Complex healing ceremonies that include sandpainting and chanting led by a Navajo medicine man; the sing most often used to re-establish *hózhó* is the Blessingway

Skinwalker: In Navajo culture, a witch who has the ability to turn him- or herself into an animal is known as a shapeshifter or skinwalker

Slaney: Navajo slang for a person who is habitually drunk

Squash blossom necklace: A large, heavy silver necklace that intersperses tri-petal blossom beads (usually a total of twelve) with round spacer beads and a central pendant known as a naja

Tsénaajin and Tsénaajin Yázhí: The Two Grey Hills—two mesas located east of the Historic Toadlena Trading Post

Utes: Indigenous tribe that lived in what is now the Colorado-Utah area, often trading with and raiding Navajo settlements; the state of Utah is named for them

Whippets: Cartridges of nitrous oxide inhaled to get high, a.k.a. laughing gas

Yá' át' ééh: The traditional Navajo greeting, it translates literally as "It is good"

Photography courtesy Mark Sublette, unless otherwise noted

Page 1:   *Colorado River, Utah*

Page 8:   *United States Post Office, Bluff, Utah 84512*

Page 13:   *Abandoned Hogan*, Near Toadlena, NM

Page 19:   *Two Burros, Utah*

Page 24:   *Historic Toadlena Trading Post and Weaving Museum Sign*, NM

Page 33:   *Tsénaajin and Tsénaajin Yázhí and Tip of Shiprock*, NM

Page 37:   *Tsé Bit'a'í*, NM

Page 42:   *Tsénaajin and Tsénaajin Yázhí Near Post*, NM

Page 47:   *Rug Room*, Mark Sublette Medicine Man Gallery, Tucson, AZ

Page 52:   *Palace of the Governors*, Santa Fe, NM

Page 57:   *Twinkle Lights*, Santa Fe, NM

Page 62:   Maynard Dixon (1875-1946), *White House Ruins, Canyon de Chelly*, 1922-1946

Page 73:   *Cattle, Navajo Nation*, AZ

Page 78:   *Mexican Hat*, UT

Page 82:   *Nasazi Ruins*, AZ

Page 88:   *Nasazi Handholds*, Northern AZ

Page 94:   *Nasazi Post Holes*, AZ

Page 102: *Coyote Stalking*, Canyon del Muerto, AZ

Page 108: Verso Maynard Dixon (1875-1946) painting *Grey Day in October*, number 598, original price $100

Page 111: *Shell Station Near Toadlena*, NM

Page 121: Maynard Dixon (1875-1946), *Fire and Earthquake*, April 19, 1906

Page 126: *Plate of Enchiladas*, The Shed, Santa Fe, NM

Page 132: Navajo Turquoise and Silver Squash Blossom Necklace c. 1960s

Page 138: *491 Gallup*, NM

Page 144: *Arizona Diamondback Rattlesnake*, Tucson, AZ

Page 150: *Goulding's Trading Post*, UT

Page 156: *Nasazi Ruin and Bones*, AZ

Page 160: *Nasazi Holes*, Near Toadlena, NM

Page 166: *La Bajada Hill*, NM

Page 176: *Inside Historic Toadlena Trading Post*, NM

Page 180: *Maynard Dixon Museum Sign*, Tucson, AZ

Page 188: *Trailer Rez*, AZ

Page 199: *Near Mexican Hat*, UT

Page 205: Maynard Dixon (1875-1946), *Late Light on the Catalinas*,
        Tucson, AZ, November 1943

Page 218: *Museum of Northern Arizona*, Flagstaff, AZ

Page 224: *New Mexico Abandoned Home*

Page 233: Maynard Dixon (1875-1946), *Distant Mesa, Kayenta Ariz.*,
        August 1922

Page 249: *Ventana*, Tucson, AZ

Page 256: *Hat Rock Inn*, UT

Page 260: *To Mexican Hat*, UT

Page 267: *Reservation Hogans*, NM

Page 272: Maynard Dixon (1875-1946), *Navajo Ponies at a Trading
        Post*, Tuba City, AZ, 1922

Page 279: *Window*, Near Toadlena, NM

Page 282: *Hat Rock Cafe*, Mexican Hat, UT

Page 287: *On the Scent, Deer Near the Navajo Nation*, UT

Page 297: Jeremy Bentham's Auto-Icon, UCL Culture, London

Page 305: *Ancient Bones*, NM

Page 309: *Abandoned Hogan Door*, NM

Page 317: Maynard Dixon (1875-1946), *Study for Father Sun (The
        Legend of Earth and Sun)*, December 1928,
        Biltmore Hotel Mural

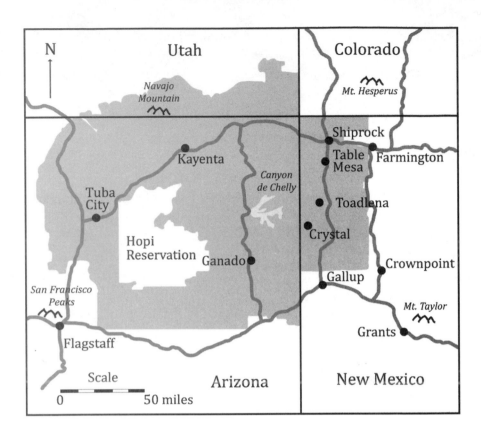